You Broke Me First

BOOK 4 - THE PAIN SERIES

LYNDA THROSBY

Warning

This book is not intended for anyone under the age of 18.

This is for adult reading only and contains counts of violence and sexual content.
This book deals with matters that may cause distress to some readers.
Be Warned.

You Broke Me First

PART XI

Vidana

One

Vidana
Present

I CAN'T BELIEVE IT'S BEEN OVER TWO AND A HALF YEARS SINCE I was rescued, and Lana walked away. I couldn't believe she left me. I was so fucking angry with her. All her promises about us getting a place together, moving away and her helping me out. It was all bullshit. Why did I ever trust her or listen to her? She's just as selfish as she's always been. If it wasn't for her and Mama's selfishness, none of this would ever have happened. It was Poppy who told me Lana ran away with Sergei, Igor's guard. I was confused. She'd never mentioned Sergei, only that she was in love with Ryker. Something didn't ring true to me.

I hate to say it but after Lana left, I relapsed in a big way. I went downhill fast, knowing I was all alone, yet again. I used to sneak out of the refuge. Not that I wasn't allowed out. It wasn't a prison, like the place I used to be in, but I needed drugs. I needed them to help me forget everything and forget about being alone. It was the loneliness that screwed with me more than anything. The drugs helped me forget my previous life. The only thing I had to pay for the drugs was my body. I didn't have any money. After getting my bearings and sniffing out the dealers, I exchanged my body for a high. I didn't give a shit. It had been used by hundreds of men in the time I was held captive. I was numb to it all. Sex meant nothing to me. I never got aroused and I never came. I'd just lie there with my legs spread and let them do what they wanted. This went on for months after Lana left. I just didn't think at that point my life was worth living, so the drugs helped me forget. How I got away with it for so long, I have no idea. The staff must have known I was out every night and coming back high. I didn't join in with any of the group sessions for so long. I'm surprised they didn't all just give up on me. I think looking back now, I must have been the worst case they have ever encountered.

I watched the girls who came in with me get lives. Why the fuck couldn't that be me? When I saw parents come for their lost or taken girls, it made me worse than ever. I think that's why it took me so long. My mama never once called. If I wanted to speak to her, then I had to call her, but I never did. She never came for me. I secretly hoped and prayed she would come. It was the being alone that crucified me. I think the staff got fed up with my attitude and Poppy followed me one day. I did think I hid it well, but what the fuck did I really know or care. I was waiting for them to kick me out as a no-hoper. Poppy did, however, put a stop to it. She took me in her arms and let me break down. I told her how lonely I was and that I wish I was dead. I told her I was selling my body for drugs because it didn't matter. I didn't feel anything but numb. I'll never forget what she said to me that day.

"Vidana, I'm here for you, regardless. I will always be here for you. I'm not going anywhere. You will always have me if you ever need me. You are a young, beautiful girl who has her whole life ahead of her. Cherish your body. It's the only one you have. The day you fall in love and let that person take you by worshiping you in a loving, caring way will be the day you realize your body can be used for enjoyment. The way you deserve to use it and be treated. It will be one of the best days for you, and you will never let anyone use your body again. Never use it as a tool, Vidana. You will one day regret it. It's your choice of what happens to you and your body. Your choice, Vidana, do you hear me? No one else will make you do anything you don't want them to. We will make sure you can protect yourself. Do you hear me, Vidana?"

I nodded my head. My face was against her shoulder in shame, and I was sobbing hard. I knew in that moment she was right. Whereas I didn't have a choice in being captive and used for sex, I do have a choice now. She's right, it's my choice.

In total, I spent over three years at the refuge. They were three very long years that felt like a lifetime, and I still felt so alone. I feel like I've aged by about twenty years. Don't get me wrong, they helped me a lot and for that I am grateful. Poppy was there the few times I really needed someone. When I was about to relapse or break down, she was always there for me. She never let me down. It was hard for me to ask her for help, but I did it and she helped me. I trust her more than I will ever trust Svetlana. They also taught me self-defense, just like Poppy said they would teach me to protect myself. I loved it. They arranged for different classes at the refuge to help us all with self-defense. This was so no one could take us again. They showed us how to stop someone attacking us and how to get out of restraints. I've toned up so much. I took every class I could, it became the new drug to me. I craved the classes.

I despised Igor when I first arrived, for what happened to my family after he came into our lives. That first time I saw him, I think it just brought back memories of my papa, remembering it was him that killed Papa. I just went for him. I wasn't in a good place when I attacked him. I was still withdrawing cold turkey, and in my head, I couldn't see reason. No matter what went through my fogged up brain, there was just no reasoning. Even after attacking her husband like I did, Poppy still helped me. The patience she showed me and the other girls, she really understood us all. If I had to guess, I would say she must have gone through something similar herself.

Lana hated Poppy, even after she gave her a job and became her friend. I know why she hated her. She thought it should have been her by Igor's side and not Poppy. Lana was always delusional and self-centered. In all honesty, I think Igor and Poppy are a great match. I've seen them together on numerous occasions, and you can see the love they have for each other and their family. What they have is something I've never seen, not even my own parents had that, but then theirs was an arranged marriage when my mama was only fourteen.

Igor wouldn't go near me for a while after I attacked him, and I could see he was wary of me each time we did see each other. I hated him, and he knew that. It was nothing to do with him being afraid of me. Oh no, not *The Igor Ustrashkins*. It was more, I think, so he didn't kill me. From what I've heard, if I had been anyone else, he would have killed them instantly, with no hesitation. I know he's Bratva. I knew when I heard Mama talking to one of her friends after Lana left with him. Bratva is good if you're on their side, but bad if you cross them. I don't want to cross the Bratva. I've had enough shit to deal with, which is why I ignore him when he's around. I also found out he is not only Bratva, but he is a godfather, a Pakhan. I think myself very lucky he didn't kill me, and he's been okay with me since.

I've learned to respect him and from what I've seen, he's a decent guy. I will always be grateful to Igor and Poppy for rescuing me. Lana told me they never gave up looking for me. I just don't think I can forgive him for how my family has turned out. Maybe in time, I will come to terms with it, that it wasn't all his fault, but ever since he entered our lives, my family has gone to shit. If he hadn't stumbled upon Lana that day, my papa would be alive, Lana wouldn't have left Russia, and I wouldn't have been kidnapped, drugged, and raped for years. It makes me so angry when I think of it in that way and it all points back to Igor.

Poppy has helped me find a job. It's in a coffee shop. I'm a barista and, to my surprise, I really enjoy it. With self-defense and knowing I can protect myself; it has given me so much more confidence when meeting new people, which I figure is why I like my job. I also volunteer at the refuge whenever I'm not working. It's the least I can do after they helped me. I have the experience of going through what the new girls have been through, it gives me a great advantage to help them with their recover. It's now me helping them, to show them they can turn their lives around, just like I have. If I can survive, then so can any of them.

I did think about going back to Russia for a while, but only for my sisters. God only knows what Mama is doing now and how they are. She's never bothered to phone me all the time I've been in America, and I know Lana told her I was here. Lana said she was the same with her, that it was her that always had to phone Mama. I will never forgive Mama for my papa being killed at the hands of Igor. I do get it, Igor was doing it to protect me and my sisters. I understand that more now. Lana was also to blame, but she was just so young and selfish. As long as she got what she wanted, nothing else mattered. I wondered if she did already know Papa was dead at the hands or Igor, or if she was actually innocent to it, like said. She told me she didn't know until she received the video, but I don't believe her. Mama is the one who should take all the blame at the end of the day. She knew what she was doing. She never loved Papa; I knew that from when I was young.

———

Growing Up

"Vidana, don't you be home late from school. I will be out and need you to look after your sisters. Give them some supper. There's everything you need in the kitchen."

I roll my eyes. This is happening more and more. She's got a new man; she's out screwing more than she's home to look after all of us. We moved after Svetlana moved to America with Igor. Mama got a lot of money from him, and we moved from the small, run-down, two-bedroom house we lived in to a nice area in a big house with five bedrooms. Mama has her own bedroom with her own bathroom in it, Zoya shares a room with Klara, then Iskra, Dominika, and I all have our own bedrooms. I am the luckiest because I, too, have my own bathroom. What a difference to this time last year. There were eight of us in that tiny house, my poor papa with seven girls. Svetlana and I shared the downstairs lounge area. That was our bedroom. The kitchen became the living area and everyone's bathroom. It's where everyone washed and there was a pitcher for the toilet, unless you were brave enough to go out into the freezing cold and deep snow in the winter, to use the outhouse. The outhouse was just a wood hut with a small door, and you sat over a hole in the ground. Mama and Papa called it the shitter.

After Svetlana left, we never saw Papa again. Mama doesn't know what happened to him, or so she says. I loved Papa more than Mama. It broke my heart when he didn't come home. I was convinced something bad had happened to him, but Mama told me he just left because he couldn't cope with all us females and was probably with another woman. She never loved him; they argued a lot. Being in a small house with paper-thin walls, you heard them argue. When they weren't arguing, they were screwing. It's how they ended up with six girls. I used to lie in bed with my fingers in my ears, so I didn't have to hear the arguing or the screwing. Lana used to come into my bed when we were younger to comfort me when they were like that. I didn't understand the screaming going on with being so young. I think Lana did though. We would hide under the covers, and she would tell me stories that she made up. That was when we were close. It was like that for a while. There was Lana, me, then Dominka then Iskra, so we all had to endure it for years. Then when Klara came along that's when Lana and I moved into the living room as our bedroom. It wasn't quite so noisy downstairs unless they were screwing. Then the screams and the banging of the bed kept us awake.

Mama was hard on us all, more than Papa was. We were all scared of Mama. That's why I loved Pap more. She ruled the house with an iron fist, which was bad for Papa, because in Russia the man always ruled, no matter what. After his accident, he became a different person and he let her do what she wanted, although he did become meaner to us all, because of all the vodka he drank. I never told him or anyone about the times I saw Mama out screwing men in one of the old disused mine buildings. I knew it would break him. I believed he genuinely loved Mama; it just wasn't reciprocated. Mama used to make him punish Lana if she answered back. I got punished a few times, but not as much as Lana. Mama told him he had to take her outside and whip her bare ass. He didn't want to do it, but he had no choice. The first time he refused, she beat him with an iron pot. He was full of vodka, so couldn't fight back. She was the one that stripped Lana naked from the waist down and made my papa whip her. She ranted about it being how she was brought up and it didn't do her any harm. That he should be the one to do the punishing, that it was his job, like it was her papa's job. He was the so-called man of the house. She just wanted him to look bad in front of us, so we feared him like we did her. It didn't work.

Lana sees that time differently from me. I was a lot more observant; I saw so much more than she did. She was always away in la-la land reading her dirty romance books. She used to leave the rest of us to do what we wanted. I would sneak out a lot and she never even knew, or I would pretend they held me back at school, which they didn't. I would meet up with my friends. There were a few of us that were close. We would hang out in a derelict house. There were enough of them around here. In fact, I think there were more disused derelict houses than there were lived in ones. The lucky ones moved on or died.

I got out when I could. We also used to meet up at an old disused mine not too far away. That's the place I first saw Mama screwing someone else. There were some boys that hung with us, one in particular I fancied, but he was two years older than me. He was Lana's age, but he was nice. I had kissed boys before, but only little kisses. I didn't really know any better. This one boy, Dima, who I thought was hot, he wanted to spend time with me. A few times when I snuck out, it was just to meet him, alone.

I was so embarrassed the second time I walked with him to the old mine building. This was the first time I saw Mama with another man. As we approached, we could hear noises, lots of slapping and grunting and moaning. We crept to the glassless window and peered in. There was a woman bent over and a man had her long skirt up and over her head. He was slamming his body into the woman's ass. I was frozen, wondering what I was seeing. I had never seen anything like it. He was grunting. I recognized him. I didn't know his name, but I had seen him in the local store. They were turned sideways. I watched as he pulled his thing out of what must be her ass, then shoved it straight back in, hard. I winced. He was doing it over and over, but the woman seemed to be enjoying it. He was grunting louder and louder and kept slapping her bare ass. Dima was pushing me away, he wanted to see what was happening. The woman was moaning and shouting yes, yes, and then she started to scream; I knew that voice. I was mortified. She managed to shrug the skirt from her head, and I recognized my mama straight away. I ducked down quickly, pulling Dima with me.

"Hey, I want to watch them fucking." He jumped back up and carried on watching. I started to move away as quietly as I could. I couldn't let Mama see me. Dima caught up to me. "What's your problem, Vidana, weren't you enjoying that? Didn't it turn you on? It sure as hell made me fucking horny. How about we find our own place to go and let's do what they were doing. I'm sure from their noises you would enjoy it." He wiggles his eyebrows at me, and I slap his chest.

"Not happening, Dima. I've only ever held your hand. If you think

I'm doing anything like that, you are mistaken. You need to find someone else to use. Besides, it didn't look like fun to me. How can him shoving his thing in her ass be fun? It must hurt like crazy?"

I couldn't tell him that was my mama that we just watched. What do I do? Do I tell her I saw her? Do I tell Lana or Papa? Why would she be doing that with another man? Is it normal? Is that what women are supposed to do? Dima suddenly takes my hand, pulling me out of my thoughts.

"Hey, what's wrong? I was only joking, kind of." He shrugs, looking at me under his blond bangs.

I pull my hand out of his and storm off. I'm suddenly elevated from the ground as he grabs me around the waist and twirls me around. I scream. Oh shit, I'm too close to the building where Mama is, she might hear me. I struggle to get him to put me down and I run as fast as I can with Dima giving chase. He thinks I'm running from him; I just need to get as far away as I can. I run into a derelict house, the one that we normally mess around in when I'm with all my friends. We have chairs in here that we took from other abandoned houses. I sit on a chair and Dima comes in breathless after me.

"What was that all about, Dana, why did you scream and run?"

I just shrug, not looking at him, and play with the cotton of my long skirt.

"I just wanted to get away from that man and Ma… that woman."

He comes over and crouches down in front of me. I look him in the face. "Are you mad at me for what I said?"

I roll my eyes. It's all about him. I look straight into his deep-green eyes; I lick my lips. He watches my tongue, and he sighs without realizing it. Before I know what's happening, he's kissing me. I've never kissed anyone properly before. I'm young, so it's not like I know much. He moves his lips on mine. It's awkward. I mimic him. Is that it? Is that all it is? Why, when I see my friends kiss, does it look like they're eating each other? He pulls away.

"I've wanted to kiss you for a long time. I know it's not proper, but we need to wait until you're a little older."

Great, now he has morals.

I caught my mama more times after that first time, most times at the old mine building. It must be her go-to place. Each time, it was a different man. A few of those times, Dima was with me. The last time we caught her, he still didn't know it was my mama. He made a comment about maybe he should be next in line. I hit him in the chest, then ran away from him again. I still haven't told anyone else about it. It's a secret I've kept to myself. I don't know if Papa knows something is going on because he spends more time at the old bar in town than he does at home. When he does come home, he's usually drunk. My mama has even given up shouting at him for being drunk all the time. I think she's just given up on him altogether. They hardly even talk to one another, let alone either of them really talking to any of us now, unless it's barking orders or shouting because we haven't done something. She did work a lot, my mama, or so I thought. Maybe she was screwing when she was telling us she was working, or maybe she screwed after she finished work. Lana was looking after us more and more. She said Mama was working, but what does she know? She barely leaves the house.

It's one of the rare occasions Mama is home and she's sent Lana to go get some groceries from the store and see if she can drag Papa from the bar. She's been gone a long time. I'm sitting in the kitchen with my sisters playing Old Maid, a new card game I found. It was a packet in one of the abandoned houses. Mama is puttering around the kitchen.

"Mama, how long will Lana be? We're hungry."

"Stop whining, Vidana. She shouldn't be long, you can all wait till she gets back. Maybe she'll have your useless papa with her for once." Just then the door goes and Lana shouts for my mama from our bedroom, telling her there's someone that wants to see her. Mama shouts back, "Who is it, Lana? Is it your papa?"

She turns, telling me to stay put as she leaves the kitchen, shutting the door behind her. How can I tell who it is now? Lana comes through the door a few minutes later and I roll my eyes at her, she's smiling so hard. Lana doesn't smile, like ever.

"Who is it, Lana? Who is in there to see Mama?"

She doesn't speak. She just sits and ignores us. She has her head resting on her hands, she looks like she's away with the fairies, with a big goofy grin on her face. She hasn't even acknowledged any of us. I finish the game we were playing, then I get up and put my ear to the door. I can hear a deep voice, not one I recognize, but I can't make out what they are saying. Zoya is still asleep, so I sit back down. Lana didn't even know I had moved. She suddenly gets up and goes into auto mode, starting with putting the bread dough in the oven, and then making the dumpling stew. She still doesn't speak to any of us. Mama has been gone for a while now, I wish she would hurry up.

Mama finally walks into the kitchen. She doesn't look happy. She's scowling at Lana. I suddenly see a man walk in behind her. Wow, he's really nice for an old man, and he's smiling away, just like Lana. I notice Mama look at Lana and she nods slightly in the direction of the man behind her.

"My angel, would you walk me to the door, please?" He's looking at Lana as he says this, and I snort-giggle.

He called her his angel. That is hilarious. He's old, but I wonder who he is. Lana turns and scowls at me for my rude noise, it makes me do it again, I put my hand over my mouth to stop myself.

"Would you like to stay for supper, Igor?" she asks him, but that is not the Lana I know speaking. She's trying to put on a sweet, girly voice. She sounds stupid. My mama shakes her head slightly and they both notice. He smirks to himself at that, but he's not angry. He looks amused.

"No thank you, will you walk me out?" he asks her and turns his back to walk out. She turns to Mama as if asking what she should do. Mama nods for her to follow him. I find this all fascinating and I want to know who he is. Mama starts busying herself, puttering about, taking the bread from the oven,

"Mama, who is that man and why did he call Lana his angel?" She doesn't speak or even acknowledge me. "Mama," I shout. She turns suddenly to see why I'm shouting. "Who is that man and why did he call Lana his angel? He was nice, Mama." She rolls her eyes at me and scowls.

"He is no one, Vidana. No one for you to worry about. Just a friend of Lana's." I don't believe her. Lana doesn't have any friends. She turns away from me. Well, that's all I'm getting from her. Mama starts to dish up the food for us. Lana comes skipping into the kitchen with the goofiest grin on her face yet again. She sets the table. No one has spoken. I watch her very carefully, her expression is what I would call dreamy and she's in a world of her own.

"Is Papa coming home for supper tonight, Mama?" I ask, breaking the silence. Even the little ones have been quiet. I think we can all sense Mama is in a bad mood, and we don't want to wrong her and risk punishment. She doesn't answer me. Lana has set a place for him at the table, just in case. We all eat, mostly in silence. Lana is still smiling as she eats. Mama is still frowning at her and snapping at anyone else who dares to speak, neither of them have spoken to each other yet. After supper, Lana helps Mama put the little ones to bed and I'm sent to bed myself. They shut the kitchen door so I can't hear them. I eventually fall asleep.

The next day, Lana is all happy and skipping about. I heard her shouting when she ran into the kitchen first thing, but not angry, it was excitement, saying, "I'm going, Mama, I'm going to leave with Igor, and you will be able to have nice lives." I didn't hear the rest. It was muffled.

Where was she going with Igor? Was he taking her somewhere? Was she coming back? Mama kept us all out of school and she didn't go to work. They got us into the kitchen and told us Lana was leaving to go and live with Igor, in America. I was shocked. Lana was leaving us. How could she? We were her family. I cried and told her I was happy for her, but I wasn't. It was a lie. She was leaving us, all of us, to go and enjoy her life with an old man she didn't even know. What if he beat her or was mean to her? How could she do this to us? She thought I was upset she was leaving us, but I'm angry and annoyed, not upset. Now it will all be down to me to look after our sisters. I'm only twelve, well, almost thirteen. I want to be out with my friends. I hate her for leaving us.

She hugged us all goodbye when he arrived to pick her up. I didn't cry. She was crying, as was Mama. I've never seen Mama cry before. She doesn't even like Lana, so why is she crying? I think it's all for show. I watched as the old man who was taking my sister handed my mama a bag. What is that for? This is all very strange to me.

My papa never came home again. Mama didn't really care, but she was out more than she was in. I had to look after my sisters. My mama wasn't working. I remember hearing Lana saying now she didn't have to work and thought it a strange thing to say. I went into Mama's bedroom to search for the bag Igor passed to her. It was a big bag and looked heavy. I found it in the bottom of my mama's wardrobe. I was right, it was heavy. I managed to open it without taking it out, which was a relief because if she came home, I don't think I could put it back. I put my hand in and pulled out what felt like a bunch of paper. I pulled it out and it was money, lots, and lots of money. I pulled out another wad, and another, and another. There must have been hundreds and thousands of rubles. I flicked through them, and they were all thousand-ruble notes. I heard footsteps coming up the stairs, so I quickly put it all back and closed the bag just as Dominika shouted out my name.

"I'm in here, just looking for a sweater. I was cold and wanted to wear one of Mama's."

I walk out, closing the door behind me, so she didn't go in snooping around. I set to making supper for everyone and did enough for Mama in case she decided to come home. I even set a place for Papa in case he turned up as well. I think he left us. I bet if he knew Mama had so much money, he would be back. Why did Igor give her all that money? I don't know who he is, but he must be rich. It must be why Lana wanted to go with him. So she could be rich too.

It was weeks before Mama sat us down and told us Papa wasn't coming home. She said she didn't know where he was, but I knew she didn't even care. She told us we would be going to America and that Igor had arranged passports for us all so we could go and surprise Lana for her birthday. We were all so excited. None of us had left our town ever, not even Mama. The trip was amazing. We were all scared on the plane and Zoya played up. It was a long way to go. I loved it in America, and I too wanted to go and live there one day. I got it, why Lana wanted to stay. Comparing America to where we lived was like chalk and cheese. I never understood that saying. Just that America was so different, and I knew it was where I wanted to be. Maybe Igor would let me live with them?

We stayed with Lana in Igor's huge place. We surprised her, but we had to pretend it was her seventeenth birthday. I frowned at Lana and Mama, but they both shook their heads at me, warning me to keep my mouth shut. The others didn't know any different, but I did. I knew she was sixteen. They were lying to Igor. What were they playing at? They must have thought I was stupid. When we were alone, I asked Lana why we were pretending she was older. She grabbed my arm hard and told me I was wrong. She told me to shut up, that I had it wrong, and she was seventeen. No, I didn't, I knew how old she was. I knew she was lying. I then had my thirteenth birthday when we got back home. I was a grown-up now, a teenager, the eldest, and I looked after my siblings just like Lana looked after us. Only Lana did it because Mama had to work. I have to do it because she's out screwing.

Two

Vidana
Present

I'VE BEEN LOVING MY JOB. I'VE BEEN HERE FOR OVER EIGHTEEN months now and I've grown so much more confident in that time dealing with the public. It took me a long time to do front of shop. I spent the first eight months in the back making orders for food and ordering stock. I've taken on more hours, which means I have to cut my time down slightly helping at the refuge center. I still have a room there, which is handy for me helping out. Poppy said I could stay until I find a place, while I still help out there. I honestly don't know where to start looking for my own place. One night I checked out some properties on the computer at the refuge, but there is no way I can afford those prices. Even the not very nice, tiny studio apartments, are way out of my price range. I don't know what I am going to do.

I may end up back where I was. I don't make enough money to be able to live anywhere here in LA. I was thinking I may have to go back to using my body. I've thought about it a lot lately, but this time getting paid for it. I've seen adverts for dancers in strip clubs. It's the only thing I can think of if I want to stay here. I need to speak to Poppy and see what she suggests about my living arrangements, only I will leave out the bit about using my body, I will see if she has any ideas. I feel bad because she's helped me out so much, I feel like I am always putting on her. She tells me constantly to speak to her, If I need to, about anything. I know how busy she is. She owns the refuge with Igor, and she's there a lot to oversee things, but she also has children, five of them. Boys and girls, two sets of twins. They must be a handful; I don't know how she copes with it all. I wonder if she needs help at her house looking after them, like a nanny, I could do that, I looked after my sisters. Poppy is more like a sister to me than Lana has or could ever be. I watch Poppy a lot whenever she's around. I see how she is genuinely concerned about everyone. I know if I suggest using my body to her, she will not be happy, and I feel like I don't want to let her down. She's like a real-life superwoman. She cares about everyone.

I do also want to talk to her about checking on my sisters. To see if Igor can find anything out. I dare not ask him myself after what happened. I know being Bratva, he will have many contacts back in Russia. I really need to know how they are. I've tried to call my mama on many occasions, but she never picks up, or she's changed the number. I want to make sure my sisters are all okay. I'm getting so worried about them. It's been years now since I've heard anything about them. I suspect after I went missing, Mama made Dominika look after the other three while she was out screwing. God knows what's been going on. I bet she never even worried about me, she clearly wasn't worried when Lana told her I had been taken, she never once tried to come see me when I was rescued. What kind of a Mama does that? She would have presumed I just ran away when I disappeared, like Lana did. Well, Lana was bought. I bet Mama was mad she didn't get any money for me. She would have been so mad about missing out on selling yet another daughter. I am scared she will do the same to my sisters, to make money and to be free. I think with Papa gone, she found she liked the freedom more. She didn't have to hide as much, although she still did at first for some reason. I heard the whispers around town about how she was a bike. I didn't understand it until I asked Dima once what the term meant. I didn't say it was about my mama, just that I had heard people using the term, he told me it meant a woman was a whore and she would ride any man that wanted her. I was still confused.

Growing Up

After Lana left, I had to quit school to look after our sisters. It made me angry and bitter toward Lana but mainly toward Mama. At least when Lana was looking after us it was because Mama was working, well supposedly. Now it's because she's out doing God knows what with God knows who. I miss school. I miss my friends and I missed Dima. I know we are going to be moving away very soon. I heard Mama talking about it. I still manage to sneak out sometimes on the rare occasions Mama is home. The first time I snuck out, it had been weeks since I had seen Dima and I missed him. Only he was with someone else. I hate him. He used me.

That first time I saw him with Sochia, I was so mad, I sat watching them, sat on the chair I let him fuck me in. Her on his knee playing with his hair. He didn't even acknowledge me. He looked my way once; I know because I couldn't take my eyes off them. He didn't even smile, it was like I was nothing. He looked straight through me. I couldn't take it anymore, watching them be all lovey-dovey. I slowly rose from my chair and ambled toward them. He looked at me then. I saw the raised eyebrow asking what the fuck was I doing? I stood there and leaned in and gently kissed his cheek. I heard the gasp from Sochia and the rest of them, whom I knew would be watching me. I licked up his cheek. As I was doing this, distracting him. I grabbed her long ponytail, wrapping it around my fist and I yanked her head so hard she tumbled to the floor backward. I heard the thud of her head on the concrete floor.

I moved quickly and I stomped my foot right in her face. Not just once, either. I didn't care what I did to her, I became crazed with jealousy. He was mine, the fucking bitch. I wanted to damage her face so he wouldn't look at her again. I then bent down to jerk her head up by the hair and I punched her repeatedly in the face. She was a mess. There was blood everywhere. Her face just looked like a big bloody mess. I was being pulled back hard, first by the arm and then I was grabbed around the waist. It was Dima, of course it would be him, trying to get me off her before I did any real damage. Too late, I must have broken her nose, and I certainly smashed her mouth in.

He lifted me up high, trapping my arms to my sides, then he swung me around and hurled me across the floor. Ouch, that fucking hurt, asshole. I landed awkwardly on my arm, but I wasn't letting that bother me. I turned and glared, ready to pounce on him. He growled at me, shaking his head in warning, before turning and rushing to Sochia to help her. He crouched down in front of her and tried to lift her head very gently. The fucking pussy, I was so angry with him. She looked at him, well, she tried to look at him. Her eyes were so swollen and her face such a mess with blood dripping everywhere. I smirked at my handiwork. I watched as he started to stroke her hair.

That did it. I got up as quickly and quietly as I could, and I lurched forward onto his back. I wrapped my legs around his body, and I hammered him on the head over and over, scratching and pulling at his hair.

"You fucking asshole, as soon as I disappear for a couple of weeks, you go after someone else for a screw. Fuck you, Dima," I screamed at him while pulling chunks of his hair out.

He managed to get to his feet with me still clinging to his back. My friends tried to get me off him. I like to think it was mainly so he didn't hurt me, but I know it wasn't. He was pulling at my legs, then he reached up and grabbed at my head. He pulled my hair, I felt some of it rip out of my head as I yanked away out of his reach. I fell backward and landed on the floor on my back. It winded me. I couldn't move. I was trying to catch my breath. I didn't want any of them to see me cry so I bit down on my lip to try to hold it in. Dima was standing next to me, looking down into my face.

"What the fuck did you do that for, Dana? We haven't screwed around for months. We're not together. We never were. You were an okay fuck, but that was it. I love Sochia. So, fuck off and don't come near either of us again."

That fucking bastard, he loved her. He told me he loved me when he was fucking me. I told him all the time how I loved him. I lay there on my back with my eyes screwed shut, trying to stop the tears. It was no good, they leaked out the sides of my eyes and ran down the side of my face into my ears. My head was throbbing from where he pulled my hair out. How could he do this, I loved him. I heard them all leave. Not one of my so-called friends checked to see if I was okay. They all left me on the floor alone. I rolled over onto my side and curled up into a ball. I stayed like that for some time, just remembering and thinking about good times. That first time we fooled around in this fucking room, over on that chair where it started.

I lay just thinking about our time together and how I was mortified. Every time we went to the old mine, we kept on seeing her there, my mama. Screwing yet another nameless man. Dima made us go there more and more, I think in the hopes we would catch them at it again. It was getting so that he would stand and watch them more and more. I would be crouched on the floor under the window with my fingers in my ears. Dima and I had fooled around a lot, mostly just kissing and him doing a bit of groping. The groping didn't come until much later on, he respected my age. He still wanted to be with me and seemed happy to just make out as teenagers do. As time went on though, he asked me more and more if he could do other things and I wouldn't let him. I was starting to feel pressured. The thing is, I was spending less and less time with him and my friends because I had to look after my sisters. We had also moved away, which made it harder for me to get to see him and my friends. We lived in a nice area, and it was a really long walk. It was another reason I rarely went to see them. I did sneak out more when Mama was actually home but then I did do it more when she wasn't home. I made Dominika watch the other three for me. I know I shouldn't have because she was still very young. As long as she didn't try to cook anything, I would be okay.

I remember this one time not long after my fourteenth birthday as I was crouched down under the window of the old mine, with my fingers in my ears, I looked up to look at Dima as I heard my mama screaming her fucking head off, even with fingers in my ears. I was shocked when I saw Dima had his cock out and was stroking and pulling it with his hand. I had never seen a cock before, never mind be this close to one, eye level. I was fascinated watching what he was doing. He was too engrossed in watching my mama fucking, he didn't notice me watching him. I was captivated by it and what he was doing. It scared me, the last time we caught my mama here she was on her knees in front of a man, and he had his cock in her mouth. I watched, transfixed, as she licked it like a popsicle. Then he grabbed her head and he rammed over and over into her mouth.

I felt like being sick watching him ram it straight down her throat. He shouted out, lifting his head to the ceiling, and I watched my mama's face going red with each thrust. Then she was sputtering all this white liquid out of her mouth, it was dripping out. She was puking up; it must be vile having something stuck down your throat like that, making you gag until you are sick. Dima stopped stroking his cock and looked down at me.

"Is that your mama, Dana? She sure looks like you."

"Don't be silly Dima, my mama is out at work," I lied.

Just then, my head was being gripped tightly on the top and being pulled toward his cock. It was even redder with him pulling it and it was big and standing up. I screamed out, got up, and I ran as fast as I could to get away from him and my mama in case she heard me.

It got harder and harder for me to get out and see him. He used me; I know that now. He never did love me, not like I loved him, but I feel so stupid. I hate him. He was fucking lots of girls from school. I found that out, then that last time with Sochia, I knew it and I felt a fool. He made me lose my mind. I never did find out what damage I did to Sochia. I was told they didn't last long. He moved on again not long after I messed her up. Maybe what I did worked, in my mind I wanted to damage her so badly he would come back to me. I guess I did damage her so badly, but he just moved on to the next one.

Three

Vidana

Present

RYKER HAS BEEN INTO THE COFFEE SHOP AN AWFUL LOT OF times now. I can see what Lana saw in him, in a way, he is such a nice guy, he's just not my type. Ha, I don't even know what my type is but I don't particularly find him attractive, I don't seem to find any man attractive. There isn't one man I've thought 'wow' about. Well, there have been two in my life, and I think the second one was because of the situation. Ryker has just walked in. I know he drinks a black decaf, so I get it for him. I turn and he's smiling at me.

"What?" I ask. He laughs. I frown.

"You remind me of Lana. There are so many similarities to you both. Have you heard from her at all?" he knows I don't speak about her. The first time he came into the coffee shop, he knew right away I was Lana's sister. I guess we must look similar, although I've never thought we do. He's asked me on numerous occasions if I've heard from her. I usually just shake my head and turn away, but I've had enough, and he needs to know.

"Look, Ryker. You're a nice guy and I don't want to offend you, but, no, I haven't heard from her and even if I did, I probably wouldn't tell you. I don't want anything to do with Lana, and you just telling me I remind you of her makes me annoyed and angry. I'm sorry she ran off with someone else, but you need to get over her, it's been over three years since she's been gone. Now please stop asking me about her." I move away from him; I don't want to see the hurt on his face, but he seriously needs to get over her. I still don't know how she could leave him and run off with this Sergei, not if she loved him like she told me she did. I don't know Sergei and I don't believe I ever saw him, so I can't possibly say. I know she said her life was in danger, but still. I'm sure Ryker could have helped her and protected her, looking at the way his T-shirt is stretched over his chest and the way it's nearly tearing at the tops of his enormous arms, you can see it's tight all over.

I turn back around with the coffeepot in my hand, ready to apologize to him, but he's gone. Instead, there is another man standing there.

"Hey, black coffee please, love." I freeze on the spot and drop the coffeepot. It smashes at my feet and hot coffee spills everywhere. I can't move. My hand is still held out as though still holding the pot as I stare at the man, who is now looking straight at me with a quizzical look on his face.

"Vi, what the hell? You must be burned, look at your feet." She's in front of me with rags, mopping at the coffee on my shoes and up my legs. I look down and just watch in a daze. "Don't move until I've swept the glass up, I don't want you cutting yourself as well. Just one minute." She's frantically trying to pick up the pieces of glass so I can move. I hear the man at the counter cough. I can't look at him. I don't dare to look at him. My head stays bowed as Sybil goes about doing what she's doing at my feet.

"Vi, are you okay?" She's the only one that calls me Vi. Everyone else calls me Dana. I look into her eyes and nod my head slightly. I feel tears slipping down my cheeks. I don't move. I can't move. She quickly gets a brush and dustpan and sweeps up the glass so I can move. The man coughs again. I don't look. "I'm sorry, sir, but we have a slight emergency here. If you could just wait for one minute, I will be able to serve you. Thank you."

I hear him sigh. I still don't look.

"Hey, Steve, haven't seen you for a while." It's Ryker talking. I don't look.

"Hey, Ryker, actually I never come in here but saw you come in. I was about to get a coffee and join you, just got to wait until they clean this mess up." I still don't look, but it's that voice.

"There you go, Vi. You go into the back and clean up. I'll see to the customers."

She doesn't have to tell me twice. I bolt as fast as I can to the back room before Ryker can say anything and give my name away. I make it to the bathroom just in time to throw up in the toilet bowl. I can't stop shaking. I try to grab some toilet paper to wipe my mouth, but my hands are shaking so much I'm unable to grab it. I close the toilet lid and sit on it. I try to understand what's going on. I saw him only once, but I heard him a couple of times. It's him, I know it is. I will never forget him. I don't understand how he's here and how he knows Ryker. Is Ryker in on it? Is he one of them? I need to hurl again. I get up quickly but don't manage to lift the lid in time. Great, now I have to clean this mess up. I look down and see my legs are red, must be from the coffee I spilled. I don't feel in pain, in fact, I don't feel anything, just numb.

I know it's him. There is no mistaking it. He was the only American I ever heard and saw in all that time I was there. The men, to me, appeared to be afraid of him. I remember that time I saw him, the door was slightly ajar to the room I was in. I was being banged from behind and I could see through the narrow slit. He was standing there with his hands in his jeans pocket. He was angry and started to shout at whoever was in front of him. I was high, it's usually what they did to us, but I remember him like it was yesterday. I thought to myself how hot he was shouting his orders and being very commanding, and with his tall stature, his long dark-brown hair and the partial chiseled chin that I could see. That was all I could make out of him. I remember thinking how he reminded me of Igor. He was powerful, just like Igor. The vibes he gave off would make anyone afraid. He was hot though, well, to me at that time he was, I think. For whatever reason, probably the drug induced state I was in, I remember thinking I wouldn't mind if it was him banging me from behind. Then I threw up at the thought. The old man behind me grabbed my hair, pulling it toward him, in essence lifting my head up to the ceiling. He spat in my face and spewed what I could only imagine was vile abuse at me. He shoved my head forward hard and ramped up the onslaught of his cock in my ass. I didn't look up to the door again. I was sure I was being watched, I felt eyes on me. I didn't want an audience and I didn't want the American to see me.

After that I never saw the American again, I only heard him. I never forgot his voice among all the foreign voices. It could only have been a handful of times I ever heard him again and it was a long time between each time. I found myself constantly listening for a hint of his voice. It became like velvet to me, like a craving, just like the drugs became, only it was a very authoritative voice, very stern and demanding, he was definitely in charge, of what I don't know, but no one spoke back to him. There was this one time he was shouting, then I heard a loud bang. I presumed he had just shot someone, but couldn't say for sure. I had his voice in my head for what must have been months and the image of him. I think they kept me sane in a way. Maybe without that, I would not have survived. That's how I know it's him out there, his hair is shorter, he has piercing blue eyes, I'd say the same as Igor's, it's the first time I've seen them, and how the fuck did he come to be in the same coffee shop I work in? We were in New York, yet here he is in LA.

Did he know I was there in that room that time? He never saw my face, I'm sure of it, my hair was covering me as I had my head down. My hair is so different from back then. It was long and brown like rat's tails all the time. It was so dirty. We never got to bathe, just a quick shower, that was it. Now it's short and pink, although I am growing it again, but I like the hot pink I have. It kind of makes me feel sassy. Not that I feel like that now. I feel like a jellyfish, like Jell-O, all wobbly and no substance. I feel like I am back in those times, back being trapped by those men. The instant flashback he brought as soon as I saw him had me terrified. I need to get out of here. I need to leave out the back, I can't chance him seeing me again, he might remember me. Who the fuck is he anyway?

I grab my fanny pack from the storeroom and I hightail it out the back door. I'm a mess, both externally and internally. I can't fathom in my head what's happening. I can't fathom the feelings I seem to have. I'm all confused, scared, and I feel dazed. I know I'm free. Free to leave the shop, but yet I feel like I should gravitate back to him. I feel I want to see him again to make sure it was him. Was it him? I'm just questioning everything. I know in my head one hundred percent it was him. Hearing his voice brought it all back. Remembering what I had long tried to forget.

———

Taken

They were all foreign. I didn't understand any of them, not that they cared. They used actions, not words, well fists, more than anything. Some of them spoke broken English, but none of them spoke Russian. I didn't know what they were saying. I had picked up some English from visiting Lana in America and when I returned, I watched some of the American TV shows on my computer Mama had bought me. She had been treating me badly and disappearing for days. I think it was a peace offering, a guilt thing. I got hooked on *Teen Wolf* and *Riverdale*. I also started to watch *Vampire Diaries*. I loved them and I taught myself a lot of English from them.

I was out at the store getting some groceries to make dinner for everyone. I didn't know what time Mama would be home, if she was even coming home. It had been like this for the past few years. I was just left to look after my sisters. Dominika helped me a lot with the others. Now she was fourteen, she was a good kid, she never went out. She was more like Lana, always had her head buried in a book. She used to watch the American TV shows with me, and she could speak very good English. She said she wanted to be an English teacher. She was teaching our younger sisters as well. She was so good with them, very patient. She took after our papa. I was on my way home from the store when a man came up to me, he was nicely dressed, but he didn't look Russian. He was dark-skinned, like he was tanned with very black head and facial hair. He did, however, speak broken Russian to me.

"Excuse me, but do you know where I can find this address? I seem to be a little lost." He got close to me to show me what looked like a napkin. I couldn't see anything on it. I leaned forward slightly as he brought it closer for me to see. Suddenly the napkin was smothering my nose and mouth and he held the back of my head so I couldn't fight him. It all happened so fast. I remember dropping the basket with the groceries as I tried to pry his hands from me by scratching them, but then nothing. It all went black.

I slowly come around; my head feels like there is an ax stuck in it. I try to raise my hand to rub my head. I can't move it. My arms ache so much, I try the other one, but I can't move that one either. What the hell is happening? I try to remember where I am. I can't think, my head hurts so bad. My lips feel cracked, I lick them, they sting, I taste blood. I lick them again and one of the cracks opens and starts to bleed. I try to move my legs but it's no use, I can't move any of my limbs. I turn my head to the side, but I can't see anything. It's pitch black here, wherever here is. I try my hands again, they are raised above my head. No wonder my shoulders are aching so much. They are tied up, my legs are spread, and each ankle is tied. Whatever they are tied with is chafing my skin.

What's that? I freeze, listening. I'm not sure if it's the room that is pitch black or because there is something across my eyes. I'm blindfolded. I hear it again. It's like a scratching sound. Suddenly there's a loud noise. It's like maybe a metal bolt on a door, being scraped along as if to open it. I wait, holding my breath. There's another noise. This one is a key in a lock. It's metal on metal. Then what must be a door creaking open. I hear footsteps approaching me. I presume I'm on a bed. It doesn't feel like a floor on my back but it's not that soft either. I hear two or maybe it could be three sets of footsteps. I hold my breath. The noises in my head of my heart beating fast and blood whooshing around my ears, are deafening to me. I need to listen. The footsteps get nearer, then stop. I breathe out, just waiting for some more noise or someone to speak. It's silent for so long.

I jump as I feel a calloused hand slowly drift up my leg from my ankle. I try to move to shake off the hand.

"Stop," a voice says in English, then proceeds to speak in another language. It's not Russian, I don't know what language it is.

The hand carries on moving up my leg and gets to my inner thigh, then suddenly it's gone. There's more talking, only this sounds angry. I'm panting hard. I'm terrified. I feel warmth down below. I know I've just peed myself. They laugh. It sounds like more than the two or three footsteps I thought there were. This sounds like a lot of men laughing. Suddenly I hear lots of movement and steps, along with angry shouting. The room goes silent. My heartbeat and breathing is deafening me once again. I don't know if I'm alone or not. I try to stop breathing to listen, to see if I can hear anyone else breathing. I don't. I just hear my heartbeat thumping in my ears. My head feels like it's about to split open. I'm crying, although the blindfold seems to be mopping up my tears.

I hear footsteps once again, only one set though.

"I will untie you. Do not try to do anything. You will be hurt if you do. We need to get you up and into another room."

It's not an angry voice, but he's harsh and definitely foreign. His English is very broken, but I just about managed to understand what he said. His accent is not one I can say I have ever heard. I feel him at my ankles. I try to move, wriggling my body. He slaps my leg

"Stop," he shouts.

It was him telling the other one to stop. I feel him untie the one ankle, then move onto the other. My legs are free, they ache, they were elevated. He moves to my wrists; he's standing beside me. I can smell him. He smells musky, dirty, and sweaty. I know I am hot, wherever I am, it is stifling in here. He unties my hands and I sigh with relief. I grab each wrist, rubbing where they were tied. They are sore and raw. It must be a rope that was chafing me. The man grabs one of my wrists and I feel myself being elevated. I try to stand on my feet, but my legs are jellified, and I collapse. He drags me by the wrist, up to a standing position. I try to stand but I fall again, only this time I must fall straight into the man. He grabs my waist and props me to standing, holding me, making sure I don't fall again. I get my balance, my legs feel so weak, I don't know if I can walk.

"Move, now. We are late." He snaps his fingers and I hear footsteps again. He hasn't removed the blindfold from me.

Suddenly I have hands under each of my arms and I'm being dragged along with my feet trailing behind me. They hurt so bad; my toes are bent on one foot, but my mouth is so dry I can't speak. I try to tell them to stop but nothing comes out. It feels like forever they are dragging me. We are following footsteps in front of me. We go down some steps, my ankles and the tops of my feet drag along the edges of the steps, and it fucking hurts. I try to cry out but it's just a small squeal. Suddenly I am being unceremoniously dumped onto a chair. My hands are put behind my back and tied together. I don't have the energy to fight. There are too many of them anyway. I have no idea who they are or where I am. I'm petrified.

My shoulders are yanked back, I'm sure they are now dislocated. I scream out in pain, finally finding my voice. There is a bottle put to my lips and water is poured out. It runs down my chin at first and onto my chest. My chest feels bare. I can feel the water. I open my mouth to take it in before it all spills. I need the water. It's very warm but I don't care at this point.

They stop pouring and I hear the plastic bottle being thrown behind me. Someone talks, he is foreign, and I don't know what he says but it is not the same voice as the man who untied me.

"What is your name?" It's broken English again but I don't speak.

Suddenly my head jolts to the side as I am slapped hard across one cheek. That fucking stung so bad.

"Ow, that fucking hurt, you bastard. Who are you? What do you want with me?" I scream out now that I have found my voice. Another jolt as I am slapped on the other side this time. "Ow, stop it, leave me alone," I cry out. Suddenly I am winded as I get what I think is a punch to the tummy. I have so much pain coursing through my whole body.

"You do not speak unless to answer me. Do you understand?"

I don't speak. I get another punch to the tummy.

"Do you understand?"

I nod my head. Suddenly I think I feel a sting on my thigh. It's hard to describe. It feels hot one second but cold the next. Then I feel a trickle running down the inside of my thigh. Whatever the sting was, it's slowly being removed, like a needle was stuck into my thigh. Maybe that's blood running down it.

"I said speak to answer me."

"Yes, yes, I fucking understand." My head snaps back with the force of a punch to the face. I think he broke my face.

"Stop this, we don't want her face marked just yet, you fucking moron." Someone else shouts in broken English. I don't understand why they are speaking foreign and then English?

"What is your name?"

"Vidana," I answer immediately so I don't get hit again.

"How old are you?"

"I was seventeen a few months ago."

"Who is your oldest sister?"

"Svetlana."

He speaks then in his language, and I have no idea what he is say-ing. Why did they ask about Svetlana? What does she have to do with this? Is she in trouble?

"You listen to me. I will say this only once. When I kick your shin, you speak. You tell Svetlana you are being held captive. That Igor Ustrashkins killed your papa because he was a child molester, that he molested his own daughter. That she must do what the man next to her tells her to do. Do you understand?"

I can't speak. What does he mean Igor killed Papa? Papa just left us, Mama said he left, he didn't want to be with all us females. Igor didn't kill him. He isn't dead. What are they talking about? Is Svetlana here, is she in the room, oh god what is going on? I'm winded yet again with an-other punch to the tummy. I try to lean forward but my shoulders and arms won't allow it.

"Do you understand what I just said to you?" He's right in my ear, gritting out the words. I nod.

"Yes, yes I do, but Papa isn't dead, you don't know what you are talking about. Svetlana, Lana are you here, speak to me, Svet…." Another punch to the tummy. I struggle to catch my breath.

"Yes, he is. Igor killed him himself. Supposedly for being a kiddie fiddler. Now when I kick your shin, you say what I told you to say to Svetlana." He kicks me hard, and I squeal.

"Svetlana, are you here, help me." Someone grabs my hair pulling my head back.

"She is not here you stupid fucking whore. You say exactly what I told you to say or I will let the men do as they please with you. Do you fucking hear me?" I try to nod but his hold on my hair is tight.

"Yes" Suddenly my head is pushed forward and I'm kicked again. I raise my head up.

"Svetlana, I am being held captive. Igor killed Papa. He killed him for being a molester to you. You must do what the man next to you tells you to do. Please do it, Svetlana. I think they will kill me. Ow, you fuckers," I scream as I am kicked very hard yet again. I have no idea what is going on. I am being untied and then pulled up by my arm with a very firm grip.

"Where am I? How long have I been here? Are you going to kill me?"

Whoever has hold of me doesn't speak. He just pulls my arm harder. I try to resist but it's futile. I am pulled along, only this time I can stand on my own feet and walk, well it's almost a run. If I don't, I will fall, and no doubt just be dragged along the floor. I need answers, I need to know. I have a free hand. There is only the one man that I know of. I lift the blindfold. He doesn't realize I have lifted it. I suddenly remember a man asking me for directions back home. It could be him but from the back, I don't know. He has jet-black hair and his hand on my arm is tanned looking. I keep up, trying not to give him a reason to look at me. I quickly look around. I'm in a hallway. It looks like a house, but an old house in ruins. He's taking me to a door, there are steps. I was dragged up steps. He's taking me back to the place I was. I try to pull back. He looks at me and realizes I can see him. I think it's the same man. He has black facial hair, but his eyes also look black. They look mean and menacing. He smirks at me as he drags me down the steps. It's so dark down here, but then my eyes have been behind a blindfold, and I suppose anywhere would look dark. He drags me farther down and into a long corridor. This looks like a basement. We pass doors on either side of us. I try to pull back, trying to grab on to anything I can, but my nails are being ripped out and I scream. I hear someone shout. It's a female. She's banging on a door and shouting to let her out. She sounds American. Holy fuck, how many girls are here?

"Hey, where are we? How many are there here? Quick, answer me."

Just then he whizzes around on me and bang.

Four

Vidana

Present

I'VE BEEN HIDING IN MY ROOM SINCE LEAVING THE COFFEE SHOP. I haven't seen anyone; I don't want to see anyone. There's a gentle knock at my door and I freeze. I don't move or speak. I'm like that broken girl all over again. The memories just keep coming and I don't want them to. I hear the soft knock again.

"Dana, are you in there, sweetie? It's Poppy." I sigh out with relief. I get up and unlock my door. We have always been told not to lock the doors unless we feel unsafe. I feel unsafe. I slowly open the door very slightly to make sure it's just Poppy. I don't see anyone with her. I move away, not opening it to invite her in. I sit back on my bed with my knees pulled up to my chest and my arms wrapped around them. I rest my chin on my knees and watch as she very tentatively enters my room. She smiles but I don't return it. I have tears running down my face yet again. She comes in and closes the door behind her.

"Hey, sweetie, do you want to talk?"

I don't say anything. I just look at her with tear-filled eyes. I feel lost again, like I did for all that time. I feel embarrassed and stupid for letting it get like this. I want the drugs to numb the pain I'm feeling, but I know I can't go there. I can't let Poppy down or myself. She moves over to me and sits on the bed beside me. She moves my arms from around my knees and she leans in to hug me. I let her. I cry on her shoulder as I hug her tight to me. We stay like this for a while until my sobs ease. All this time I've been wondering what to say to her. I can't tell her about the man in the coffee shop. I just remembered Ryker called him Steve. I have a name to the face and that voice.

"Do you want to tell me what happened? Ryker called and said you had an accident in the coffee shop. Are you okay?"

I see her look at my bare legs. She gets up and moves to the bathroom. She comes back with some wet cotton pads, and she starts to dab at my feet and legs. "Oh Dana, you have blisters all over your legs. Was this from the accident?" I just nod. "Stay right here. I need to get some lotion to put on them to help with the blisters. I'll be right back." She leaves but doesn't close the door. I get up and run to close it. I'm scared he knows who I am. I don't believe he just happened to come into the same shop I work in, or that Ryker isn't a part of this, this, whatever this is.

It takes no time before Poppy is knocking on my door again. I open it, only it's not Poppy standing there. It's Ryker. How the hell did he know where I was? I never told him I lived here. I only speak to him on a casual basis. I slam the door in his face quickly before he has a chance to stop the door from closing. Fuck. Why is he here? What does he have to do with that other man? Is Steve even his real name? I hear voices outside in the corridor. I put an ear to the door to listen. I can hear Poppy; she's asking Ryker what he is doing here. He says he just wanted to check I was okay. She tells him to leave. There's a gentle knock.

"Dana, it's Poppy. Ryker has left. Can I please come in?" I open the door a tiny bit to see if she is telling the truth. Of course she is. Why wouldn't she be? Poppy has only ever been truthful and so helpful to me. I open the door slightly to allow her to come in and I move back to the bed. I scoot back so my back is on the wall. She sets about putting lotion on my burns.

"Do you want to tell me what happened?"

"I dropped a coffeepot that was full of hot coffee. I felt stupid and I ran out." I shrug.

She looks at me closely.

"Ryker says you were freaked out about something. He was the one that phoned me and asked me to look in on you. I just met him in the corridor, but I asked him to leave. Was that okay?" I nod. "Is there anything else you want to talk about? You seem awfully upset about a broken coffeepot and some blisters." She knows there is something else. Now is the perfect time.

"I've just been so worried about my sisters, Poppy. I wanted to speak to you about them, but I know how busy you are, and you have enough to worry about with all your family." I look down to my hands that are playing with the hem of my tee.

"Anything else, Dana?" I look at her. She knows there is more.

"Just, I'm—" I break off and look back down.

"You know you can talk to me about anything. I've always told you this. Please never bottle anything up." I look her in the eye. I can't tell her that.

"I was looking at apartments to rent around here and there is no way I can live here, Poppy, in LA. The prices are way out of my league. I don't know what I am going to do. This is the only place I know, and the only place I feel safe. I have you here. I don't want to leave. There's that and worrying about my sisters. I haven't heard from any of them for so long. My mama never answers when I call. I want to ask if Igor could please have someone check on them. I'm scared, Poppy. I know what Mama is like."

She carefully dabs lotion onto my legs and feet. It's soothing. I can see her thinking.

"Is it that you need to leave here? I mean the refuge?"

I shake my head.

"It's not that I want to leave. No, I think it best that I do leave. I feel like I shouldn't be here because you need this room for someone else you could be helping. I know you said to stay as long as I want, but I feel bad taking up a room. I checked out the prices and—"

Should I tell her what I was thinking? I don't want her to get angry or upset with me.

"And what, Dana?" she asks gently.

"I was thinking the only way I could possibly be able to rent an apartment would be to, oh god Poppy, you will hate me for it. But I was thinking of maybe becoming a dancer at night in one of those clubs that advertise for dancers." I see the look on her face. It isn't anger or upset, but more pity. She shakes her head, gently.

"Is that what you want to do or just what you think will get you the money for rent?"

"It's the last thing I want to do."

"Why didn't you speak to me sooner? We could have sorted all this out without you worrying about any of it." She strokes a finger down my face. I close my eyes as the tears slip out yet again. "First, I will get Igor to check on your sisters and see what your mama is doing. That's easy enough and he would do that, no problem. Once his men get back to him, I will let you know and we can deal with whatever it is when we know. Second, you can move into a room on the ninth floor of our building. That is where Svetlana lived, along with a lot of other girls we have helped. This refuge was new when you arrived. It was to help people like you. Most of them that live on the ninth floor stay because they can't afford the rent, like you say, and they either end up working for Igor and me or they get a job and pay rent. As you have a job and you work here in the refuge, if you continue to do that, then you don't need to pay any rent. How does that sound?"

I throw myself into her arms, nearly knocking her over. How could Lana ever hate this woman? She does nothing but good for everyone. I've heard the rumors about her being someone you never want to cross. She's Igor's right-hand woman, after all. I've been told she is called the dragon lady and is feared throughout LA. I know you never know what to believe, but she's a mom of five and she is so caring. I love her like a sister. More than Svetlana ever was to me. I squeeze her tight and cry on her shoulder. She hugs me back.

"You mean the world to me, Poppy. I class you more of a sister than Svetlana could ever be. I am so grateful to you and to Igor for all you have done for me. I know I haven't been easy and I'm sorry I put you through all that. I love you, Poppy." I look down, embarrassed that I just blurted that all out. She just hugs me close to her.

I've just moved into my own room at the building Igor and Poppy own. I have access to the gym and swimming pool and my room is self-contained, not like a hotel room, which I imagined it to be. This is a minisuite. I have a bedroom, bathroom, a seating area, and a small kitchenette that has everything I need. I can cook my own food here. Igor sent his men to check on Mama and my sisters. He still doesn't talk to me, but Poppy told me that my mama doesn't live in that house anymore. They are looking for her. I'm in a panic even more now.

I took two weeks off from the coffee shop. I was just too afraid to go back. I knew Ryker would be coming in to see me. He tried twice more to visit me at the refuge, not that I was there but they didn't tell him that I had moved out. I know he only cares about me, but I am nothing to him, not even a friend. I don't want him to look out for me because of Lana. She left him and he needs to get over it. I was mainly terrified of Steve coming back. What if he knew who I was? What if he recognized me? I saw him, I knew he was important. I haven't told Poppy about him. I've been thinking about it a lot. I've been waking up in hot sweats almost every night, screaming out. I'm just relieved I moved into my new place the next day after speaking to Poppy. If I had stayed at the refuge, someone would have heard me screaming in my sleep and come to check on me. The memories in my dreams are so real. I'm living the fucking nightmare of my captivity all over again.

———

Taken

I don't know how long I was knocked out for. I woke up with my mouth dry and tied up how I was the first time I woke up. I had the blindfold on again, so I couldn't even see where I was. I remember I removed it and I was being pulled along by a man. I remember a long corridor with doors on either side and there were girls shouting and crying. I try to move but it's no use. My body is aching everywhere, my face feels like it's swollen, my lips are cracked, they are so dry. I lick them, then wince. They are huge and swollen. I remember being slapped and punched a lot. I must be bruised all over. The place smells rotten, it smells like one of Zoya's diapers. I know it must be mostly from me. I try to sniff more but my nose is all blocked. Maybe it's broken like the rest of me. I just feel like I want to die. I don't know where I am or even who has taken me. Svetlana, they knew her. What does she have to do with this? I cry. I remember them telling me Igor killed my papa. My eyes sting bad, I can't sniff, and my lips feel enormous and cracked. My tummy is hurting so bad, but what hurts the most is remembering my papa is dead.

It keeps going round and round in my head. Igor killed my papa. They said he was a child molester, that he molested Lana. There is no way he did that. He would never do anything like that. Why would they even say that? Why would they say Igor killed him because of it? I have so many things racing through my mind. My tummy grumbles. I don't know the last time I ate anything. I hope Dominka is looking after the small ones. What will they do without me? Mama is gone most of the time. What if these men go and grab my sisters? Oh god, did they have them in the other rooms? Were they the ones crying? Are they already here? I cry again. I'm cold, hurt, and hungry.

I must have fallen asleep. The noise of the bolt on the door and the metal on metal of the key wake me up. I wait with bated breath, trying not to breathe so I can listen. My heartbeat is going ten to the dozen in my eardrums, I can't hear properly. Just then someone is standing at the side of me. I can feel them. A finger presses on my nose and I try to shake it off, wriggling my head. It then travels down over my mouth. It hovers on my lips, then presses into a crack.

"Ow, that fucking hurt," I shout in Russian at whoever it is.

It's a man, he laughs. His finger then travels over my chin, down my neck, then very slowly down my body. I am naked. I can feel his finger all the way down. He pauses between my breasts then carries on down to my belly button, where he then inserts his finger into it. He digs in hard. I wince. He then starts to travel down lower. I'm starting to freak out.

"Stop that. You were sent to collect her, not play with her. There will be time for that later." Someone else in the room speaks, but it's broken English again. I don't understand unless they all speak different languages. The man removes his finger from just under my navel. He then unties my ankles and I try to kick out at him. He grabs them

"Stop, or I will break your fucking legs."

I still. He then unties my hands; they collapse above my head. I have no feeling in them. I couldn't lash out if I wanted to. He takes an arm and pulls me off whatever it is I'm on. I bang with a thud on the concrete floor, my head cracks on it. Then nothing.

"Get off me, leave me alone. What are you doing? Stop hurting me."

Someone is slapping my cheeks, not hard but trying to rouse me. I'm sitting on probably the same chair as yesterday with my hands tied behind my back. The blindfold is removed. I can't see much to focus on anything. I hang my head. When I feel I can, I look up. The room is horribly dark, I can see there are people standing around. There seem to be about six of them. There is a camera in front of me. I look down and I have clothes on.

"Do you remember what we asked you to say last time?" The voice makes me jump, it's someone standing right behind me. "ANSWER ME," he shouts in my ear. I shake my head.

"NO," I grit out.

"I like her. She's feisty," the voice says behind me. He sounds different. I can understand him, but there is a twinge to his accent.

"I want you to look into that camera and you say 'Svetlana, you need to do as they say. If you don't, they will kill me. Igor killed Papa for molesting you. He killed him, Svetlana, he's a bad man. Do it or they will kill me and our sisters next.' Now do you think you can remember that?"

I don't say or do anything. I'm shaking with fear, my sisters, what if they already have them? What if they are making them do this? The man grabs my hair and yanks my head back, he leans over my face. My vision is still a little blurry, but I can see he looks angry. He also has darker skin, like the other men.

"Fucking answer me, bitch." He spits in my face.

"Yes, okay. I will do as you ask." He pushes my head forward hard.

"Now you look at that man there with his hand raised," he turns my head so I can see a man stood to the side of the camera. "When he drops his hand, you say what I just told you to say, okay?"

"Yes," I say, but I don't look up to the camera. He pulls my head back again by the hair.

"Fucking look into the camera when you speak. I want her to see your beat-up face to know we are serious." He pushes my head again. I look up and straight ahead of me. I see the other man's hand drop. That's my signal to speak. The tears are streaming down my face as I start. I hiccup a couple of times and wince at the pain I feel. When we are done, they put the blindfold back on me and unceremoniously one of them marches me back to where I was before. This time, they keep my hands tied behind my back. As soon as we've descended the steps, I start to shout.

"Hello, can you hear me? Please shout. How many of you are there? Dominika, are you here, shou…"

My head is pulled to a chest with a hand over my mouth to shut me up. My heart is beating so fast, I hear the pulsing yet again in my ears. I also hear some girls shouting. There seem to be a few of them but I have no idea how many. What are they doing with all these girls? I don't know if my sisters are here. I didn't hear any of them. Once again, I am shoved into a room and before I can say or do anything, I am shoved onto the bed and tied up. I am at least dressed in clothes this time.

I fall asleep. I have no idea how long I have slept for, but the door being unlocked wakes me up. Someone comes over to me. I didn't hear footsteps. They set something on my bed, then I feel something hard at my lips. It's forced between them and liquid spills down my throat. I lick my sore, swollen lips. There's a food taste on them. The hard object is put to my lips again and this time I open them. It feels like a spoon being put inside and liquid trickles down my throat. I gulp, big mistake, I start to choke. I can't move with being tied down, but I cough and cough. I then dry heave as bile comes up my esophagus and into my mouth. It tastes vile. The spoon is once again put to my lips, but this time, I sip the liquid. It's some kind of soup, there isn't much taste, it's like dirty water, but anything will do at this point. I have no idea if I have been here for days or weeks. This is the first thing I have been given.

It doesn't last long and before I know it, whoever gave me the soup is gone. I hear the door being bolted and locked again. My body still aches all over. The choking and coughing really hurt my tummy, ribs and chest. The soup stung my lips, but I needed it. My nose is still swollen, I can tell. I can smell but with difficulty still. I smell vile. I smell of pee and shit. They obviously don't care.

It seems like months have passed. I've been cooped up in this room for so long. They untie me now during the day but tie me up at night. I have a bucket in the corner to use as my toilet and they bring me dirty water to drink, along with watered-down soup and stale bread once a day. That's it. The same every day. The only thing that changes is the girls who bring my food. One of the men stands at the door while she puts the food on the floor. The first month or so, a girl would spoon-feed me. I used to see the look of disgust on the faces as they approached me. I was soiled and smelled terrible. I lay in my own shit. No one cared. Once they started to untie me and remove my blindfold, the girls would just put the food on the floor and back out the door. I've tried to speak to a number of the girls, but none of them speak to me. Most of them look as bad as I'm sure I look. I was shocked the first time I saw any of them. I gasped out as she moved inside my room.

My room, there are no windows at all, there is no light, it's dark all the time with or without a blindfold. If I ever do get out of here, I think I will be light blind. Not so long ago, well, I don't think it was long ago some men came to my room and they brought in pitchers. I was told to strip. They put my mattress on the floor, and they hosed it down. Then they had me standing naked. They ogled me for a little while. One of them stepped forward and started to slap my breasts, hard. I put my hands over them to stop him. He was standing in front of me, eyeing me from top to toe. I thought he was going to do something to me. One of the other men stopped him, they spoke in a different language, so I don't know what they were saying. They then threw whatever was in the pitchers over me. It smelled a little soapy, so I rubbed it over my body. Then they hosed me down with freezing cold water. I tried not to think of the look on their faces. I bet they would have all had a go on me if it weren't for the one who spoke, telling them to stop. Every man I have seen has looked tanned with jet-black hair and most of them have the same facial hair, long beards, some of them wear what look like dresses, others are in jeans and tees. That was the first wash I had since being here, however long it had been.

It's now been days again, or weeks, who knows. The door is unlocked, and a man comes in. I know it's a man because all the girls don't wear shoes. He stands at the side of me where I am tied to my bed. I don't have any clothes on again, not since they told me to strip when they hosed me down. I hear him move.

"What do you want? What are you doing?" I ask, afraid.

He hasn't moved, just standing there. Suddenly a hand lands on my breast. He squeezes it hard.

"Ow, you fucker, that hurt. Get off me, leave me alone."

I start to try and wriggle. My body doesn't ache anymore. I am used to being tied up and they haven't hit me much, just the odd slap every now and then if I open my mouth. He moves to the other breast and squeezes and pinches that one even harder.

I scream out, "Ouch, get the fuck off me. Leave me alone."

I scream loud like a baby, hoping someone will come in and stop him like they have been stopped all the other times. No such luck. My head is jolted as he punches me in the cheek. I see stars. I straighten my head back.

"Leave me the fuck alone, you asshole!" I shout at him.

He grabs both nipples and squeezes them so hard. He twists them, the pain is excruciating. He stops for a second, then he's back, grabbing hard and rolling them in his hands.

"Get off me."

I try to buck with my body. He slaps my face hard with the palm of his hand right onto my nose. I think he's broken it. I feel something trickle from it down to my top lip. My tongue comes out on instinct, and I can taste the blood. He lets go of my breasts but replaces his hand with his mouth and teeth. He starts to suck one of my nipples, then he starts to bite it hard. I swear he's broken the skin there. His saliva is making it sting. I try to buck my body to get him off me. As I do this, he places a hand on my tummy to flatten it. His hand then drifts down lower to my vagina. I feel him stroking my hair there. Oh no, this is what I've been dreading. I'm surprised they have left me alone this long. My legs are spread with being tied to each end of the bed. I can't squeeze my legs together to stop him. His hand wanders lower, stroking while he still bites on my nipple. I feel him there at my nub. It sickens me.

"Get off me, you fucker. Leave me alone. HELP," I scream out over and over.

The blackness descends as I'm punched in the face.

Vidana
Present

ILOVE LIVING ON THE NINTH FLOOR. I HAVE EVEN MADE A COUPLE of friends. I didn't realize there was a room where we could just chill out with each other if we wanted instead of being alone. It's like I've seen on the TV when they are at college, they have houses they all live in, the boys have one and the girls another. They give them funny names but it's like a communal area where we can just talk if we want to. I love it. I never thought I would ever say that.

Ryker has been coming into the coffee shop practically every day I am there. He's growing on me, he's really thoughtful and caring. He even brought me some flowers after my injury. I have never in my life had anyone buy me flowers. He was even embarrassed about it. He hasn't asked me about my reaction that day I dropped the coffeepot, and I haven't had the courage to ask him who Steve was, but I do need to know one way or another. He's just walked in now. I turn to get his coffee ready, on turning back he has a big goofy grin on his face.

"What's wrong with you? Why are you smiling like that?" He looks down to grab his coffee, then looks around to see if anyone is near him.

"Dana, would you like to go out for a drink with me tonight?"

I must look shocked and before I can answer, he speaks again.

"Or not, if you're busy, it's okay we can take a rain check. Just as friends, of course."

I feel sorry for him. The more I see him, the more attractive he becomes to me and he's a nice guy and I could be friends with him.

"Just as friends? Nothing more?"

He nods like a little boy, and his cheeks flush slightly.

"Then yes, I would like that, Ryker."

The realization on his face that I actually said yes makes me smile.

"Great, that's great. Should I pick you up and we can go to this nice cocktail bar I know?"

I frown at him. He looks worried.

"Erm, Ryker, would you mind if we just got something to eat rather than a bar? I would just feel better with that." I don't smile at him, instead I shrug and turn around to clean the side.

"Okay, Dana. Yes, let's get something to eat then. Do you want a fancy restaurant, or we can just go to the diner down the road? I could pick you up when you are finished from here and we can go straight there. It's up to you."

"Can I please go home to change first? Just so I don't smell of coffee all evening. The diner sounds great. I haven't been to one before."

"Yeah, sure. I can pick you up from the refuge." I look down. He doesn't know I moved out a few weeks back. I wasn't sure if Poppy would have told him or not.

"I don't live there anymore. I moved into the building Lana used to live in." I see his face drop. "I can meet you, just tell me where."

He looks a little sullen, but I don't know why. Maybe it's the memories of Lana.

"No, I will come and pick you up. Let's say seven, does that work for you? I will stay in the lobby and wait for you."

I agree and he sits to have his coffee. He always stays in to have his drinks, he never takes them away. I'm also always more on edge when he's in here in case Steve comes in to see him again. So far, he hasn't been in.

I dashed home to get a shower and fresh clothes. We are going to the diner so casual clothes will be fine. I throw on my jeans, a nice top, and put my wedge sandals on. Just as I exit the stairwell, I like to walk down the stairs rather than take the elevator, I stop dead. I see Ryker, he has his back to me but he's talking to a man. It's him. It's Steve. I edge back into the door so he doesn't see me but I keep it slightly ajar so I can see what happens. They are too far away for me to hear anything. There is no way I am going out until he has gone. Ryker will just have to wait.

I see Ryker check his watch. I check my phone. It's now seven fifteen, I'm late. He turns to look in the direction of the elevators. He wouldn't know I walked down. Just then I see Steve pat Ryker on the back, and he heads in my direction. Fuck. What do I do? I can't run up the stairs quick enough and I don't know what floor he'll be going to. I let the door close, gently, and I go up a couple of steps. If he comes in, I will keep my head down, looking at my phone and walk past him. It's all I can do. I wait a couple of seconds; he would have been here by now. I move to the door. I look through the small, elongated glass pane. I don't see him. I open the door gently and slightly peer out. The elevators are just to my right. I see him there; he steps into the elevator. I breathe out with a sigh of relief. I head out the door after waiting a minute just to make sure he's gone. I pretend I'm texting someone as I walk out so I don't have to look up. I know where Ryker was standing.

"Hey, I thought you had stood me up. I was about to leave; I couldn't phone you as I don't have your number." I look up and smile.

"Sorry, I was just on the phone with a friend, then she texted me. I'm here now and ready when you are."

We walk out of the building. As we walk down the street, I feel a little awkward. Neither of us has spoken and I don't honestly know what to say. I've never done this before, never been out for something to eat with anyone, let alone a man.

"What do you like to eat, Lana? Do you like…"

I stop in my tracks. He just called me fucking Lana. I turn around to head back home. In a flash, I'm being whizzed round by a strong hand on my arm and my instinct is to grab the thumb and bend it back. We were taught self-defense at the refuge. It's Ryker, he's a tough muscly guy but I still manage to hold his thumb back. He holds up his other hand in surrender. I instantly let go. He shakes his hand out as if in some discomfort. I didn't bend it that hard.

"Hey, I'm sorry, it just slipped out. Please don't go."

I frown at him. "I told you before, Ryker. I am not Lana; don't think I am a substitute for her. She was a long time ago now. Surely you are over her?"

He looks hurt. "I don't think that at all. I just like you, Vidana." He emphasizes my name this time.

I do actually find I like him. Just not in an attraction kind of way, I don't think. Oh, I don't know. The only person I was ever attracted to was Dima, and look how that turned out. The words Poppy said keep coming back, that one day I will find the right person and want to give him my body. I just don't think Ryker is that person. Maybe I will never find that person. I sigh and start to walk back in the direction we were heading.

"Please just call me Vi. Then you might not get confused. Sybil at work calls me that and I kind of like it." I look over and smile at him. His eyes light up as his goofy smile reappears. We walk on, I have no idea where the diner is, it's not like I've ever been out to eat anywhere really.

"What do you like to eat, Vi? Is there anything you don't like?"

Hmm, I've lived on watered-down soup with stale bread for a few years, so I don't suppose I am fussy anymore. Once I was rescued and brought to the refuge, all I could eat was soup. They tried to get me to eat normal food, but I just used to throw up. I do eat a lot better now; I even cook me some home-made Russian food we used to have growing up. That makes me sad, I think of my sisters.

"Hey, why the sad face. It wasn't that hard of a question, was it?"

I have no idea what he knows about me or my past.

"No, I was just thinking. I am not too sure if there is anything I don't like. I suppose I just need to try things to find out. I've never been out to a diner; I did go out to restaurants when I visited Lana and Igor with my mama and sisters. I don't remember much of what I ate back then so I don't really know."

I see the look of pity as he registers what I just said. We walk a little more until we come to what looks like a shiny train carriage to me. It says Dickies Diner on it. He opens the door and motions for me to enter. We are greeted by an older lady in what looks like a maid's uniform, complete with hat. I hear Ryker laugh; I turn and he shoos me to follow the lady. She seats us at a table and gives us menus. She starts to recite some things that I have no idea what she is talking about. She leaves as Ryker orders something. He suddenly leans forward and very gently pushes my chin up.

"You are gawking. This is funny. I'm glad I brought you here. This is one of the oldest diners in LA."

I smile, picking up the menu. I've seen something like this on that TV show I watched, *Riverdale*. The kids were always in a diner in that one. I just can't believe I'm sitting in something like this. The lady returns with two big glasses and places them in front of us. She asks if we are ready to order. I just look to Ryker. He tells her to give us a few more minutes.

"These are milkshakes. Have you never had a milkshake before?"

I shake my head and pull the glass toward me and have a taste. Mmmm, this is delicious. I don't think I will be able to eat though if I drink all this.

"This is so nice. What is the flavor? I've seen the kids on TV have these before."

"You have chocolate, because I don't know a female that doesn't like chocolate and I have banana, here, do you want a taste of this one?" He slides the glass over to me and I take a sip of his. Mmmm, I think that one's better than the chocolate. They are huge glasses with whipped cream and a cherry on the top.

"I like this one better," I say before taking more of it. He laughs at me. I slide the chocolate one over to him as I sip the banana one through the straw. I take a breather; I'm going to get full on this. "What do you suggest I try?"

"I think, as a diner with the old all-American fast food, hot dogs, ten different ways and burgers with fries, maybe you should try a dog, how about that?"

I screw up my face.

He laughs again.

"You eat dogs here? That is so gross, Ryker. I don't think I want to eat a dog. Maybe one of those burgers you suggested." Well, he roars with laughter. What the hell did I say? People are looking at us and I sink into my seat and cross my arms over my chest.

"Oh Vi, you crack me up. We don't eat dogs here; no. A hot dog is just the name they gave it. It's processed meat rolled in a skin and it's long. See, this picture here shows you what it looks like. You can have ketchup and mustard on it, it can come with onions, or you can have a chili dog.

I will get a burger and we will get you a normal dog with onions. Then you can try them both. Let's get some fries and onion rings. Does that sound good to you?" He shows me the images on the menu. I feel stupid now, thinking it was dogs.

I nod in agreement.

"This is so delicious, Ryker. Thank you for bringing me here. It's good to taste this food, but I'm stuffed now." I only managed a couple of bites of the dog and a little bite of the burger with a few fries. I know I need to eat more but I still struggle on that side of things. Maybe in time it will come but until it does, I will just nibble. I've even struggled with the portions I cook myself and end up throwing a lot away.

We start talking and he tells me all about his job and how he worked for Igor when he injured his back. He said that was how he met Lana. He told me he was married before that and it shocked me, but his wife died. I felt so bad for him, he looked so sad. I didn't give anything away about me, I just talked about my sisters, not Lana, the younger ones. The burning question I needed to ask was who this Steve was. I needed to know if Ryker had any connections with him.

"Ryker, who was that man that came in the coffee shop the other week? When I had my accident. He looked familiar but I couldn't place him." He thinks for a second.

"Oh, you mean Steve? He works for Igor. He's his guard, that's how I know him. When I used to do rehabilitation with Igor, Steve was around a lot. He's a nice guy, quiet and keeps to himself mostly. I hadn't seen him for a while, we just had a catch up that day in the coffee shop. Funny though, he said the same thing about you. When he sat down, he just said you looked familiar. I thought maybe your paths must have crossed at the refuge center. That must be how you know him, maybe you've seen him around when Igor has been there. Sometimes he shadows Poppy as well."

Oh my god, I can't believe he works for Igor and Poppy. How can that be? They are the ones that saved me and the other girls. They can't be in on it, can they? I need to get home.

"I'm sorry, Ryker, do you mind if we call it a night, please. I think I ate too much, and I don't feel too good. I've really enjoyed it, thank you."

He looks a little forlorn as we leave. We walk back and just talk about random things. I tell him more bits about growing up in Russia, not too much. I never like to talk about my life. Once back home, we say good night. It's a little awkward. I just turn and wave bye from the revolving doors as he watches me go through them.

In my room, I'm pacing. Steve was the leader; he was in charge. I could tell the other men were afraid of him. How then can he work for the Ustrashkins? How could he work for them, and they don't know about what he does? I don't understand, my head is in bits. The Ustrashkins must have known. How else could Steve do what he does? Maybe he's the middleman, maybe Igor is in charge and doesn't want anyone to know he does the sex trafficking. I'm tearing my hair out, literally. They had me tell Svetlana that Igor killed Papa. Why would they do that? Surely that was to get back at Igor in some way. If they all worked for him, why would they do that? Nothing makes sense. I'm just relieved I didn't mention any of this to Poppy. What if she's in on it? But how could she be? She set up the refuge to help girls and boys like me. Kids younger than me that are taken and used for sex trafficking. She set it up for us. Why would she do that if she was involved in that business? Maybe she doesn't know Igor is involved. That must be it. She doesn't know, she can't know. There is no way she would be involved, I'm almost sure of that.

Taken

I have no idea how long I have been here now. It's got to be months. I think so far, I have been lucky. I'm sure some of the other girls come and go, yet I seem to be a constant and I don't know why. I say I've been lucky because so far apart from me being beaten a few times, and a couple of the men have tried to touch me, no one has actually done anything that bad to me. I've heard other girls screaming to be left alone. The screams haunt me every night and day. During the night when I was tied up, all I could do was listen. The screams, followed by slaps and lots of grunting. I know what was happening. There was the one man who got close to me that one time. He was biting my nipple hard and nearly bit it off, but he started to play down below at my vagina. He didn't actually do anything, at least I am sure he didn't because I felt okay once I awoke after being knocked out by him. I can only assume someone came in and stopped him, as has been the case each time someone tried to touch me.

I guess I might have had a birthday at some point, although I have no idea what the date is, never mind what day or time it is. There is no time here, it doesn't exist. The only thing that keeps me going is my sisters. I just pray they are all safe. I often wonder if Mama ever tried looking for me or if she just thought I ran away. I don't think she would have looked but I also know she would have been angry I wasn't there to look after my sisters. Poor Dominika will have had to step in full time. I have thought about trying to end my life a lot, I just don't know how I can. I don't have anything that I could do it with. I have to drink my soup from the bowl, there are no spoons. When they untie me, they take the ropes out of the room, and I barely have any clothes on. Every time someone walks in that door, I think this is it. They are going to kill me or rape me. My life is just complete dread. I know I can't go on like this for much longer and I'm sure the little luck I have will be running out soon.

The weeks have gone by again. This is it; I know it. They have come for me. They have dressed me and led me out of the room, blindfolded and my arms tied behind my back. I'm being dragged along by a chain tied to a collar around my neck. I can hear other chains, like I'm not the only one tied up. I am pulled up the stairs. I try to resist but end up being punched in the tummy, pushed over and my knees cracking on the stone steps. One of them pushed my head hard and I hit my forehead on a step. I felt dizzy and sick, but had no chance to say anything as I was being dragged up the steps. I blacked out.

I have no idea how they got me into a vehicle, but the motion woke me up. I'm lying on a floor. It must be a truck of some sort. I try to sit up. I hear sobbing. I'm not alone. The chain around my neck must be tethered to something on the vehicle because I am very restricted in my movements. With my hands still tied behind my back, I feel around and there is a bench of sorts behind me. I try to get up to sit on it, but the chain doesn't allow it. I feel with my hands on the floor and I'm shocked when I touch something. I feel and it's someone's feet.

"Hello, hello, who is that?" I hear a sob again. I speak in English because I have no idea what nationality anyone is around me. "Hello, can you answer me? I can feel you have no shoes on, you must be like me?"

"Shhh," someone whispers. "They will hear you and beat us all." All, there's a few of us?

"Where are we? Where are they taking us? How many are in here?" I whisper, hoping someone will answer me.

"I don't know where we are or where we're going. There are five of us on this truck." It's broken English like me, but I don't recognize the accent. It's the first time I have spoken to anyone in so long. I cry. "Shhh," the voice says again. "You're going to get us all beat up if you continue." I stay quiet, listening to what I can.

We're in a truck and moving, at least that was confirmed, but to where? What are they going to do with us? Why are they moving us now, or me at least? I have been locked in that basement for so long, why now?

The truck stops. I wait with bated breath to see what happens next.

"Can anyone see where we are or are you all blindfolded like me?" I whisper. No one answers. "Can you hear me; please can someone tell me if you can see where we are?"

"Be quiet, they are outside. I can hear them but can't see them. I don't have a blindfold on, but this is a truck all enclosed. No Windows, slats, or anything. This is like the trucks you see things being delivered in. It is white outside of it. Shhh, I hear someone coming." I listen and can hear the footsteps. Then there is a loud bang, then a door opens, it's very creaky. Suddenly I am drenched, and the door slams shut. They threw water over us. The truck starts moving again.

"What did they do?" I whisper.

"They threw buckets of water over us so we could scoop it up to drink. You need to get what you can from the floor. Who knows how long we will be in here in this heat?" She's right, I am sweating with the heat in the back of this truck. I lean down and suck up some of the water from the floor. It's no different to what I've been used to all this time.

It seems to be hours that pass by. I have no idea even what country we are in with all the men I have seen so far being foreign. I must have fallen asleep with the motion and the heat. There are loud bangs again and the door suddenly opens. I feel the truck dip as someone jumps inside. My chain is being untied.

"Get off me, no, don't put that on me again. Please don't, I need to see where I'm going." It's the girl who was talking to me earlier. I hear the thwack as she is being punched, most likely to silence her. I am pulled out of the truck, I fall to my knees, I don't have the energy or strength to get on my feet. I am being dragged along the floor. I know I will be grazed and cut, it feels rough under me. I can't protest. They shoved a rag into my mouth. I suspect they did to all of us, so we don't scream. That tells me we must be in earshot of other people. I need to try to make noise, try attracting attention to us. I start to wriggle as they drag me, I try to turn over, they didn't tie the rag that's in my mouth, just shoved it in there. Fools. I wedge it out with my tongue, it takes a lot of effort.

"HELP, SOMEONE, HELP US. HELP US, QUICK. WE HAVE BEEN TAKEN." I scream out as much as I can. It's hard, my throat is so dry, but I do it. I scream and scream until…

My head is thumping, my body is aching, I feel like I have been in a fight and lost, big time. I try to move but it's no use. I am tied up yet again, this time though the bed under me feels a little softer than the previous location. I can't move my arms or legs and I'm blindfolded but also with a rag this time tied around my mouth. I can just about breathe through my nose but it's a struggle. I feel like I'm going to hyperventilate, I'm scared, I feel like I'm suffocating. I try to scream from my throat to see if anyone comes, but the noise I make is so feeble. I start to panic, this is it. I'm going to die by suffocating. I try to think of something to take my mind away from the panic, but nothing comes to mind, just sheer panic. My nose is burning trying to take in air and breathe it out through it. The rag in my mouth is touching my nostrils. I feel like I can't get the air out and I suck the rag in as I try to sniff up the air. I try to wriggle my arms free, but I know it's no good and I just break the skin by trying. I start to buck my body off the bed, up and down. My energy is low. It takes all I have. The tears are soaking the blindfold. My wrists are now raw and I feel myself slipping away second by second. Just a couple more sucks up the nose, then out, in and out, in and out. I'm calming myself but my mind is going blank. The lack of oxygen is making me dizzy and sleepy. I need hel...

I'm woken with freezing water being thrown on me. I startle at the coldness. I splutter and screw my eyes shut, then open them. I can see, there is no blindfold, and my mouth is also free. I lick at the water around my mouth, my throat is so dry. I can breathe again. I thought I had died. I thought it was the end for sure, with the panic attack. In all honesty, I wish it was. I wish I was dead. I slowly turn my head to see who is in the room with me. I'm surprised when I see a woman standing there with a bucket in her hand.

"You need to get up now. I need to get you cleaned up. You have visitors to see you today." What is she talking about? She's American, I recognize her accent. I remembered there was another man that sounded either English or American, but with a slight accent still. I look around the room. There is a window that I can see, but it looks boarded up. There is nothing else but the bed. It's a big bed that I am currently on that is now soaked with the water. The woman doesn't look old, but she looks mean.

"Who is coming to see me? Have you rescued me? Is it my mama who is coming?" I'm getting excited at the prospect of Mama coming to take me home. I look to the woman, she looks pityingly at me, then she suddenly bursts out laughing.

"Get up, you stupid little bitch. You haven't been rescued. Who would rescue you? You're worthless and nobody wants you or has even looked for you. You're a nobody in this world now, just a body. Now, you will get cleaned up for your visitors, we need you scrubbed clean and shaved."

She points to my vagina area. I look at her closely. My eyes are blurry from the tears forming, she's not going to help me. She suddenly grabs the top of my arm and starts to drag me from the bed. I move with her, my arms ache as it is. I stand on wobbly legs; she pulls me forward to her. She's not much bigger than me, but she's very hefty. She has big arms that are flabby with lots of skin hanging down at the underarm. She's wearing a tight vest that shows all the rolls of fat. She has a heart tattoo with a dagger through it on one forearm and then on the other, she has a fish. She has dirty yellow hair that doesn't look real, her makeup is all smudged and looks like it's been drawn on by a child. I reckon if I tried anything with her, she would be able to knock me out. I move with her; I look around as we exit the room. It looks like a house, there are other doors we walk past. I can hear girls crying as we pass. One door is slightly ajar, and I can see a man's naked back sitting up on a bed. I don't have time to see anything else as the woman drags me forward. We enter a room, a bathroom. There is a wall with showerheads above on the ceiling and one toilet. Nothing else.

"Strip now and get under the shower. I will make sure you are clean-shaven once you have cleaned yourself. Give yourself a good scrub because you stink of shit and you're filthy. Move it."

She pushes me forward. I just stand there. Suddenly I get a shove in the back, and I'm sent flying into the wall. The shower starts up and freezing water pours down on me. I try to get up but slip, banging my head against the tiled wall. I sit on the floor under the showerhead and just hang my head. I don't move. I sit and cry.

"Get the fuck up and take your clothes off. Scrub that fucking rancid body. If I have to come under the shower and do it, you will regret it. Now move, you fucking stupid cunt."

I slowly make it to my feet. I start to take off the very loose-fitted dress. It's about ten sizes too big for me. It was already stuck to my body from her throwing a bucket of water over me. Now it's just a case of peeling it from me. I let it drop and hold my head up to the ceiling, letting the water cascade over my face and down my body. It's freezing but refreshing to have clean water. I get hit on the head. I turn the top of my body in her direction, covering my chest with my arms. I scowl at her. At this point, I really don't give a shit what she does. She points to the floor.

"Pick the fucking soap bar up and scrub. Do I have to fucking tell you everything? Are you incapable of cleaning yourself? I could always call one of my men in to help you. I have a number of volunteers, just waiting." She whistles, in seconds there are three men entering the room.

I watch as they all walk toward me, bypassing her. One of them starts to take his tee off, then unbuckles his jeans. Oh no.

"Wait, I will do it. I can do it myself. Please let me do it."

"Too fucking late, cunt. First Joe will help you, then who knows, the others may just watch or they may join in."

She leans against the wall and lights up a cigarette with a sneer on her face. Joe is now naked, he walks toward me. My eyes go wide as I watch him holding his hard cock as he approaches me. I see over his shoulder one of the others starts to strip too. Fuck. This is it. I pick up the soap quick but not quick enough. He's at my ass as I bend over, and he puts a hand on my back to stop me from getting back up. I feel him line up his cock and the next thing I know, he's ramming it inside my ass. I scream out in pain. He doesn't even falter as he pushes inside harder and harder. I drop the soap and I reach my hands out for the wall to steady myself. He's slapping my ass as he rams deeper and deeper. I cry out in so much pain.

"Get off me, you fucker. Leave me alone. It hurts, stop, please stop."

But he doesn't. He goes on and on. I can't stand it anymore. My legs give out, and I collapse to the floor on my hands and knees. This makes him leave my ass but before I know what's happening, I am being shoved over onto my side, then pushed on my back. It's the other one who was stripping. He raises my legs and forcefully enters me. He pushes hard and my head slams on the tiled wall as he starts ramming inside me. I cry so hard, the water from the showerhead is pouring into my face. I try to open my eyes but the water hinders me. I feel like I'm going to drown with the water pouring into my mouth. I want to drown; this is my way out. I open my mouth wide and let it all in, pouring down my throat. He's going at me so hard; I scream out as he rips me.

The water stops on my face. I open my eyes and see it's the other man who is standing over me that's blocking the water. He's playing with himself, standing, straddling my body, so his cock is directly above my face. The other one feels like he is tearing my insides. He's like a rabid animal. He suddenly shouts out in a foreign language as he thrusts sporadically harder and harder as his cum seeps out of my vagina. That must prompt the one above me as he ejaculates and his cum squirts all over my face. He bends down and squeezes my cheeks together, making a duck face and he aims his cum into my open mouth. The hot liquid slides down my sore throat. They both move away from me when they are finished. This is what I have been expecting for so long. Like I said, I was lucky then, but my luck has just run out. The woman comes closer.

"You going to clean up now, cunt. Your visitors won't want another man's cum on you when they arrive. Scrub up now or Jess here will have his turn and believe me, you don't want that to happen. He likes it so rough he leaves his girls unable to walk for a week. He tears them up good and proper. I use him for the unruly girls, so be warned. He told me he can't wait to rip you open."

I hear them all laugh as I slowly roll onto my side. I curl up into a ball. I just want to die. I feel a foot on my side; I don't look. I don't give a fuck what they do now. Suddenly I feel a hand on my arm, and I'm being lifted up like a rag doll. I loll to the side. He lifts me high up so I can look in his face. It's the Jess guy and he's sneering at me through his black beard. I manage to put my feet on the floor.

"Okay, I will clean up," I whisper as I look for the soap on the floor, but don't see it.

The next thing, he has his hand between my legs and he's moving it back and forth. Not sexual, he's rough. I look down and he has the soap, he's cleaning me. I look up to him and with gritted teeth. "I can do it myself. Give me the soap."

He smiles and slams the soap bar into my hand. I turn my back and proceed to clean myself all over. I scrub hard with arms that feel like they have lead weights on them, almost scrubbing parts of me raw. I scrub my ass till it's sore, it was already sore from that man. I see blood on my hand and on the soap bar. He tore me up. I clean up the rest of me. I use the soap to wash my hair that hasn't been washed in forever. It takes every ounce of energy I have left. I take my time. I don't turn to see if they are all watching me. I don't dare look. I silently cry to myself. My shoulders must give me away, but I stand with my face up to the shower, letting the freezing cold water numb my body. I just want to die.

Six

Vidana

Present

I HAVEN'T SEEN RYKER FOR OVER A WEEK, HE HASN'T BEEN IN THE coffee shop, which is strange, he usually comes in most days. Maybe he thought better of it after he took me to the diner. I did cut it short. I've been thinking a lot about this Steve and the Ustrashkins. I've spent more time with Poppy, and I truly believe she knows nothing about it. Yesterday I saw her in the lobby, and she had an older man with her. I watched closely. He was definitely her guard. I had heard they all have guards. It's some kind of Bratva thing. The main players in the Bratva all have different ranking guards, some to guard them and some to take care of different aspects of the business. I don't know an awful lot about Bratva, only the rumors I have heard. I can't believe Poppy is as feared and as ruthless as they say, it's hard to believe, but then I haven't crossed her.

The man with Poppy is one I have noticed a few times, but I have never seen that Steve until the day in the coffee shop. I'm always wary now about living in this building in case I run into him. It spooked me when Ryker told me Steve thought he recognized me. Did he see me at all in captivity? Was he the one who ordered me to be taken? With all the new memories coming back to me, I had to have been taken for a reason. It wasn't random like I first thought. They needed me to do the video speaking to Lana. They needed that for a reason and, to me, the only thing was to get at Igor.

I am on my way to the refuge. I just finished my shift at the coffee shop and Poppy called me earlier to ask if I could go to the refuge straight after my shift. Apparently, there are some new girls arriving and she wanted my help. I start with the set up as the girls haven't arrived yet. I help with the food prep and making sure the rooms are ready. I haven't seen Poppy. I've been told there are ten new girls arriving, all rescued from a particular sex trafficking ring they have taken down. They told me all of the traffickers were killed by Igor's men. Why didn't they do that with my captors. Some of them died during the rescue mission but not all of them, and Steve certainly didn't. He's American, so I don't know how he fits in; all the other men were Iranian. Poppy told me that they didn't think they had the leader or don of the cartel. They thought they did, but it wasn't him. He is still at large. She didn't go into too much detail about it. I understand she wants to keep things from people, but this cartel took me and used me for a long time. I found out I had been gone for just over two years. It felt a lot longer than that. It felt like a lifetime.

The girls have started to arrive. Each time we get new ones from sex trafficking, it takes me back. I see myself in them all. One of the reasons I want to help, is because I needed the help. I had to believe in myself again. Thanks to Poppy, she let me do that, she taught me how to and I decided I needed a new look. A look totally different to what I was before. Poppy paid for me to have my hair done. I chose to have it pink, then blue, then lilac until it was a bit of everything. I started to wear makeup; it became like a mask to me. The more I wore, the more I decided I was hiding the real me. With my new hair and the makeup, I felt like I was in control of myself, I felt sassy, stronger, and I became quite outgoing. The change in myself has even surprised me. I don't think Lana would even recognize me if she saw me now. My makeup is dark at times, I think nothing of wearing black lipstick and either really bright eye shadows or really dark, it depends on my mood in the morning. Since I ran into Steve, I'm so relieved I did change my look. I even wear nonprescription glasses at times, to change up my appearance.

I sat talking with one of the new girls but not getting any response. I just want her to feel safe. It's the stages we go through. I know exactly how she feels. I look to the door just as Poppy enters. I smile, but then my face drops and I freeze. What the fuck? It's him behind her. He hasn't noticed me, and I immediately look away, then move my chair to position it so my back is to the door. Fuck. I feel someone approach. I go rigid in case it's him, my breathing is starting to get erratic, I feel myself starting to panic. Fuck, I can't have a panic attack here, what kind of an example will that set with the new girls. I'm frozen to the spot, trying to hold my breath.

"Hey, Dana, are you okay? You look as though you've seen a ghost. Hi, Anne-Marie, I'm Poppy. We will do everything we can to help you. If you need to talk to me, I'm around most days. Okay, sweetie?" she says to the girl I'm sitting with. I try to breath out slowly, not wanting Poppy to see my anxiety and panic. I smile as she squeezes my shoulder gently. It comforts me. Knowing she's there for me gives me so much relief.

Anne-Marie nods as she looks up at Poppy. At least Poppy got more from her than I did. I smile up at Poppy to let her know I'm okay. She nods, then squeezes my shoulder again, but I see the slight furrow of her brow before she leaves and makes her way around the room to introduce herself to the new girls.

I stay talking to Ann-Marie. It helps calm me. She nods, but that's about it. She rubs at her arms as they are folded. I haven't looked around to see if he is still in the doorway, but I get up to fetch some soup, bread, and a bottle of water for her. The stupid fool I am, I look to the door, and he's there. He's looking at his phone, leaning against the doorjamb. I remember my session on combating panic attacks and I do the breathing in and out to calm myself. He's just a man, I'm not even certain it's him. He shouldn't be here, he's intimidating being here, in front of these girls. Most of them don't trust men after what they have been through, I'm still not there myself. I can't help but stare at him. He must feel it as he looks up and straight into my eyes. I have my big nonprescription glasses on today which helps, because I look nothing like the girl I was. He smiles at me. Fuck, what am I supposed to do? I just need to act normal. Not give anything away that I know who he is. I smile back then turn to get the food for Ann-Marie.

My heart is beating out of my chest. I can feel his eyes on the back of me, like I did that day. I'm sure he was the one who did this to me, or he certainly had a hand in it, but yet he was also the one that kept me from dying in that place. Waiting to hear his voice or even catch a glimpse of him. What I have seen of him now has me thinking unthinkable things. He had a hand in what happened, yet I want him. I've never wanted anyone since Dima and especially not since what happened to me, yet for some reason, it's him. The quick glimpses I've had of him, he is much nicer than that time I saw him through the crack in the door. He is so much hotter now. How can I think that? I must be out of my mind. One minute I'm in a panic attack because I'm sure it's him, then the next minute I'm thinking I want to have sex with him and start getting butterflies. I'm screwed up, that's for sure. Since seeing him, it's just brought everything back to me. There isn't a night that goes by currently that I don't have nightmares about my time in captivity. My time being trafficked for sex, my time of craving the drugs. It's even made me want to take the drugs to make me forget, but I know it's the wrong thing to do.

Taken

It must have been a few weeks now since being in this new place. It's worse here than the first one. Here I have to have a shower and be clean-shaven every day. They don't let me shave myself, just in case I try to slit my wrists with the blade. That's exactly what I would do. I get soup and bread twice a day. If I'm lucky and I've been a good girl, they feed me some scraps from their dinners. But mostly it's just soup and bread. It's not often I am good. The first few days were the nastiest. After those men took me in the shower, I did have visitors that afternoon and into the night. They said they were breaking me in gently for a day. For fuck's sake, breaking me in gently was having five men, one after the other, do what they wanted to my body. I screamed, punched, kicked, and bit anything or anyone that came near me. The men were not happy. They called in the woman who owned me now, I have to call her Madam, to have words with me. She did with her fists. I ended up black and blue everywhere. I was already torn from the bathroom episode but that didn't matter to any of them. They plowed me in every hole I had. The one brave sick bastard that dared to put his cock in my mouth soon regretted it. He was the last of the men that night. He almost lost his cock. I had blood dripping from my mouth as he got off the bed. I looked at him, then to his cock, which was bleeding a lot. I didn't remember anything after that last look because he punched me so hard, he knocked me out. God knows what he or anyone did to me after that.

They didn't use me the next day, but when they brought me food, they also brought a needle. They injected between my toes. It fucking hurt. After that, I was floating around my room with butterflies. Then I think I just slept the rest of the day. Every day since, they have done the same, only I am more aware of what happens than I was the first couple of days. I don't know if it's because they don't give me as much or that I am getting used to what they are giving me. They usually inject me when they come to collect my plastic dish that holds my soup. Madam wants me to eat so I have strength. If I refuse, she force-feeds me. It happens a lot, she grabs my nose, holding my head up and she pours the soup down my throat, then she tears the bread up, stuffs it In my mouth and makes me eat that. The first time she did, I spat it out all over her. I don't remember the rest of that day either. I've done it a few times since just so she knocks me out and I don't have to remember anything. I even goaded her men expecting the same, only they used their cocks on me, not their fists, so that plan failed. It was only with Madam it worked until she grew wise to it and threatened to not give me any more injections if I did it again. That way, I would know and feel everything that was done to me.

Because of being somewhat lucid, I just lay there and let each man do what they wanted. I did notice that a lot of the men who visited me were American. Not the foreign ones. The foreign ones were the ones holding me captive with Madam.

I'm lying on my bed naked. I'm always naked. I don't have clothes anymore. I'm floating in and out but playing with the butterflies just above my head. Swaying my arms to and fro, humming to myself. The door opens. I don't look. I know it's someone coming in to use his cock. I'm suddenly pulled up by my arms. I'm like a limp rag doll and I laugh, loud. Then I'm put on my feet. Someone yells at me to be quiet, but it makes me laugh more. I feel pain on my chest, and I look down. I smile as a man starts biting my tits. But then I stop, I realize there are hands all over my body. They are feeling my tits, inside my vagina, running up my legs, holding my arms. I look down and I try to count. I get to five, then have to start again, then again and then again. The hands keep moving. I don't manage to count them; I'm being flung around like a rag doll from one to another. There must be three or four or maybe more of them. Who the fuck cares? I don't remember there ever being more than one before. I'm flipped this way, then that way for what feels like hours. I have cocks in me at the same time, what feels like multiple cocks stretching and tearing me. I just try to play with the butterflies and ignore what's happening. Once I catch my butterflies, I must fall asleep.

"Well, you certainly did good yesterday. They are coming back today with more friends. Carry on like you are and you may get some privileges. Keep it up."

Madam has brought me some soup. I feel like shit. My head is throbbing, and my body is sore and aching all over. I look down and see bite marks all over my body and it's full of bruises.

"Just make sure you give me enough of whatever you inject me with so I don't know what's happening or they may end up with bitten-off cocks," I snarl back at her, which then gets me a backhander across my face. My nose bleeds yet again.

"Get up and get in the shower. Any more lip and Jess will be escorting you and shaving you today. You really don't want that." She laughs as she puts a cig in her mouth and lights it, blowing out the smoke in my direction.

I try to cough but my ribs are killing me, and my stomach hurts so much. I hold myself to try to put pressure on my chest, so the coughing doesn't hurt so bad. She drags me up and pushes me to the bathroom. There are three other girls washing under the showers. They are being watched by her men, one of them being the big guy Jess. I watch as he strips to get in the shower. He grabs the one girl by the head and forces her legs apart with his leg. He then kneels in front of her and takes the razor and proceeds to shave her pubes. She doesn't move, I don't blame her, I stay as still as I can when Madam does it to me. I don't want my pussy cut up. I'm learning more and more that if we are good and the clients want us, the less damage they can do to us. They are obviously paying big bucks and the last thing they would want is a cut-up pussy.

I watch as he finishes shaving her. He then bends his head and he licks all along her pussy. I hear him say something but don't understand a word of it. He then unceremoniously turns her around with her back to him. He spreads her ass cheeks with one hand and with the other he pulls her down hard onto his huge, hard cock. She screams out as he rams it into her. With both his hands now on her waist, he moves her up and down harder and harder each time as he thrusts up into her ass. She's hanging her head, crying. The onslaught carries on for ages. The other two girls are standing stock-still. Madam goes to shave them, making them watch what is happening to the other girl. I try to turn around but one of her other men is behind me. I didn't know he was there. He stops me and holds my head to make me watch. I screw my eyes shut.

"Open your fucking eyes, bitch, or Joe will open them for you."

I open them immediately. I watch as the big guy Jess goes from being on his knees to being on his back. He still has his cock in her ass and he's holding her waist. He puts his feet on the floor to help him thrust up as hard as he can each time. He brings her down with a thud on his cock. He starts rotating inside her, she's screaming, and I'm not surprised, he's huge. I think he would break anyone with that cock. He goes on and on and on until he tells her to get on her knees, quick, then brings her head down onto his cock where he thrusts right down her throat, and he comes so hard she's drowning in it.

Once he's finished, he pushes her back. She hits her head on the wall. She's not knocked out, but it must have hurt. I see the blood start to mix with the water and flow to the drain. He then leans forward, pulling her legs wide apart and bringing her pussy to his mouth. He sticks his tongue inside her, along with what looks like a fucking hand. She screams as he stretches her out. He must rip her open with the bloodcurdling screams. He laps and laps. I don't know if she's come or if he's just doing it for the fun of it. He soon finishes and she's left curled up in a ball on the floor. I haven't seen her before. I think she must be new, and this is her being broken in. One of the other guys marches the other girls out. I'm alone once again with Madam, Jess, and Joe. The other two just watch as she shaves me. I clean myself. She even gives me some liquid body wash that smells nice. She obviously wants me smelling fresh for my visitors. From the sounds of it, there are going to be a few of them.

The only thing I remember is Madam coming in, making me have the soup and bread and then she injected me. I don't remember anything after that.

I swear I have been in this place for months. I still have no idea what day it is from the next, never mind what date or even year it is. I feel like I have been held captive for years. How I even think straight these days, I don't know. I've given up arguing back or being snarky. I don't give a fuck about my life. If I could get hold of the razor they use to shave me, I would slit my own throat. I would rather die than carry on like this for the rest of my life. Having man after man use my body for his pleasure. I can't even walk straight anymore; I feel like I'm drugged up all the time. I crave it more and more; I've even started to beg Madam for more of it. There are a few times I've had to lick and suck her pussy to get more from her. I don't give a shit, I need it.

I'm on my knees on the bed, facing the door. I'm holding the bed rail to support me as the old foreign man behind me rams his rancid cock in my ass. I look up as I hear a raised voice and realize the door isn't closed. Through the hinged side of the door, I can see a man standing there. He's fucking hot, and he's American. He runs his hand through his long brown hair, as he's turned sideways I can see he has stubble and a chiseled chin. I don't know why but I suddenly think I wish it was him ramming his cock in my ass. I have never wanted that ever.

Ah, Dima, I loved him. I wish I was back home with him. I could be married and living a normal life right now. Instead, I'm in the pits of hell.

I watch as the man shouts, then he lowers his voice to a menacing tone. It scares me. But I think his voice is music to my ears. I throw up and the old guy behind me pulls my head back and spits in my face. He pushes my head down. I don't look up again. I don't want him to see me. I hear Madam talking to him. I can just make out her saying something about our most popular one, no she's going nowhere anytime soon. She's making us a fortune. He tells her to keep him posted. They all called him sir, except her. She called him Alborz. What a weird name for an American.

I've heard the American only a few times. It always feels like months in between each visit. The door has never been open since, but I've heard him shout at the men. I'd know that voice anywhere now, it's velvet, I wait to hear it day after day. I was in the bathroom under the shower with my back to the door this morning when I heard his voice. He was in the room with us. I didn't turn around. I was rigid for a minute but then I thought I had better carry on before they notice and Madam makes a scene. Joe and Jess, who were the regulars in the bathroom, were terrified of him. It was, yes sir, no sir all the time. Madam was just normal with him. I heard footsteps coming closer, I quickly scrubbed at my face and in my hair so I could pretend I hadn't heard anyone behind me. I was sure it was him. He stood still for a few minutes; I swear I could feel his eyes on me. I think he was standing, examining me. I hoped he wouldn't make me turn around. Suddenly a finger gently trailed around my ass and up to my spine. I shivered as it sent tingles and I felt electric shocks running all over my body. How could I have felt like that with his touch? He's a fucking monster, yet I felt in that moment like a stupid little girl. I froze and I heard a little chuckle from him. The fucking monster was laughing at me. He turned and walked away and out of the room.

"Make sure you keep me posted on this one, Vera."

I smiled to myself at hearing her real name. Vera and Alborz, I needed to store them in my fogged-up brain.

The weeks went on forever. It felt like years had gone by again, I was in a drug-induced haze for the rest of the time I was there. I never heard the American Al… something or other again. I was used over and over, day and night, but the days just rolled into each other. My body was just a tool to be used. I didn't give a fuck what anyone did to me anymore. I just wanted to die. Madam never once let me have the razor to shave. That would be my only way to end this. She knew it. She probably had loads kill themselves over the years. I don't even know how old I am. I don't remember much about anything anymore, it's just me and my butterflies, that's all that matters. They are colorful when I'm not being used but then they turn black when I'm being raped.

My life has been nonexistent until today. I was being used again, drugged up as usual, when I heard lots of noise from outside my door.

The men who were in my room started to panic and get off me, trying to get dressed. I rolled onto my back with my head hanging off the bed, laughing at them. I found it hysterical they were falling over trying to put clothes back on. The door suddenly flew open and into the room, right off its hinges. Well fuck, there goes my privacy. I laughed loud. It looked funny just flying into my butterflies. It scared them and they disappeared. Fucking assholes.

There was shouting and then loud noises like pop, pop, pop, I laughed more. My butterflies appeared again, and I started to reach out for them. I could see some things standing in my room. I was seeing them upside down, it was funny. I also noticed white and red on the floor. What the hell was that? One of the things came closer. It scared me, and my butterflies, my little purple and blue and pink butterflies, all flew away. I was angry, but I still laughed. The thing did something, and he became a man, or a woman, I wasn't sure.

"Have at me, everyone else does," I said, lifting my legs up and spreading them.

It was a woman; she came over to me and threw something over me. I tried to lift my head to see but I couldn't, it was too heavy. She sat next to me, and she helped me sit upright.

"Out now, let me dress her," she shouted.

I looked over and saw the other things that were standing there moving out of the room, I laughed.

"Ha, no door, now everyone can watch me," I said, pointing. I then looked down and I saw the white was the clothes the men who were in me had on, but the red was blood or paint. "Hey, I want to paint on them. Can I have a go?" I turned to face the woman beside me. She was lifting my arms. "Here, I can do that." I took the top she was holding and trying to put on me and I put it over my head. "It doesn't fit?" I laughed through the material.

The woman helped me get my head through the right hole and we managed to get my arms through their holes. She then stood in front of me and took both my hands to lift me up to standing. She then bent down and tapped each leg for me to put my leg through the holes of the trousers she was putting on me.

"Hey, clothes. Hello clothes, I haven't seen you for a long time, never worn anything for so long. I'm just always naked." I laugh, trying to reach out for my colorful butterflies that have returned.

She then puts slippers on my feet. I like them. "Hey sweetie, do you remember your name?"

Hmm, that's a hard one.

"Bitch, I think?"

She shakes her head and moves my hair back behind my ears so she can see my face.

"No, that's not your name. Don't worry, it will come back to you. Come on, let's get you out of here."

I pull back to look at her. Who is she? She has on all this stuff like the other ones did. I laugh because they look like aliens. I poke at what she's wearing. It's hard and it bends my finger. I put it in my mouth to suck.

"Are you replacing Madam? Has she gone? I hate her so fucking much. She's a monster, they're all monsters, especially the American one, but he's nice. I kind of like that monster."

I just realized this woman is speaking to me in my language. I understand her. I can't remember what it is, but I understand her. I smile. She looks at me worryingly. I don't know why. I haven't done anything. I look to the door, ha, what door? The hole where the door was. I hear all the pop, pop noises again. She looks over too. I think that's what she's worrying about.

She moves us both slowly to the hole. I stumble and she tries to stop me from falling, but it's no use. I land on one of the men on the floor. I laugh and start painting on his white shirt with the wet red paint.

"Come on, sweetie, we need to get out of here. You're going to be safe now. I promise you, nothing bad is going to happen to you ever again."

I snap my head to her as she helps me up. What does she mean? I'm safe, from who? I can't leave, they won't let me leave. They will find me. No, I try to shrug out of her hold. I scramble backward on my hands, clambering over the men on the floor. My colorful butterflies have left me again. I search up ahead for them. They are my comfort, I need them. I hit the bed with my back and sit. She watches me. I don't know what that look on her face is, but I see a tear slip down her cheek.

"You can leave here now, come with me. No one will get you; I promise. We will take you to a safe place to be looked after and get you better. No one is going to do anything bad to you again. Come on, sweetie, come with me."

She holds out her hand. I shake my head no; I bring my knees up to my chest and cradle them to me with my head resting on them. My hair is glued to my face and in my eyes. She crouches in front of me. I hide my face. She very gently moves my hands and lifts my head up, again pushing my hair back behind my ears.

"My name is Alina. I am Russian. You too are Russian because you understand me. I am not going to hurt you or let anyone else hurt you. Please come with me so we can get you and the other girls out of this place. We are here to help you all."

She holds out her hand and I finally let her help me. I'm terrified the others will come back and beat us or kill us. But she said we are safe, me and the others.

"It's Dana, Vidana. That's my name. I just remembered," I tell her.

She smiles at me and pulls me into her side.

"We've been looking for you, Vidana, for a long time. Your family will be so pleased to know we have found you. Come on, let's get out of here." She takes me slowly and carefully out of the room.

We pass the bathroom and I freeze. I expect Jess or Joe to come storming out and take me in for a shower. I peer around the doorframe, it's empty. I sigh out and carry on with Alina as she takes me down some stairs. We pass a lot of people running around and there were a lot of the foreign men on the floor full of red paint. I laugh again. Someone's been having a good time painting.

I've never been anywhere else in this place, just my room and to the bathroom. It's a house, I see now it's a big house with lots of stairs and different levels. We reach an open door; I feel cold and shiver. She pulls me tighter into her side and we go through the open door. There are other girls wrapped in blankets outside. There's a big vehicle that they start to climb onto. I stop walking.

No, they are not taking us somewhere else to be used. No, I'm not going. I start to pull back, trying to get out of her hold. She tries to hold me tighter. I manage to duck and slip away, and I head back up the steps and into the house, trying to get up the stairs we came down. There are men all over. They want me, I know they do. They want to use me again. I start to scream for them to move. My butterflies are with me, only they are black now. I try to reach out for them. I want my colorful butterflies back. Just then, someone grabs both my arms from behind. They are pinned to my sides. A man is telling me to shush and to try and calm down. I hate men. I try to escape but I am too weak. He then puts his arms around my body and gently lifts me up. I kick out with everything I have, trying to get him to put me down. Just then Alina is in front of me.

"Vidana, sweetie, calm down. Please calm down. We need to get you out of here quickly. All the other girls are in the RVs. You will be safe; I promise you with all my heart. You will be safe, but we need to leave now before any more of the bad men come back. Do you understand me?"

The bad men, they will come back. I don't know what to think. Are these the bad men? Am I safer back up the stairs in my room? I don't know. I just want to die. That's why my butterflies are black. They turn black when I want to die. I stop struggling and hang my head. What choice do I have? What can be worse than what I've already been through. I don't have a choice. They will just take me anyway. I go limp in his arms. He scoops under my legs and carries me in his arms back outside and down the steps to the waiting vehicle.

"Please, just let me die. I can't take this anymore. Let me die." I close my eyes as I hear him whisper,

"Not a chance princess, not a chance."

Vidana

Present

TWO WEEKS SINCE I LAST SAW HIM AT THE REFUGE, AND I HAVE thought of him every single day. He's a fucking monster, yet I seem to be looking for him at every opportunity. Every time the door opens at the coffee shop, I hope it's him. There is no way he will recognize me, not with my short spiky, pink and purple hair, and I've taken to wearing my big glasses most days too. I just need to be more confident in myself. I'm working on me like I have done for the past few years, since I was rescued from his men. Alborz was his name, I remembered it in my dream last night, yet he goes by the name of Steve. Steve is more suited to him than Alborz. If I can work on me more quickly, then I can make a play for him. I hate the attention I get from men, I see the way they look at me and, in all honesty, after what I went through, I'll be surprised if I do let a man near me ever again. Maybe I should try a woman. I drop the spoon I have in my hand.

I just had a flashback again. I fucking hate them. I remember that sometimes there were women in that room with me when I was high. I'm sure they did things to me. In fact, I would say I was positive they did. I seem to remember thinking this wasn't so bad, there was a woman with black hair, and she was so gentle with me, then I remember her, and a redhead and she was a monster like the men. I remember her hitting the black-haired one. Maybe the one with black hair was like me, captured and the redhead wanted us both. I don't know and I don't want to know anymore. I want it all to go away. I would much rather not remember any of that time. I hate it's all coming back; I just want it locked away for good.

I have on my cropped denim overalls with one strap down and a bright-pink tee to match my hair. I love dressing like this, all grungy, with my black Doc Martens. I decide to go sit in the park for a while, I enjoy sitting and watching life go by, wondering what each person's story is. Making up stories about them. One bad habit I have picked up is vaping. I just reckon it's better than the alternative, smoking or using drugs again. It's a hot day out today, but then most days here in LA are hot. I have a bottle of water. I sit watching people. I take a swig of my water when I see him. Fuck. What is he doing here? He's standing across the way behind the park railings, leaning on them. He's looking straight at me. Fuck, fuck, he's moving. Do I stay? Should I leave and go the opposite way? I watch to see where he heads. To my horror, he heads to the opening to the park. I don't look. I grab my fanny pack and it's a fight-or-flight thing. I've chosen flight. There is no way I am ready to speak to him face to face. I don't mind a bit of flirting from afar but that's it. I'm just not ready.

I walk quickly but I don't look back. I head home. I wanted to get changed before heading to the refuge. I hurry once in the building, heading for the elevators. Luckily one opens right away. I get in and press the button for the ninth floor and don't look back. I am almost positive he was following me. Will he put two and two together? Knowing I work for the Ustrashkins, it was them that saved us, and I live here in their building? Will he know I am one of his girls? How could he not? He works for the Ustrashkins himself; he has to know it was them that saved us, and I was in the refuge. Maybe I'm overthinking this like I always do. Maybe he won't know exactly who I am and also, he wouldn't know I was Svetlana's sister unless someone tells him. Then what? Will he kill me? I'm sure he doesn't know. I just think we have this strange attraction to each other. I need to do some breathing exercises before I leave for the refuge. I need to calm myself down. I can feel myself worked up to near hyperventilation. I breathe in and out slowly, sitting on my bed.

I make it to the refuge without any sightings or incidents, thankfully. I'm lucky it's only a short walk away. I've been working a lot with Ann-Marie and another girl called Cheryl. They are coming along okay at the moment. They have become buddies in the refuge. We like to pair up the girls, so they have each other at all times and never feel alone. There are staff there at all times, so they are never actually alone, but we find it helps so much. I didn't have it when I arrived. As we were all the first rescued, it was something that came in later. I was lucky I had Lana for a couple of weeks, until she left me again, but then I had Poppy a lot. She seemed to take me under her wing more than any of the others. I wasn't sure why and I've never asked her.

Poppy has been in tonight working. I want to speak to her, but I don't want to bring Steve up. I don't know how to ask about him. I'm just walking down the corridor when I see him sitting there not far from her office. He looks up as soon as he senses me near. My step falters, fuck, what do I do? I slow my walk, and I smile at him, a very nervous smile. I have to play this cool and not act afraid of him in any way. Inside, I am freaking the fuck out. What do I do? I'm not ready for this, it's too soon, but fuck I have to do something. I just need to be nice and flirty. I'm sure I can do that. I hope I can do that. Flirt, I don't think I ever did that, even with Dima. I feel my chest tighten; I think I'm going to stop breathing. I try to take in silent deep breaths and slowly exhale as I walk slowly closer. He watches me intently, slightly squinting his eyes. I want to turn and run. I want to hide away from this man, this monster. What if he knows who I am? What if he grabs me and tries to take me away? Fuck, calm the fuck down Vidana, smile and walk, concentrate, in and out, breathe slowly, walk, one foot in front of the other. I got this; I can do this. He doesn't smile back at me. I can't read his face. I look away, I just carry on walking toward Poppy's office. I focus on her door as I pass him.

"Hey, I've seen you around a bit lately. Are you new here?"

He actually fucking speaks to me. I can feel myself start to blush. I stop just a couple of feet away from him. I need to act normal and speak. I don't want to give anything away. Do I need to turn around to face him? I don't want to. He will see my cheeks are probably the color of my hair. I can't be rude, so I stop and slowly turn my head.

"Hi, I've been helping out here for a few years now."

He cocks his head.

"Is that an accent you have there? Where are you from originally?"

Fuck, I knew he would ask that if ever we spoke.

"I'm originally from Kiev in the Ukraine, but I have been in America for a few years now." I smile and blush. "Are you from around here?"

"Yes, I was born in LA, and I've been working for the Ustrashkins for a long time."

I frown, as if not understanding him.

"You know, Poppy and Igor?" I play dumb, pretending I didn't know who he was talking about. Of course, I did.

"Ah, yes, I've known Poppy since working here but never realized her surname."

"I'm Steve, by the way. Ryker says he's a friend of yours too."

Oh shit, I hope Ryker hasn't told him I was brought here.

"I'm Vi, and yes, I know Ryker from the coffee shop, and we had dinner once. He's a nice guy. Are you friends with him?"

He looks at me suspiciously. Shit, I bet Ryker told him.

"I've known him a while. He worked for Igor Ustrashkins at one point, so our paths crossed a lot."

I need to leave. I'm starting to get panicky inside. I feel sick talking to him. "Nice meeting you, Steve, maybe I'll see you around."

"You too, Vi."

With that, I turn back and walk to Poppy's door, where I knock and enter straight away. Usually, I wait for her to shout for me to come in, but I rush in. She looks up as I sit in the chair in front of her.

"Dana, are you okay? You look very flustered."

I smile at her, nodding my head. I just need to sit and take a few breaths. These are techniques we were taught here. Whenever we felt we were in a situation we couldn't handle, to move away and take breaths to calm us. She can see this is what I am doing. She waits a few minutes, passing me some water from the cooler behind her. She sits and waits patiently.

"Do you want to talk about what just got you like that?" she asks me very quietly and calmly.

I nod. "It's nothing bad, just the man outside talked to me. I've seen him a couple of times and it's the first time I've ever thought someone was nice. He was asking me where I was from and my name. I just got a little flustered and started to panic inside. I kind of didn't tell him the truth. I told him I was from the Ukraine and that I had lived in America for a few years. Please, if he asks, don't mention anything about my past. I know you wouldn't, but I will go into meltdown if anyone was to mention it. I saw him a few weeks ago. He came into the coffee shop. He saw Ryker, apparently, they are friends. I need to make sure Ryker never tells anyone I was in here other than to work. That will freak me out. Does he work for you?" I breathe out. I said all that in such a rush without taking a breath.

"It's okay, a lot of girls want a different identity like you've done with your look. It's natural. A lot fear someone who used them will recognize them at some point. Never worry about anyone here giving information out to anyone else. Don't worry about Ryker, I have also told him to never give information out to anyone. No matter who, I highly doubt he would have told Steve anything. Yes, Steve is Igor's man at arms, his second, he's worked for Igor for some time now. He was assigned to be my bodyguard when I first moved here. I will tell you something Igor has drummed into me. Never trust anyone apart from your partner. That way, no one knows anything. If you want to give someone a different name for yourself and where you're from, then that is perfectly acceptable. Steve is a good guy, but Igor's words have always been embedded in me. He only trusts me, and I only trust him. No offense."

I smile at her.

"None taken and thank you, Poppy. I've had men leer at me a lot and you know how that feels, look at you, you are beautiful. But I've never felt embarrassed to speak to one before this. I don't know what it is about him. I think he's attractive but there's something about him. I saw him at the park earlier and I panicked and got home as quickly as I could. I swore he followed me, but I didn't turn around once to check. I just had this feeling. He may not have been. I just feel kind of weird. I can't explain it or the feelings." I shrug.

"Give yourself time. There is no rush for anything. If you find you like each other, then you take it further on your terms only. Do you hear what I'm saying, Dana? Under no circumstance let any man take the control from you. When you find the right man, he will wait for you no matter what. Never give him control."

I hear her loud and clear and smile at her, nodding. I drink my water, get up and walk around to Poppy, giving her a kiss on the cheek and a hug. I've never done this before, but I truly adore this woman.

"Thank you for always being there for me."

"You never have to thank me, Dana."

I walk out with a light skip in my step. I feel more confident and a little more at ease after speaking to Poppy. I skip past Steve, who is watching my every move. I smile at him.

"See ya around sometime," I say as I pass him. I don't look back and don't hear anything he says. I grab my fanny pack and head home.

With all these nightmares I keep having, I'm remembering more. I also remembered that Madam's name was Vera. I don't know If she survived when they rescued us, there were an awful lot of dead bodies around. I remember jumping over some and falling on one, thinking it was paint. I now know it was blood. I was told they killed everyone in that house that day, but I never asked about Vera. I also hope that meant Joe and Jess got killed. I hated those fuckers. I'm about to go to the tattoo shop. I've decided I want to have butterflies on my shoulder and forearm. I remembered all the butterflies I used to chase while high. I'm having a black one, they used to turn black when I was being hurt bad or I thought about dying. Then I want to surround the black one with other smaller ones in pink, purple, yellow, blue, orange, and red. All the colorful ones that I used to chase. It's me embracing my past. As much as I hate it and I still struggle and will for some time, I can't change what happened in any way. I just have to either deal with it or lock it away for good. The latter only comes back to haunt you, as I have found out.

During those months at the refuge, when I wasn't high, and Poppy rescued me from the drugs yet again, we had learning phases we went through. I've seen it for myself with the new girls that come in.

Phase one, I was taught that with years of physical and sexual abuse, our brains get into a state of chronic overstimulation and once the abuse stops, we have to train our brains again not to be so stimulated. That overstimulation puts us into a high alert status. We have to break that. This is very difficult. There are different ways they helped us with this. Some worked on some and not on others. Everyone is different. I felt none of it worked on me personally at the time, but now I know it did work.

We had different weekly counseling sessions, we had to gain responsibility for ourselves, get our self-confidence back, I'm still working on this one even now. Learn to solve problems and self-control, again the self-control was hard for me. I was craving the drugs, hence the relapse but I was also craving the stimulation which they told me was why when I wanted the drugs, I gave my body up easily. I told them I never got stimulated from sex. But I think they were right.

We had to learn routines, like getting up at a normal time in the morning and going to bed at a normal time at night. So many of us struggled with that. There was no night or day in captivity, everything rolled on and on. Our bodies were used constantly no matter what time it was, as long as the customers wanted us, they got us. Sometimes I never got a break from it for days. It was nonstop. Exercising was another thing we had to learn, but that also came with self-defense classes.

Phase two was a lot about reconstructing practical everyday life, along with the shopping, we had to relearn that we had our own personalities and our own identities. I never had an identity while captive. I didn't even know my own name. We were taught about shopping, banking, using money again and self-care, grooming ourselves. All the simple things everyone takes for granted. I shower two or three times a day even now.

Phase three, this was actual integration. Some girls went back home, some stayed and went to college, others to work like myself. We had to learn to survive on our own outside. We still had the refuge to back us up all the way. It was slow integration, week by week, then day by day. Until we could go out on our own. The lucky thing about it all was that for those that stayed, the Ustrashkins made sure they were set up. Like myself, housing was an issue, we couldn't afford anything like that. I've seen a few of the girls who were rescued with me on the ninth floor. They now work for the Ustrashkins in some way.

They also went into Stockholm syndrome as part of our rehab, but I dismissed that at the time. Now I'm not so sure. Is this what I have and feel for Steve? Is it that I'm attracted to my captor? Even though he didn't physically touch me, he was the man in charge. Is that why I feel like I do toward him? I have this attraction and I feel he helped me survive, but how? I also have a kind of sympathy for him. I tell myself he had to have had a reason he did what he did. Now, knowing he works for the Ustrashkins. He had to have had a reason. Then, on the other hand, I hate him because he's the fucking monster that made my life hell for all that time.

It suddenly hits me. What if he's still doing that now? Oh my god, I hadn't thought of that until now. He could still be trafficking and the Ustrashkins don't know. Fuck. I've got to know; he has to be stopped. I need to get close to him to try and expose him to the Bratva. It was Bratva that rescued us, Igor is against sex trafficking, or so I've been told. How do I know he isn't involved, and Poppy doesn't know? I should tell Poppy what I know. I owe her that much. If it wasn't for them, I would either be dead or still being used. It will never ever leave me, the trauma I went through, but now I'm so much better than I ever was or could ever have hoped to have been.

PART XII

Steve

Eight

Steve

Present

I SAW THAT GIRL IN THE COFFEE SHOP WHEN I SPOTTED RYKER. I'M
sure I know her from somewhere, but I just can't place her. I'm sure
she's not one of my girls, because she seemed to recognize me and
none of my girls have ever seen me, like ever. I make sure no one ever sees
me; I couldn't have them giving the game away.

This girl looked fucking stunning, maybe it was just that. I have girls
coming out of my ass, literally, well maybe it's the other way around and
I come in their asses, schematics. There was just something about the
barista. From the back of her with her grungy look and tight body, from
what I could see in the baggy clothes she wore, and the big pink and purple spiky hair. Then when she turned and dropped the coffeepot and just
stared at me, I stared right back. She looked like a fucking model from a
catwalk with that face of hers. All I could picture were those full, volup-
tuous pink lips wrapped around my cock. Her eyes were stunning, like
the color of the ocean, but more green than blue when you got through
all the pinks and purples around them. She was gorgeous. I cocked my
head, watching her. She looked down as the other woman helped mop up
the spilled hot coffee and glass. I was getting impatient. The other woman
told me to wait a minute.

Just then, Ryker grabs my shoulder and I spin around.

"Hey Steve, haven't seen you for a while."

"Hey Ryker, actually I've never been in here, but saw you come in. I
was about to get a coffee and join you. Just got to wait until they clean this

mess up." I turn back just as the pink girl turns and runs away; she didn't even look back. Fuck. I get my coffee and go sit with Ryker.

"Do you come in here often, Ryker? She was fucking hot, that pink one who just ran out, Vi or something. I'm sure I've seen her before, but I've never been in here until now. She looks familiar and she seemed to recognize me. I just can't place her. Maybe I've fucked her at some point. I never remember who they are." I nod in the direction of the counter. He just puffs out a laugh, but it's a false one. I watch him carefully.

"Yeah, she's nice, Vi, and yes, I come in a lot actually, mainly to see her. She's sort of a friend, so be nice to her, Steve." The fucking wuss. Why doesn't he just bang her already. If she hadn't have run out, I would have hit on that for sure.

"What have you been up to, Ryker? I haven't seen you for a while now? You finished working for Igor completely?"

"Yeah, he wanted me to work for him permanently, helping train his men and keeping them fit, but I didn't want to be tied to one business, you know, he's not exactly a normal business guy, is he?" He raises his eyebrows at me.

I know he knows what Igor does, he has to, to be making that statement. If you know what Bratva is, then you steer well clear unless you're born into it or brought up in it like I was. My pops was Igor's papa's man at arms, his second, he looked after Kirill, helped protect him. Not that he ever needed protecting. Not *the Kirill*, he was someone no one messed with. Igor doesn't quite have that reputation as yet, but he's not far off.

Igor never told me what went down, not all of it. I only know he got shot and that he lost Andrey and Ivan, those fuckers were useless anyway. Igor was so up his own ass; he didn't know half the shit those fuckers did. I knew, I watched them all, I watched everyone, just little old me, lurking in the background like I always did. When Igor took over after his papa died, he made Andrey his second and Ivan his third. He didn't even think of me, but he kept me on anyway. I was good and loyal to Kirill. I was one of his best soldiers. I kept my nose clean and did everything for him. My father was his second and I thought I would have been picked for Igor's second or third with all the loyalty I showed his family all those fucking years. I've been involved with the Ustrashkins since I was knee high. Igor and I were friends way back when we were young, we used to sneak off and play when his papa was away. For him to not choose me the first time around, that gutted me. I was so angry I went on my own killing spree and put a plan into motion. Then he recruited me as his second once the goons had been killed, well that pissed me off even more. I was his third choice, not his first or second. How could he do that to me?

"You're miles away there, Steve, everything okay?" It's Ryker breaking through my thoughts and my hatred of Igor. I smile and take a sip of my coffee.

"Yeah, sorry, I was just thinking about something. So, you going to hit on the pink girl or what? I'll tell you now, if you don't, then I certainly will. I reckon she'd be a screamer." I look behind me to see if she's returned, then look back at Ryker. I can see the disdain on his face at my words. I think he has it bad for her. To be fair though, she's a fucking looker alright. She looks like she's got some sass on her. I would eat her for breakfast, lunch, and dinner, maybe even supper, if she let me. Ryker is nothing like any of us in the Bratva, he wouldn't survive, no matter how big of a guy he is. I think he's too much of a pussy.

Growing Up

Me and Igor just got our asses kicked by my pops, again. We didn't go to school again, no biggie, but my pops says we need an education, not just Bratva education. Who fucking cares, we're both gonna be in the Bratva for life, so why not just get Bratva educated instead? We were out at a mall, only we were causing trouble. Igor is a year and a bit younger than me, but we were in the same classes at school, not that we are there much. As young teenagers, we're a fucking riot, everyone wants to hang out with us. Being Bratva, we can get almost anything we want, girls, cigarettes, liquor, even drugs, but neither of us wants to go down the drug route, we've seen too many of our brothers getting into that shit and end up dead. If it wasn't Kirill killing them, they killed themselves. It was mostly his drug pushers, they never lasted that long, one way or another, they almost always ended up dead. Me and Igor always joke about it being a 'dead-end job', we should be on the stage. It's his fourteenth birthday next week, so I've been trying to decide what to get him. What do you get the kid who has everything? He wants for nothing. Not like me. Me, who gets the beatings of his life for looking at my pops the wrong way. My pops is only Kirill's second. He's not loaded or anything and he seems to take it all out on me.

We were in this mall, and we were smoking when you're not allowed to smoke in there and we were pissing everyone off, because we wouldn't let them in our elevator car. We rode it up and down for about an hour. We also did a little graffiti in there. First, we colored the camera, then let's just say our version of tits, pussy and a cock didn't go down too well. We were having fun until the security guards came and nabbed us. I almost got away, but I ended up going back because I couldn't let Igor take the rap, that's what best buddies do, they stick together. One brother falls, the other does too. So yeah, my pops came to get us from the security office. We got a ban from ever entering the mall again and we had to pay to have the graffiti cleaned up.

Pops wasn't too happy about that. It's a good thing it was my pops they called to collect us as Kirill would have had us beat up bad to make us learn a lesson. I can honestly say we've learned a lot of lessons over the years. My pops would deal with me when he got me home, but he marched us out of the mall by an ear each. It fucking hurt and it was embarrassing. Other kids stood watching us. I mean, we are Bratva. People should be piss scared of us, but they laughed. Fuckers, we will punish those who laughed, especially that ginger nut, Thomas. What kind of a fucking name is Thomas anyway? He's gonna get his fucking head shoved down the toilet when I get hold of him. I'll make sure someone's had a crap in it before I do it though.

Igor and I have been inseparable since we were about four. I've never known my mama, Pops says she died in childbirth. I have no reason not to believe that. He said she was an American whore, one he screwed twice, and she got pregnant with me. He had no choice but to take me in, he's a very hard, stern man and I fucking hate him. I've been beaten to a pulp on more than one occasion by him. When he gets pissed and starts on me, that's when I know I'm in trouble. That's how I found out about my mama, he was pissed and laying into me ranting and raving about what a useless fuck I was, just like my mama. How she tried to trick him just like the other useless whores and how he didn't even know if I was his kid. Yep, my pops was one big fuckup who used to take anything and everything out on me all the time. I was there for him to use as a punching bag. He would beat me so bad and lock me in the basement for days. Is it any wonder I stick with Igor and get out when I can?

It's his fourteenth birthday. I don't have any money to buy him anything, so I organized a little get-together with Dimitri, his brother, and some of the older Bratva kids, who in turn brought the liquor, the whores, and the cigarettes, some were probably on the hard stuff too. It turned out to be a good night with both Igor and I getting laid, until the cops showed up. We had music blaring, liquor flowing, then the fucking cops raided us. Who the fuck told them? It wasn't the music blaring, we're in one of our legal warehouses, legal in that it's a cover really, but to anyone outside it's just a vehicle parts warehouse. There are trucks and cars all over, being repaired, well they are permanent fixtures really, but they look like they are being worked on. There are tools all over and if you come in the daytime, there are guys in coveralls and greased up with spanners in their pockets. The real reason the warehouse is here is the firearms that are hidden underground in a safe bunker, but the bunker access is out in the yard, and you would never know it was there. Unless someone grassed.

They turn the place upside down, with us all lined up against a wall. The cops are loving it and leering at the whores who are practically naked. Kirill usually has the cops in his pockets, so I'm not sure why they are doing this. They all know the places Kirill owns. The one in charge seems to be some kind of chief or detective, he's not in uniform. Maybe he's new or something. We all have our hands on our heads, as the main one bawled at us and told us not to move a muscle. Some of the whores are crying and it's getting right on my tits. Igor is next to me.

"Who sent them? How did they know we were here? Someone must have grassed, there must be a snake here. We need to find out who it is."

I look past him, slightly edging ever so slowly forward, but not so much to draw attention. I look at each person down the line trying to weigh up who isn't that bothered about what is happening. Dimitri is next to Igor, and he raises his eyebrows at me, asking what the fuck am I doing? I shake my head slightly at him, telling him not to ask or worry. It's me who will get it if this goes bad. I can't see anyone who doesn't look slightly anxious, the girls are mostly crying, there is one though who looks very indifferent. I recognize her. She was with Alex, and I don't like or trust him. He's fairly new to us all. I don't even know where he came from. It's not like I'm privy to that info.

Suddenly I'm being shoved in the back hard by a stick or something. I drop my hands and turn quickly. It's a cop, he snuck up behind me. I raise my fists, ready for him. He laughs at me.

"You were told not to move a muscle." I scowl at him, then charge. My head is down and I headbutt him right in the stomach, he grabs me around the waist and before I know what's happening, I'm upside down in the air then being dropped on my head. Ow, that fucking hurt. I think he's broken my neck. I'm on my back, when suddenly all hell breaks out. The girls are screaming, I see Igor charging and laying into the cop who just attacked me, then Dimitri is wading in to save Igor, it's one big clusterfuck. I manage to sit up, I'm okay, I move my neck from side to side, it's just achy. I look around and see all the Bratva guys are at it with the cops. It's like something you see in the old movies my dad likes to watch. The whores are all scrambling for their clothes, all except the one who was looking bored with it all. She's just standing, watching it all play out. I look around and I see Alex. He's by one of the trucks, just watching. She spots him and moves over to him. He smiles at her and nods. It is them; they're undercover. They're cops.

I whistle loud and our guys all stop and stand still. Dimitri takes over. He's just like his papa, only not quite as mean and the others all respect him. He moves over to the man in charge.

"What is the meaning of all this? We are on private property, not harming anyone or doing anyone an injustice. We are simply celebrating my little brother's birthday with a few friends. What right do you have to enter here and start all this? Where is your warrant?" The detective guy goes nose to nose with Dimitri, but he's smaller and no match to him.

"We were informed there was a lot of illegal drinking and drug use in here. Some of these look like young boys. As for the girls, they were nearly naked."

"That doesn't give you the right to enter private property. The girls are all over twenty-one, you can check their IDs. The younger boys were not drinking or using drugs of any kind. They were simply talking. The girls are naked, because, well, they wanted to get that way and who are we to stop them. There is nothing illegal happening here. Kindly leave this minute before I get my father Mr. Kirill Ustrashkins and his entire legal team down here to file a lawsuit against your department for harassment, assault on minors and for basically just beating up who they want as well as touching up the naked girls. By the way, this is all being recorded, and I dare say watched live by my father. Smile at the camera." He motions with his head to the cameras up above. I watch the detective look up and he smirks while rubbing his chin. He knows some of his guys were out of line.

"Okay, round up. Let's get out of here. Our sources were incorrect. There is nothing happening here, just some kids enjoying a party." He turns his back and starts to walk out of the building. His men follow. They know they are all screwed. I move to Dimitri and tell him my suspicions about Alex and the girl. He looks over to where they are, still standing by the truck.

"Okay, Steve. I got this. You guys clean up and call it a night. I think looking at Igor he's had a little too much liquor. We need to get him home." He walks over to where Alex and the girl are. All the other girls have left, just this one who stayed behind. I watch as he grabs the back of Alex's neck and then the same to her. He walks them to the center where we were all standing. Most of the kids have left. I'm standing with Igor, watching. Dimitri's second and third are flanking him. He is the heir to the Bratva family in LA, he will take over one day when Kirill either dies or gives the position to him. Igor is second in line.

"Get me two chairs," he orders us.

Igor and I scramble to get a chair each and set them in front of Dimitri.

"Go home, you two. Steve, make sure he gets back okay."

He motions with his head for us to leave. We turn our backs and head out. I want to watch what he's going to do. Igor is fine, he's not that drunk. We crouch behind a truck near the door, and we watch. This is what I want to do, be like Kirill and Dimitri. I know Igor is my best friend but I'm not sure he's cut out to be like them. He's too soft.

Dimitri shoves them both down into the chairs. One of his guys ties their hands behind their backs and to the chair. I can't quite hear what is being said. But Dimitri gives Alex a backhand across the mouth and splits his lip. He spits out blood. She shouts, I can hear her telling him to fucking leave them alone. She also gets a backhander. Dimitri pulls out a knife and bends down in front of her. He takes a foot and plays with the knife between her toes. He speaks calmly, which is why I can't hear what he says, but he's talking to Alex. I reckon he's giving him an ultimatum. He speaks, or she gets hurt.

I was right, Dimitri slices off her little toe. She screams out, but a rag is shoved into her mouth to silence her howls. Alex shouts now.

"Fucking leave her alone. She's nothing to do with this. Let her go and I'll talk." I see Dimitri laugh.

Yeah, I'm with him, I wouldn't let her go, use her. Alex is pathetic, willing to talk now when Dimitri hasn't even gotten started yet. What a fucking pussy he is. Dimitri takes her other foot and threatens to slice her little toe off that one. Alex talks to him. I can't hear what he says, but he obviously starts giving him information because Dimitri drops her foot and stands in front of Alex. The next thing I know, Alex's head is held back and Dimitri has hold of his tongue and is slicing it out of his mouth. He's an informant, that's what happens to informants. If he lives, he will never talk again. I love watching this shit, it's fucking sweet. It's what I want to do, I want to be in charge. I want to have that power, the power to make everyone fear me. Now Kirill, he only has to walk into a room to command it and everyone in it. That power is what I strive for. The problem is, to have that power, you have to overturn the current godfather and his heirs. That means I have to kill Kirill, Dimitri, and Igor. I'm still too young to think about that but who knows, one day I might be able to do it. I'm patient and can bide my time and see how it all plays out.

Nine

Steve

Present

ALL I'VE BEEN ABLE TO THINK ABOUT IS THE PINK GIRL. ALL I see when I close my eyes are her stunning eyes staring into mine and those fucking lips of hers. I picture them wrapped around my cock as I fuck her mouth and those eyes staring up into mine as I do, while grabbing onto that pink and purple hair. Fuck me, I've woken up with a few hard-ons just thinking about her. I've never done that about any woman. They come, literally, and go and I never bat an eyelid. I've never actively pursued a woman before; I mean, they only have to look at me and their panties fall off. Yeah, I'm that arrogant, but pink girl has got me all in a tizz and I can't for the life of me fucking fathom out why. The number of times I've had to jerk off in the shower thinking about her or picturing her as I fuck other women. I even tried to find someone with pink hair so I could imagine it being her. It didn't work, so I just fucked her hard and kicked her out.

I've walked past the coffee shop a couple of times like some fucking ponce of a stalker. Me, a fucking stalker. Never. But the times I did, I walked fast so she wouldn't notice me, but she wasn't there when I looked. Is that just bad luck with the timing or hasn't she been in? I wonder if she left. Fuck, I think I need to find Ryker and ask him. I stop in my tracks. Who the fuck am I? Am I really that fucking desperate for pink girl?

I've been shadowing Poppy this week, just like old times. Gregor, her normal guard, got hurt. Not in the line of duty as we say, oh no, the fucker got so pissed he fell and broke his shoulder. What use is a guard with a broken shoulder? Igor asked me as his trusted second to step in and guard Poppy just for this week, because he didn't have any meetings planned and was staying home to work. I didn't mind, I like Poppy. Although she's my boss, she's one of the only women alive that I would let tell me what to do. Not that she does that often and maybe because I don't really have a choice. I used to enjoy tailing her when she first arrived, she was a woman full of sass. I really grew to like her. I would have banged her myself if it weren't for Igor. The fucker screws everything up. Well, his time is ticking down and fast.

When I found out it was Poppy that had her suspicions about the sting that went wrong with that fucking idiot Farhad, and she was the one that warned Igor and in fact saved him, I was kind of in awe of her, but fucking angry with her all at the same time. I think that's where my adoration for her comes from. That and the fact she's a fucking hard-ass now and doesn't take shit from anyone, male or female. I've heard them all call her the dragon lady. I think her reputation is stronger and harder than Igor's. He did good marrying that one. The fact she has five kids, runs a refuge for fucked-up girls and the odd boys, and carries on with the Bratva business, makes me admire her more. She is definitely a force to be reckoned with.

Shadowing her this week will be interesting. I know I will get to visit the refuge for the first time since they had residents. I only ever went when it was being built and I was shadowing her then for a while, when she was heavily pregnant. I've stayed as far away from it as possible, only staying in the car when Igor went, or outside by the doors. I never entered it, I didn't want to chance it, you know, just in case. Seeing what this dragon lady does daily is a real eye-opener. I only hope I get a woman like her by my side when I am king, one day soon. Maybe I could have her when he is dead, now that's a thought I have never thought before. Then out of nowhere, the pink one pops into my fucking head. Fuck.

I'm entering the refuge following behind Poppy, cautiously watching everything around us.

"I'm just going to see how the new girls are doing, then I will be in my office. You go grab coffee or something, if you want."

She turns and walks away. I follow behind her but I'm on my guard, looking for the first hint of recognition. I'm supposed to be looking for threats to Poppy, but fuck that, I need to know for sure I am okay in here. She walks into a big room. I don't scan it like I should, I just lean against the doorjamb and read messages on my phone, I'm on alert all the while. After a few minutes, I feel like I'm being watched. I don't want to look around, I know it's my job, but I have this feeling of unease. Nothing to do with a danger to Poppy or myself, but what if someone recognizes me? What if someone has seen me before? For all I know, it could just be a girl I've fucked that's ended up here for some reason. I slowly lift my head up and look straight into the eyes of pink girl.

We stare at each other. She's just standing there with a tray in her hands, watching me. What the fuck is she doing here? What are the chances she's here at all? How is she here? Is she one of the girls? Is that why she looked at me like she did in the coffee shop? But I know I haven't seen her before. I would have remembered her for sure. Does she live here? I'm so confused watching her watching me. She suddenly looks away and starts walking. I watch as she sits at a table with her back to me and places the tray in front of another girl. I watch her for some time, I just can't tear my eyes away from her. I think she works here; she works for the fucking Ustrashkins. What are the chances of that? How, though, wouldn't I have seen her before now, unless she's new?

I must look like a right turd standing here staring at the back of her head. Suddenly Poppy is by my side.

"You okay, Steve? You didn't see or hear me approach? What if I was a danger to you and you hadn't noticed me?"

I turn and scowl at her.

"Of course, I saw you and heard you. It's my job. I just didn't acknowledge you approaching, that was all, the element of surprise. You know I am always on my guard. Yes, I am good, thank you. Are you going to your office now?"

She nods and I follow behind her. I sit outside her office, I keep watching the corridor, just in case pink girl comes this way. I'm kinda hoping she does, but she never does. It's a good hour and a half before Poppy finishes and I walk her to our car and drive her home. We don't speak, but that's normal. I pull up to the security gate and enter the code.

I drop her at the front door and watch her enter the house before I drive off and head home.

Home, I have two addresses here in LA. One is in an okay apartment block, nothing spectacular but safe enough. It's lightly furnished but nothing personal in it. The other is a penthouse in Santa Monica. Far enough away from the Ustrashkins building, but near enough for work. This is my apartment, the one I live in. No one knows about this one, it's under a false name. When I fuck women and want to take them back, it's never here, always to the other place. That way it looks used and lived in if anyone was to look into my living arrangements. Not that anyone will, I don't give anyone cause to. I stay low and watch, like I've done all my life. Watching over Igor, I've spent my entire life doing that, but that's going to change, very soon.

Growing Up

We're at the funeral of Dimitri. I'm standing next to Igor, who is standing next to Kirill. I have my arm around his shoulder, he needs support. Kirill doesn't even glance his way. Igor is broken. Since we found Dimitri dead, he has been inconsolable. Dimitri was out on a job, nothing unusual about it, it's one he has done a hundred times. He had his men with him, only it turns out some of them turned on him. They turned on Dimitri. Who would have thought it possible, but then you never know. Sure, Dimitri was going to take over from Kirill, him being the heir but he was a good guy. Igor doted on him. He was like my brother too. He was strong and forceful but he knew how to handle people in the right way. He didn't have many enemies. He was nothing like Kirill. Igor is the same. Thank God, because Kirill is an evil bastard. I've seen him lose it a number of times and he thinks nothing of shooting someone right between the eyes, just cause they looked at him strange or the wrong way. How Dimitri turned out so different from him, I don't know, but in turn he taught Igor. We stand looking at the coffin in the grave for some time after everyone else has left. Kirill barked his orders at Igor, telling him not to be a pussy and to get a move on, but he ignored him. How could Kirill be so heartless, that was his son and heir he just buried in the ground. He didn't even flinch as he was being lowered. I watched him closely, he looked bored and inconvenienced by being here, like he should be somewhere else and not bothering with his son's burial. What the fuck is that about? Telling Igor not to be a pussy. Fuck, I suppose that can be chalked up to the fact that Igor is now the heir. Unless something happens to him, he will rule the Bratva. Fuck. My best friend will rule us all one day. I'm not sure he has it in him. He always knew it was Dimitri who would rule. I kind of get the impression he was more than happy with that. Now it will be him.

It's been a few weeks since we lost Dimitri and to be honest, Igor is not himself at all. There have been a few times I've had to cover for him. He seemed to want to hide from everyone. His hiding was burying himself in whores, whores who were more than willing to spread their legs for the heir of the Bratva. I've had to lie to Kirill for him on a few occasions. If Kirill knew, I'm sure he would kill me.

Igor is really starting to irritate me; in fact, he's getting on my fucking nerves. I know he's my best friend and we have always been like brothers, but just lately he's treating me like one of his soldiers, like I'm a nobody and he is above me. I know he is, but fuck, he's never been like that. I've been seeing less and less of him. It's been seven months since we lost Dimitri and the change in him is not one I like. I always thought he wasn't cut out for this, being like Kirill, but I've seen a totally different side to him. I've seen him shoot someone in the head all because he happened to say something wrong about Dimitri, others he has tortured. Anyone dares say anything about Dimitri and they suffer or die. It's like Dimitri was a god in Igor's eyes. He's even been like that if anyone speaks bad about the Bratva, you respect Bratva and the godfather and you never say anything bad, it can and will cost you your life. It's why I never trust anyone. To be honest, Igor is starting to make my decision to overthrow him and Kirill a lot easier. It was the thought of killing Igor that was my sticking point. I wasn't sure I could do that. I thought I was being a pussy the times I doubted myself, but now he's made it easier for me.

I haven't hung out with Igor for nearly two years now. You couldn't separate us at one point. I was moved by my papa to work on the arms trafficking. I fucking hated it, but he said I had to do a stint in each area so they knew where my position in the Bratva would be. I was of age now, nearly eighteen. It was time, he said I had to have a taste of it all. The arms bored me. I was getting more and more impatient with this whole shit. Each time I saw Igor, he either ignored me or called me in to bark orders at me. He was a total dick. You would never know we were inseparable growing up, Kirill was training him to take over one day, he was making Igor more and more like him. I've heard the soldiers talking, they now fear Igor almost as much as they fear Kirill and that says a lot.

I've now worked on the drugs trafficking, and the money laundering, and they all bore me. I want to be out there doing shit, killing people, having meets. I did some of that in the arms division, and in truth learned a lot, so am grateful I did it. It's been years now; I'm coming up to twenty-two and my love for Igor has turned to loathing. He is a total ass, just like his papa. I suppose Dimitri is long forgotten now.

I was out getting drunk one night, nothing unusual about that, but I heard the rumors it was Kirill that had Dimitri killed. There was a mixture of us out drinking and some of the old arms soldiers I knew were sitting with us. One of them let slip that Kirill gave the order to have Dimitri executed. I spat out my beer and asked him to repeat what he said. He looked at me afraid, I shot up out of my chair, grabbed him by the throat and pinned him to the floor. I was spitting in his face, telling him to tell me the details. It wasn't him that had the order to kill, he had been told by someone else. He told me that those that killed Dimitri are now dead, but one of them told someone else before he was killed, knowing he was going to be killed. Kirill was trying to cover his tracks to make sure no one knew it was him that gave the order to have his heir killed. It all fell into place, perfectly. This was my rumor, I was the one that started it back when Dimitri was killed. I can't believe after all these years it's finally coming to fruition. It will all fall into place with Igor, the indifference Kirill had at Dimitri's funeral, he didn't give a shit about him. I need to tell Igor about the rumor, now it's finally out. I wanted him to know what Kirill was capable of, but I'm going to bide my time. If this plays out as I hoped it would, then it will mean I only have one more to overthrow. Igor.

Ten

Steve

Present

I'M TRAILING POPPY. SHE'S WALKING TO THE REFUGE, SHE DIDN'T want me to drive, she was at their building so it's not far. She walks to the Starbucks by the park on her way. I glance over and I see her sitting there. The pink girl. I watch her as I stand waiting for Poppy outside the store. She's watching people go by. She looks fucking hot from here, even though she looks young. She has on jean overalls, but she has a neon pink top that matches her hair. I'm too far away to make out her face but she has sunglasses that are at the edge of her nose as she watches people over the top of them. I watch her until Poppy appears at my side.

"Hey, you okay Steve? You look miles away there. You didn't even notice me standing here." I look down to her. She's smaller than me.

"Yeah, I'm good. I knew you were their Poppy. It's my job to know."

I try to distract her from looking to where I was looking. "You ready to go to the refuge?"

She nods, takes a sip of her iced coffee, and walks in the direction of the refuge. I have one last glance over to the park. I see her vaping. Fuck, why does she have to be one of those? I fucking hate anything like that. Just have a proper smoke, for fuck's sake. I turn and follow Poppy. At the refuge, she tells me I can leave but to just come back in an hour. Thank fuck for that. I head straight back to the park, hoping she's still there. I set a timer for an hour on my phone, so I know when to head back to Poppy. If anything happens to her, Igor will kill me.

I make it back and thank fuck, she's still there. Leaning against the railing, I stand just watching her. I'm closer this time. I watch with fascination, watching as she takes a sip of her water, watching as her tongue slips out onto her lips, licking the remnants of the water from them. I watch as she takes out her vape and takes a pull on it. Watching her lift her head up as she blows out the vape and it billows out into the air. She looks back to watching a young mom with her baby, as she takes another sip from her bottle, then suddenly her eyes meet mine. I stay indifferent as I start to move toward the park entrance. I watch her closely as I move. I see the startled look on her face when she realizes I'm heading to the entrance. She grabs her purse, rises to her feet, all the time watching me, I can see her thinking about what to do. Should she stay or should she run, then she turns and walks to the opposite entrance. I'm baffled as to why she would leave. I don't want to run, that would make me look like a freak running after a girl. She's fast, I'm fast, but there is no way I am catching up to her unless I run. I watch where she goes, never taking my eyes off her back. I follow as fast as I can without looking like the fucking freak I am. She's heading to the Ustrashkins building. What the fuck? Why would she be heading there. Maybe she lives near there and not actually in their building. She's unbelievably fast, never once looking behind her. I lose where she goes. She just disappeared as I rounded a corner. We are so close to the Ustrashkins I quicken my pace to see if I can see her in there. I stop, but there is no sign of her in the lobby. Fuck. I wanted to see where she went. I stand there rubbing my hand over my face and through my hair. No use, she's nowhere to be seen. Who the fuck am I right now? Why do I have this obsession with her? She's not even my type. Fuck. I shout, scaring an older couple walking past me.

I head back to Poppy's. I sit in the corridor near her office, just waiting. That's most of my job anyway, patience and being patient. I have to wait all the time. I don't mind, especially not here. I can see anyone approach. Now the younger me had no patience at all and didn't everyone fucking know it. Since becoming Igor's second, I have all the time and patience in the world. Just biding my time until I make him meet his end. I play games on my phone to kill the time once I've finished answering my emails and messages. Poppy said she'd only be an hour; I've been here three hours already. I get up to go get something to eat from the kitchen and get a drink. I just grab a sandwich and water and head back to sit outside Poppy's office. I knock on her door first and stick my head in to make sure she didn't leave.

"Had a pee break and wanted to make sure you were still in here."

She smiles and nods.

"Sorry, I've been longer than I thought. I will try not to be too much longer now."

I nod and close the door, sitting back in my chair. I finish my sandwich and check my messages again. You wouldn't believe the number of messages I get being the don of a cartel. I have two phones, one for the cartel and one for Bratva. The raid on the house in New York hurt me. Customers died as well as my team there and two girls. News got around and it made me appear weak. It's taking a while to get back to where I was before the raid. I'm not there yet, but not far off. I bought a club in New York and disguised it as an adult sex club, similar to what Igor has. Only it's used for my sex trafficking. It's a clever layout. I also have a lot of new houses that are just starting to get a reputation. Thank fuck for that.

Just as I'm about to send a message, I sense her near. I look up straight into her beautiful ocean eyes. Each time I've seen her, it's like they change color. Sometimes more green than blue and then other times more blue than green. Her eyes are surrounded by the pink and purple makeup she wears and those fucking pink lips are full. I noticed she changed and now has on a vest top which shows off her arms. I watch her feet stutter slightly as she notices me and she fucking smiles at me. My heart skips a beat. Who the fuck am I right now? My heart has never skipped a beat unless I was being beaten by my papa. I don't smile back; I watch her walking nearer, then passing me. I have to say something. I speak and she stops, slightly turning and speaks to me, for the first time, she fucking actually speaks to me, but I detect an accent. Is she fucking Russian? I frown as I ask her but she says she's from the Ukraine. She tells me her name is Vi, that's what Ryker told me when I asked him about her. He didn't give me too much info on her though. He was being rather cagey. I tell her my name and she leaves, telling me it was nice to meet me. I watch as she knocks on Poppy's door and enters in a hurry. I can feel my heart racing still. How can a young, colorful girl like her have this effect on me? I move my palm over my forehead. I actually have a fucking sweat on. What the fuck is she doing to me?

I need to pee. I get up looking to Poppy's door. I don't want to miss Vi leaving, maybe I should wait, but I'm desperate. I walk away, quickly, thinking about Vi and that smile she gave me. She acted like earlier never happened, like I didn't scare her away or follow her. Maybe she didn't know I followed her? I'm so confused. Even standing while peeing, her smile and those eyes are all I can think about. I need to hurry; I want to see her leave. Maybe ask her on a date. Fuck. That's it. I'm a fucking ponce. I don't date, I don't ask, I fucking take when I want. She's screwing with my head.

I'm back in the corridor sitting on my chair. I was only gone for a few minutes, I don't think she left. The door opens. I don't look up, it's one of two people and I don't want to appear eager. If it's Poppy, she'll tell me I didn't know she was there, if it's Vi, then I don't want her to think I'm eager. I can't help it, I fucking look, because I know it's Vi. She smiles at me as she quickly passes and tells me she'll see me around. Just like that, she's gone in a flash of pink. I stare in the direction she's gone for a few minutes. I don't realize Poppy's standing at her door watching me until I turn around and see her. The look on her face is suspicious. What the fuck is that about?

"What's that look for, Steve? You look like you're catching flies, your jaws almost on the floor." She laughs at me. I like Poppy but I think she's a bitch right now. Mainly because she caught me out.

"Give me ten minutes, then we're out of here. Igor phoned and asked if you could stop in to see him when you drop me off. Take me to our building."

I nod, still embarrassed at being caught out. She disappears again into her office. Why the fuck didn't Igor phone or message me? Why ask Poppy to ask me? What's that about? Why there? I know what goes on in there. Has he found out something? Every time I get called to see him, I wonder if this is the time, time for me to kill him. I only accepted being his second so I could be close to him and learn more. I've learned so much more for it, the boss man, the Pakhan and how he operates everything. There are some things he doesn't let me see and some things he doesn't tell me, just like the raid on my fucking New York house. I should have finished him a long time ago. The problem I have now is his fucking family. He has heirs himself. If I kill him, will Poppy step up like she did when he got shot? Will they make her the Pakhan? I don't see it myself, as far as I know, there are no women at the top, especially not American ones. Will I have to kill her and his kids? I will do whatever has to be done for me to be the top dog around here.

We're on our way to see Igor. Poppy said she has some stuff to do there first, then will drive home with Igor. Basically, dismissing me for the night. When Sergei left with that bitch Svetlana, Igor went into a rage, and he made Pavel his third. I had worked with Pavel before, and I knew he didn't like Igor. Maybe I could recruit him once I am Pakhan. When Sergei ran off with Svetlana, it was bad enough but the fact they disappeared from the face of the earth, and no one could find them, made him angrier. That's when I learned she had done this to him before. If a stupid bitch like Svetlana can fool him, then he's easy prey. That's what he didn't want to get out. It made him look weak. I made sure a few of his men knew about it on drinking nights, that way it would spread that Igor was weak.

When we arrive at the Ustrashkins building, I'm told Igor wanted to see me in the basement. That immediately put me on guard. Why the fucking basement? I head down there and he's in the control room, I stand in the doorway.

"Hey Igor, you wanted to see me? Poppy just went up to the apartment."

"Yes, come with me, Steve." Fuck, what's his problem? He seems pissed. He walks past me and knocks my shoulder. He heads to the double doors, and I follow. We pass the white rooms, heading for the dungeons as we call them. We approach one and he stops to open it. He looks back to me.

"Is he the one who told you Kirill killed Dimitri?" I look in past him. I don't remember who the fuck it was. I was drinking and it was a while ago. Why's he doing this now? I shrug.

"I don't remember who it was, Igor, it was a while back and we were all drinking. Why are you asking about that? Don't you believe me?"

He stares at me, then looks to the man.

"This is Gustov, one of our arms traffickers. I've recently found out he's a plant. He's been with us for fucking years and he's a fucking plant. How the fuck does this happen? If he told you Kirill killed Dimitri, then it's probably a fucking lie. I just want to know if it was him?"

I look and I know it's not him.

"No, he didn't tell me. I'm sure it was Rolan that told me. In fact, I'm positive it was him. He told me that Yasha was one of the ones that were given the order to kill Dimitri. Yasha was also one that was killed, disposed of."

Igor looks at me, slightly cocking his head and weighing me up. He steps right into my space and is almost nose to nose with me.

"Are you fucking sure? You just said you don't remember."

I could just fucking nut him and send him down now. I could do it and finish him, but I know there are cameras everywhere and I wouldn't get out alive. I stand up tall to him, he is slightly taller than me but only slightly.

"It was Rolan, I remember," I spit out, annoyed he's questioning me.

He's angry, really fucking angry. He turns and casually walks over to Gustov, who is sitting on a chair with his hands tied behind his back and both his ankles pulled back and tied to the back legs of the chair. He pulls his head back.

"You have thirty seconds to tell me who planted you. Who do you work for?"

Gustov just laughs in his face. I watch as Igor turns away and casually walks to the side table. He picks something up, but I don't see what. I watch him turn back to Gustov, one hand in his trouser pocket, the other obviously with something in it. I watch him walk behind Gustov. He bends to his ear.

"Time is up. Who do you work for, Gustov? This is your final chance. I don't have time for this. Your whole team will be extinguished. If you're a mole, then I can only presume the rest of them are. You will be their downfall; their deaths are all on you."

Gustov doesn't say anything. I watch as Igor bends and with two swift movements he slices both the Achilles. I watch as Gustov screams out. He couldn't get up and walk if he wanted to now. Igor moves around to the front, and I see him position the knife he holds in his hand so he can stab with some force. I watch as he lifts his arms slightly, then brings it down hard. He's blocking my view, so I move slightly to the side. I see the knife is in Gustov's groin. Igor lifts it out and plows it straight back down on the opposite side of his groin. These are the things we have to learn, the best places to make someone bleed out. The groin area holds the femoral artery, a major artery if you want to cause death by exsanguination. I watch as Igor steps back and then walks to put the knife back on the table. I watch how he is so unaffected by anything he does.

I watch Gustov scream, lifting his head to the ceiling. I see the blood seeping into his boxers, then dripping down his thighs between his legs and starts to pool on the floor. I watch as it forms a little rivulet to the drain in the middle of the room. Igor turns back to him.

"You can scream all you want in here, Gustov. No one can hear you or is there to help you. Now you don't have long left before you lose consciousness. I can inflict more pain on you, or you can tell me who you are working for."

I watch as he picks up a spreader and some pliers. He's going to pull his teeth. He casually walks over.

"You going to tell me? Last chance."

Gustov spits at Igor but it just falls short. Igor holds his head back and pries the spreader between his lips, turning the screw to force his mouth open wide. He then uses the pliers to start pulling his teeth. Gustov tries to fight at first but then I can see the lights are slowly going out. Igor moves away again, and this time comes back with a poker. He proceeds to shove this up Gustov's nose, jarring it right up as far as he can. He's barely conscious now, so to me, this is futile. I understand Igor is pissed but it's wasted. Gustov is practically dead, he won't feel anything now. He pulls the poker from his nose. There's brain matter on it now. Gustov is as good as dead.

We leave the room but before we get to the control room, Igor stops me.

"We need to find his team. You had dealings with the arms crew, I want the brigadier brought to me. He needs to start talking. It needs to be done now before this gets out. I need you to do it for me. Go now," he barks at me.

Why the fuck is it my job to go get the brigadier? I don't have anything to do with them now. I'm Igor's second, I'm above all this, the fucker. I leave to go bring the brigadier in and I'm going to bring in Lukan, who is the spy that oversees the arms and drugs trafficking. He should be the one brought in for questioning, in my opinion, he's the one that ensures loyalty between the men. If he's in on it, then the entire crew is tainted, and we have a huge problem. I eventually find them both and bring them in for Igor. He dismisses me while he speaks to them, not in his basement but in one of his meeting rooms. Who the fuck knows what will go down there? I just hope someone does away with Igor and saves me the bother. It grates on me to think how he's treated me over these years.

<hr>

Igor killed Kirill; I know he did. I don't have the proof, and no one has said anything that I have heard, but I saw the murderous look on his face when I told him the rumors that it was Kirill that killed Dimitri. It had been a couple of years. Kirill and Igor were feared more than ever. I needed them both to die. It was my turn to take over. I was more than ready for it, so I told him, knowing full well he would kill his papa. I took great joy in watching his face as I stood in front of his desk telling him, and rubbing it in about how Kirill was at Dimitri's funeral. I played it cool, with compassion in my voice. He didn't speak for a while, he just stared straight into my sorrowful eyes. He didn't thank me, he told me to leave, dismissed me without so much as a thank you for telling him. Who the fuck did he think he was, dismissing me like I'm a nobody? I covered for him so many times growing up. I was enraged at how he was with me, but I smiled to myself as I left. I knew the look on his face. I knew I didn't need to be the one to kill Kirill. I can't believe how fucking easy it's been. Here I was thinking I would have to kill them all, turns out you can't even trust family, they are killing each other. I would have killed my own papa for the way he treated me my entire life, but again, it turns out I didn't need to, he ended up dying of lung cancer. Serves the fucker right for chewing tobacco all his life.

Just before he died, I was put on the sex trafficking department, and I knew this was where I was going to stay. This was my calling. This was where I plotted against Igor. I came up with the idea of running my own sex trafficking ring. It was easy to get these girls and make big bucks off of them. I created a cartel, the Darvish Cartel. With being Bratva, we run into various cartels in our business, and we take down as many as we can. I created an alias, I became Alborz Darvish, the don of the Iranian cartel. I recruited Iranians to work for me. I made them believe I was part Iranian, with my dark hair, slightly tanned skin, it was just the color of my eyes, bright blue is rare in Iran. I told them my father was Armin Darvish of the old Darvish Cartel and that my mama was an American he took for himself. It worked. In no time, I was running one of the biggest sex trafficking rings. It was outside of the USA, but I was working on worming my way in. I had all the contacts and all the knowledge with being in Bratva. Bratva is my true calling and once I have disposed of Igor, I will amalgamate the two. I will be able to do what the fuck I want once I become the Pakhan.

Igor has completely wiped his hands of me. He recruited those fucking morons, Andrey and Ivan, to be his second and third. How the fuck could he do that? We were brothers growing up, it should have been me as his second. It should have been me at his side, helping him rule. If there was one thing to break the bond, it's that, choosing someone else to be his second over me.

My cartel was growing strong. I was careful, I had to make sure only a very select few knew my identity and I had to make sure my two worlds didn't collide in any way. That was much harder than I anticipated. It took me a few years to get to the top with my trafficking, but everyone knew not to mess with me. To say I'm ruthless is an understatement. I'd go as far as to say Kirill had nothing on me. I eventually moved my operations into the US. Twice, Bratva plotted to take me down. I was Igor's second when he did this. He didn't run a sex trafficking ring like his father. He abhorred it. Being his second, I knew when the attacks were happening and helped coordinate them. That gave me the upper hand. I used false addresses with stooges set up, so that when Bratva raided they only found a couple of people at the premises, ones I didn't need in the cartel anymore, ones we as Bratva just killed. I didn't go in myself. I stayed and watched the comms from a secure vehicle, making sure none of the stooges said anything they shouldn't. Not that any of them have ever seen me before. The two times Bratva raided, there was nothing for them. The second time I had a stooge in place who was told he had to say he was the mastermind behind it. Just to give my men something to brag about. It was all so fucking easy. Igor thought that was the end of the Darvish Cartel. How wrong he was.

I spent a few years building my cartel up in the US. It was huge. There were a few times other Bratva tried to take us down. We never got told when another division was doing any raids, or at least I didn't think we did.

I had Svetlana's sister kidnapped from Russia. I set up an arms deal using Svetlana to take out Igor, that was going to be his downfall. It fucking failed and I killed all of my men that were involved, those that survived the Bratva assault. How could they fucking screw up so badly? I later found out it was Poppy that had warned Igor. She fucking saved him. I should have killed her as well, but I actually admired her.

My team, who ran the New York operation from several houses, told me that Svetlana's sister was still around. I visited the house where she was being kept. I only ever saw the back of her at the house. She was in the bathroom that time I was visiting one of our houses in New York. She had been there a while and was one of our best girls, from what I was told. She was the most popular, so they kept her around for a while. Normally once the girls were used for a while they were disposed of. They were no good to me once they became a problem or once they were used too much. A lot of the customers wanted them fresh, not too used.

That house got raided. I knew nothing about it. I was Igor's second and yet I was never privy to the raid. How the fuck could it be kept from me? Any raids that went down for anything, I knew about them all. I was always involved in them being Igor's second. Why the fuck did I have nothing to do with this one? Did they find out? Did Igor know it was me? If he did know, he would execute me on the spot with it being a sex ring. I was so enraged. I found out they killed everyone at the house. No one survived apart from the rescued girls. In a way, I was relieved because no one could identify me. I made sure none of the girls we had anywhere ever saw me. Svetlana's sister was the closest to ever seeing me, but she never did. If she had turned around in the bathroom that day I trailed a finger down her back, I would have killed her on the spot. I was so careful, making sure none of them ever saw me. Only Vera, Jess, and Joe from the house and, of course, some of my men I recruited early on saw me and knew who I was. Any others just thought I was a customer.

It screwed with my head. How they managed to attack my house and kill everyone, nothing was reported on the news about it, and it was only when I heard some of the men talking about the success of bringing down the biggest cartel that I knew about it. Some of the girls apparently ran away, having not trusted anyone, and two of them were killed as they attacked the men trying to rescue them. I was livid. A few days after the raid, I had the other five houses closed and moved to new locations. I couldn't chance them being raided as well. Who knew what Igor had found out? He never told me. I tried asking him about it, trying to be indifferent and congratulating him on the successful raid. I had to know. I asked him how come I never knew about the raid. He stared at me for a while before speaking. He was thinking about what he should say to me. I could see the anger on his face from me questioning him. He told me I didn't have to know everything that went on, that I was there to serve and protect him and his family, that what went down with Bratva was his business. He dismissed me straight away.

I needed to plan to get this fucker once and for all. I needed to now seriously plan his demise. It was my turn to rule. I was even more ruthless than Igor could ever be. I remember the pussy he was growing up. The question I needed to answer for myself is, do I just take him down or do I take his whole family including Poppy and his heirs?

Eleven

Steve
Present

I HAVEN'T RUN INTO HER SINCE THAT TIME AT THE REFUGE. I KEEP looking for her everywhere I go. I look at the refuge, passing the park, at the Ustrashkins building and I've even walked past the coffee shop a couple of times, well, maybe more than a couple. I think I'm losing my mind, but I need to see her again. I can't get the image of her smiling at me out of my head. Vi is becoming the color in my life I've never had and I'm all fucking confused about it. I've been worrying lately that Igor has found something on me. I now need to step up my game and plan his downfall. I'm rattled because of Vi. She's throwing me all off-kilter. I don't want to make any mistakes. But I need to see her again, whether to see if I can screw her out of my system or if it's just some stupid infatuation. Something I've never experienced before.

The other thing that's been bothering me of late is that since my papa died, I've never been to his place, I hated ever stepping foot in there, so I've left it to rot all these years. He owned his little shitty house, the one I grew up in, the one where he beat ten tons of shit out of me constantly my entire life. I vowed I would never set foot into his place again, but I know that's something else I need to get sorted. Either sort it or torch it, one of the two. It's probably been trashed by the kids or vagrants by now anyway. There was nothing in there I ever wanted. I decide I need to get this over and done with after all these years. See what state it's in, it may just need pulling down if it can't be torched.

I haven't been shadowing Poppy the last couple of days now that Gregor is back to full fitness. I bumped into Ryker yesterday as he was the one that gave Gregor the all clear. Although he doesn't work directly for Igor, he kind of freelances for him. I know he does this, so Igor can't tell him what to do or control him like he does everyone else in his life. I arranged to meet Ryker tonight for drinks. It's the first time we've socialized before, but I do kind of like him even though he isn't Bratva. It's unusual for me not to mix with Bratva for drinks. I really want to find out what he knows about Vi.

I walk into the bar to meet Ryker and I don't believe my fucking eyes. She's sitting there with him, Vi. My fucking heart skips a beat at seeing her. Neither of them notices me. She says something to him, and he laughs. I watch them for a few seconds before moving to join them.

"Hey Ryker. Vi, I didn't realize you were joining us for drinks. How are you?" She looks at me first with shock on her face, then it morphs to a quizzical look before looking back at Ryker.

"Hey Steve, Vi was just leaving. She's on her way to work. We met outside and she just had time for a quick drink. Here, sit down, let me get you a beer." I pull out the chair opposite Vi, she was sitting next to Ryker. It's not a big table and my knee accidentally bumps her as I shuffle my chair under the table. It's my long legs. She looks to me and I see anger in her eyes as she squints at me.

"Sorry, one downfall of having long legs," I say as I shuffle back slightly and shrug because I am not sorry one little bit. Fuck that, I want to touch her. I want to lean over and stroke down her cheek, I want to kiss those lips. They are a dark purple tonight. I smile at her, leaning my forearms on the table, I pick up a beer mat and start playing with it. I look up at her. She's staring at me, she looks weird, only in the way I can't read her face.

"You off to the coffee shop or the refuge, Vi?"

She looks at my lips as I speak and my eyes dart to her tongue, licking her lips. She picks up her glass and finishes the dark liquid inside. I take it she was drinking a soft drink if she's off to work. She doesn't speak.

"You in there, Vi?"

She blinks, then the corners of her mouth slightly turn up into a half-assed kind of smile.

"Sorry, yeah. I'm going to the refuge. I had a few days off but I have a shift there tonight. Ryker didn't mention he was meeting you. I wouldn't have come in for a drink otherwise."

I frown at her. What the fuck does she mean by that? Is that her way of saying she didn't want to fucking see me?

"Oh, gosh, sorry. That came out wrong. I didn't mean it to sound like that. I just meant that if I had known he was meeting someone, I wouldn't have intruded. That was all."

She must notice the look on my face as she tries to rectify what she said. I smile at her; she looks so awkward. I then laugh. She raises her eyebrow at me and looks pissed.

"Sorry, I just found it funny you trying to backtrack. It's okay, no offense taken. I get what you mean." I watch her finish her drink, then she stands to leave, grabbing a purse off the back of her chair. Fuck, I don't want her to leave. I notice as she puts the purse over her shoulder that she has Saran wrap on her arm. I scowl as I stand up. Who the fuck am I, standing up for a woman as she leaves? She notices my look.

"It's my new tattoo, in fact, it's ready to come off now. It's healed nicely. I just wanted one more day for it to heal." That's it. She doesn't elaborate or show me. Just then, Ryker comes back with two beers.

"You off now Vi? It was lovely to see you. Shall we do dinner again soon?" I watch her closely as she nods.

"Yes, that would be lovely, Ryker. Let me know when and I can check my schedule." I notice her accent isn't as strong when she speaks to him, but the couple of times she's spoken to me, it's a little thicker. He nods and walks her to the door. That fucker. I want her. I watch them at the door. They seem quite intimate as they stand for a few minutes talking. I try not to watch but I can't help it, I'm drawn to her. He leans in, I can't make out if he kisses her or he's speaking to her. The fucker, again. He turns and heads back to me. I look away, looking at my glass and twirling it around on the table as he approaches.

"Hey Steve, so how's it going?" He slaps me on the back as he goes to sit down.

"Okay, just working nonstop, as usual. So, what's the game with you and Pink?" He looks at me funny as he sits. I take a swig of my beer.

"Pink, is that what you call her?" He laughs, and I notice he's avoiding my question. I raise an eyebrow. "Does she know you call her Pink?" It's my turn to laugh.

"I have no idea; I've only spoken to her a couple of times. It's just what I call her in my head. She told me her name was VI." I notice a slight twitch in his left eye as I say this. I've learned to read people over the years and I'm pretty fucking good at it. He's a little uneasy. "So, what's the score with you two. You laying her or what?"

He scowls. "No, we're just friends, getting to know each other. I like her, a lot."

I'm cheering inside my head, just friends. If I can get to her before he does, then it won't matter. It's not like we're bosom buddies or anything. It's no skin off my nose if I fuck her first. I want to try to find out more about her. I get the feeling she wasn't being quite truthful with me the other week at the refuge.

"Where's she from? She has an accent and then I find out she works at the refuge for the fucking Ustrashkins. Is there anyone around here who doesn't fucking work for them?" he huffs out. I can see he's conflicted about telling me anything.

"She's from Eastern Europe, I think, that's all I know, really. I haven't asked where exactly. Yes, she works at the refuge, she helps with the girls that are brought in, so technically, yes, she works for the Ustrashkins. She's just an enigma to me, she won't let anyone get close to her. I've been talking to her for a while now and she's only gone out with me on one date. We just arranged another one at the door. We're going out next week. I've been trying to get her to go out on a second date for a while now. She's very closed off." I take another swig of my beer. It's gone.

"Do you want another one, Ryker?"

He nods and I get up to go to the bar for more drinks. I don't usually do this, socialize with people, it's not my gig. I just want to see if he tells me anything. He's not told me anything I didn't already know so far. Except he's into her in a big way. I laugh to myself. Aren't I?

I stay for a couple of hours talking and drinking with him. He doesn't tell me anything else and I don't ask. I don't want him to get suspicious of me. Even after a few beers, we don't bring her up again. I like Ryker, he's got balls. I heard the way he used to speak to Igor when he was rehabilitating him. I don't know anyone who could talk to Igor like that and get away with it. I guess he's a likable guy, with lots of huge muscles. I could do with someone like him on my team when I take over.

"Hey Ryker, why is it you don't work for Igor? I mean, you kind of freelance for him when he needs his men trained and keeping fit, but you're not an employee. Why is that?"

"Well, Igor asked me to work for him, be on his payroll, if you know what I mean. I didn't want that. I had heard a lot about him. I know who he is and what he stands for and I didn't want to be involved in that life. I've heard the rumors about how dangerous it is, and I just want a quiet life. I know you are his bodyguard or something and I respect anyone who works for Igor, but I've seen the way he commands any room he is in and the way he can be with people. I just didn't want to have anything to do with that life. I am more than happy freelancing for him and working when he needs someone, rehabilitating or training." I actually have an admiration for Ryker. Not many people can stand up to Igor like that.

It's been a couple of weeks again without seeing her. It played on my mind that she was going out with Ryker on a second date last week. I couldn't stop thinking about them being together. What if he managed to fuck her? What if they start seeing each other? For some reason, the thought of them fucking makes me angry. I have no claim on Pink, but the thought of her with anyone else has me seething. What the fuck is happening? Only last night I picked up a girl but the entire time I was sucking her clit or plowing into her ass, I was thinking about Pink and those fucking ocean eyes and pink lips. I need to just take the fucking bull by the horns and go after her once and for all. I can't and won't carry on pussyfooting around, trying to catch a glimpse of her here and there. I haven't been to the refuge because I am not shadowing

Poppy and I don't have an excuse to go there. I need to find out when she is there and be on my way there or something as she leaves so I can speak to her again.

I've been trying to think of the best way to take Igor down. I'm ruthless, and don't give a fuck about his family, even if I do like Poppy. I've decided it's going to happen soon. I'm not going to set up a sting like last time. I need to have my men take him out once and for all. I've also decided his family has to go so there are no heirs left and that includes Poppy. They have been destroying sex rings in New York, LA, Vegas, Atlanta and Seattle, they found two more of my houses and I have no idea how and why the fuck I have not been involved. I can't ask him about it because he will suspect something. It fucking grated on my nerves, the last one he took down. I had to congratulate him on the hit. He just thanked me, he never elaborated on any of it. I must have a plant in my cartel. I need to find out who it is, and the fucker will die. Someone is giving away intel and I have no idea who. I had two days off and flew there to try to find out what the fuck was going on. Vera managed to get away from the first house they took down and she's been running one of the others. Luckily, not one of the two Igor has taken down. I met her at an apartment only she knows about, she's the only one left who knows who I am. It's nothing flash, just an apartment in a run-down area, I don't fucking trust her but what choice do I have?

"Vera, someone is giving away intel. Someone is a mole and is telling the Bratva where my houses are. Do you have any idea who it is? Has anyone been acting suspicious lately, a customer or one of the Iranians? I haven't recruited anyone new so it must be someone already embedded."

She doesn't say anything for a minute.

"I have my suspicions about a customer. He came to my house first, then he's been visiting the others. I think he's Russian. You can never fucking tell these days. He was looking around. He was supposed to be with one of the girls when I caught him snooping. When I asked him what he was doing, he lied and said he needed the bathroom. I watched the CCTV back and he didn't. I asked the girl he was with what he did but she couldn't remember. I only gave her a mild sedative.

I didn't shoot her up. He must have given her something else to knock her out. I had to wake her up when he left. Apparently, he went to the Dickins Street house and did the same there. I watched the CCTV there as well, only no one asked why he was wandering around. He just left. When I spoke to Michael at the Vale Street house, he said there was someone there who was a bit suspicious, that he didn't even fuck the girl he was with. I watched his CCTV back and it was the same guy. Here, I have the footage on my laptop."

She shows me the images and I know him straight away. He's Henrique, he works for Igor. Last I knew, he worked in the drugs division. Why the fuck is he in New York snooping around? How the fuck did he get the addresses for the houses? I need to get him.

Twelve

Steve

Present

I'VE BEEN BACK NOW FOR A COUPLE OF WEEKS. I HAVEN'T SEEN Henrique yet, but I will. I'm outside the refuge because I know Pink is in there. I fucking followed her from the Ustrashkins building. I was just leaving to go hunt down Henrique when I spotted her exiting the outer doors as I stepped off the elevator. I couldn't believe it, but with her hair, you can't exactly miss her. I followed her to the refuge, so I know she's in there. I'm waiting just on the corner of the opposite side, I know she will head home. I can't fucking believe I am doing this, just to talk to a fucking girl when I can fuck anyone.

It's three fucking hours before she finally comes out. Three fucking hours standing on the corner like a fucking ponce. I spot her straight away. I move fast.

"Hey, Pink," I shout out. She doesn't hear me or she's ignoring me. "Hey, Vi."

She still doesn't seem to hear me. I catch up to her and tap her on the shoulder. She turns suddenly and before I know what's happening, I'm being high kicked in the stomach and she's just about to punch me in the face, but I catch her hand to stop her. It's then I see she has AirPods in, which explains why she didn't hear me call her. I lean forward, making a big show of her kicking me in the stomach as though she winded me. I'm fine really.

"Oh my god, Steve. I'm so sorry. You freaked me out. I thought someone was attacking me."

I'm still bent over, holding my stomach, but I lift my eyes up to hers.

I hold a finger up, telling her to just give me a minute. I pretend I need a minute to catch my breath. I make a big thing about it. She moves next to me and starts to rub my back. Her touch sends little shock waves all the way to my fucking cock. That's the last thing I need right now. Perfect, showing myself up on the streets of LA. I stay bent over, putting my hands on my knees and pretending to breathe funny. She carries on rubbing my back.

"Steve, are you okay? Do you need some water? I can grab a bottle from the refuge for you." I hear the panic in her voice. She really thinks she's hurt me bad. Maybe this will play into my hands.

"Yeah… water… would… be good," I stutter out, pretending it's bad. I know I'm terrible, but it will also give me time for my semihard cock to fucking deflate. She turns to leave. I turn slightly to watch her as she runs to the refuge door. It's only a couple of minutes before she's out and back at my side. I'm standing up tall now. I look down at her as she hands me the water.

"Are you okay? I'm so sorry. I would never intentionally hurt you. Please forgive me." She looks so worried. I examine her face as I take a swig of water. Her lips are black today and her eyeshadow is darker pinks and purples than the usual vibrant colors I've seen on her, her hair is up in two small pigtails either side of her head. She looks so young like this. I lower the bottle and smile at her, I never fucking smile at or to anyone.

"It's okay. You just caught me off guard and winded me there. Thanks for the water."

She has a backpack on, and she holds both straps at the front, looking sheepishly at me. She looks hurt and upset.

"Hey, honestly, Pink, I'm fine. I was just going to say hi. I saw you leave the refuge and was not far behind you, I called you but didn't realize you had AirPods in. It was my fault for startling you. I should know better. A young girl out on the streets of LA late on. I'm the one that's sorry."

She looks up into my eyes and squints at me, as though thinking. What the fuck, I just apologized and took the blame for her kicking me. She lowers her arm and it's then I see the tattoo she told me about. It's butterflies, I can only see a couple, but I suspect there are more under her top.

"Nice tat." I smile at her.

She looks to where my eyes are looking, then lifts her tee sleeve up and I can see there are more of them. All colorful, just like her.

"Thanks, they turned out great, just how I wanted them." She smiles at her arm as she admires her butterflies. Out of nowhere, I suddenly have the urge to touch her, so I trail a finger very gently and softly over the butterflies. I feel her goose bumps at my first touch, and she inhales. She suddenly looks straight into my eyes. We stare for what feels like an hour, but it's only a few seconds. I want to just lean down and swipe my tongue over her lips. I imagine doing just that as I then look to her mouth. She suddenly steps back and my hand falls to my side.

"I'm sorry. I don't know why I did that. They are so colorful, just like you. Can I ask, Pink, how old are you?"

She stares at me and doesn't answer. I tilt my head to the side and place both my hands in my front jeans pockets, with my thumbs on the outside. I'm waiting for her to answer me. I raise an eyebrow, still waiting.

"Why?" is all she says on the defensive. She's fiery and I like that.

"I was just curious. You look a lot younger with your hair like that." She frowns and instinctively she puts her hand to one of her pigtails and plays with it. I watch her face closely. She's not going to speak. "Look, sorry. Would you like to get a drink with me?" Her eyes widen at my suggestion, and she tentatively steps back and starts to shake her head. Fuck, is she going to run from me? "Pink, look it's okay, we could just get a coffee and have a talk, all innocent. I'd like to get to know you, unless you're with Ryker off course, then I'm sorry if I overstepped. I just thought you two were frie…"

"Yes, a coffee would be good. There's a Starbucks up the road. Shall we go there? I think it will be open," she says, pulling her phone out to look at the time. I smile again, fucking hell. I motion for her to walk with my hand, and she falls in at the side of me. We don't speak for a while, and I find it a little awkward.

"How come you ended up working at the refuge, Pink?"

She stops walking and I stop and look at her.

"I'm sorry, if you don't like me calling you Pink, then I can just call you Vi. What does Vi stand for? Is it Victoria?" she shakes her head.

"It's okay calling me Pink, but what happens if I dye my hair blue?

Will I become Blue? And my name is Viya." She carries on walking, and I now step into line next to her. We approach the Starbucks, but it's closed. Fuck, I wanted to spend time with her. What now? I know there's either a bar not far from here or a pizza restaurant.

"Are you hungry? We could go to the pizza place just up the road. We can eat in and have a talk. I'd like to get to know you."

She nods and we carry on up the road, not speaking. Fuck, is it going to be like this when we sit to eat. I hope not. Although I prefer not talking to people as a rule, I actually want to speak to her and get to know her. We sit at a table and the waitress comes over to see what we want. She gets a Coke and I just get a water. We each order a pizza; I also order some garlic bread to share. We don't speak. Fuck, she's going to make me do the talking. The waitress brings our drinks, and she immediately starts drinking. Her way of not having to speak.

"How long have you been here, in the US? You speak very good English."

She looks at me as she drinks through her straw.

"It's been about four years now, I think. I came with my older brother to LA. We lost our mama, and I didn't have a papa. Vlad, my brother, thought if we could come here, then we would have a better life. When I moved here, we had a tiny apartment and he bought me an old TV. I watched a lot of TV and learned a lot from that." She shrugs. Sounds like she's had a bad time with no parents. "I'm twenty-three," she says very softly and quietly but I catch it.

Twenty-three. Fuck, she's young, but legal.

"Where is your brother now? Is he still here?"

She looks at me for a second with what looks like sadness before lowering her eyes to the straw in her glass she is playing with.

"No, he got into an accident almost two years ago now and didn't make it. It was a hit and run. He was working late at a store, and they think it was a drunk driver. I've lost everyone. I worked in the coffee shop and was homeless for a little while, that's when I got to know Poppy. She was really nice and helpful to me and gave me a job at the refuge and a place to live as payment. I couldn't be more grateful than I am to her. She's become like a sister to me. I could never repay her for her kindness." I wonder if she knows that the Ustrashkins are Bratva or even if she knows what Bratva is. That's something I can find out another day. I feel bad for her, she has no one. She's all alone. She would be a great candidate for my houses, no one to come looking for her. I'm looking at opening a few right here in LA, right under Igor's fucking nose. It won't matter, he won't be around soon. I will rule this fucking city once and for all. Maybe I will have a woman like Poppy by my side. Maybe someone like Pink here who is a little fiery. I bet she's a real firecracker when she gets going. I wonder how she learned to defend herself like that. Kicking me like she did.

"Where did you learn the self-defense? You have a damn good kick on you."

"The girls at the refuge are given self-defense lessons, I thought it was a great opportunity with being on my own, to join them. I was right?" She smiles at me. That fucking smile gets me every time. I can feel my cock stirring. I shuffle a little in my seat just as the waitress brings over our food. Thank fuck for that. I need a distraction. We eat in silence at first. She's making me do all the talking and I fucking hate talking, usually.

"Are you planning on going back to Russia, or sticking it out here in LA?"

She stops eating and squints at me.

"I'm from Ukraine and I am going to stay here for the time being. Unless it becomes too much for me. It is so expensive living here. Poppy can't help me forever. I may just travel the US and see different states. I like it here; it is a lot better than the Ukraine." She takes another bite of her pizza and a sip of Coke. I watch her like she's something new. "Tell me, Steve, what is your story? Have you worked for Igor and Poppy for a long time? I had never seen you before until that time in the coffee shop and then you appeared at the refuge. Where are you from?" Now we're getting somewhere and I tried to trip her up with Russia, but she corrected me.

"I grew up right here, with my papa, who is now dead. It was just the two of us, I never knew my mama. I have known Igor since we were young boys. We were best friends growing up. Now I work for him, protecting him and his family." I watch as she cocks her head and squints slightly. I frown.

"Sorry, I didn't know what you did for Poppy. I didn't realize they had bodyguards. I did wonder why you were sitting outside her office though." I smile. "We are the same as well. Neither of us have family."

She's right, I never thought of that. We finish our pizza and I order some more drinks. I don't want her to leave. I want to keep her here. There doesn't seem to be much to find out about her. She has no family to speak of, only the coffee shop and the work at the refuge center. She doesn't go into that in detail. I guess confidentiality and all that shit. It's not like I don't know what they are there for. We just make small talk, for only being twenty-three, she is very mature. I'm fifteen years older than her. Fuck me. I find her quirky and she makes me feel good. For the first time in my life, I'm talking to someone who has no idea who I am or what I do and she's talking to me because she wants to talk to me and not because I'm making her or fucking her. I have grown women talk to me like they are teenagers, wanting me to fuck them. I'm like Igor. We used to call ourselves babe magnets. We are never short of fucks. They throw themselves at us, or they did him until he got married.

"Would you mind if I left now, Steve? I have to be at work early in the morning. I've been opening up the coffee shop lately and I start at five, ready to open at five thirty. It's kinda late now. I hope you don't mind and don't think I didn't enjoy talking to you." I nod, grab my cell off the tabletop, and stand up. Funny how I never once looked at my phone all the time I was with her. I smile to myself. This girl has gotten me into a tizz. I look at the time and it's eleven already. She stands up and I follow behind as she walks to the door. I watch her ass the whole time. Just out-side, she turns to me.

"Well, thank you for the meal and the drinks."

Is that it? No way. I'm not ready for her to go just yet.

"Let me walk you home. You never know who's out at this time of night." She scowls at me.

"I walk home late all the time. I can defend myself, you know." She laughs and I join in. I actually fucking laugh with her. This is all new to me. I have feelings for this pink girl. She's young and vibrant and confi-dent. I like that.

"I would still like to walk you home if that's okay? I'm just not ready to say good night just yet." I stare into her eyes. She looks away quickly and starts to walk. I step in time with her and look down as she looks up to me. "Is this okay with you?"

She nods. We don't speak and before I know it, we are at the Ustrashkins building. She turns to face me.

"Thank you for walking me home and thank you for tonight. It was nice and unexpected." I smile at her.

"Thank you for allowing me to spend time getting to know you. I would like to do this again, only if you would like to?" I watch as what I'm saying sinks in. Her eyes go wide when she realizes I've just asked her out.

She nods, then turns and runs into the building. That's it, the pink streak disappears from my view. I have no idea why the fuck I am being like this. I've never asked a girl out before or wanted to ask one out. I just fuck and leave them. I have the odd ones I've fucked a few times, but with no strings. I don't do attachments with anyone. I tried it once when I was younger and it didn't work out, it ended suddenly. In fact, after that first time, I vowed never to go that route again.

Sixteen Years Earlier

I kinda like Fallon. She's a little different, not like all the other sluts who throw themselves at me. She's four years older than me. I'm twenty-two now, so that makes her twenty-six. I've run into her a few times at the bar we use when I meet up with the other members of the Bratva. The women in there all know who we are, and they come on to us, trying to get in with us. They know if you become a Bratva wife, you have power and sometimes money. Money is not a problem for me. I have a lot. My papa died and as I was his only heir, I got the lot, which wasn't much to begin with. Including that fucking house that I refuse to go to. Fallon keeps herself to herself and lets her friends do all the work. They are fucking whores, the lot of them. I can't stand them. She seems different. I watch her sit there quietly each time she's with her friends. She never comes on to anyone. She just sits playing on her phone, usually alone. I've watched others try it on with her and she either blanks them or tells them to fuck off. I like that. I've been watching her for a while now. Just watching how she reacts. Even when I have a slut sitting on my cock, she doesn't do or say anything. Most of the sluts that come in here come in for a fuck or a suck, no matter who is around. It gets like one big fucking orgy at times.

It took about a month or so of me watching how she reacts to finally sit at her table to see how she reacted with me. She didn't even look up. I've watched her do this countless times, ignoring everyone. I move her glass away as she is about to reach for it. I take it and sip to see what she's drinking. Coke, that's it. She watched me sip it and then place it back in front of her.

"Hey, would you like something stronger? I can get you something else to drink." She watched my lips as I spoke, then looked into my eyes.

"I'm good, thank you," is all she said, then looked back to her phone. What the fuck. No one ignores me. I grab her phone out of her hands.

"I didn't ask if you were good. I asked if you wanted a drink." She watches my lips again, then looks up to my eyes and scowls.

"I said I'm good. I don't want another drink. Thank you." With that, she turns, so she isn't facing me. What the fuck. I shouldn't be surprised; I've watched her do this enough times.

"Okay, would you like to go out for a drink with me? Just the two of us with none of these clowns around?" Nothing. She doesn't even acknowledge me. Bitch. I stand up and move to her side, where she can see me. She looks at me and rolls her eyes before turning back toward the table. I move with her and sit in my chair. I hear laughing behind me and I turn to see three of the men laughing at me. I get up and walk to them. I grab Dom in the middle by his tee and get right into his face. "You fucking laugh at me again and I'll bury you. Do you fucking hear me?" He looks terrified as he nods. I shove him backward and he hits his head on the wall behind him. "That goes for any of you fuckers," I say before turning to head back to Fallon. Only she's not at the table. I look around and I just see her heading out the door.

I go after her. She hasn't gotten far; I call her name, but she doesn't turn. I grab her arm. She turns, swinging with her hand clenched to try to punch me. I step back. She looks terrified.

"Sorry, I called you, but you didn't answer."

"Can't you get the message. I'm not interested. Now leave me the fuck alone." I like her a lot, she's feisty.

"Wait, I just wanted to take you for a drink." She watches me again. I'm sure she has problems hearing. She always watches my mouth when I talk and then doesn't hear half of what I say. "Can I ask you? Do you have a hearing problem?" her eyes go wide as I say this. She turns and starts to walk quickly away. I catch her again. This time, as she swings her hand, it connects with my face. I instinctively grab her wrist, but let it go the minute I realize. She steps back.

"I do have a slight hearing problem, yes. I can hear noise and it blocks out what people are saying." She's angry. "I don't mix with your kind, they are dangerous. The only reason I am in that place is to watch my younger sister. Just to make sure no harm comes to her. I don't want a drink with you or anyone, now just leave me alone." She turns again and walks off. I watch her go. I'm not chasing after a fucking skirt for no one. I never have to chase skirt.

Five weeks go by, and I haven't been out to the bar, I've been kinda busy. I walk in and immediately spot Fallon sitting at a table, only she isn't alone. I scowl as I look to fucking Dom, of all people, sitting with her. She looks up at me and smiles. She fucking smiles, yet she's sitting with him. Looking at her body language, I'd say she didn't want him there. I watch as he reaches over the table and he grabs her tit in his hand. She scoots back, getting up quick and knocking her chair over. She grabs her glass and throws the contents in Dom's face. I laugh, serves the fucker right. He gets up and makes as though he's going for her. Not on my fucking watch. I walk over to him and grab him by the hair. Pulling him up, I palm him right in the nose. His nose bleeds instantly. I knock him to the floor.

"You ever fucking touch her again without her permission and I will fucking kill you. Do you hear me?"

He's holding his nose as he tries to nod. I see the blood pouring out between his fingers and running down his arms.

I turn to look at Fallon. "You okay?" I ask.

She nods. She's crossing her arms over her chest tightly. "Do you need a drink, or do you want to get out of here?"

"Out of here, please." She doesn't have to tell me twice. I walk to her and take her elbow gently, leading her to the door. When we get outside, she sighs with relief.

"Thank you for getting me out of there. I hate going in there. Men always leer at me and come on to me. I thought that was what you were doing the other week. It's just, I promised my mama I would look after Bean." I frown, who is Bean? "My sister. We call her Bean, ever since she was born. Anyway, she's gotten into coming here and playing around with the Bratva." She stops, sealing her mouth and looking to me. "Oh god, you're Bratva too, aren't you?"

I nod gently.

"I knew it, I will not be involved in Bratva. I have heard too many horrifying stories. I try to stop her coming here but she has a mind of her own and basically does what she wants. I swore to Mama that I would look out for her. It's an almost impossible task."

"Shall we go somewhere else? I promise you I am not trouble unless you want me to be." I wink at her, and she smiles. We head to a much quieter bar and that is where it started with Fallon.

We were inseparable for so long. I fell for her; she was the only person I ever had feelings for. Although, at first I still screwed around, but I stopped after about five months. She used to come to my apartment and stay over, she practically moved in with me. I was away a lot setting up my own cartel, she knew nothing about what I did, and she never asked. I was plotting to overthrow Igor at this point. One day, when I entered my apartment, I found Fallon on the floor in the bedroom, sitting there crying. I ran to her, thinking she was hurt. I searched all over her to see what was wrong. I couldn't find anything wrong. I lifted her up and placed her on my lap on the bed. I turned her head to me and asked what was wrong. She pulled out a white stick from her pocket. She looked at my face and she just said, I'm sorry. I had no idea what she was talking about. I looked at the stick and it said pregnancy test. I couldn't fathom what was happening or what she was telling me.

"I'm pregnant," she whispered and I felt my world tilt.

Pregnant. No way, I did not want kids. This wasn't happening. I almost felt I loved Fallon, but in that moment, I hated her. I wanted to throw her off me. To get away from her. I pushed her aside. Removing her from my lap. I sprang from the bed and headed for the door.

"I don't want you here when I get back," I turned and said.

I saw the shock on her face when she registered what I had said. I turned and left. I didn't go back to my apartment for six days. I gave her that time to leave. I don't know what I would have done to her if she had been there when I returned. Luckily for me, she was gone. I didn't give a shit about her or the fucking baby. I spent six days pissed out of my head and buried in God knew who or what. There was no way I was having anything to do with a baby. I had some loyal men that would stay with me and who I would make my guards once I got rid of Igor. I had one of them watch Fallon and see where she was. I had him follow her. I gave him an envelope with a letter and some cash inside. He had instructions to hand it to her personally and then he was to watch and follow her until I told him not to. He reported back to me each night what she had been doing. This went on for a few weeks until the day he told me she went to a clinic and was in there for a few hours. She did as I asked. She got rid of the baby. If she hadn't, I think I would have got rid of her with the baby inside. I was never going to be anyone's papa.

PART XIII

Vidana
&
Steve

PRESENT

Thirteen

Vidana

I CAN'T BELIEVE I ACTUALLY KICKED HIM AND WINDED HIM. HE'S huge and it's the first time I've ever had to use the self-defense I learned. I did it though, it was instinct. Except turning and seeing it was Steve, I was terrified and thrilled all at the same time. I ran to get him some water, I felt terrible for hurting him, but I felt scared. I thought he might hurt me back, but he was actually nice about it.

Sitting in the pizza restaurant with him, I was scared out of my skin. I couldn't believe I was sitting there eating and talking to him, but also, I had to lie through my teeth, so he didn't get suspicious. The lies flowed so easily I even surprised myself. This man sitting here in front of me was the reason I was kidnapped and trafficked. This man here was also the reason I think I survived. It was his voice I yearned to hear each day or to even catch a glimpse of him. Sitting here in front of him and I know I've fallen for him, or at least his voice. It's captivating to my ears, I want him to keep talking. He's even better than I imagined in all that time I was being held captive. He's strong and has an air of authority about him, I would say as much as Igor. His eyes mesmerize me. They are as blue as Igor's. If he had blond hair like Igor, you would say they were brothers. They look so much alike, and he's just told me they grew up together. I didn't know that, but then why would I know that? I don't know anything about Igor except all the trouble my family has known since he came into our lives.

I start to feel uneasy with the way he keeps looking at me. I know I need to get to know him and try to pull him in. I know I have to do this for the sake of all the girls he held captive. I don't know if he still does it or if that was it when me and the other girls were all rescued. Why would he have a sex trafficking ring if he works for the Ustrashkins. I just don't get it. He says he and Igor are friends and grew up together, maybe Igor does know about it, and he's involved. Maybe Poppy is, but why would they build a refuge and rescue us? I'm all confused. I do know I like Steve. I've fallen for the monster, but I also know I want to find out what his game is. I want to find out if the Ustrashkins are in on it, if they were also my captors. I'm so confused, I just need to leave.

I tell him I have to get up early and need to go, I get up and he follows me then walks me home. I'm nervous with him even more, now that I've spoken to him, and I know he wants to see me again. I'm shaking inside from the nerves. It's both from fear and excitement. He just asked me out, like he wants to see me. I just nod and run inside, not turning back. I hit the button for the elevators and wait. They take their time coming and I know he's standing there watching me. I just don't want to turn to face him and acknowledge I know he's there. The doors open and I stumble inside quickly before I even look to see if there is anyone exiting them. I hit the button and wish the doors to close quicker.

In my room, I throw myself on the bed and just lay there thinking about Steve. Have I got him all wrong? Is it him? Why am I questioning myself when I could never forget his voice? I know it's him without a doubt, only the doubt in my fucking brain. I feel stupid and I have no idea when I will see him again. Can I do this? Can I get to know him and find out more about him? What if I fall for him hard and everything he did or does doesn't matter? What if I fall into his business with him? After all, I experienced it so maybe I could help him. Who the fuck am I right now? He broke me; he destroyed me. He's a fucking monster. I am and was so young, yet I feel I've lived forever and it's all because of him. He put me through hell. Why can't my brain compute it was all his fault? He gave the orders; he was the leader, yet my brain can't comprehend that. My brain just keeps telling me it's Igor's fault. All this is his fault, not Steve's. I'm mad, I know I am. One part of my brain knows it's Steve, but the domineering part is blaming Igor. If it wasn't for Igor, it would never have happened. If it wasn't for Igor, I would never have met Steve. Steve, who makes my heart beat like it's never beat before. Steve, who makes me nervous and who gave me goose bumps at a slight touch.

His touch that sent tingles all through my body, just as he did that time in the bathroom. I've never wanted anyone like I want him. Poppy was right, she said not to use my body, that someday I will want to give it to someone. In my heart, I want to give it to Steve, but in my head, I want to kill him for what he put me through.

I must have fallen asleep thinking about Steve because I wake to my phone alarm telling me it's time for work. I'm still fully clothed and I feel so tired, like I haven't slept all night. The comforter is on the floor, so I must have been tossing and turning all night. I get up and take a shower and head out for work. Just as I get through the doors, I see him leaning against a post. What the fuck is he doing here?

"Good morning, Pink, I thought I would walk you to work. You said you start at five, didn't you?"

I smile at him. He's eager, that's for sure. I need to do this; I need to put my big girl pants on and do this. I have to get close to him, I have to, even if that means using my body for one last time. I have to do it for the sake of all the girls I need to save.

We walk side by side, quietly at first. I feel awkward but I need to say something.

"Did you get any sleep, or have you been standing outside the building all night?" I laugh, looking up into his bright-blue eyes. I'm mesmerized by them; they are like pools of water I could dive into and get lost. He coughs. I step back.

"You looked a little lost there for a minute, Pink."

I go red with embarrassment. I feel my cheeks burning. The last time this happened to me was with Dima, that seems like a lifetime ago now. I wish I was back there, being that young, with not much to worry about. My life was a lot simpler then, when I was looking after my sisters. I thought I loved Dima until he used me and threw me away. It's been the story of my life. Used for my body. Will anyone ever love me?

"Hey." He stops in front of me and slowly lifts my chin up gently with a fingertip. "You look sad and lost. Are you okay, Pink?"

I smile, it's fake. What do I tell him, that I wish I was younger with no worries, looking after my sisters who I miss with all my heart? I nod, then start to walk toward the coffee shop.

We walk the rest of the way in silence. I side-glance Steve and see he is walking with his hands in his front jeans pockets with his thumbs sticking out. I noticed he did change his top so he must have gone home. I have no idea where home is for him. I stop.

"Where do you live, Steve? Is it far from here? Please tell me you don't live in the Ustrashkins building? Just with you being there so early."

He turns and smiles at me.

"I have an apartment not far from the Ustrashkins building. I did live in their building before they moved to their house. Igor always had his guards living in. Now they have a big house in the hills which is like Fort Knox. You wouldn't believe the security they have in place. They do have twenty-four-hour guards on the perimeter, but no guards inside. When I drop them home, I am free to go home myself. It's better this way; it means I am able to socialize more." He smiles down at me, and I look away and start walking. We reach the coffee shop. I take out my keys.

"Are you getting off to work or would you like a coffee before you go?" I have my back to him, unlocking the coffee shop door. Suddenly I feel his front against my back, and I freeze. He bows down to my ear,

"I have time for a coffee," he says and then places his hands on my biceps and rubs.

I can't move. I feel like I'm frozen to the spot. I flash back to that first time I heard him. Fuck, what do I do now?

"Hey, are you okay, Pink? What's wrong, you're shaking."

I shake my head to rid the images and the fear I feel.

"Yeah, sorry. I'm just used to my own space. You scared me." I don't turn to him. Instead, I open the door and rush in to disarm the alarm. I sigh out and lean my head on my outstretched arm that I placed on the wall to steady me. I take in some deep breaths before he comes to find me. I turn, wipe my brow, which is sweating, and I walk to the front of the shop. He's standing in the entrance with the door closed behind him. I smile, it's hard and fake. "Now, let me get the coffee going and I'll pour you a nice fresh cup before you have to leave. Would you like that to go? It's just I have a lot to do before the rush. My delivery will be here any minute with the fresh bakery goods." I smile at him. He stands again with his hands in his jeans pockets, but he cocks his head slightly, looking at me.

"To go would be good. I have to get to work myself. Got a big day. It was one of the reasons I was up so early. I need to fly to New York later today. I'm not sure when I will be back. I have a couple of days off while Igor is staying home with Poppy and the family." I smile then turn to busy myself with the setup for the day. I know it sounds stupid, but starting at five thirty I will be nonstop until Toni comes in at eight for her shift, followed by Sybil, who will be in at ten as she's working the close. Why is he telling me he's going away? It's not like he has to report back to me or anything. I wasn't even expecting to see him for a few days. To say I was shocked he was waiting for me was an understatement.

I turn to give him his coffee, smiling as I put it on the counter that separates us. He's at the counter in two strides, picking it up.

"Thank you, Pink," he says a little standoffish. I pull back slightly at how abrupt he is, and I squint at him.

"What's wrong?"

He just stands staring down at me. It takes a minute or two before he speaks.

"Sorry, I just didn't want to leave. I know I have to, and I know you are busy. I'll come back to see you when I get home." He smiles, then turns and walks out with his coffee in hand. I'm standing watching the back of him disappear out the door. I'm already missing him. The morning goes so slow and everything that can go wrong does. My head just isn't in the game today and Sybil asked me a couple of times what was wrong with me. In all honesty, I'm not sure.

My day is made better when I see Ryker come into the shop at two thirty. Why does seeing Ryker make me feel better? I haven't seen him for a few weeks, yet I feel my tummy do funny turns at the sight of him. I've not felt that before with him, only recently with Steve. Strange, but I can't stop smiling. I only have half an hour to go before I finish my shift and I can't wait to get out of here. I make him his usual coffee, motioning for him to sit. He does and I take it over.

"Hey, Ryker. I haven't seen you for a while. How are you doing?" He looks at me a little apprehensively. I guess I would be the same, I haven't been this friendly with him before. I think it was because I thought he was comparing me to Lana all the time.

"I'm good Vi, how are you?" He's another one being a little standoff-ish with me. What is it with these guys?

"I'm good. I'm just about to finish my shift but have a few things to sort in the back first. I'll come see you if you're still here." I don't give him a chance to answer as I skip into the back and get the orders for tomorrow phoned through. It takes longer than I realize. It's nearly four by the time I grab my stuff and head out. When I get to the front of the shop, Ryker has gone. My heart sinks. I don't understand these feelings I'm having.

"Hey Vi, Ryker said to say goodbye, that he will catch up with you another time. He had an appointment to get to," Sybil shouts as I head for the front door. I feel deflated. Both Steve and now Ryker have gone. What is wrong with me? One, why am I so bothered about either of them, and two, why all of a sudden am I so bothered about Ryker, even more than Steve?

Heading home, I walk slowly, just ambling along, thinking about both of them. Steve, I know is dangerous and I'm not sure if it's that which is drawing me to him as well as wanting to get close to find out if he runs the sex ring on his own or if he's doing it with someone else. Ryker is completely the opposite to Steve. He is caring and tentative. I know he likes me, not to mention he's hot. Whoa, where did that come from? I've never thought of him as hot. I liked him but now I've seen him again today, I think he is hot. My head is screwing with me. I think I want to look more into Stockholm syndrome. I think that is what I have with Steve. He was my captor at the end of the day, even if he wasn't actually there, holding me down. It was all at his hand.

I'm just approaching my building when I see Ryker walking toward me. I don't stop, I just carry on into my building. I don't know if he's coming to see me or visiting someone else.

"Hey, Vi." I hear him shout, so I stop and turn around.

I smile as he approaches me. I'm standing a couple of steps up so when he reaches me, I'm almost at eye level with him. "I was just coming to see you. Sorry I left earlier, but I had a client to get to. I couldn't wait any longer. I waited till three fifteen then had to leave." He looks a little upset.

"It's okay, I was longer than I expected with the orders for tomorrow, there was a mix-up. Sorry if it made you late."

"Not at all. I only popped in to see if you were there, as I hadn't seen you in a while. I actually saw you last night. You were with Steve." He looks a little annoyed.

"Yeah, I was just finishing work at the refuge, and he was apparently there and caught up to me. We were going to go for a coffee, but it was closed so we went for pizza instead." Why does it feel like I have to explain myself to him?

"Oh, I saw you both walking here, it was late. Can I ask ar… no it's none of my business."

I squint at him. "Go on, ask what?"

He looks away, then looks back, and he looks embarrassed. He shrugs. "No, it's okay, it's not my place or business to ask." Now he even sounds angry.

I scowl at him. "No, go on, I want to know what you want to know. You started, so now ask me."

He puts his hands in the side pockets of his sweatpants. That pulls them tight, and I look. I feel so embarrassed that I actually look at the outline of his bulge in the front of his sweatpants. I turn and move up a step, I'm burning up with embarrassment.

"Hey, Vi. Wait, please don't go. I'm sorry. I just wondered if you and Steve were together, you know, seeing each other. I didn't want to step on his toes. That's all. He's not the kind of man you want to piss off, if you know what I mean. I'm sorry." I wait a few seconds before turning back to him. I try not to let my eyes wander and I don't think he actually noticed when I did. He looks down to his feet as he kicks the bottom step.

"Ryker, no. I am not seeing Steve. That was the first time we actually had a conversation, to be honest. He asked if I would like a drink and I just said okay. We are not together. What do you mean, he's not the kind you want to piss off? Why?" I look at him as he looks back to me. He looks conflicted and shrugs. "Do you want to tell me or not? It's okay if you don't." I give him an out. I already know what type of person Steve is. I've witnessed firsthand what he does. I just need to know if he's the boss or working for someone else. I doubt Ryker would know. He doesn't work for any of them that I know of.

"I was on my way to see you. It's been playing on my mind since seeing you last night. I just… he likes you. He told me that the first time he saw you he thought he might know you and he asked if we were together. I told him no and he said I was a fool. I know I am, but I know you only think I like you because of Lana. I don't. I want you to know that. I see how completely different you are. I like you, Vi, really like you. I was going to ask if you wanted to grab something to eat?"

Oh wow. They both like me. I can't comprehend that. I think Steve does, probably because he wants a fuck, but I have to get close to him. That may mean hurting Ryker in the process. Why is my fucking life so complicated? How do I let him down without letting him down? I nod. What the fuck am I doing? I watch as the smile spreads wider on his face. At first, its apprehension, then I see it morph into glee.

"Do you want to get changed first or just go now?"

I smile a timid smile. Why did I nod? Surely it would be better to not go with him. Not give him false hopes when I have to get closer to Steve. I know I'm playing with fire with Steve, but I have to do this. "Let me run up and get changed first. You wait here, I won't be too long."

I turn and head inside. Just as I am about to get on the elevator, I feel him behind me, Steve. I know it's him. I don't turn, pretending I don't know he's there. I feel three people get onto the elevator behind me. I don't turn around until it starts to move. When I do, I come face-to-face with Steve. He's looking at me, confused. I act shocked and smile a timid smile.

"Oh, hey Steve. I thought you were going away?"

He doesn't speak, he just glares down at me. He's scaring me but I don't want to show it. I smile wider, then raise an eyebrow because he hasn't answered me. The doors open and the other two people get off. It's just me and Steve, alone. We only have to ascend two more floors, then I'm at my floor. He still doesn't say anything. He has his usual stance of legs wide and hands in front pockets with thumbs hanging out. The doors open for my floor. He doesn't move. The doors start to close, and I move past him to press the button to open the door. He still doesn't move even though I knocked him.

"Excuse me, Steve, this is my floor."

He still doesn't move, so I move around him and exit onto my floor. I hear him move. I carry on walking and can't help but look behind me. I knew I shouldn't, but I did anyway. He's following me. I stop.

"Steve, what's wrong? You look angry and why are you following me?"

He steps right into my space, and I have to look up into his face. He looks so annoyed; his eyes are a darker blue and I'd say he looks menacing. He scares the life out of me, but I need to act indifferent. I step back and cross my arms over my chest, and I glare at him, waiting for an answer. He raises his eyebrow, as if to say, *What the fuck do you think you're doing?* I do the same back to him. I watch as a smile starts to break out on his face. He can't help it, then he laughs.

"What's so fucking funny? Why are you acting like an ass?"

He stops laughing and scowls.

"I saw you outside with Ryker. Why are you with Ryker? Are you fucking him?"

"No. No, I am not, and if I was, it's none of your fucking business. We, me and you, had something to eat together last night, that's it. Then you waited for me this morning. Big deal. That doesn't make you my keeper or me your property all of a sudden, so don't come trying to intimidate me. It won't fucking work, and if anything, it will make me push you away. Now stop following me. I am going to get changed and then I'm going out for something to eat with my friend, Ryker."

I turn and storm off to my room. Just as I'm about to shut the door, he wedges his foot in it to stop me. I look up at him, shocked he would do something like that.

"Steve, what is your problem?"

He thinks for a minute before removing his foot. He steps back and I shut the door. Hopefully, he will get the message and leave. Now he also knows exactly where I live and that fucking terrifies me.

I have a real quick shower and get my jeans and a tee on. We're not going anywhere fancy, so I don't want to dress up. I also want to try to get Ryker to not like me that way. I know it's hard for me to do, but it's also hard for me to like anyone. I have so many feelings and emotions going through me. I open my door to leave and am shocked Steve is still standing there, only he's leaning against the wall opposite my room. I'm scared but have to act tough.

"Steve, what the hell. Why are you still here? I thought you were busy today and you had to get to New York? Look, Ryker is my friend. Nothing more and nothing less. I'd like to say you were a friend, only the way you are acting is kind of scary and is making me rethink being your friend, you're trying to intimidate me, it won't work. What is wrong?"

He pushes off the wall and in one step is in front of me. "I'm sorry, I didn't want to scare you or intimidate you. It's just, well, there is something about you that I can't pinpoint. Suddenly I'm a little crazed that you're going out with someone else. I know Ryker really likes you and it scares me that you like him." He looks down the corridor, left, then right, then back to me. "I like you Pink, I mean really fucking like you and I want to get to know you. I just need to know if Ryker is going to be a problem." He raises his eyebrows. I glare at him. "Well? Is he going to be a problem for us?"

I sigh out. I have to play it cool. I have to make him think I'm not into him. Even if I really am. "He's not a problem, Steve. He's a friend. That's all. I don't think of him in any way but as a friend. As for us, well, there is no us."

"But I—"

"No, let me finish. There is no us. Not yet anyway. I'm not saying there will be or won't be. We need to get to know each other first. Then take it from there. One night eating pizza does not mean there is an us. It will take a lot more than that. To be honest, the way you are acting right now is making me nervous. Now please go do your things and when you get back from New York, come find me. I'll either be in the coffee shop or at the refuge. But I guess you already know that."

I smile at him, and I don't know why, but I reach up and stroke down his cheek. He inhales at my touch, and I think instinct makes him turn into my hand and he kisses my palm.

"Now, I'm leaving to go have something to eat and a drink with my friend. There is nothing more. See you when you get back."

I close my door and put my key card into my fanny pack that's over my shoulder and I walk to the elevators. I get in as the door opens but I wave to Steve as I do. He hasn't moved. I find it odd and would have thought he would come down with me. But he does what he wants to do.

I head out and see the smile on Ryker's face when he spots me. We head to a little Italian place he says is really great. We spend the rest of the evening talking and I really like him. I can see why Lana fell for him. He's so easy to talk to, he's not bigheaded and he actually treats me like a lady. He opens doors, pulls out seats and makes sure I am settled and talks me through the menu. He's attentive in every way. He's what I would call a gentleman, he makes me feel safe in his presence. That's more than I can say for Steve. Steve terrifies me and not in a good way. That's because of what I know about him. If he finds out I know who he is, I have no doubt he would kill me. I plan on staying alive. I plan on getting my sisters out of Russia and bringing them here. I have to stay alive to save them.

Fourteen

Steve

I WATCH AS SHE DISAPPEARS DOWN THE CORRIDOR TO THE elevators. I don't move. I should go with her, but I don't. Once the elevator doors close, I move. I have a master key and I open her room. I need to get out of the corridor because I'm still not sure if anyone on this floor knows who I am. I mean, I'm almost ninety-nine percent sure no one has ever seen me at the houses, but there's always that one percent chance. I want to know who Pink is, that's the only reason I stayed and am now standing in her room. I had no intention of doing this, it's just, well, following her up here presented me with the opportunity. She must have some ID lying around or something I can check. I search her drawers but there is nothing, under the bed, in the bathroom, all nothing. I open the closet and there is nothing, no boxes, even the in-room safe is unlocked and empty. Maybe she carries her ID with her? I need to leave.

I'm just entering the lobby from the elevator, and I check to make sure there is no one around that I know. I don't want anyone asking questions. I didn't lie to her. I have to catch a plane to New York in two hours. I was going to chance going to my papa's house this morning. But, well, I couldn't sleep thinking about Pink. I got up and had a cold shower while fucking my hand, thinking about her. I'm consumed by her; all my thoughts are of her. She's the most beautiful woman I have ever met, and I just want to sink my cock into her fucking pussy. I was right about her being feisty. She can't possibly know who I am. There is no way she would talk to me like she does if she knew. She'd be fucking terrified of me and she's not. I keep staring at her when I'm with her, I watch for any sign of recognition, anything that might trigger a memory, but there is nothing.

She can't possibly be one of my girls from the houses. Why do I have a problem believing that? She told me her story, she has no one, just like me. She works for the Ustrashkins, well, Poppy at least, and she seems happy working the two jobs she has.

I'm sitting on the plane thinking about Pink. It's all I do. I need to get my head in the game. I've got to get this meeting done; I'm meeting with some of my men first, the older ones that have seen me before, then we are going to see another Iranian. This one, Hafez, is supposed to be ruthless and I want to use him to kill Igor and his family. I need them all gone, that way I will be able to take over. I'm sorry I have to Kill Poppy and their children, but I can't chance leaving any of them alive. There can be no heirs or Poppy. I will then kill Hafez and any men he uses so there is no connection to me. Then I will rule LA as the Pakhan. I was born to rule.

Fuck, Hafez turned out to be a fucking nobody. My intel was wrong. He's no good. I didn't tell him what I wanted him to do, only when I am sure of the person I hire will I tell them. I ended up shooting him right between the eyes, him and his three stooges he had with him. I'm going to have to rethink yet again. The only option I can see is me doing it. I need to take them all out at their home. There's no other way. When people find out it was me, they will be scared shitless of me. Not that they aren't already. I'm going to head back to LA early. I can't wait to see Pink again; I feel like I'm pussy whipped. What the fuck is that all about? I just can't get her out of my head. I want those full lips wrapped around my cock as I fuck her mouth. It's all I can think about.

It's a good job I took the early flight because there's trouble in LA. Igor phoned, he wanted me back there ASAP. He didn't know I was away; he doesn't need to know everything, my business is just that, mine. He told me to meet him at his building, he was supposed to be spending time with his family, which is why I've had some time to myself. Now he's been out without me and there's fucking trouble. I get to his building within twenty minutes of his call. I had just walked back into my apartment when he called and summoned me. I call him to see where he is.

"I'm here. Where are you?"

"Basement." That's it. He cut the fucking call on me. What the fuck. I enter the elevator and insert my card key to take me to the basement. I find Igor in one of the white rooms. He has fucking Sergei sat on a chair with his hands tied and raised above his head. What the fuck. Does that mean Svetlana is back? Igor looks to me as I enter the room, he raises an eyebrow and then turns back to Sergei. I look at Sergei, his face is bloody, one eye is out of its socket, he has no clothes on and I see his cock is missing. I look around and see it on the floor behind him.

"Where the fuck did this ass come from? How did you find him? Have you got her as well?" He doesn't turn to speak to me. He keeps his eyes on Sergei.

"We don't have her, because lover boy here won't give up her whereabouts." He kicks Sergei in the shin. "As for him, I've been tracking him for a while. I had eyes on him a couple of months ago when he came back to the States, alone. I was just biding my time to see if she materialized. I got fed up with waiting, so I had Renat bring him in. He's been lying low in Pennsylvania. How he didn't think I wouldn't know is beyond me. Guess he's the stupidest fuck going. To be taken in by that fucking whore like he was. She used him. She never loved him. There's only one person she ever loved besides herself and that was me. We all fucking know it. You dumb fuck."

He's pissed, really pissed. I've seen Igor angry before but this is way up there. Sergei will be lucky he has any limbs left by the time Igor's through with him. I wouldn't mind joining in myself. In fact, I'm not sure why Igor called me in.

"Okay, Sergei, now is the time to tell me where she is. I've never had anyone escape from down here before you two, and let's just say it fucking pissed me off, big time. So, you have a choice. I either ask Steve here to put a bullet in your head as soon as you tell me, or we prolong the agony, and you know only too well how that goes. You've already lost your cock as that seems to be the thing that led you to help her escape, so the balls will be next, then I'm going to cut your nipples off one by one and feed them to you with your balls. After that, well, I think I'll get the thumb screws on you while I shove the poker up your ass. Then I might finish with the poker from your ass being shoved up your nose into your brain. Now it's your choice. You choose option one or option two. Steve, he has the time it takes me to go piss to decide. I'll let you have a little go, maybe do an eardrum first."

He turns and walks past me with a smirk on his face. He's not going for a piss; he'll be standing outside in the corridor listening. Hoping I get some info out of him, knowing we worked together. Sergei isn't stupid in that way; he knows all the tricks and what went on down here. I'm going to play it cool, pretend to be on his side.

"Why the fuck did you come back to the States, you dumb fuck? You knew the minute you stepped foot back Igor would find out. Why, Serg, that has to be the stupidest thing to do. If you split from Lana, you should have gone anywhere but back here or Russia. You know he'd find you there as well. Why did you do it? I mean, why run away with her when we all fucking knew it was Igor she wanted all along? She never loved anyone else. She was the biggest fucking user and whore going. Where did you end up? Igor was going nuts looking for you both. You know she disappeared once before, and then to do it again, to him. He killed some of our men, Serg, he killed the guys in the comms room for allowing it to happen. He tortured them, thinking they were all in on it. You got them all killed." He looks at me with his one good eye. I can see tears flowing down his cheek.

"Why, Serg? I thought you knew better than that. You knew he'd find you one day." He drops his head. I kneel in front of him and put my hand on his knee. Fuck, he's a mess. He's going to bleed out soon anyway, he has to know his end is imminent. "Just tell me where you were, where she is. You know you're going to die, Serg, it might as well be easy and quick. You know how this works. He can prolong this for hours. Just tell me." He looks down into my face and he sighs.

"I loved her, Steve. I fucking loved her so much. I thought helping her out of here, and getting away, she would love me back. She made me believe she loved me. We were fucking long before Igor made me his guard. We fucked like rabbits all the fucking time. I loved her. It killed me when she started seeing Ryker. But she said she didn't want me to get hurt by Igor and she only called it off for my safety. I fucking believed her. She begged me to help her that night. I knew he was going to kill her, and I couldn't let it happen. I loved her." He hangs his head and cries. I actually feel a slight twinge of sorrow for the stupid fucker, but only a slight one. He was taken in by a manipulative bitch. He fell for her lies. I stand up and put my hands in my jeans pockets, so he knows I'm not going to do anything to him. I'll leave that to Igor. I just hope he stays out there because I think Sergei is opening up to me. I move to the table with the tools and I grab a bottle of water. I tilt Sergei's head up gently and I show him the water. I place it to his lips and tilt it for him to sip. Might be his last fucking drink. I'd prefer vodka myself.

"Where is she, Serg? Where is she now?" He looks up to me.

"We made it to the UK. We never stopped looking over our shoulders. We stayed there for a while, then we moved to Dubai. She soon got fed up there. We then moved from there and went to China. She left me in China. She was screwing a Triad boss. How the fuck does she do it? First, she gets in with Igor the Pakhan of the Bratva, then she somehow gets in with a Dragon Head of the Triad. Does she have some fucking Mafia magnet attached to her pussy? Anyway, I had to get out of there before they killed me. I had nowhere else to go, it was either the States which has been my home for most of my life or to Russia. Either way, I was screwed. She turned Longwei, the Dragon head, against me. I fucking saved her and that's how she repaid me. She just wanted to get rid of me, cut all ties to this life and be with Longwei, I think she knew Igor could never go after her. I think it was her plan all along. She was the one that made the decisions on where to go. She led us to China. I swear she planned to seduce the Dragon head all along. I had to flee in the night, I had to cross the border to Bangladesh and then to India where I managed to fly out, first to New York and then to Pennsylvania. I've been there for a few months. I thought I was safe until I saw Renat, then I knew I had been found and my end was near." He hangs his head again just as Igor walks in, clapping.

"Thanks, Steve. I knew you would get it out of him. Well done, Sergei, you just opted for option one. Steve, do the honors."

I pull out my gun and with a look of sorrow on my face, I aim it right between Sergei's eyes and pull the trigger. His head snaps back with the force. His arms are tied up so his body can't slump. It was better this way for him. He was kind of a friend at one point. Well, sort of, I don't have fucking friends. Igor would have tortured him relentlessly if he hadn't spoken.

"Are you going after her?" I ask.

He looks at me and he puts his thumb to his mouth.

"Nah, she's not worth the time or effort and I'm not treading on the Dragon head's toes. We have an understanding with the Triad in certain areas. I don't know this Longwei. He'll either get fed up with her and let his soldiers use her or kill her. She won't last long. I don't see her coming back here, that's for sure." He turns to walk out of the room. "Get the cleaners in to clean this mess up and put his body in the vat. Then come up to the apartment. I have something I want to speak to you about before taking me back home."

He marches out, just like that. I still admire him, even if I fucking hate him now. We were brothers and he disowned me. He threw me away. He never even came to me when my papa died. I went to Kirill's funeral, we all had to. Igor was indifferent, he didn't want to be there. He acted just like Kirill did at Dimitri's funeral. I see how alike they are. Igor has become Kirill and I thought he had a softer side. I was wrong. I get the cleaners in and head up to his apartment. I have no idea what he wants to see me about. It always makes me nervous. If he has anything on me, I will take him out, but I'd rather do it taking them all out.

I walk out of the elevator and I hear Igor talking. He's in his office. I stand at the door and let him see me. He's on his cell, it sounds like he's talking to one of his kids. I move away to the kitchen to get a drink and wait for him. It's not long before he's heading to me. I turn just as he comes into view. I hold up the water.

"Do you want anything?" He scowls at me, maybe because I work for him and I'm being too familiar right now. I don't fucking care. I just killed Sergei for him. He nods his head and I take another swig from the bottle. He motions with his head to follow him. He heads for the corridor where the bedrooms are. I know he also has an arms room, or he did. He opens one of the bedroom doors. It used to be his bedroom. What the fuck does he want with me in there? I stop at the door; he turns to look at me. I peer past him and the room is empty apart from a small table with two chairs. I raise an eyebrow.

"Come inside," he says all authoritatively. He moves away from the door and sits on one of the chairs. I'm armed, but who knows what's waiting for me in the bathroom. He motions for me to take a seat. "Shut the fucking door behind you." He's not angry, he's just normal Igor.

I move over casually and sit down slowly. I noticed he's facing the bathroom and I have my back to it. I'm on alert, listening for the slightest sound. I keep my hands under the tabletop just in case I need to reach for my gun.

"This is a safe room. I sweep it regularly for bugs, as you know I do. This was the room Poppy and I had all our discussions in. I wanted to speak to you because I think we have someone working for us and working for the Iranian cartel. I haven't found out who it is yet, which is where you come in. I need your help weeding them out. I know it's one of our men. The raids we have been doing trying to destroy the cartel's sex trafficking are all well-organized once we get in. It's like someone has the intel we are going to do the raids and sets it up for us to find just enough at the raid to make us think we are getting them all. I know we're not. It's been too easy and the ones we captured, well, three of them had cyanide capsules in their teeth. As soon as we started the interrogation, they bit them and died. They were stooges."

He looks past me for a second. Is there someone behind me? He looks back, straight into my eyes.

"You are thick with some of our men and I'm hoping just like with Sergei you can weed out who is responsible."

He's fucking serious. I don't move my face an inch, he's watching me closely. I know his tactics. He watches closely to see if I flinch, or my eyes widen, or I squint, or my breaths stutters. He listens to see if my heartbeat has quickened and watches the pulse on my neck. It's not happening. I'm good, better than he gives me credit for.

"Yeah, of course I will help any way I can. Fucking hell, Igor, are you sure it's one of ours?"

He scowls at me. "It has to be, how else would they know? The only thing is, the last few raids, there weren't many of my men that knew about it. I kept it that way. It means the few that did know, one of them is either the mole or he told someone else in Bratva. We will find who it is. Here is a list of the names of those that knew about the raids. See what you can find out." He passes me a piece of paper from his inside jacket pocket. I open it and see there are only a dozen names on the list, including mine. I look up to him and scowl.

"What the fuck, Igor? You ask me to help find who it is, yet you have my name on the list. How does that fucking work?" I crumple the paper up and throw it on the table, showing him how pissed I am. He reaches into the same pocket and pulls out another piece of paper and passes it to me. It's the same list minus my name. "So what? You gave me the wrong list? Why the fuck is my name on that one?"

"Because you knew about the raids, and I put everyone on it that knew. I wanted to see how you would react and you did good." The fucker, it was another test. Seeing how I would react. Being pissed was correct. If I had laughed about it, he would have known I was involved.

"Are we done? Can I drive you home now? For your information, I never knew fuck all about the last raids you did. So my name shouldn't have been on anyway." He nods and gets up. I follow behind him with a sneer on my face as we head to the elevators. "I'll make a start on the list. Call me when you need me, I may be out gathering intel." He nods.

I drop him home. I punch in the security number at his gates and I drop him at the door. He hasn't spoken since we left his building, not that there is anything unusual about that. We don't make small talk. I head home so I can sort myself out. I pull out the list of names and I don't see Henrique's name on there. I still need words with him. I'll get on that when I start talking to the other names on the list. I have to interrogate them all, even though I know it's none of them. But some are going to have to pay the price.

I'm staring at the names, and I know all these men are loyal to Bratva. I need to see Pink. Just like that, she pops into my head. I wonder where she is now. I look at the time, it's eight thirty p.m., she might be at the refuge. I'm close, I may just pop in to see if she's around. Just say I'm checking security. I head out. She won't be expecting me, I said I was going to New York for a few days. I'll try not to startle her this time, avoid another kick.

I head inside the refuge. I'm safe being in here. Most people have seen me around and most of the staff know I'm Igor's second. I look around but don't see her anywhere. I ask one of the other staff members if Vi is in and she doesn't know who I'm talking about. I tell her it's the girl with the pink hair. She smiles at me and nods, telling me she's in the dining room. I head there and I stop at the door when I see her sitting there with another girl. She has her back to the door, so I lean against the doorjamb, watching her. She's very gentle and attentive with the girl she's with. I can see the girl is a little fragile. She's well worn, her skin is very pale, and her features are gaunt. She notices me watching them and her eyes go wide. Fuck, does she recognize me? She starts to breathe heavily, then she pushes away from the table they are sitting at. She rises up, knocking her chair to the floor. She backs away, keeping her eyes on me all the time. She looks terrified. Fuck. I hold up my hands to show her I'm good. She backs herself up to the window. Pink turns to see what she's looking at and she scowls at me.

"Leave, Steve. NOW," she shouts at me; I turn and move away from the dining room.

Was she one of my girls? Did she recognize me? Fuck. I stay with my back to the wall next to the door and I listen just in case she says something. I hear Pink get up and move to her, trying to calm her down. She's good. She's telling the girl no one is going to harm her. She's safe here. This is a safe place. The girl starts crying. She's Russian, I can speak fluent Russian. What surprises me is that Pink then speaks back to her in Russian. She told me she was from the Ukraine, but she is speaking perfect Russian. Most Ukrainians speak Ukrainian, a lot of the younger generation speak Russian, but it is still different to normal Russian. It's kind of mixed between Russian and Ukrainian. Did she lie to me? Is she from Russia? She's calmed the girl down and it sounds like they have now sat back down. I'm listening for any giveaway that the girl knows me. I know she doesn't. It's impossible but you just never know. From the way the conversation is going, it's because I'm a man. She's terrified of men in general.

I go wait in the lobby for Pink to finish and come out. She's fucking ages. I'm just about to leave when she appears. I don't see her but sense her. I look up from my phone and she's standing in the corridor watching me. She smiles when I smile at her.

"Hey, sorry. I thought I would wait for you. You looked like you had your hands full there, so I thought it best I wait here. I hope that's okay?"

She starts to walk toward me, smiling as she does.

"Yes, of course it's okay. I'm just surprised you hung around as long as you did."

"I wanted to see you. I got back from New York early. All I could think about was seeing you again," I tell her in Russian. She cocks her head to the side. I know she understood me.

"Why are you speaking Russian to me?" She looks at me quizzically. I raise an eyebrow.

"I heard you speaking perfect Russian to that girl. It kind of surprised me because you said you were from the Ukraine but there was no Ukrainian dialect in there?" I question her. Why the fuck am I questioning her? She squints at me but doesn't say anything. I raise an eyebrow, waiting for her response. She starts to walk to the door without saying anything. What the fuck. I get up and follow her.

"Pink, wait up." She's walking quickly, heading for home. I catch up and very gently put my hand on her shoulder. I immediately step back in case she tries to roundhouse me again. She stops still but doesn't turn. I breathe out. "Look, I just got back and wanted to see you. That's all." I sound angry even to myself. She still doesn't turn. I walk around and stand in front of her. Her head is bowed down, I crouch to look her in the eye. She lifts her head up and she's pissed.

"Who the hell do you think you are questioning me? I told you the truth, yet you question me? Well, STEVE, go fuck yourself. Leave me alone." She emphasizes my name. I was right about her being a little spitfire and I find my cock responding to her. Fuck, not now.

"Look, I'm sorry, you just surprised me, that's all. I didn't expect you to speak fluent Russian." She sighs out then looks up to me.

"I was born in the Ukraine. That is where I am from. When I was four, we moved to Russia for my papa's work. That is how I speak perfect

Russian. I went to school there and lived there before me and my brother moved here."

Well, why didn't she fucking say that the other night. I smile at her and automatically lift her chin up gently with a finger. I lean in and very gently brush my lips over hers. I watch as her eyes go wide, and she inhales deeply before exhaling out. I smile and she smiles back. I want to devour her, but I know it's too soon. I'm not used to this at all. I'm used to taking what I want when I want and fucking them real hard. With Pink, I want to take it slow, don't get me wrong, I want to fuck her, but I want to do it slow.

"Do you want to get a drink or something to eat? I actually fucking missed you, Pink, and I was only gone a short time." I smile at her, and I watch as her smile spreads across her face.

"Drink would be good. I had a salad at the refuge not so long ago." We walk along and I start to make small talk, asking about her day. I have no idea who the fuck I am right now. All I know is I want to spend time with her. I want to get to know her for real. She fascinates me in a way no woman ever has. I don't even care that she's only twenty-three. She's legal and age is just a number. I'm just going to try not to lose it with her. I don't want to lose her. I have to do this before Ryker gets in there. Tomorrow I am going to sort my papa's house out, go back there once and for all instead of putting it off. Then I'm going to sort out getting Igor, finally, tie up all my loose ends, so I can take over and maybe have Pink by my side, ruling. I can see her being a great asset, just like Poppy is to Igor. Who knows, take over Bratva, get the girl and the family just like he did.

Vidana

I HAD NO IDEA HE WAS EVEN BACK, NEVER MIND STANDING THERE watching me in the dining room. It was only because Melina started to freak out at him standing there that I knew he was even there. He looked really sorry and ashamed for being scaring her. Melina only arrived today, and I've been working with her, trying to help her realize she was now safe. When she saw Steve standing there, she thought he was coming to have a go at her. It took me a while to calm her down and tell her she was safe, that Steve was only a friend who also worked there sometimes. I took her to her room and made sure she was settled before leaving. It's been a real hard day today with a new influx of abused girls arriving. It always leaves me feeling sorrow and hurt for them. It drains me and really takes it out on me mentally. More often than not, it takes me back to me being captive. I guess it always will, but at least I can help these girls get to where I am. I mean, look at me now, who would ever have thought I was just like them.

To see him sitting there waiting for me shocked me. I thought he had left a while ago. What is he playing at? Why is he so keen? He notices me and smiles. I smile back. How can I not? I mean, he is gorgeous to look at and he's my savior. Oh my god, why did I just say that? It's why I'm so attracted to him, which I think I knew all along deep down. But I've admitted it now, it has to be Stockholm syndrome. I have it. I still need to play along to find out if he is the leader. I know I'm playing a dangerous game, but I have to know. I now realize I really like Ryker; I mean, really like him. It's just dawned on me, after me thinking he was hot, I know he's the perfect guy.

Oh my god, he's questioning me about where I come from. What the fuck. Does he know? Is that why he's asking? I think he knows who I am. I need to be cool. I leave without saying a word. *Way to play it cool, Vidana.* He shouts my name. I freeze when he taps my shoulder. I know it's him, so I don't turn around or try my self-defense moves on him this time. He apologizes and I'm playing it cool, although I lose my patience with him. I had time to think about my story. I only told him I was from the Ukraine originally; I didn't say I actually lived there so I tell him we moved to Russian. He lifts my chin up and my eyes go wide as he moves his head toward mine. Holy fuck, he's going to ki... WOW, he kissed me very lightly on the lips. I feel myself blushing, my tummy is doing somersaults. How could I have these feelings? How could I let a man touch me like that after everything I've been through? My head is all over the place. I loved it but my tummy doing somersaults was more me feeling scared and anxious at what was to come rather than excitement, although I think there was some excitement in there.

I agree to have a drink with him. I need one. My knees are wobbly with my legs feeling like Jell-O. What the hell is happening? I'm so confused and conflicted. I wouldn't mind, I've never even had any alcohol before, well only a small taste. I'll just have a Coke, the last thing I need is to be addicted to alcohol. My addiction levels and cravings are too high for me to start on that shit. I still struggle with wanting a fix of drugs, but I have more willpower than I ever did. I just don't want to tempt myself with a different addiction.

We're sitting in a bar. I've only ever been in the one bar and that was with Ryker, where Steve came and joined us. I feel a little uneasy. It's really busy, but there are a lot of men in here and only a few women. I'm not sure what kind of a place this is, but I don't like it. It's different from that first one I went in, that was a lot quieter and cleaner. I order a Coke and Steve gets a tall glass of beer.

"Have you drank alcohol before, Pink?" I look at him weirdly. Why would he ask me that? Is that a normal thing to ask someone? Here goes another lie.

"Yes, I've had wine, which is okay, but I wouldn't go out of my way to have any more and I also had a rum and Coke once, oh and I tried a beer," I say, pointing at his half-empty glass. I don't want him to think I'm a total wuss or try and force me to have a drink or a taste of his. "Why would you ask me that, Steve?" He laughs at me.

"Just trying to get to know you, Pink, that's all. Seeing what you like or don't like, so that's good to know. By the looks of it, you seem uncomfortable. Do you not like it in here or is it the company?" He kind of sneers at me. I don't like that. I sneer back at him. "Sorry if I come on a little strong or ask too many questions. It's my job to be observant. To read people and how they react. You seem to not like me asking you questions."

"I know you mean well. I'm just not used to it. I've had to fend for myself a lot since losing Vlad. Poppy is the only one I've had to talk to. I'm not used to people asking me questions. I'll get used to it, I guess." He sits back and just looks at me.

"Come on, let's get out of here. I know you're uncomfortable." He jumps up and takes my fanny pack and holds out his hand for me to take. I'm grateful we are leaving. I really don't like it in here. I'm being stared at by a lot of the men, probably my hair grabbing their attention but the few women in here are also sneering at me. What for? I haven't done anything. "Okay, what now? I don't want to take you home yet. I saw the way you were being looked at and to be perfectly honest, if we had stayed in there any longer, I wouldn't have been responsible for my actions." He's still holding my hand and has my fanny pack slung over his shoulder. We walk but I don't know where we're going. I feel kind of scared but excited all at the same time. I've never had anyone holding my hand since, well, since Dima, and we know how that turned out.

We walk in silence for a little while. He swings our hands as we walk. I look up to him and see he has a goofy smile on his face. I really look and wonder how can this man be the monster he is? He's truly an evil bastard running a sex trafficking business. How can men be so callous or indifferent to women, and how can they treat them like they do? We're all humans. You should never treat another human any differently than yourself. I just cannot understand it. How they use women just for their bodies, to get off on it, just for sex. Why are men so fucking ruled by sex, is it a problem with their brains? Do they have this animalistic thing where they have to have sex or they will die? The thing is, they use us and they get away with it. They use us, then kill us , mostly. I drop his hand from mine. He looks down to me.

"Hey, what's wrong. Why are you crying?"

Oh fuck, I didn't realize I was. I'm so fucking angry with him and men. He turns my body to face him, and he very gently cradles my face in his hands and wipes the tears from my face softly with his thumbs. I nuzzle my cheek into his hand. What the fuck am I doing? One minute I'm crying because of the evil monster he is, then I'm letting him get under my skin and fall even more for him. This is only one side to this monster. Maybe when I see the other side, it will make me despise him. I really hope the Ustrashkins have nothing to do with the sex trafficking and that when I tell Igor what I know he will kill Steve. Yet, I don't want him dead. I cry harder. He pulls my head into his chest and cradles it with his strong hands. He rubs down my head. All I can think is that he's going to flatten my hair. I need to get out of his hold. He's making me question myself and what I'm actually doing here with him. No man has ever touched me like this. Affectionately. Not even Dima. He only wanted one thing in the end. Every time after that was obviously against my will and was very violent. I was just a body to be used. I calm myself down. How do I explain this episode to him now? I sniffle into his tee; I pull back and see the colorful wet patch I left from my tears and nose. I look up to him.

"I'm sorry, I wet your T-shirt." I wipe at it just to make sure there is no snot on it.

"Hey." He takes my head gently and tilts it up to look in his face. I must look like a mess. My makeup must be all over. I hang my head in shame. "Pink, don't do that. You're fucking beautiful to look at, never hide from me. Are you okay? Did I do something wrong?" I look up and he looks worried.

"My face must look a mess. My makeup must be all over." I sniffle again, trying to look back down, but he doesn't let me.

He lifts my head up again and this time he bends down and kisses me. I nearly have a freak-out. He's full on kissing me, prying my lips open with his tongue. He's dueling with my tongue in my mouth. He has my head held in both hands; I couldn't move away if I wanted to. I join in with the kiss but in no time, I start to try and pull away. I start to freak out, thinking back to being held and forced to do things. I start to have flashbacks. I grab his hands, trying to pry them from the side of my head, I dig my nails in, trying to make him let go. All I can picture are old men sticking their tongues in my mouth and my other holes. It repulses me and I manage to turn away from him as he releases me, just in time as I throw my guts up. I feel so ashamed. I'm bent over, holding my stomach. He steps next to me and starts to rub my back. I don't want him to touch me. Every time he touches me, I have flashbacks. I wretch again and again, until it's just bile coming up. I stand up straight and wipe my mouth on my sleeve. I dread to think what I must look like now. He holds my head again and makes me look up to him. I try with all my might not to shake out of his hold. I breathe heavily through my nostrils. He must see the panicked look on my face. He has to see the tension in my jaw while gritting my teeth.

"Come on, let's get you home. You obviously have some kind of bug to make you throw up like that. Maybe something on the salad didn't agree with you. Let me take you home." He picks up my fanny pack again and then turns me to walk home, he has me pulled into his side with his arm around me for support. You would think I was drunk or stoned the way I was walking and being held up. My entire body feels like Jell-O and my mind is telling me he's going to use me and fuck me, then probably kill me. My mind can't compute that he is supporting me and helping me.

We arrive at my home; he walks me up the steps and to the elevator. I need to think quick; I don't want him up in my room. "Steve, I will be okay now, thank you for helping me. I feel awful for ruining the evening. I don't know what came over me. I still feel queasy. It's best if I go up on my own. Thank you."

"I don't mind helping you to your room, Pink. I promise I will just see you there and make sure you get into bed okay, then I will leave." I stop. No.

"No. I am fine, honestly. Thank you, Steve."

I enter the elevator and press my floor, then the close door button. I smile a pathetic smile at him as the doors close, just as I see him running his hand through his hair. I make it to my room. I'm not hurt or hurting anywhere; I know why I was sick, but it's best to let him think it was a stomach bug. I look at my face in my bathroom mirror and I'm horrified to see most of my makeup has come off or is smudged on my face. My makeup is my war paint. It hides who I am to the outside world. I cleanse my face, then get into bed. It's still early. I'm wide awake, playing it all back in my head. Does he know? Is that why he questions me. It makes me wonder. When he kissed me, I loved it fleetingly, but then it turned to something more sinister. All I could think was back to being captive. He is the link back to that time. I don't know if I can do this, if I can get close to him. How long will it take? He's not going to open up that easily to me. Would he even tell me anything? I highly doubt it, not unless… hmm, I have to be like Poppy. I have to be Poppy, then maybe he will tell me.

I'm up for my early shift in the coffee shop. I do all earlies now so I can get to the refuge and do my bit there. I have to work there; it's why I live in Poppy's building rent free. I'm headed outside, putting my fanny pack over my shoulder when I stop. He's here again. I smile at him when he looks up from his phone.

"Good morning. What brings you here so early, again?" He gets up from the wall he's sat on and moves over to me. He bends down and brushes my cheek with his lips. I blush.

"Good morning to you too. You look and sound a lot better this morning. How are you feeling?" I smile and start to walk toward work. He walks at my side. I look up to him.

"I'm good, I had a shower then went to bed and I wasn't sick anymore. I had a good night's sleep. I don't know what happened. All I can think is it was something I ate." He looks down and smiles. He takes my hand like he did last night, and I smile inwardly at the touch, but it only lasts a second. I then start to feel myself get panicky. I try not to show it, but he feels my hand tense. He looks at me and frowns. I drop my hand from his and move my fanny pack as an excuse to let go.

"Hey, are you okay with me being here?" he looks angry. I nod and smile. But keep my hand on my fanny pack. "Are you sure? I can leave. I'm sorry if I'm coming on a little strong but I think about you all the time. I don't know what it is about you. I just really like you and believe me, that's a big fucking deal." He sounds sincere.

"Yes, I'm fine. Just, I'm not used to all the touchy-feely stuff. I've not had anyone to answer to for so long, it's just an adjustment I need to get used to." I shrug. We walk in silence for a little while. "Steve, I like you too," I say all of a sudden and look up to him. He stops and I stop with him. He gently takes my hand, which is still holding my fanny pack, and grasps it with both of his. I don't pull it back and he stands staring into my eyes. I get lost in his bright blues.

"I will take it as slow as you need. It's new to me too. I've never had a girlfriend, well only one, a long time ago, but it was so long ago now it doesn't count. I am so busy, I never really have time. With you, I want to make time. If you allow me to. I tried being away from you this week, but it didn't work. I would rather take it easy and let us get to know each other than risk losing you." I tilt my head as I get lost in his eyes and words. He just said about being his girlfriend, I think. Fuck me. What do I do now? I have to do this though; I have to find out. If it means giving myself to him, to end what he does and save God knows how many girls from going through what I did, then I have to do this. I have to push through and do this. Poppy has taught me to have self-respect, and to fight for what you want and what you believe in. I have to be like Poppy. It just occurs to me; I don't know how old he is.

"How old are you?" I ask, just like he asked me. He smiles.

"I am thirty-eight. I know I'm a lot older than you, but it's a number. I don't care as long as it doesn't affect you. I know you are young and may not want to be with an old man, but..." I rise up on my tiptoes and gently brush my lips over his to stop him talking. He is old, as far as age goes, but I would have said he looked more like twenty-eight than thirty-eight. It shocked me, I have to admit, but if I am to go through with this, then age doesn't come into it. We walk to the coffee shop, and I do what I did the other day and make him a coffee to go. He can't hang around my workplace all day. He takes the hint, leans over the counter, and kisses my lips.

"See you later. Are you working at the refuge tonight?" I nod. "What time do you finish? I would like to try and come meet you if I may?"

"It should be about eight thirty, but it all depends how it goes. I can never tell from one day to the next. If we have anyone new come in, I am usually the one to tend to them. Poppy likes me to do that. If you drop by, come find me, just be careful not to scare any of the girls again." He kisses me gently once more, then picks his coffee up and leaves. This is going to be hard. Just my luck, Sybil walks in. She's not supposed to be in until later. I roll my eyes as she stands there with her arms folded, staring at me.

"What?" I snap and turn away to head into the back to place the orders. I hear her follow me.

"I saw the two of you through the window. What are you playing at, girl? It wasn't that long ago the sight of that man terrified the hell out of you and now you're, what" —she spreads her arms— "you seeing him or something? What's that all about, Vi? I thought you were into Ryker, cause he sure as hell is into you. Vi, look, that one who just left is bad news. He has this bad fucking aura around him, I see it, girl, and you know I know my auras. You need to stay away from him VI. I'm telling you he has bad, bad juju vibes or some shit." She's spot on, but I can't tell her that. I am getting closer to Sybil, but she doesn't know my past and I'm not at the stage that I can discuss it with anyone yet. That's why I have Poppy. She rescued me. She knows what I went through.

At the refuge, there are no new girls. I just work with the girls that need me the most. Time flies so fast in here sometimes that I didn't realize what time it was until I saw Steve at the door to the communal room. He backed away when I spotted him, I guess he didn't want to freak any of the girls out like yesterday. I say my goodbyes and head out. He's waiting outside for me this time.

"Hey, beautiful. How was your day today?" he asks, walking toward me, then bending to kiss my lips gently. Is this too much? Is this fast? It feels fast to me, but then I need to get this over with as quickly as I can so I should be grateful really. I smile as he kisses me.

"I'm good, thank you. How was your day? Did you do anything interesting?"

"Just the usual, tied up some loose ends and sorted some stuff out.

It was quite a good day, really. Made even better now I've seen you. Have you eaten anything?"

I haven't, come to think of it, I shake my head.

"Good, would you like to come to my place? I got some food in just in case you hadn't eaten anything."

I freeze, staring at him. His place, it's too soon. I can't do it. What if he wants to use me, or just have sex anyway? But isn't that the whole idea, let him use me so I can find out the truth?

"Hey, Pink, what's wrong? You're shaking, are you okay? Look, you don't have to come to mine. It was just an idea. I promise nothing will happen. Just eat and talk, nothing more, if you don't want it. If you want to go somewhere else, then that's fine too. It was just a suggestion." He strokes down my cheek gently, then grabs my hands. He stares down into my face. I look up and force a smile.

"Okay, just eat and talk. Nothing more?" He nods and smiles. "I have my car, it's just over there." He motions with his head, and I follow the direction.

I see a black car with blacked-out windows. It's huge. He starts to walk us with him walking backward. He lets go of one hand, then walks us to the car, still holding the other. He opens the passenger door for me and helps me inside. He's being so nice, but then he's been nice since I met him. We drive for about twenty minutes or so, he told me he lived near the Ustrashkins building, but we would have been there long before now. Where is he taking me? I start to breathe heavily, I place my hand on my chest to try and calm down, but it doesn't work. I start to freak out.

"Hey, Pink, what is it? What's wrong? Hey, just wait one second. Let me pull over."

He dives out of his side and is at my door within seconds. He opens it and leans in, taking the sides of my face.

"Breathe, okay, just breathe. Follow me, watch, deep breath in and deep breath out. Follow me."

I watch as he slowly inhales and then exhales. I follow him. I must look a right fucking idiot. I start to calm down, watching him and following him. It's working. I don't know what happened. I just started to freak wondering where he was taking me. "Hey, look at me, don't look outside. That's it, you're doing great. In and out." He smiles and I feel calmer.

"Where are we, Steve? I thought you said we were going to your place. You told me you lived near Poppy and Igor's building. We are nowhere near them. Where are we?" I raise my voice, wanting an answer. He smiles at me.

"We are going to my place. I do live near the Ustrashkins building but I only use that place when I am needed in the city. It's very basic and it's not home. I have my apartment about ten minutes away from here. It's my home, the place no one knows about, and I have never taken anyone back to it. If you want me to turn around, we can go back, and I can take you home. I will not force you to go anywhere you don't want to go, but I promise you, Vi, I will never hurt you. Do you trust me?" Well, that's a loaded question and he has two apartments, and no one knows about this one. That means no one would find me here. Not that anyone knows who I am with anyway. Fuck, what do I do? He's going to think I'm crazy.

"No, it's okay. I'm sorry I freaked out, just I've never been driven to a place I don't know on my own."

"We can go back, honestly, if you feel better going back it's not a problem." I shake my head, then stroke down his cheek. He sighs out and smiles. He closes the door and gets back behind the wheel. "We're nearly there, just another ten minutes I promise, I think you will love it." I laugh, he glances at me.

"Ten minutes away, that's all it was, and I had a freak-out, I could have waited." We both laugh together. He pulls into a parking garage. I look around. There are a lot of nice cars in here. It's bright, but quiet. We get out and walk to the elevator. "Where are we, Steve? I mean, I know you said it's your apartment but what part of town are we in?" I see the name of the building on a plaque next to the elevator. I make a mental note of the name. Valadares Plaza.

"This area is Santa Monica. It's not too far. Have you been to Santa Monica before?" I shake my head just as the elevator door opens. He takes out his key card and inserts it, pressing the top button. It's not as high as where I live, this only has twelve floors. The doors open, but they open straight into an apartment. I look up to him, then back. I step out and this place is huge. I automatically move toward the floor-to-ceiling windows and it takes my breath away. He said Santa Monica, but I didn't realize we were this close. I can see the pier all lit up as the sun's setting. There are people and cars everywhere, this place is alive.

"Wow, you can see for miles, we are quite elevated here, but the building is not very tall." He suddenly steps up behind me and places both his hands on my arms and his chin on the top of my head.

"I love this view and especially at this time of night. The place is alive, but I'm far enough away to not hear it all. Come with me."

He turns me and takes my hand. He walks me to the far end and to a corridor. I start to pull back, trying to stop him and break out of his hold. He stops immediately and turns to me.

"Trust me?" is all he whispers and I nod like the fucking idiot I am.

I don't trust anyone, and least of all him. I let him take me to a door. I freeze, thinking this is his bedroom. He has to feel my resistance, but he doesn't say or do anything except he opens it and I see stairs. I allow him to take me up the stairs. There is another door, and he pushes it open. I feel the air immediately wash over my face, we're on the rooftop of the building. It's all landscaped up here, it's like a garden and it's beautiful. There is a lawn, in the center, around it are small tables and some lounge chairs. There is a fire to the side, it's beautiful and looks real, there is a hot tub in another corner. I've never been in one of those. Just seen them on the TV. There are wooden structures all over, covered with trailing plants. I gasp.

"It's like a little oasis up here. It's beautiful." I look to him and see the smile on his face. He pulls me over to what looks like a viewing platform with a telescope. He shows me you can see for miles up here. I'm stunned at the beauty. I turn around and I notice a dining table next to an outdoor kitchen. The table is set for two, there is a man standing there in chef whites. I gasp and put my hand to my mouth. Steve takes the other hand and leads me to the table. He pulls out my chair for me to sit. He's such a gentleman. How the fuck can this man be the monster he is? He sits next to me, and the chef sets about serving our dinner. He has wine or Coke, so I go for the Coke, obviously. Why did I fear coming here?

"This is amazing and just beautiful, Steve. I'm sorry for the way I reacted, but it's not like I really know you or who you are. All I know is you work for Poppy and Igor. I have no idea what that entails so I'm sorry if I have been freaking out."

He smiles, then takes my hand and kisses my palm.

"You are right, Pink; you don't know me or what I do. You don't know me to trust me, fuck I don't trust anyone myself." I scowl at him. "Sorry, I have never brought anyone here. Even Igor doesn't know I have this place. It's my little sanctuary to escape to with no one to bother me. You are the first woman to come here." I find that hard to believe, although he did say he hadn't had a girlfriend for a long time.

"Are you saying you haven't been with a woman for a long time?" He laughs, finding that funny.

"I don't want to scare you off, but I've had women, too many to count, it's just I never have them stick around and they only ever go to my place near Igor's building. I would never bring anyone to my sanctuary, but with you, well, I feel you are special. I feel for you, something I have never felt for anyone. Not even the last girlfriend that I did have. I know that's hard to believe. It's hard for me to fucking believe, so I don't expect you to. I just can't put my finger on why. Yes of course you are beautiful, in fact, you are the most beautiful woman I know, but it's just you and who you are that is more beautiful and yet I hardly know you." He looks away and he looks embarrassed. Well, I never would have thought this evil man would ever be embarrassed.

"Hey, Steve, thank you for this. It's beautiful here and thank you for the dinner." We finish eating and talking. He is such a nice person; I have to keep telling myself he's a monster. "So, tell me, what does your day look like? I mean, working for Igor. I work for Poppy and she's the best." I watch as he thinks about what to tell me.

"I grew up with Igor, we were like brothers. That all changed when his papa died, and he took over the family business. We hardly spoke and he had other guards in arms to look out for him. He got injured at work and lost his guards and he asked me to be his second. I just drive him to business meetings, make sure he and his family are safe while in my care, and so on. That's my days. It can be a long day or a short day depending on when Igor needs me." I raise my eyes. Is he telling me Igor knows his business?

"So did you feel bitter when he had the other, what did you call them?"

"Men at arms. That is what we are. We look after the boss at all costs. He becomes our priority when we are appointed. At first, I was so angry with him because we were inseparable as kids. Then his brother died, and it changed him. Then his papa died, and he became a totally different person. Not one I liked. We hardly saw each other or spoke to each other for so long. I was in charge of a different department of his business, which I ran extremely well. Then I branched out on my own, you know, doing work on the side. I wanted to be my own boss and run my own business so that is what I did. Then he asked me to be his second, meaning I was his highest-ranking man of arms. There are always two men of arms, a second and a third. There was another man called Sergei, who was his third, but he disappeared. We have another who is third, but I've been second for a while now." Wow, I can't believe he's opening up to me like this and so soon. I take it from this conversation the business he runs on the side is the trafficking one. He's not given anything away about what Igor does, or what he does but I know anyway.

"Wow, you sound amazing and so in charge, kind of. So, the business you ran on the side, do you still do that? Does Igor now know?"

He looks at me and tilts his head. I can see his eyes flicker, which means he's thinking what to say. He rises from his seat and stands next to me, holding out his hand for me to take. I do so hesitantly. He pulls me up to standing and gently kisses my cheek. He walks us to a lounger by the lawn and we sit. He faces me with his leg raised on the seat and I turn my body toward him.

"Yes, I do still run my business. That is how I have all of this." He motions to the rooftop. "If I did not, then I would be living probably in Igor's building." That makes me think that Igor doesn't have anything to do with the trafficking, but then he could be talking about something else.

"What is it you do? Do you make something?" He smiles and shakes his head.

"No, it is more a people business, consulting, and such. Now would you like to go indoors or stay up here. It can get a little nippy up here so I can get a blanket." He avoided telling me but a people business, I think, is definitely code for sex trafficker. Maybe I don't need to go any further with him, maybe I could leave now and go straight to Poppy to tell her what I know. Maybe…

"Pink?" He breaks my thoughts.

"Oh sorry, I don't mind but I do kind of like it up here. I'm not cold just yet, but I have an early start again tomorrow so will need to get going soon if that's okay with you?" He smiles and nods. We talk about nothing in particular, just random stuff like movies and music, but it's me doing all the asking, but he doesn't seem to watch or listen to anything. I'm forever listening to music. I joke with him telling him how old he is, and I will make him a playlist to listen to. He just seems to work nonstop. I don't ask him anything else about what he does. I don't want him to get suspicious, so I make the conversation light. Before I know it, it's ten thirty p.m.

I feign shock. "Oh wow, would you mind taking me home please, Steve. By the time we get there it will be gone eleven and I have to get up early."

He doesn't say anything but pulls me off the lounger with both hands. I stand in front of him, and he lowers to my face and kisses me on the lips. He has both sides of my head in his hands and he's being very gentle. He pries my mouth open with his tongue and enters my mouth and starts dueling with mine. I grab his hips, which are trying to get closer to me, to try and control them. I don't want him rubbing himself on me. I try to stay calm. I think back to Dima and how he used to do this exact same thing. Only he used to get so aroused and rub his cock against me vigorously. I think that's what Steve is trying to do.

He deepens the kiss more; he lets go of my head and his hands wander down my arms to my waist. He tries to pull me into him, he's too strong for me so I have no choice. I put my hands around him and rest them on his back above his ass. I don't want to touch his ass and give him the go-ahead. He pulls me into him tight. Then his hands start to wander around to my ass, and he grips my ass cheeks tight. I freeze and he pulls back. I have my eyes closed so I don't see what he's thinking. I fucking freeze. I can't stand it, I try to think it's Dima, he was the only one I ever let touch me. I never let anyone since. They just did it. If I didn't let them, I was violently beaten, they raped me anyway. I slowly open my eyes. He has hold of my hips and his fingers tighten as I look at his face. I smile a very slight smile. He doesn't smile back. I step back and his hands drop.

"I'm sorry, can you please take me home now? Or, I can call a cab." He nods and motions for me to head to the door. I do, I'm conscious of him behind me, all the time I'm thinking, *Is he going to strike? Is he going to push me or grab me? Is he going to take me anyway, regardless of how I feel?* So many questions running through my head as I listen to every single sound he makes, just waiting for a sudden move. I walk down the steps. Once in the apartment, I pick up my fanny pack and walk to the elevators. I expected him to grab me every second and every step I took, but it didn't happen. I press the button for the elevator and the door opens immediately. I step inside but don't turn. I feel the elevator dip as he steps in behind me. The doors close. He's right behind me, I feel his breath on the back of my neck, which means he's bent down. I feel his lips pepper small kisses along my exposed neck. I freeze yet again. Fuck, he hasn't done anything wrong to me at all in the time I've known him, and he's been a gentleman every step of the way. He never wronged me when I was captive, but I know it was at his hands. He places his hands on my arms and gently strokes them. He still kisses my neck, traveling to my ear. It actually feels good. He's so gentle. I lean my head back into him and I feel the smile on his face.

"Thank you. I know you don't trust me, but thank you for being here with me tonight. You don't know how it's made me feel. I hope we can do this again." He gently turns me to face him. He cups my head and lifts it up to look at him. I smile and nod.

"I would like that, Steve. Please just be patient with me. I like you; I really like you and I just want to take it slow if that's okay with you. I am nervous, yes, but I will get there."

He smiles, then bends down and kisses my lips. The doors open behind him and I break the kiss so we can exit the elevator. He takes my hand and walks me to his car. Before he opens the door, he pins my back to it gently and presses his body up against mine. He kisses me again, this time inserting his tongue, but I open up willingly and let him. I'm feeling brave now, I'm not in the apartment. Knowing he could have taken me at any point in there against my will, but he didn't. I grip the belt loops on his jeans, and I actually fucking pull him into me more. I freeze again when I feel his cock rock hard against my tummy. He laughs, knowing what I felt and pulls back.

"Yep, that's what you do to me all the fucking time." He shrugs. "What can I say? I fucking like you and so does my cock, but we are both patient, and we can wait as long as you want and need to." He pulls away and opens my door, letting me slip inside. He drives me home. Once he pulls up outside the building, he jumps out to help me out of the car. I just laugh at him. He pins me to the car again and gives me one last long kiss, letting me feel how hard he is again. This time I don't freeze. I'm getting used to it and I enjoy it more this time. I push his chest slightly to let him know I'm ready to leave. He steps back.

"Good night, Steve, and thanks for a great evening. I really enjoyed being with you." I stand on my tiptoes and quickly peck his mouth before I duck under his arm and move around the car to my building. I don't turn but I know he's watching me.

"I'll try to see you tomorrow night, Pink," he shouts as I enter the building and straight into an elevator.

I sigh out with relief, it went well and nothing bad happened, but also, I think I now know Igor is not involved with his business. I just need to be a hundred-percent sure. I fall asleep thinking about Steve and the way he treated me like a real lady. I think I'm falling for him; I mean, really falling for him. I just know I can't allow myself to let it happen. I have to remind myself he's a monster in disguise.

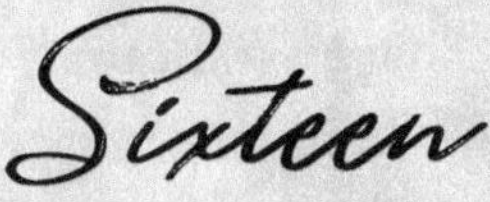

Steve

I WATCH HER DISAPPEAR INTO THE BUILDING. MY COCK IS ROCK hard and I'm feeling rather uncomfortable sitting here in my car. I wait a few minutes to see if he deflates, but he's just not moving. I need to do something about it. I don't want to fuck anyone else, for the first time ever, because I don't want to feel as though I will be unfaithful to Pink. Who the fuck am I and what did I do with heartless fucker Steve? I just need to get home and rub one out thinking about her. I decide to go to my other apartment as it's nearer and I have to be at Igor's in the morning once I've walked Pink to work.

I've been home literally for two minutes. I was just about to jump in the shower when the buzzer goes. Who the fuck is that now? Igor wouldn't come here, he would ring me to go to him and there are only a handful of other people that know where I live. I go to the panel where the monitor is to see who it is, and if I want to answer. Of course, I have a camera wired in by the door so I can see, I'm not that fucking simple. I don't fucking believe it. It's the girl I brought back a while ago. I'm sure she was the last one I had here. I'm just gonna ignore her, pretend I'm not in. She had pink hair when I last saw her, if it's the same one. Her hair looks orange now. She was hot though. I watch her. She buzzes again, then looks to her watch like she has to be somewhere. I'm standing here naked watching her, I was just about to get in the shower. She can't keep fucking still, it's like she's got ants in her panties or something. That says she's probably high. Well, she can fuck off. She buzzes again and it pisses me off. I press the button to speak.

"What!" I shout. It startles her.

"Oh, hey. I wondered if I could come up. I've been a few times since I was last here, but you always seem to be out."

"Yeah, well. I'm a fucking busy man. What do you want?" She pouts at the fucking door, trying to be all sultry. She's a fucking slut. I never look for the girls I use for trafficking, I have men that do that, but I wonder if we could use her. You know what, I can't be fucked doing any of that. If I let her in, I will fuck her hard imagining it's Pink. Then I will regret it and who knows what I will do to her. I really don't want to be carting bodies from here. Fuck no. She needs to fuck off and never come back.

"I wondered if you wanted some company, you know?"

"No, fuck off and don't come back. You were a one-time fuck and it wasn't any good. I don't want another round of sloppy, so fuck off. Don't let me catch you around here again." She gives me the bird to the door, using both hands. How fucking immature. I'm right to leave that alone. No one knows where the actual camera is because it's not supposed to be there. She's just presuming there's a camera.

I walk away and enter the bathroom; the buzzer goes again but I just ignore it this time. She's trying to get me to go to the door, but it won't work. I head into the walk-in shower and turn it on. It's fucking freezing at first, but I like this, it invigorates me. Then it starts to get hot. I hold my head up to the rain showerhead and let it pour all over my face. My eyes are closed, and I see Pink as though she's standing right in front of me. I fall to my knees, and I imagine her standing naked. I see her butterfly tattoos down her arm and over her shoulder. I trail my finger over them, then trail it down to her tit. I squeeze her nipple gently. I start to trail my hand down her front, between her tits and down past her navel, to her pussy. My fingers find her clit. I pinch it gently before inserting first one, then two of my fingers inside her. I play with her clit with my thumb while feeling inside her pussy to find her spot. She breathes heavily as she places her head on my shoulder. I nip at her nipple gently; I don't want to hurt her. I start to pump my fingers in and out of her pussy. I even hear the noises of her moist pussy lips as I do it. She's panting hard, she starts to gyrate on my hand, she squats on my fingers each time I start to pull out. She runs her hand over one of my nipples and pinches it. She gently falls to her knees, spreading her legs wider for me to carry on my onslaught inside her. She's almost jumping on my fingers. She pinches my nipple hard before trailing her fingers down my front. I suck in a breath at her featherlight touches.

Her fingers find my hair and she follows the trail down from my navel to where my cock is standing rock hard. She pulls back and looks at me with hooded eyes, licking her lips, before looking down, first to watch my fingers pumping in and out, then to look at my cock. She spreads her legs even wider to give me more access and I insert another finger. She starts to play with my cock. She pulls him gently at first but I thrust in her hand, making her grab harder. She squeezes him hard and runs her hand from base to tip and over the head. She falters at the head and plays with my pee hole. She nearly inserts her finger into it, what the fuck. She smiles up at me as she licks her lips again. I pump my fingers inside her harder and faster.

She's literally bouncing on my hand with my cock being pulled in every direction in her hand. I start to gyrate in her hand just like she's doing on mine. In no time, she's screaming my name and her juices are running all down my hand and to my wrist. Before I know it, I'm blowing my load over and over into her hand. I scream up to the ceiling at the feeling of her hand on my cock. I don't look when I feel her lips wrap around the head and she sucks hard to take all my cum. I pump and pump until I fall forward on my hands. I open my eyes. The water is dripping down my face and into my eyes as I look ahead and realize I'm alone. Fucking hell, that felt so real. The look on her face when she came. Her pink makeup smeared all over her face with the black liner as she screamed in ecstasy. I can't believe it wasn't real, that she wasn't here. Fuck, I have it so fucking bad for her.

I wake up early, rock hard yet again. I had to rub it out before I got ready to go meet Pink to walk her to work. I arrived as I had the last couple of mornings, only she didn't appear at her usual time. I walk to the coffee shop to see if she is there, but it's the other woman puttering around. I tap on the door. She scowls at me but comes toward me. She doesn't unlock the door.

"She's not in today. She didn't feel too good, so she phoned me to do her shift."

"Oh, okay. Thank you." I turn and walk toward her building.

Why the fuck am I doing this? If she doesn't want to see me and is not going to work to avoid me, then I should just fucking leave well enough alone. I don't need anyone, just her. Oh, for fuck's sake. I may as well just go back to get the car and head to Igor's. I'm going to finalize my plan to take him and the rest of his family down. It's got to happen soon. I'm not going to wait much longer. I still also need to go to my papa's house. I just keep putting it off, I know it's going to be a shit tip.

At Igor's, he's not going out today. Change of plans. Poppy has gone to the refuge, so he is staying home to spend time with the kids. I stayed for a little while and went over the week's meetings with him, then left. Well, there's no time like the present I suppose, to go to my papa's and get all that shit sorted.

I'm driving to my childhood house and as I do, I feel my mood changing the closer I get. Not that I'm a happy, jolly person or any of that shit, but I start to feel depressed and down. Like the dark is swallowing me up. It's getting darker and darker the nearer I get. I turn down the street where we lived and it's better than I expected. It seems to have had some work done on the area to make it more appealing. As I approach our house, it stands out like a sore thumb. It's not a tiny house, in fact, it's quite big and imposing. It has a basement, which is where I used to get beat and spent a lot of time locked up down there. The place looks a mess. It's falling apart and it really brings the neighborhood down. The other houses around have all had work done on them and look pretty decent. Then you look at my papa's and fuck me. The wood is all rotten, the windows are mostly smashed up top and boarded up on the bottom. The porch looks like a death trap, if you were to stand on it, you'd probably fall through it. The whole surrounding grounds, front and sides, are filled with trash and overgrown bushes. I pull up outside and sit staring straight ahead of me with both hands on the wheel. I just need a few minutes. I don't know if I can go in there. I try to compose myself, taking deep breaths.

I finally turn back to face the house, and I'm appalled at the state it's in. It just needs pulling down completely. I would torch it if I could but I'm pretty sure I would get fined for doing that and putting the surrounding houses in danger. I don't want the house or the land. I should just give it to the states department and let them do what they want with it. I get out of the car and just lean against it with my arms folded. What a fucking joke this place is. The memories of my papa come flooding back. I don't think I ever loved him. It was always just the two of us and he hated me from as far back as I can remember. I was always just a burden to him. He used to bring back different whores all the time, sometimes more than one, and just fuck them all day and night. Most of that time, I was locked in the basement. Never getting any food or water. I would be down there for days, just lying in my own shit, listening to him up above me. It was only as I got older, I started to stay out and stayed with Igor a lot.

I don't know if I can bring myself to walk into the place. It would probably kill me if I did. I'm like a fucking pussy standing here. There have been a few people walking by, eyeing me up, wondering what the fuck I am doing here. Even the neighbor to the left came out puttering around his garden, watching me. I don't know him, or at least I don't recognize him. I push off the car and take the first couple of steps toward the house. I have to do this. I just need to make sure there is nothing in there. Not that there will be. I know my papa had a safe in his bedroom closet hidden in the floor. I also know the combination. It's a big safe so I will just check that out then leave. There will be nothing else in there. The deeds for the house should be in the safe. Maybe if I just get them and hand them to some homeless person, that will be my repentance for running my business.

I kick trash out of the way as I walk the path. It stinks of shit around here. I watch that I don't step in anything. I climb the first step to the porch and the wood creeks; fuck, I hope it doesn't collapse. Then the second step and it cracks. I jump onto the last step. There are broken boards on the floor, I have to be careful where I stand. I kick more trash out of my path. The door is boarded up, great, I need a fucking tire iron to get in. I see the old man near the bushes.

"Excuse me, do you happen to have a tire iron I could borrow?" He looks up at me, shocked I spoke to him. He looks behind him to see if

I'm talking to someone else. I raise an eyebrow. "Look, I used to live here with my papa before he died. I just need to check it out."

"Steve, is that you, boy? Well, I never. Look at you now. It's me, Carl, Carl Dunster. I've lived here many, many years. I remember you as a little boy, son. Look at the man you are today." He walks toward me through the bushes. I vaguely recognize him. "I'm not surprised you never came back here. I'm not sorry about your papa either. He was an evil man. The way he used to treat you was disgusting. Me and Marjorie my late wife used to want to get you and bring you to our house to be safe. She even told your papa that one day and he just laughed at her. Then as he turned to head inside with one of his many women, he told her if she ever called the cops she would become one of his whores and once he finished with her, he would dispose of her. That shook my Marjorie up good and proper. She was afraid of your papa from that day." He looks sad.

"I'm sorry you had to put up with living next to him. I'm also sorry I haven't been back before now. I just couldn't bear to step foot back here. I just thought it was about time I checked it out. I was thinking of burning it to the ground but looking at the area now, it's a lot different to when I lived here. Not sure if I should just get it bulldozed and sell the land. Do you have a tire iron handy, Carl?"

"Wait there, I'll see what I can find to help you." He turns and ambles off to his house.

I decide to see if I can get around the back. I watch where I walk and just get to the back when I hear Carl shout my name. The back is like a jungle and it's full of crap. God knows where it all came from. I mean, it was always a shit tip but there was always room for me to play ball or hide. I turn and head back to Carl. He has a tire iron and I smile, taking it from him. He follows me a couple of steps to the porch.

"Best you stay here, Carl. I'm sure the floors will be rotten, and I don't want you to get injured. Thanks for this."

I hold up the tire iron. I make it back to the door. I pry the boards from the frame and the door underneath is hanging off its hinges. Like I thought, it was used by kids, druggies or homeless. Who the fuck knows? I move the broken door out of the way and carefully step inside. The floorboards are cracked and broken, with some missing in places. I can see down into that fucking basement. The one place I didn't want to see. I move toward the back of the house where his bedroom was just off the corridor. I tread carefully with every step. This place is a mess. You couldn't do anything with it except tear it down. I bet there are rats and all kinds of vermin and things in here. The walls are covered with graffiti, what there are of them anyway. Most of them have holes right through to the next room. The kitchen I walk through is barely that, the cupboards are ripped from the walls, the sink is not there, and I reckon most of the smell is from being damp from the looks of the rotten floorboards. I look up in the kitchen, I'm surprised there are no holes in the ceiling.

I enter my papa's bedroom.

"Hey, Steve, you okay in there?" He made me fucking jump.

"Yes, thanks Carl. Don't come in, it isn't safe," I shout back to him.

I edge in the room very slowly, why I don't know. Maybe I think my papa's ghost is gonna come jump out at me. This room is a mess. There was a bed here once and a dresser, but they are just shattered to pieces and by the looks of the scorch marks, I'd say someone thought they would have a little fire in here. I move over to the closet. The bi-fold doors are non-existent, but I can see the floor is still intact with the crappy threadbare carpet over it. The rails from above are on the floor, I move them out and throw them into the room. I lift the decrepit carpet up and see the tiny mark which indicates where to lift. I pull out my keys and use the knife to lever the tiny hook under the wood. I pull up the board. The safe is still there. How the fuck has no one found this? I have a key to unlock it, along with a combination. You need both, it won't unlock otherwise. I pull open the lid and fuck me, there is so much money stashed here. I start to take it out and pile it up next to me. There must be thousands and thousands. Not that I need money. I find his guns and lots of papers with some old notebooks. I need a bag. Why the fuck didn't I bring a fucking backpack? I have one in the trunk. I move to go get it. As I turn, there are three men standing at the entrance to the room. Well, more like boys than men, but they are trying their best to look mean, I don't know who the fuck they are, but they don't want to mess with me. I'm meaner.

"Who the fuck are you?" I stand tall and face them. The one in the middle steps forward. He has a fucking pink fluffy hat on his head. One, it's hot as hell and two, how does he think anyone is going to take him seriously in that. I laugh, actually fucking laugh. He scowls at me.

"What's so fuckin' funny, yo dipshit? Yo askin' fow a motherfuckin' beatin', ain't cha?" I laugh more.

"Excuse me, can you speak English so I can understand you?" I'm trying not to laugh. The dumb shit. He's trying to be fucking hard with his stupid talk. I eye the other two who look just like him, minus the pink fluffy hat. They are all in denim shorts that are more like three quarter-length jeans, but the crotch area is so low I'm surprised they can walk straight in them. They are torn all over with patches of some shit or other. They have long white T-shirts, then the three of them have vests over the baggy tees. They can't be much older than seventeen or eighteen. The cocky bastards. I see the middle one has a line shaved through each eyebrow with pierced rings at the ends of each one. The other two have a line shaved in one eyebrow. Maybe it's like a uniform where a captain or major wears stripes. I laugh again. The middle one takes another step toward me and the other two do the same, flanking him. I step forward and raise an eyebrow.

"Yo motherfucker, yo wan a beatin' or wot? Whatcha doin' in ere, this is r ouse, yo can walk now or die."

Is he for fucking real? I move another step forward. He mimics me. He's within reach. As quick as a flash, I bring my palm up and smash him in the nose, hard. It breaks, I feel the crunch. His hands fly to his nose and I see the blood seeping through his fingers. I stand, waiting for any of them to attack. I've already seen that one on the left has a gun in his waistband under his baggy tee. I'm on guard in case he goes for it. I haven't seen the other two have anything. The main two stripe guy is now bent over holding his nose. He grunts something and I see the one with the gun move his hand. I quickly step forward and kick the other one in the chest as a distraction, which sends him flying backward. The one with the gun watches the other guy go down. I quickly round on him, shoving his nose up into his head with my palm. He covers his nose as blood pours everywhere. I take the opportunity to lift his tee and retrieve his gun. I empty the chamber and throw it through the glassless window.

"Now get the fuck out of my house before I kill you all. Don't ever come back here. Do you hear me?" The three of them groan and slowly compose themselves, giving me the eye before retreating back out the way they came in. I shove the money back into the safe with my foot and close it. Just in case they try anything again. I close the board over it and lay the crappy carpet back over the top. I walk out to my car, watching every step I take and listening in case they haven't left.

I reach my car and Carl appears in his garden.

"I'm sorry I couldn't warn you, Steve. Let's just say they've put me in my place a time or two. Last time I ended up at the ER with a broken arm. They were always coming round and going into your house, even with it boarded up. They play music loud till early hours of the morning and God knows what goes on in there. I've called the police many times, but they don't have the time to be checking in on a bunch of kids. When I see them, I lock myself in my house? I'm sorry." He hangs his head in shame. He's old, he's got to be in his seventies, the poor guy. He's had to endure all this because I was too much of a fucking coward to come back here. Don't get me wrong, being here is making me remember so much of what I locked away. I always remember growing up with Igor and being beat by my papa, but the rest I blocked out.

I remember being in the basement listening to him screwing whore after whore up top. I would be lying in my own shit when he would bring a whore down to me every now and then. They would screw up their noses as the smell infused them. He would push their naked asses to the floor next to me. We would then have to have sex in some way, however he commanded it. He liked to watch and get off on it. He never joined in, but he would beat me if the whore wasn't sucking me right or I wasn't licking her right. He even hit the whore if she wasn't putting everything into it. There were a few times he would have two whores on me. He would make me lie on my back and one would be sitting on my face riding my tongue while the other would be sucking my cock. If I made the slightest noise, one of the girls would get whipped with a cane. I had to stay as quiet as I could. The girls, on the other hand, had to be noisy, letting him know how much they were enjoying it. He would then make them suck his cock right there in front of me and made me watch. It repulsed me. Never once did it turn me on. He was a monster, I guess it's why I grew up like I have, not caring much about the whores I traffic, to me they are all the same. Women don't give a shit as long as they get what they want out of it. They are all users, all except my Pink. Why do I have to think of her while I'm here? The others are all whores. Maybe it's because I didn't have a mama in my life, just a ruthless papa. I have no respect for women and he made me like that. I've been brought up with women being easy, with them screwing constantly to get what they want. It has to be why I don't give a fuck about the sex trafficking and think nothing of it. As long as they make me plenty of money to live my life how I want, then I don't give a fuck. At least I didn't until I met Pink.

Just thinking of her makes me want to leave this place and go see her. Today has been a long fucking day already and it's still early.

"Carl, I'm sorry you had to endure that. Look, can you get a bag for me please. I promise this will be the end of them coming around here." He disappears while I get the backpack from my trunk. He comes out with a plastic bag. It will do. "Thanks. You go inside in case they come back with reinforcements. I don't want you in the middle of this. I will try being as quick as I can. I need to get some stuff and make a few calls." He saunters into his house. I go back to my papa's bedroom and open the safe up. I take out the money and place the majority of it in the plastic bag. I put a few bundles in my backpack. I take all the paperwork and notebooks, placing them in my backpack. Who knows what info is in those books? They could be useful.

I've emptied the safe and I make a couple of calls before leaving. I have contacts everywhere. I want this place bulldozed immediately. I know there is paperwork and shit to get this done, but Carl has been through enough. I can buy anything these days. This place will be flattened tomorrow. I have a team on the way to fence the whole place off so no one can enter once I leave. I put the backpack in my trunk and head to Carl's.

"Here, take this. It's the least I can do for all the trouble you've had over the years. I should have come and sorted it sooner. You know I don't have happy memories here, which is why I stayed away. This will help with the medical expenses you've had and maybe you could move if you wanted to. I've taken care of next door and it will be flattened tomorrow and then it will get landscaped to make it nice at least."

He takes the plastic bag from me and opens it. He looks up and goes to speak but I hold up my hand.

"It's yours, Carl. No questions and no worries. Do with it as you please. I'm sorry and thank you for you and Marjorie always looking out for me when I was little. I just remembered a lot of the shit that happened in there. Shit I haven't thought about in such a long time and never want to again." I say goodbye and leave.

Just as I get to the end of the road, I see the trucks arriving with the metal fencing and I also see the goons on the corner. They notice my car and the two-strike guy flips me off. I smile and salute him. He has on sunglasses, but I reckon he will end up with two shiners by tomorrow to go with his broken nose.

I drive to my place in Santa Monica. Igor doesn't want me for the rest of the day, and I feel I want to be home. I will go to the refuge later to see if Pink is there. Until then I'm going to sit in my office and go through my papa's stuff. I empty the contents onto my desktop. There are passports, lots of envelopes and the notebooks. I pick up the books and notice they are all dated. There must be about ten of them. I find the earliest one and sit down to see what they are about. The date is a few years before I was born. It's a diary of all the shit my papa and Kirill did. Who to, what, and when? Fuck me, why would anyone write this shit down. Unless it was going to be used as evidence of some sort or used to blackmail. Who the fuck knows? I carry on reading for a while and nothing really strikes me as odd, I grew up with most of what's in here. The bits about Kirill and what he got up to, well, that's a little different.

Kirill would bring over girls mainly from Russia but from other countries as well. He would have his pick at a lot of them before they got used. It goes on about how Kirill used to make my papa do the same thing. It was an order, yeah, I don't think my papa would take much ordering in that respect. What was interesting is that Kirill used to do to my papa what he used to do to me in the basement. It's the exact same thing. Kirill would have these girls doing all sorts of things but then he got off on watching them on my papa. I suppose that explains the sickness of my papa doing that to me, but I was his young son, not a guard or part of Bratva. I have to take a break to grab a drink. It's quite detailed what went on and it's bringing back the images of me as a young boy doing these things. I pace along the floor-to-ceiling window, it's still light out, I look at the time and it's almost seven thirty. If I want to head to the refuge, I will need to leave soon.

Back in my office, I pick up the second journal, as that is what they are. In this one it goes on about the killings Kirill has done and had my papa do. They all seemed to thrive on it. It then goes into detail on how Kirill runs his businesses. Was my papa looking at killing Kirill so he could take over? Just like I am going to do with Igor. There is a lot of mention of Dimitri when he was born and about his mama. Kirill killed her. She was a whore he fucked, and she tricked him by getting pregnant. My papa says Kirill was a fool being ruled by his cock all the time and his businesses were starting to have cracks in them. It's pretty much the same stuff, but it does jump time somewhat. I get to the year I was born. I look at my cell and see it's past eight. I need to get going. I'll come back to this tomorrow. I would like to bring Pink back here again if she would like that. I gather up the journals and the other stuff and place them all in my safe. My safe is huge, it's a walk-in safe, nothing like my papa's and unless you know it's there, you wouldn't find it.

I'm sitting outside the refuge waiting to see if she comes out. It's nine twenty. If she's in there, she's late. I think I'm going to go in and see if she's around. I walk in and it's fairly quiet. There's no one in the dining room or the communal room. That's strange, there's always someone around. I walk to the offices, and they are empty. She mustn't be here. I walk to Poppy's office and knock, there is no answer, but then I knew Poppy wouldn't be here. I start to head out when I hear a chair fall over from one of the therapy rooms. I very quietly listen by the door. I hear movement but it's only slight. Then I hear someone whimper and another voice telling them to be quiet. Fuck, what's going on? I walk back to Poppy's office and fire up her PC. Good thing I have all the access information. I watch the CCTV footage at the entrance. At this time of night, you need a code to enter the refuge, so no one can just walk in. You wouldn't know what this place was unless you actually knew it was here. I go back to earlier, and I see Pink arrive. You can't miss the flash of pink, I stop it and watch her enter. Some time later, I see two men come up to the building. They look suspicious with their body language and the way they are looking around. They enter the building. That was at seven fifteen. Fuck. They haven't come out but then neither has anyone else. They have to be in here. Fuck. I call Igor, telling him to send some men quick. I will monitor the situation and get back to him. I move out again, only this time I know I have to be stealthy. It's what I do best.

I move past the room where I think some are being held. I need to know where else. There were only two of them so it can't be hard. I know there is no one in the dining or communal area, apart from the separate rooms the girls stay in that only leaves the recreational hall. This is where they learn self-defense and have other classes and part is used for a gym. I listen at the closed door. There can only be one man in here if the other is in the therapy room. That means most of the girls and staff must be in here at least. I wonder where Pink is. They must be terrified. This is supposed to be a safe place. Who the fuck would come in here? It's not like it's my lot for stealing my girls. I didn't give any orders. Maybe it's one of the other trafficking rings who has found out it was Bratva that took their girls or broke the ring. I hear movement and I can hear crying. I listen more. No one is speaking. I move quietly back to Poppy's office and turn the camera on for the recreational room. Why the fuck didn't I think of this sooner. My head is all over, wondering where Pink is and hoping she's safe. I watch. I can see some girls on the floor all huddled together. One by one, they are disappearing into a room. It's a safe room. I didn't know there was one in here. I see there are two staff members that I recognize who are directing them quietly. I don't see Pink. Fuck.

I eventually find the camera to the therapy room. The two men are in there, that's a relief. A relief in the way they are nowhere else, which means the people in the recreational room will all be safe, but not in the way that I can see Pink in there along with two other girls. They are sitting on the floor. Pink is in front of them, as though protecting them. Fuck. I can see the two men have guns on them. One has his tucked in his waistband, the other has his in his hand. Fuck. I need to get in there. Do I wait for Igor and his men to arrive, or do I go in all guns blazing, literally? I don't want the girls, well, Pink, to get hurt. The two men only look young. Young and stupid, the fuckers. I'm going in. I can't stand here just watching.

I leave Poppy's office; I go to the janitor's closet and put on some coveralls that are hanging up and get a broom. I start to sweep as I walk down toward the therapy room. I whistle as I go, making noise so they know someone else is here. I try the other doors as I go, pretending to be checking them. I get to their room and try the door. It doesn't open.

"That's strange. I didn't lock this door," I say out loud. I then get my keys out and pretend I am inserting a key into the lock. Bingo, it worked. The door flies open and one of the stupid fucking idiots has his gun pointed at me. I pretend to be startled; I hold up a hand.

"Hey now, what's all this. Who are you? Don't hurt me, please." I make a very slight nod with my head, hoping Pink sees it. I can see her in my peripheral vision and see her rise slowly to her feet, that's all I need. In a flash, I have taken the gun from the guy and have his arm twisted up his back and the gun pointed at his head. Pink saw my nod. She moved as soon as I did, and she had the other guy on the floor with her foot pressed to his throat. She managed to take his gun from his waistband, and she points it at his head. The other two girls are on their feet.

"Girls, go to your rooms. There is no one else to hurt you in the building. There will be some men coming very soon to secure the place and take these fuckers away from you. You are safe now." The one nods at me as I tell her they are safe.

"Gretta, take Nina with you, the others are in the recreational room, please let them know they are all safe. Igor will be here soon with his men. No one will harm any of you. Go, hurry," she tells them in Russian. She turns to me and smiles. "Thank you for coming, Steve. I don't know what would have happened if you hadn't come. The girls will be terrified. This is supposed to be a safe place. Now what will they think? They will never trust anyone again." Just then I hear footsteps.

"In here?" I shout, hoping it's Igor and his men. He comes in first, followed by some of our guards with guns. "All secured. It's just these two." Igor motions for the guards to take them. They will be questioned and killed, no doubt. I will find out who they are from him.

"Any idea who they are?" he asks me.

"Not a clue, they look like young fuckers, maybe thinking they could get opioids or some shit from here. Maybe thinking it's a clinic."

"Yes, they wanted meth and opioids. That is what they were asking for," Pink tells us. Fuckers were just druggies. I walk to her and take her in my arms.

"You okay? Did they hurt you?" She looks up and shakes her head. She smiles and I melt.

"Ahem," Igor coughs. "I didn't know you two were an item. I didn't even know you knew each other."

I look over Pink's head to him and see the strange look on his face.

"Yeah, we've been out a couple of times."

I'm not telling him anything else. It's none of his fucking business.

"I think we need a security guard on this place, twenty-four seven. These girls need to feel safe."

"Yeah, well, you leave that to me, it's my place and I'll sort it." He turns to leave. I fucking hate him. He reaches the door and turns back. "Lucky you came here, Steve. Thanks for helping and letting me know." He leaves us. If it wasn't for Pink, I wouldn't be anywhere near this place. I'm still afraid one of the girls might have seen me at some point and suddenly remember. No matter how careful I was. He shouts back.

"My place in the morning, six thirty."

I don't reply. I pull back and look into Pink's face.

"You were fucking amazing. I knew you would see my nod and react. I just knew it." She scowls and I bend down and kiss her. Those fucking lips are like a magnet to me. I just want to kiss them all the time. They are bright pink today like her hair. I think I've figured it out. The days she wears dark purple or black are the down days. The days she wears hot pink are her good days. At least that's my theory.

"Do you want to come back to my place? We can get something to eat on the way. I just want you to be with me, so I know you're safe." She smiles at me and nods.

Seventeen

Vidana

I DIDN'T GO INTO THE COFFEE SHOP TODAY. I KNEW STEVE WOULD be waiting for me this morning and I really didn't want to see him. After last night and being with him, I fell for him. I don't know how I could, knowing what I know, but he was just such a gentleman and never pushed me for anything. What the fuck do I do? I can't fall for him, I know I already did, but that was Stockholm syndrome, I think, now I'm just falling hard. I know he's a monster, I know he runs the trafficking ring and I know it was him that had me captured and then kept me there. So how the fuck can I have proper feelings for him just because he was nice to me one night? He may turn into an evil killing monster if I don't do what he wants when he eventually tries to take it from me. I am so conflicted about him, which is why I called in sick at the coffee shop. I just needed time to think. Do I carry on with this charade to get the proof I need, or do I let him have me for real and just bury my head in the sand about what he really does? Wouldn't that make me an accessory? Why would I want to do that? Why would I let anyone treat women like they are nothing but fuck sacks for vile men? I am so confused. I think I need to speak to someone, but it can't be Poppy and I have no one else. Fuck Svetlana for leaving. I fucking hate her. She's the one that I should be hating, not Igor. It was her infatuation with him and her fairy-tale dreams of being swept away that did this to me and all my family. That's the other thing, I am going to find Poppy and talk to her about my sisters again, see if she has any updates on them.

I stay in bed, just tossing and turning like I did most of the night. I didn't get much sleep. I just don't know what to do about anything. Why is my life a fucking mess? I get up and dressed and head out to get something to eat before going to the refuge. I will see if Poppy is there. I'm on my guard, looking everywhere in case I see him. The number of times I've seen him because he's been following me, it puts me on edge right now. Not that he would hurt me, but he seems to always be just there lately. I go to the diner not far from here, the one Ryker took me to. I haven't seen him for a few days now and I do miss him. Do I like Ryker because he is the safe option, or do I really like him? I have feelings for him, but they are nothing to what I feel for Steve and that fucking terrifies me. Falling for the devil when I could have the sweet angel.

I sit in the diner but hardly touch my hot dog or fries. I play with the straw in my Coke glass. I'm miles away just thinking. I need to find Poppy and get that sorted first so I have the food put in a box to go. I may eat it later at the refuge. I walk in and look at my cell and can't believe it's five thirty. Where has my day gone? I head to Poppy's office to see if she's in. I knock but there is no answer. I pull out my cell and text her.

Hey Poppy, just wondering when you are next at the Refuge? Just wanted to have a chat with you. Xx

She texts back immediately.

Hey Dana, on my way home, you just missed me. I Won't be in tomorrow, out all day. I will text you when I am free. Look forward to catching up with you. Hope everything is okay. You could always come to the house anytime I'm in for a chat. I can get a driver to pick you up. You can come now if you're free? X

I wish I could. I would love to get lost for a few hours.

I have my shift to do, and it will be later when I finish. I will try to catch up with you the day after, if that's okay. I am good. I just needed a chat with you to see if any news on my sisters. Speak to you soon. Xx

She just replies with a smiley emoji and a heart. I go find Sevra, it's not difficult she is usually in her room. We head to the dining room and spot Gretta, who is also a helper and Nina. Nina is fairly new and is starting to trust us now. We sit with them, and I eat my hot dog and fries from earlier. Sevra doesn't say too much. We need to head to the therapy room so I can go through helpful info with her. The evening flows great and Sevra did really good. She's gone back to her room now, but she really started to open up to me. I head back to the dining room, there's no one around. I walk to the recreational room; we use this for learning self-defense or there is the small gym and sometimes we use it for theater play. That's what's happening now. I stand at the doors watching. This role-playing really helps get some of the aggressions out. I think everyone is in here right now.

I spot Gretta and Nina sitting watching and go sit with them.

"Oh hey, Vi, I was just going to see if the therapy room was free. Glad you're here. I wanted to see if you would like to sit in while I talk with Nina here. She's happy for you to be in there with us." I look at Nina and she smiles, giving me a slight nod. I smile back.

"Yes, that would be great to see how Nina is coming along. Do you want to go now?" She stands and I follow. Nina stays seated. I look to her and hold out my hand. She immediately takes it. Nina has a close bond with me, I was the one she spent time with the first couple of weeks. We like to change it up, so they trust more people but also, so they don't get attached, which is exactly what Nina has done. She got attached to me. She's very young, she thinks she's thirteen, but she couldn't remember because she couldn't remember how long she had been captive. It makes me want to cry, knowing exactly what they have been through, but even worse at such a young age. I know I was young, but to think of these girls going through all that fucked-upness is heartbreaking.

I grab us some waters and we sit in the therapy room. We talk and Nina really starts to open up with some gentle encouragement. I tell her that Gretta and I have been through exactly what she's been through, and I let her know there is hope and light at the end of it all. I hear a noise outside of the door, it's like heavy footsteps. I see a shadow move under the door, it stops as if listening and then moves. Gretta looks at me, I put my finger to my mouth to tell them not to speak. I slowly rise from the chair and very quietly open the door. I see the back of a man; I don't recognize him.

"Where the fuck is anyone? Where's the fucking drug store? You told me there were drugs in here, you fuckwit. You said it was a clinic with drugs. You fucking lied, didn't you?" I try to move back slightly so I can close the door before he and whoever he was talking to come in here. Too late.

"Well, well, well. Who do we have here, Miss Pinky?"

I didn't know there was another one standing on the other side of the door. I only looked the one way. Fuck, how fucking stupid. He grabs the back of my neck as the other one turns to see who he's talking to. He has a gun, and he points it straight at me. There's nothing I can do. I start to shake, but I need to be brave and strong for Nina. She needs to know we are safe. He pushes me back into the room and both of them enter. Nina flies out of her chair and runs to the corner, where she curls up into a ball. Gretta looks to me, shocked. I give a slight smile, trying to let her know it will be okay. How? I have no fucking clue.

Gretta gets up and goes to Nina in the corner. She takes hold of her to comfort her.

"I heard you out there. We don't have any kind of drugs in here. This is a safe place to help abused girls. Please just leave before you cause them all new traumas. They are traumatized enough." The one holding my neck lets go, shoving me toward Gretta and Nina.

"You're fucking lying. I was told this was a clinic, and you had lots of meth and opioids, so don't fucking lie to me." I stare him straight in the face. The other one still has his gun pointed at me.

"You were misinformed. We don't have anything like that here. We don't even have pain meds for headaches. A lot of the girls that come here have been drugged up and we have to help them recover, if we had anything like that here, they would never be clean. We don't have anything on the premises."

"Fuck, you asswipe. You got it wrong. Whoever told you this was a clinic had it wrong. Did they set you up? Are the pigs going to come in now?"

"I don't fucking know. He swore to me there were loads of stuff here. He wanted a cut of whatever we got. He wasn't setting me up, I'm sure he wasn't." He looks away. The other one lowers his gun and I feel my shoulders sag slightly. I didn't know I was so tense. I don't know what we can do now. I don't know if there are more of them or if it's just these two. I lower to my knees slowly, so they see I'm not doing anything. I place myself in front of Gretta and Nina so it's me they shoot if they decide to shoot. I need to try pleading with them to leave.

"Look, I can't even offer you anything because we don't have anything on the premises. Please, just leave and no one will know you were here. If you stay, then security will be coming on duty any time now. It would be better if you left now before they arrive. They will come in to check in with me and make sure everything is good."

They look to each other. The one with the gun seems to be in charge. They both shrug. They start to argue. I shuffle back and tell the girls not to worry, they will be gone soon. Just then I hear him. It's Steve, I know that voice, the guy with the gun pulls the door open quickly. Steve is standing there looking shocked in janitor coveralls, he's acting. He asks the gunman not to hurt him, I watch him carefully without giving anything away, I see the nod. It's slight, but he's telling me to be ready, he's going to do something. I rise up slowly and as soon as he makes his move, I do the same. I round kick the other guy in the head, he turns to see what happened and I smash him in the nose with my palm. It's what we got taught to have the most impact. If you break their nose, which is possible if you put the force behind it, then they are in so much pain they hold their nose. I then sweep his legs from under him, and he falls flat on his back. I then press my foot on his throat, effectively stopping him breathing. I look down and his nose is pouring with blood. He tries to pry my foot away, but I have all my weight on it. I bend and take his gun from his waistband, which I hadn't realized he had until now and I aim it at his head.

"Girls, go to your rooms. There is no one else to hurt you in the building. There will be some men coming very soon to secure the place and take these guys away from you. You are safe now."

I tell Gretta and Nina to go, that they will be safe now. I presume Igor and his men will be arriving soon. I thank Steve for coming just as I hear footsteps approaching. Steve shouts to let them know where he is and tells them it's just these two. Igor motions for his men to take the two guys. God knows what he will do with them. I don't even want to think about it. Igor and Steve talk and I start to shake. I think it's shock setting in. I actually took a man down and it was easy, and he was armed.

If only I knew how to do that a long time ago, maybe things would have been a lot different.

I hear Steve saying something about opioids. "Yes, they wanted meth and opioids. That is what they were asking for." He walks to me and takes me into his arms.

"You okay? Did they hurt you?"

I shake my head and smile at him. He rescued me, he fucking rescued me. That's a complete U-turn. I hear Igor speak again but I zone out. I am in disbelief. I disarmed a gunman and Steve protected me. I start to shake again and bury myself in his chest. I hear Igor shout something as I hear him leave but I don't look back to him. I hear the rumbles of Steve talking but I'm not listening, I'm taking comfort in being held to his chest, feeling safe and protected. He pulls back and I look up to him.

"You were fucking amazing. I knew you would see my nod and react. I just knew it."

I scowl and he then bends down and kisses me. "Do you want to come back to my place? We can get something to eat on the way. I just want you to be with me, so I know you are safe."

I smile and nod.

"Come on then." He puts his arm around my shoulder and walks me out.

"Can I just check the others are all okay first? Just in case any of them have had a setback." He smiles.

"Yes, of course, although the others were all okay in the rec room. They were a little scared and were disappearing into another room. I don't know how they knew about those fuckers, though, as they only went down that one corridor and heard you in the room. I watched it on the CCTV in Poppy's office. It's how I knew you were in there." We walk to the rec room; Igor is making sure everything is in order on the building. I see Dotty, she was in the rec room,

"Hey, was anyone hurt? Did you see them?"

"No, Vi. Felicity went to find you and she was just about to enter the corridor when she said she heard the men's voices and then yours. They didn't see her, and she came back and told us all we had to hide. None of the girls saw anything. They should all be okay. You go, Mr. Ustrashkins is making sure we have security tonight and from the looks of him he is not happy." I rub her shoulder and nod.

"Okay, Dotty. I'm heading home now. I'll see you tomorrow." I turn and walk out with Steve. He never lets me go, even helping me into his car. We drive in silence; he's taking me to his nice home. I think I would just rather be in my own bed. I'm not sleeping with him.

"Steve, would you mind If I just went home tonight? I will be okay."

He looks to me and scowls.

"I just want to make sure you don't go into shock, Pink. Please come stay with me just for tonight. I have lots of room. You can have my bed and I'll sleep in one of the other rooms or on the couch. I just want to look after you and make sure you are okay. Please do that for me. I also need to make sure you have something to eat and a drink. Shock can do funny things to you. It could be hours later when it actually hits you." I nod. Okay, he's not saying I have to sleep with him. I couldn't handle that as well tonight. I think he's right. I can't stop shaking.

We are not too far from what I remember but he pulls into a Taco Bell. I've never had anything from these places before. It's a drive-through. He doesn't want to leave me alone. He orders for us and passes me the bag and places the drinks in the cup holders. Once we get to his parking ga-rage, he comes around to my side, helps me out and takes the drinks while I keep hold of the bag of food. It smells good. He puts his arm around me and walks us to the elevators. Once in his apartment, he sets us up next to the windows so we can watch outside while eating.

"The rooftop is no good for you tonight. The cold will make you shake even more than you are now." He's right, my teeth are chattering, I am shaking that much. He gets a blanket and places it around me, then he gets some dishes to put our food on, he then returns with a small glass that has some amber liquid in it. I scowl at him, is he trying to get me fucking drunk. No way.

"Hold on, this is just a little whiskey to calm your nerves. Nothing more and it will not inebriate you. I promise." He holds up his hand and does the sign of the cross. He sits next to me, and I drink the liquid. I nearly spit it out, it's that vile. It burns my throat as it sinks down. I screw my face up at the taste and I hear him laugh at me. I open my eyes and scowl yet again. He laughs harder. "Here, eat this, it will take the taste away and you will feel much better." He passes me a folded thing with meat, lettuce, and tomatoes in it. I look at it and he nods. "It's a soft taco, that's ground beef, but there is a little bit of hot sauce mixed in. I take it you haven't had these before?"

I shake my head. I try it and surprisingly it's really tasty. In no time, I've eaten it all and he passes me another one. This one also has cheese on the top. I didn't even know I was that hungry, but I end up eating three of them. To my surprise, I have also stopped shaking and I am now hot. I have a slight sheen of sweat on my top lip. I wipe it away with my napkin.

I remove the blanket and he notices. You look a lot better now. You went so white earlier I thought you might pass out; shock can do that to you. I smile at him, putting my head back on the chair. I love it sitting here, even though it's dark outside, I can still see all the lights of the pier. I bet it's so busy down there, yet it's so quiet up here. Suddenly there is gentle music playing in the room. I look to Steve, who has a remote in his hand. He gets up and removes the dishes, then pushes his chair right up next to mine. He pulls me into his side, putting his arm around my shoulders. I lean my head on it.

"This is nice, just sitting here, watching the world go by. I love it here."

I smile to myself. I love it here, being with him. I wish with everything I am that he wasn't the monster I know him to be. If only he was just in a normal, nice job. It then just hits me that because of doing the business he does, that is how he can afford to live in luxury like this. I suddenly feel sick, I want to throw up. I quickly get up and ask where the bathroom is, with my hand covering my mouth. He points me in the direction, and I just run. I push open three doors before I find the right one. I throw myself on the floor next to the toilet bowl and I empty the contents of my stomach into the bowl. I feel him come in and he kneels down beside me, rubbing my back.

"Hey, are you okay?"

I don't acknowledge him. How do I say you're a monster, but I love you, which means I can't be near you? That's how I feel. He continues to rub and soothe me. I heave until there is nothing left. I cry. Silently and quietly at first, until the reality of this situation actually takes hold. Then

I sob uncontrollably. He moves away, I think he's leaving, but then I hear water running. He's now by my side, running a damp cloth over the back of my neck. He lifts me up off the floor, placing me on his lap. He sits on the floor, leaning against the wall. He takes the cloth, and he gently dabs at my face. I look him straight in the eyes, trying to see the monster, willing that monster to show itself. It doesn't. It's just a kind, worried man who sits here comforting me and making sure I'm okay. How do I process this? I haven't seen the monster. What if I'm wrong and it isn't even him? What if that day in the coffee shop, the first day I saw him, that I just wanted it to be him? What if it's just someone who sounds like him? I mean, I only ever saw his side profile and he had long hair. Steve has short hair, it's just the voice, but I was off my head on drugs. How could I possibly know that voice again? I'm doubting myself so much because he's only ever been nice to me and I don't want him to be that monster. How do I find out who he really is? He's not going to just tell me what he does, and it's not like I can just ask him, although I'm so close to asking him. It's on the tip of my tongue as I look deep into those perfect blue eyes. I'm trying to find the words to ask, I know if I do, this will all come crashing down. I know it in my heart and my head. I look back down still sobbing.

"Hey, hey come on, Pink, calm down. Hey, what is it? What's got you so freaked out? Do you want me to take you home? I don't want you to go, this is why I wanted you here because I know what shock can do. I want to make sure you are okay and safe. I want to be here for you." He brings me out of my thoughts, and I'm sitting trembling on his lap on the bathroom floor. "Let's get you up."

He helps me get up then gets up himself. The next thing I know, he's picking me up in his arms with one arm under my legs and the other supporting my back. I lean my head on his shoulder. He walks me to one of the rooms I opened the door to earlier. He walks me in, kicking the door open more and then places me on the end of the bed. He moves around to the side of it, and I hear the rustle of the comforter being moved. I don't turn around. He then comes and bends down in front of me, and he slowly takes my Doc Martens from my feet. I'm then being lifted up and I put my arms around his neck. I stare into his eyes. They are so bright, I get lost in them, like being lost in the ocean.

He gently places me back on the bed, then swings my legs onto it. He covers me with the comforter and tucks it around my shoulders. He smiles down at me while stroking my head.

"You are beautiful, Pink. I don't want to lose you." He bends down and kisses my forehead.

Why would he say that? Why would he say that about losing me? He moves away and I think he's leaving but then I feel the bed dip behind me. He's gotten onto the bed. He cuddles right into my back and places his arm over my hip. Fuck. I freeze. I didn't feel the covers move, so I presume he's on top of them. I feel cocooned in. He must be on top. That calms me slightly. I'm staring ahead.

"Breathe, Pink, you're safe. I promise you. I will just stay until you fall asleep."

I breathe out the breath I didn't realize I was holding. I even out my breathing and my eyes start to drift closed. I fight it, scared in case he does something to me when I do fall asleep. It's no use, I lose the fight.

I'm woken by the smell of coffee. I sit up, startled, trying to get my bearings of where I am. It takes me a minute or two to remember. I look around, he's not here. I look down and I'm still fully dressed, and the comforter is still around me, only sitting at my waist now. I see the coffee on the bedside table. Was it the smell or him coming in to place it there that actually woke me? I listen for any noise. I can hear running water, it's louder than I would have thought. I look around the room, there are two sets of double doors. All closed, but the one set to my right seems to be where the noise is coming from. I don't want to move so I sit back and grab the coffee.

I startle a few minutes later when the water stops running and the door suddenly opens. I spit my coffee out as I turn my head to see him standing there with his dark hair plastered to his face, his bright blue eyes staring at me intensely. My eyes drift to his naked chest. I can't help it as I watch the droplets of water meander around and over his pecs and his six-pack making their way down to the towel tied at his waist. I lick my lips, watching them. I feel ashamed and I feel my cheeks flame. He takes in a deep sharp breath; I automatically look to his face and see his eyes are hooded. I have all kinds of funny sensations in my tummy. I have only ever felt something like this with Dima, but Dima has nothing on the man standing in front of me. I feel hot and flustered. I feel I need to leave, to get out of here before he does something I am not ready for him to do. My mind is in turmoil. I place my hands on my head and start to pull at my hair. Fuck, what is wrong with me. I want him so bad, but I think I'm going to be sick again at the thought of him taking me. Poppy said, only ever give your body to someone who will worship it and never use it again. But if I let him take me, *I* am letting him take me, it's my choice. I am only here to find out what he does, aren't I? I feel confused, I start to hyperventilate. He's at my side in no time. He pulls my hands from my hair, and he kneels on the floor in front of me. I can't look at his face. What do I say to him? He must think I'm a basket case, anyway with the way I've been acting. My eyes stay on his chest, I watch the last droplets dripping from his hair onto his pecs. He gently lifts my face up with a finger under my chin.

"Hey, tell me what's going on? Tell me, what has you terrified? Is it me? Are you afraid of me? I promise you, Pink, I am not a monster, I would never hurt you."

With those words, I shriek out and cry again. Did I say he was a monster in my sleep? Is that why he's saying that. I need to leave. I have to get out of here now.

"I'm sorry, but I need to leave, Steve. I can call a taxi to take me home. I just need to leave." He looks hurt and confused. He breathes in, then he slowly rises. I open my eyes and see just as he gets up, his cock is sticking out of his towel. I screw my eyes shut. I don't want him to know I saw that. I hear him walk away and I breathe out. He heads to the other double doors and goes inside. I take this as my moment to get out. I dive for the door, grabbing my Docs on the way. I run to the elevator and press the button. It doesn't open. I press it over and over, but nothing. He's stopped it, just in case I tried to leave, oh god what do I do now? He's trapped me, he is a monster. I slide down the wall next to the elevator and pull my knees up to my chest with my head buried. I hear him come around the corner.

"Hey, Vi, what's wrong? Why did you run? I was just getting some clothes on so I could drop you home. I have to go to Igor's. I really don't want to leave, you can stay here if you want for the rest of the day, but I have to go to work."

Just then, the elevator opens beside me. I laugh out loud; he didn't stop it. What the fuck is happening to me here? I'm crazy, I feel out of control, I feel like it's not me feeling all this. He bows down and takes my hands to help me stand. He looks at his watch. Oh god, now I'm keeping him.

"Can you just take me home please, Steve?"

"Of course, come on." He puts his arm around my shoulders and walks me into the elevator, where he doesn't let me go. He even walks me to the car and helps me in. I don't speak all the way home. He doesn't speak either. He's probably just glad he's getting rid of the crazy bitch. I know I would be. He pulls up outside my building and I open the door before he has a chance to open his and I jump out. I run up the steps and turn at the top to wave bye. He's gone. Well, I think I screwed that up good and proper.

Eighteen

Steve

I DON'T EVEN KNOW WHAT THE FUCK JUST HAPPENED, BUT SHE'S like a deer in the headlights. She's terrified of me for some reason, yet she will spend time with me alone. When I saw her in that room last night with those fucking dickheads, I just wanted to barge in and rescue her by ripping their fucking heads of for putting her in danger. My heart stopped seeing that fucker with a gun and it wasn't until I had her safely in my arms that I started to calm down. She was in shock, it's why I insisted she come with me. I wanted to make sure she was okay. I lay next to her on the bed trying to give her some comfort, it took a little while, but she fell asleep. I stayed there all night just holding her. At one point, she turned over and snuggled deep into my chest. I thought she was awake, but the tiny little snores and whimpers soon made me realize she was still asleep. I just wanted to stay like that forever. I have no idea who the fuck I am right now but she's making me question myself. She seems so carefree, kind, caring, and innocent. Do I want to destroy that in her? If she ever found out who I was or what I did, she would run a mile. She would run and run, and I wouldn't be able to catch her.

I'm almost at Igor's. That's a loose end that I really need to tie up once and for all and I know I keep saying it, but it's now or never. Well, not literally now, but it has to happen soon. The sooner I can take over, the sooner I can have Pink by my side permanently. I'm hopeful I can bring her around and get her to accept me. I'm sure she has feelings for me. She just seems terrified to show them or let me know, then again, aren't I the same? I never let anyone get close. What did Kirill and Igor always say, never trust anyone, no matter who, only your lifelong partner. I want

Pink to be that. To be my lifelong partner. I have never wanted, craved, or sought out anyone to be my lifelong partner. I suppose it just happens when you least expect it.

She works with the damaged girls. How would she react if she knew it was because of me a lot of them are in that place? It's me that has damaged them. If she found out, I think she would run or kill me. There is no way I can let her find out. If I kill Igor and his family, do I still need that part of my business? Don't get me wrong, money is how I've been able to have everything I have. I can't let Igor or anyone else know exactly what I have because I know questions will be asked. If I take over the Bratva, I can do away with that side of the business. I will have the weapons, drugs, and money laundering. That way, Pink will never have to know and hopefully she will stand by my side for life. The only niggling doubts I have about Pink is the fear she has of me. Why does she have that fear? Is it just me or men in general? If it's men in general, then I would say she is damaged. If I had to go out on a limb, I would say she was trafficked. If she was, I'd like to find the fuckers who did that to her and kill them. I would give them such a painful death. Could it be? No, I'm sure she wouldn't be able to work at the refuge if she was. She told me Poppy helped her when she was homeless. That then means it's me she's afraid of, but why? I have done nothing to make her afraid of me, so I don't understand why or how?

I pull up to Igor's and key in the code. The gates open and I drive up the path to the front. I don't see the two guards he has stationed at all times, but I know where they are. I know the movements and when the changes happen. I have a connection to the telecoms that I listen into periodically when they speak to do the changes or to do the walk-throughs. Just as I get out of the car, Poppy and her eldest daughter come out the front.

"Hey Steve, you have me today. Not sure if Igor told you. I have to take Sabina here for a dance comp today and Gregor got himself injured again. Igor is staying home. Sorry it's an early start but we have to be there early for her to get warmed up." I frown, as I have no idea what she's talking about. She notices.

"Sabina here is going to be the next big thing in dancing. Not your normal run-of-the-mill ballet dancing, this is a combination of all dances, but especially street dancing. She's amazing. You should come in with us and watch. We're off to the San Diego Convention Center." I smile and open the back doors for them both to get in. I head out in the direction of San Diego. It's a good two-hour drive if traffic is good. It's just coming up to seven a.m.

"What time do you have to be there, Poppy?"

"The comp starts at ten, so we have plenty of time if traffic is clear."

"Do you mind if I pull in for a coffee to go? I didn't have a chance to grab a coffee yet."

"Not a problem. I could do with one myself. I've been too excited for Sabina here."

I smile and look in the back mirror. I've seen Sabina a few times when I've been at the house. She's a lovely little thing but looking in the mirror at her now, I notice she has long blonde hair and those blue eyes of Igor's that are also a match to mine, how odd. She smiles at me in the mirror and my heart stops. When she smiles, she looks just like Pink. Why the fuck does she look like Pink? She's not her child. Igor never said who her mama was, but we all suspected it was Svetlana. This little girl just showed up one day. No one could deny she was Igor's, but we couldn't see any resemblance to anyone else, as the resemblance to him was so overpowering. All you could see was this messy blonde hair and the bluest of eyes. She reminded me of Igor when we were little growing up together. Only a female version of him. Svetlana was the obvious choice, because, well, he was with her for a while when she first disappeared on him. Then she reappeared on her own and he was going to kill her the night Sergei ran off with her. Now looking at her, oh shit. I have to swerve the car. I was so busy looking at her in the rearview mirror that I didn't see the old woman crossing the road with her shopping cart. I just miss hitting her by swerving and slamming on my brakes. I turn around to check on Poppy and Sabina.

"Hey, are you both okay? I'm really sorry. I didn't see the woman crossing the road. She just appeared."

Poppy has her arms around Sabina. Sabina looks okay, but a little upset. The way she is looking at me is just how Pink looked at me this morning. Fuck. She couldn't possibly be Pink's daughter. Pink is far too young to have a daughter the age of Sabina. She has to be eleven or twelve. That would mean Pink had her when she was about twelve herself. There is no way Igor would sleep with anyone that age. There has to be another explanation. Maybe it's just me seeing Pink everywhere I look because I want her so bad. My mind is playing tricks on me.

"We're okay, Steve, but I really need that coffee now. Please just watch the road." She kind of scolds me and I don't blame her, I wasn't watching the road. If I had, I would have definitely seen the woman.

I keep looking in the rearview mirror at her. I can't help it. If Poppy notices, she'll kick me out of the fucking car and drive herself. She'll think I have a thing for her young daughter. I don't, it's just the resemblance but how can I tell her that?

We've been at this comp thing for about three hours now. Sabina is due to do hers next and Poppy insisted I stay to watch instead of sitting out in the car. This is the first time I've spent any time with any of their kids. I wouldn't mind. I was there when they had the twins, then Sabina showed up and then the other twins. How they cope with five kids I have no idea; it freaks me out thinking about it. I would never be a good dad, I didn't have a good role model, but then neither did Igor and look at him. Maybe it depends on the woman you're with. Now with Pink, who knows. Kids, why the fuck am I thinking of kids? How the fuck could I have kids, I'd never let them leave the house thinking someone like me would take them. After all, isn't that exactly what I do and never bat an eye at doing it. I'm damaged, that's for sure and no kids would be safe with me. I'd be terrified of me doing to them what my papa did to me.

Sabina steps onto the stage. On her own. Wow, most of the kids before her have been in groups or couples. She must be good or have some balls. The music starts pumping out loud. It's some kind of rap shit. Very different to everyone else. It doesn't surprise me coming from the family she comes from. They would support her even if she wanted to do fucking synchronized swimming or some shit. I stand at the back of the room, mesmerized by the little girl up on that stage. I look around and see everyone is the same. No one is talking, they are all just watching. She's fucking amazing. The moves she has are like nothing the others have done.

Poppy was right, she's good. I just thought it was a mama spouting off as usual that their kid is the best, but watching Sabina rock it up there, she is amazing. She has no fear and is full of confidence. That must come from having parents like she has.

It's sometime later before all her group has finished and she has to dance again as she won her group. This time, all the winners of each group dance again to find the overall champion. I didn't realize this and almost missed it getting coffees for me and Poppy. I enter just as she starts her next dance. Poppy explains what is happening. Again, I am mesmerized, as is everyone else. This is a different dance to different music, it's different from the first round. I'm not sure she should have changed it up. What the fuck do I know? I laugh to myself. The roars when she finishes are ear shattering. I get up and whistle, clapping like she's my own fucking kid. What the hell. We watch the rest and another hour later the results for the overall champion are in. They do drag these fucking things out. They give the third place, and the runner-up place out but they are not to Sabina, my heart sinks for her. I don't think she is going to win. There were some good kids up there. The announcer drags it out for a long time. All of a sudden, the room erupts as he announces Sabina Ustrashkins as the winner. Poppy is up out of her seat and running toward Sabina. I'm on my feet whooping and hollering. She fucking did it. She beat all those other kids. That's fucking amazing. Why do I feel proud? This is the first time I've spent any time with the kid.

We're on our way back home. Sabina has fallen asleep on Poppy's knee. Her huge trophy is on the seat next to her and she also won entry into the world champions. I didn't know it was for something so big. It surprises me that Igor allows this. He's well known in a lot of fucking countries so why bring attention to yourself and tell the world 'Hey, here's my kid to use as collateral against me', he needs his head seen to, the fucking asswipe.

"Poppy, you must be so proud of her. She was amazing up there. No fear at all." I look to her through the rearview mirror. She looks up and smiles.

"I am the proudest mama alive right now. I knew she could do it. I knew she was that good. She dances nonstop."

I need to ask though. "I know it's none of my business, but why would Igor or you allow this? I mean, this brings so much publicity to the Ustrashkins name, it's like announcing here is the collateral to use against us. Doesn't that scare you?"

She frowns at me. "Yes, it does, Steve. It terrifies me, but I will not stop any of my children doing what they want in life. If that means being followed by ten guards each, I don't care. We try to let them have a normal life. Well, as normal as we can make it. If one of them wants to be a football player, then they can be. I will not let this life dictate where their path takes them. This is Igor's and now my life. They don't have to do what we do or follow in anything we do. This life will never be forced onto any of them. If none of them wants it, then the Ustrashkins name dies when either Igor or I go. We both agreed to that when we had Dimitri and Nikoli. If they want to follow, then they can, if they don't, then they do what they want to do. We will stand by them no matter what they all choose."

Wow, that's a shocker. I never thought Igor would do that. I wonder whose idea it was. It must be hers. She wasn't born into this life like we were. She's definitely got some balls.

I drop them back at home safely. I make sure Igor doesn't need me for the rest of the night. It's already past ten thirty, I head home. I think it would be a waste of time going to the refuge. I'm sure Pink would have left by now. I decide to go to my apartment near her. That way, I can get up in the morning and see if she's going to the coffee shop. Igor said he didn't need me tomorrow, they are all staying home, and he has Pavel staying over tonight. That suits me fine, I have stuff to do. I would have gone back to my Santa Monica home but I'm going to see if Pink would like to come back tomorrow. I head back to my not-so-nice apartment, it's after eleven, so I just go to bed. It's been a long day.

Nineteen

Vidana

I EXPECTED TO SEE HIM AFTER WORK TONIGHT BUT THERE WAS NO sign of him. Maybe he's realized I'm broken, what with all my throwing up, crying, hyperventilating, and not talking. He must think there is something drastically wrong with me, he wouldn't be wrong. I curse myself. I thought I was doing well, turns out, not so well after all. I know he likes me but maybe he was just being nice after the break-in yesterday. Most of the girls at the refuge have been great but then they didn't see anything. The only person who has gone back on herself is Nina. I feel so bad for her being caught up in the break-in. This will set her back a lot now. It will take some persuading that this place is safe. Gretta, bless her, has been trying to help her again today. She's traumatized by the ordeal as well, but she knows it was a one off. I'm fine with it now. They have amped up security; everyone gets a lanyard now and they have to show it at the door to gain access. This is only from six in the evening until seven in the morning. The doors are locked during this time, but anyone can come and go as long as they have a lanyard.

I step outside and look around; I don't see Steve or his car anywhere. I feel deflated. I was hoping to see him and maybe go back with him again. Is that really what I want? But I was so disappointed he wasn't there, so yes, it is what I want. Maybe he's just been working somewhere with Igor all day and couldn't make it. I start to make my way home. Just as I approach my building, I see Ryker coming out of it. He spots me and breaks out a smile as he walks toward me. I smile back at him.

"Oh, hey, Ryker. How are you? I haven't seen you for a few days. You usually come into the coffee shop." I love the beam on his face.

"Hey Vi, I missed you when I was in yesterday, you must have been on a break or a day off. How are you? You heading home." He nods his head up, meaning my room.

"Yes, I just finished at the refuge."

"I heard about the break-in yesterday. I was coming to see if I could find you to see how you were. I believe you were in the thick of it. That Steve came and rescued you all."

Wow, news sure travels quick. Unless he spoke to Steve, and he's bragged about it. I roll my eyes.

"Is that what he's telling people?" I laugh. "Yes, he did actually. I am okay. I was in shock last night and a little bit apprehensive going to the refuge to work today, but Poppy and Igor have amped up security, so I felt a lot safer." He reaches out and rubs my arm.

"I'm so sorry you had to go through that. Good job he was there. You could have phoned me last night and I would have come over to sit with you for a while." Oh shit, I'm not gonna lie to him.

"Thank you, Ryker, that is so nice. I don't actually have your number, but I was with Steve last night. He wanted to make sure I didn't go into shock, so I went home with him. As it turns out, I did go into shock and threw up." I see his face drop and turn sad. I really do like Ryker and the more I see him, the more I'm drawn to him. He's growing on me and he's such a gentleman.

He drops his hand from my arm and puts it in his front jeans pocket.

"Oh, okay. So, are you and Steve, erm, you know, a thing now?"

I shake my head and smile.

"Not really, no. I'm just getting to know him a little better. I don't actually know much about him though. He told me you and he met a while ago when you were helping out Igor. He does seem nice but also a little intimidating."

"Yeah, I don't know him that well, but he seems nice from what I've seen. It's not my place to say, but be careful."

Wow, what does he mean, I must look confused.

"It's just I don't know much about him, but I've heard things. I don't want to say what because they may not be true and that's unfair. He works for Mr. Ustrashkins, so just be wary of him, that's all I'm saying. It was great to see you and put my mind at ease knowing you're okay after your ordeal. I'll see you around, maybe in the coffee shop. Night Vi." With that, he walks past me and goes on his way. What the fuck was that about? Now I want to know what he's heard. He can't just leave it like that.

"Hey, Ryker. Wait up."

He stops but doesn't turn around. I catch up to him.

"Can we talk? I would rather know what you've heard so I can be on my guard. I find it hard enough to let anyone in or trust anyone. The last thing I want is for Steve to be a danger of any kind. It would destroy me for life."

He runs his hand through his hair. "Do you want to get a drink?"

I nod and we walk to the bar at the end of the street. It's a quiet place, this is what I like.

"Do you want a Coke, Vi?"

I nod and he goes to the bar while I take a seat near the back where there aren't many people around. I watch him come toward me with the drinks and he looks a little forlorn. He sits opposite me and slides my drink over to me. I take the straw and have a little sip.

"I don't want to put you in a predicament, Ryker, but you know I was in the refuge and Svetlana told you things, so you know why I need to know. I see you as my friend, Ryker. If you would rather not tell me, then I completely understand." I feel I could open up to Ryker and he would be loyal and listen, is that just me being naive? I know he was hurt by Lana, but he's gotten over her now, it's been a few years since she left.

He sighs. "I consider you my friend, Vi. I haven't spoken about you to him or anyone. I know whatever goes on at the refuge stays there and it's none of my business and not my place to tell anyone anything. Poppy also made that clear to me, although she didn't need to, I wouldn't do that anyway. He has asked me about you the couple of times I've seen you. I've told him we are friends from the coffee shop and that's it." He takes a sip of his drink. It's not a beer, it's clear liquid but in a big glass.

I'm curious. "What's that you're drinking, Ryker?" I smile. I wonder if it's vodka. It's a lot if it is. It reminds me of Papa. He always drank vodka.

"This is just water; I don't drink very often. Alcohol isn't good for you, and neither is soda." He smiles, looking at my Coke. I smile and shrug, taking another suck on my straw. I suppose that makes sense. He's a personal trainer, so diet and nutrition will be everything to him.

"What did you hear about Steve? I like him, Ryker, but like I said before, he intimidates me. I have this feeling there is something more to him that I haven't seen. I get the feeling he isn't letting me see the real him." He cocks his head to the side.

"Are we friends, Vi? I mean, we don't even have each other's numbers, so are we truly friends? I don't want to go spouting off about Steve and you go telling him, which then gets me into trouble. I keep my nose clean at all times. When you're dealing with the likes of Mr. Ustrashkins, you have to be very careful and that means with Steve also, because he is his man at arms, or his top guard, whatever you want to call them. They were best friends growing up, but I've been told they are not friends anymore." I take his phone from the tabletop next to his glass. He looks at me, wondering what I am doing.

"Can you unlock it please?" I hold it to his face, and it unlocks. I then put my name and number into his cell, and I ring my cell from his. "There, you have my number and I have yours. Yes, we are friends, Ryker, I would never betray you."

He smiles at me. Happy he has my number.

"I would just be cautious with him. I don't want you to think I'm saying this because I like you, Vi. It's just I do know what you have been through, and I would hate for you to get mixed up with something not good. Svetlana did tell me some of it and I don't want the first man you fall for to be a bad one." I take another suck on my straw. He knows Steve is bad. Fuck, I know Steve is bad, but I do need what info I can get on him. "I've heard he thinks nothing of killing someone who crosses him, but then that applies to all Bratva." His eyes widen when he says this. I get up and sit next to him so I can speak quietly.

"It's okay. I know Igor is Bratva. I've known since I was younger when he took Lana. Well, Mama sold Lana to him. He also killed my papa."

"What the fuck. Why are you working for them then?" he raises his voice and I look around to see if anyone notices. They don't, thankfully. There aren't a lot of people in here, but we are in Igor's territory, so we need to be careful.

"Can we get out of here, Ryker? I don't trust anyone in here, being in Igor's territory. I don't want anyone to hear us speaking about them. I would never forgive myself if anything happened to you." He nods and rises out of his seat. I get up and he walks behind me as we leave the bar. "Where do you think would be safe around here?" I ask him. He looks around us.

"I'm not sure, Vi, unless you come to mine. We can get a cab and I will make sure you get home safe. I agree though. I don't know where else is okay to talk." I trust Ryker way more than I do Steve, in fact, I don't trust Steve at all knowing what he does, so I agree. It doesn't take us long to get to his place. It's a nice little apartment, cozy and compact. I look at the pictures he has on the side while he gets me a coffee and him a water.

"Is this your wife, Ryker?" I look over to him and he nods. "She's beautiful and you looked so in love. I'm sorry you lost her." He passes me my coffee, smiling at me.

"We were childhood sweethearts. She became ill with cancer, and we married before she passed away. She was beautiful and the most caring and loving person I ever knew." I squeeze his hand; he looks down at me and smiles again. "Come, let's sit."

"Okay, so yes Igor killed my papa, but I don't blame him for it." I tell him the story about what Mama and Lana did and he is dumbstruck. He can't believe they would do that, especially Lana.

"She's like a chameleon. She changes to suit her surroundings, Ryker. She lies all the time, to everyone to suit her. She manipulates everyone. She's not one to be trusted. I love Poppy, she's more like a sister to me than Lana could ever be. She's helped me so much. I attacked Igor when I first arrived at the refuge. I blamed him for everything. I now know he wasn't to blame. He thought he was saving Lana and by eliminating the danger, he was saving the rest of us, even though there was no danger to us. He didn't know that at the time. I have the Ustrashkins to thank for saving my life and I will forever be grateful to them. I just need to know what you know about Steve. I can't be put in danger's path again."

He takes in a deep breath, then slowly blows it out.

"I've done physical therapy and training on some of Igor's men. Igor wanted me on his payroll, but I declined and said I would help whenever he needed it. To be honest, he makes up eighty percent of my business these days. He's always got men out for one thing or another. Over the last few years, while I have been working on his men, I hear things. When they are on the phone or if someone comes in to talk to them. They all forget I'm there at times and they talk about business. Business I should not be privy to. I've heard the talk on Steve. It's why I keep him at a distance. They say he's dangerous. That they know he has other businesses on the side. I don't know what, I'm not sure any of them do, but they are scared of him. Some are more scared of him than they are of Igor. To me, that says a lot. That tells me he is dangerous. I've heard the talks that Steve's papa was Igor's papa's man at arms and that when Igor took over, he didn't make Steve his man at arms. Apparently, that sent Steve over the edge, and he went off the rails for a long time. Steve and Igor grew up like brothers, but things changed once Igor took over the family business. I've heard talk that when Steve used to get drunk with his men, he would talk about overthrowing Igor. That he should be the one ruling this city, not Igor. I don't know how true all this is, Vi, so please don't let this go any further than us two. I would hate anything to happen to you."

He grabs my hand and squeezes it. He really cares. I believe everything he has told me, knowing what I know it all fits. I can't tell him what I suspect though. I don't want him being in the middle of all this.

"Thank you for telling me, Ryker. I do appreciate it and I will tread with caution. I refuse to be dragged into anything bad. If you see me with him, please know it's nothing serious and nothing is going on. I do like him, he is nice and caring to me, but there is just something about him that I can't quite put my finger on."

We spend the rest of the evening talking. I actually open up to him about my sisters. I need to check in with Poppy to see if they have found them yet. I tell him Igor has his men looking for them.

"I'm afraid what my mama will do. Igor cut off her money some time ago after he found out that Papa was innocent. If she has no source of income, she may do something with my sisters, and I fear for them. Knowing what I know and what I've been through, I wouldn't put anything past anyone, not even my own mama. People do desperate things in desperate times."

He makes me a sandwich when he hears my tummy rumble. I enjoy my evening with him. He opens up about his wife and you can tell he was in love with her. The adoration he has talking about her. That's something I could only ever dream of finding if I even want it. I don't think anyone would want me if they knew what I had been through. Ryker knows I was sex trafficked. He hasn't run a mile from me, so there is that and hope. It's getting late and I have to be up early for my shift in the coffee shop. He calls a taxi but instead of just seeing me into the taxi, he comes with me to make sure I actually get home okay. I kiss him on the cheek good night. He then takes that same taxi back home.

I get up for my shift and I'm heading out and secretly hoping Steve will be there. I chastise myself, even knowing what Ryker told me, I still want him to be there. I'm not disappointed this time. He's outside waiting for me. He smiles as I walk out of the building. I smile back and skip down the steps to him.

"Hi," I say, smiling, looking up to his face. He mirrors my look.

"Hi to you too. I missed you yesterday." He bends down and kisses me gently on the lips. I take in a breath at his gentle touch. He pulls away, smiling at my reaction. I swear I'm nearly the color of my hair. We automatically start to walk toward the coffee shop. He takes my hand as we do. I smile my biggest smile, but don't look at him. I scold myself for wanting this when I know he is a monster. I just can't seem to help it. Even after my talk with Ryker last night. I hate myself right now.

"Hey, penny for them." I look up and frown. What is he talking about? He laughs.

"That's what we say, a penny for your thoughts."

Oh right, I have never heard that saying before.

"Well." He stops and looks down at me. "You looked angry at something. Are you okay after the other night?"

I nod. "Yes, I was a little apprehensive going to the refuge last night, but Igor has security in place now from six, so that put me more at ease."

"What were you just thinking about that had you looking angry?"

I frown. "Was I? I don't know, I was just thinking about the orders for work, but I wasn't angry."

He laughs and we carry on walking.

"I'm sorry I didn't get back to see you last night. I wasn't sure you wanted me to after yesterday morning, but it was late by the time I got back from work. I just crashed at my other apartment near here so I could see you this morning. I've got to go see Igor this morning, so will just walk you to work then leave. I think I'm going out of town for a little while, either tonight or in the morning. Hey, why don't you come with me if you can get time off work? I'm going to New York on business. Would you like to join me?"

Oh fuck. Me go away with him. What if he does something to me? But I need to think about this. Maybe I could get some idea of what he does in New York. I'll stall on him.

"Well, Pink. What do you say? Would you like to come away for a few days? I promise there's nothing meant by it. I have an apartment in New York, and I promise you can have your own room. No funny business. I just have some business to do, then I could show you the sights of New York." He smiles at me like a kid with a new toy.

I, on the other hand, am having palpitations. I can feel my heart racing. I try to take a couple of breaths without him noticing but that's easier said than done when he's staring at me. I nod. It's all I can do. He leans down and takes my lips, cradling my face in his hands. I can feel his smile. Oh fuck.

"Let me check with Sybil at the coffee shop and I need to let Poppy know I won't be in. How long are you going for?"

"Just a couple of days. Two nights. Is that okay? Do you think that's doable?"

"Let me get back to you. I need to check first and make sure Sybil and Poppy can get cover. I will let you know later." We walk the rest of the way in silence, mainly because I am internally having a panic attack. I stumble at one point because my knees are like Jell-O. He keeps me upright. I turn as if looking at what I tripped on.

He doesn't come into the coffee shop; he leaves straight away to go to Igor's. I run into the back and sit in the storeroom quietly. I put my head down and take in deep breaths. It's one thing playing here where I know I can at least get to people who can help me, but to be alone in New York with him. I also know that was where I was kept for some time. Poppy told me I was rescued from a house in New York. She also told me that they don't think they got the cartel leader. They believed it was a cartel. Their intel had told them that. If I go, then I have to tell Poppy and Ryker where I am going. I need to let people know where I will be. I hear the door open. Fuck, has he come back? No one is due in. I didn't lock the door. I just ran in here. I wait and listen, trying not to breathe.

"Hello, Vi, are you in?"

Thank god, it's Sybil. She wasn't supposed to be in for a while. I leave the storeroom and walk out, trying to compose myself, so she doesn't think there is anything wrong. It didn't work.

"What the, what's wrong, Vi? You look terrible."

Oh shit.

"I'm okay."

"Like hell you are. Come, let's have a coffee. Tell me what's wrong." I explain to her I haven't had a boyfriend since I was young, and that Steve had asked me to go to New York, so I was having a freak-out. She said I could go, and she will be more than happy to cover my shifts, but that I need to be careful with that one. One down, one to go. On my break, I call Poppy.

"Hey Poppy, I am so sorry to put this on you and if it's short notice, then that is perfectly fine, I will understand. So don't worry if you can't do it. I know it's not much notice so it may be hard."

"Hey Vidana, are you going to tell me what it is?" She laughs, I was rambling.

"Steve has asked me to go to New York with him for a couple of days and it's tonight so it might not be possible for you to get cover for my shifts for the next two days, so it's okay I'll just tell him no. It's too short notice."

"Vidana, I can tell you're nervous and of two minds. I'm not going to be the one who says yes or no to going. You need to ask yourself if you feel confident enough to do this. Do you know him well enough? I wasn't aware you were close, never mind that you actually knew each other. I thought it was just a hello in passing. Look, think about it. Think first, do you want to do this, then second, can you do this? Don't worry about having the time off, you've worked nonstop for a few years now. I can get you covered but I need you to think about this. Is he pressuring you to go? This has to be something you want to do without pressure from anyone. Remember what I said to you, never give anyone the power over you, always stand your ground. Never let them control you. You do the controlling."

I know she's right.

"I don't know, Poppy. Yes, I know him. I've been to his apartment a couple of times just for something to eat. I kind of like him and he seems to be good to me. He's never tried to do anything, and he knows nothing of my past and I'd like to keep it that way. I just keep questioning myself and the what-ifs. What if he changes and turns nasty, what if he tries to force himself on me, what if he hits me? It all goes around and around in my head. I know you can't make the decision for me. I think I'm going to go but will you put a tracker on my cell just in case, please? If there is anyone I trust on this earth, it is you and I would like you to know where I am."

"Of course, I will. When you come in later, come see me. I'll be in the office for a little while. We can sort out the cell and you can tell me what you wanted to chat about. I'm glad you are being sensible by telling me. Not that you have to tell me, but for your own safety you are doing good, Vidana, I'm proud of you and proud you are taking the steps to get back to normal. Just please be careful. Is this just a leisure trip he's taking you on?"

"Yes, he said he will show me the sights of New York. He has business to attend to, then he's going to show me around. He was good when I stayed at his place in Santa Monica, and he says he has an apartment in New York, and I will have my own room. I think he will be okay."

She doesn't speak but I hear her tapping away on the keyboard.

"Poppy?"

"Yes, sorry Vidana, I was just replying to something. Okay sweetie, come in and see me, then you don't have to do your shift today. I can get that covered. I will see you in a little while." She hangs up and I go back to work.

The time goes by quickly. I hugged Sybil and said I'd see her in a couple of days. I am now just walking into the refuge to go see Poppy. I stop when I see Steve in the corridor. He must sense me, as he suddenly lifts his head up and smiles. I smile back.

"Hey, I was hoping to see you. I just dropped in, and Poppy said you would be here soon. I was just going to see if you had thought about New York. I have a plane leaving in a couple of hours." Wow, that's fast.

"Yes," I say, nodding and smiling. My heart is racing, I'm starting to break out into a sweat and my breathing is starting to get heavy. I'm going to go into a panic. I need to move. "I've just got to clear some stuff up with Poppy, then I will head home and pack a bag. Do you want to meet me in the lobby in about an hour?" I say this walking past him. The smile on his face says it all. I'm trying to stay as calm as I can.

"Really? That's fantastic. Yes, I'll come for you in an hour. See you later."

I turn and walk straight into Poppy's office without knocking and I slide down the back of the closed door. She jumps up from her chair and comes to kneel in front of me.

"Okay, remember, deep breaths, in slowly and out slowly." She sees right away the panic and turmoil I'm in. I do as she says, in and out slowly, until I feel myself calming. She gets up and holds out her hands for me to take. She helps me to my feet. I hug her to me. I just feel I need the contact from someone who cares. It just dawns on me the only one who ever used to cuddle any of us at home was my papa. Mama was always distant with us. We never had any love or affection from her. I start to cry, thinking of them.

"Hey, shhh. Sweetie, if you don't want to go, then don't go. No one will think anything of you for standing your ground. Hey, come on now. Sit here and let me get you some water." She takes me to a chair and then gets the water from behind her desk. I take my cell out and pass it to her. "Let me ask you one thing and I want an honest answer. The first thing you think of, say it, because that there will be your answer. Do you want to go to New York with Steve?"

"Yes."

"Okay then. So, you just need to calm down and think good, happy things. Now promise me if you go and he does try anything, and you don't want him to, that you will stop him. Please promise me. You can say no to anything you don't want. If he turns nasty, you call me right away. I will make sure you are looked after. I want you to go knowing you have an out no matter what. Okay?"

I nod. I love this woman. She does some things to my cell and her computer and then passes it back to me.

"You're all set. Now when you are ready, walk out of here like the queen you are. Not a fear in the world because you are in control of your body and no one else. I have you on my system. I will know where you are. Just remember, anything at all and you call me, we have people in New York who can get to you quick, got it? Take care, sweetie." I get up and move to her to hug her again before I leave.

I head home, I feel good after being with Poppy. She has this way of always making you feel good about yourself. I could do with her on my shoulder every step of the way on this trip. I know I am going to go into meltdowns at each step. Do I need to tell Steve that it will happen to prepare him? He must already think I'm crazy. I mean, I threw up a few times at his place. I don't know what to tell him though. I rush inside and pack a bag; I have no idea what to take. Do I need anything to dress nice for or is it just all sightseeing? I put a dress in the bag just in case. He's waiting for me when I get down, only he's in the lobby this time, not outside. My heart stutters at seeing him, I'm sure this is to do with being scared of him rather than wanting him. He smiles and takes my bag from me then takes my other hand. We head out to the waiting car.

"Are you excited about this trip?" He settles me in the car.

I nod and smile. The palpitations have started. I feel like I want to throw up. That has to be because I'm scared. I feel scared. The only reason I have agreed to this is because I need some kind of information on him. Something to give Poppy. I know I told her about his apartments in Santa Monica and in New York. She's a smart woman who would have looked this up to see what she can find. Steve told me Igor didn't know about his Santa Monica apartment. I mentioned it on purpose. I hope Poppy has started checks. I've decided when he leaves to do his business, I will try to follow him. If he leaves in a car, then I will be stuck. If he walks, I can follow. But I know he is very good at his job and I'm sure being a guard means you're on full alert at all times.

He holds my hand the entire time in the back of the car. Every now and then he brings it to his lips to kiss. I smile, but it's a nervous smile.

"Steve, please bear with me, won't you? I am a little nervous having never done anything like this before. If I look nervous, that's why. It's all new to me and, well, I am a little scared. I don't know you that well yet."

He strokes his finger down my cheek and leans in to kiss where his finger trailed.

"I understand completely. Please know you will be safe with me, and I promise nothing will happen. I like you so fucking much, Pink. I don't care if I only hold your hand or steal a kiss here and there. I don't care if this is how it is for the next year. I will wait for you for as long as it takes."

See, this is why I'm falling for the monster. I snuggle into his hand against my cheek. My heart is pounding. I'm so confused and conflicted as usual, but I do know I have to find out if he is Alborz, the leader of the cartel. I'm ninety-nine percent positive it is him. We pull into the airport and the driver pulls up by a jet. I've been on these before when Igor brought us over those couple of times for Lana. I need to act impressed because I know these are not the normal planes people fly on.

"Wow, look at this. It's so luxurious," I say as he buckles me into the seat. "Is anyone else coming on here with us?"

He laughs and kisses my lips, then buckles himself in the seat opposite me.

"It's just the two of us. This is my jet, Pink. Nobody else uses it. It's just for us." My eyes go wide. Does he honestly make that much money from sex trafficking? It's unbelievable, he has all this luxury from making so many girls' lives a misery and then killing them, like they are nothing. I start to feel myself getting angry. I need to calm down.

"Wow, Igor must pay you a lot of money to be his guard," I joke, but he doesn't even smile. Just then, a lady brings a tray with a beer and a Coke on it and passes the Coke to me. I thank her and look to Steve.

"I already had the drinks sorted for us and there will be a meal served after we take off." He totally skips over the comment about being paid too much. It's as if I didn't say anything. I sip on my Coke. The plane starts to move, then it's not long before we are taking off. I grip the arms tightly and close my eyes. I never did like flying. I keep my eyes shut. This way I don't need to speak. I hear him laugh and on instinct, I open my eyes. "I take it you don't like the taking off part?"

"I don't really like the flying part, period. I only flew the one time to get to LA, well it was two times because we had to stop somewhere else first. I didn't like it then, and that was a big ass plane, full of people. I think I feel a bit safer in a bigger plane. Is that weird?"

He laughs at me.

"No, it's not weird. I think I understand why people think a bigger plane is safer, but to me, this is safer. One it's lighter and two it's faster. The bigger planes have so much weight in them. That's just how I feel and it's why I bought the jet. As well as the fact I don't have to book and can set my own schedule."

Just then, the lady is back and starts to mess around with the table and sets it for a dinner. She then brings out the food. I wasn't hungry until she put it in front of me.

It seems like no time passes and we are now on the way to his apartment. The flight was quite good. He did tell me there was a bedroom if I wanted a nap, but I declined. We pull up outside a tall building. They are all tall here. Not much different from where I live now. I obviously have no idea where I am. He helps me out of the car and holds my hand, taking us into the building. The doorman greets us and welcomes Mr. Darvish back. I didn't know his surname. Steve Darvish, huh, suits him although I don't think it's a Russian name and he told me his papa was Russian. I shrug it off and we head up to the penthouse. Wow, he has a penthouse in Santa Monica and one here in New York. I step off the elevator into an enormous room with floor-to-ceiling windows just like his Santa Monica home. I move over to them. It's really dark outside. I can see a big black space in front of us but then the surrounding areas are all lit up. I can't wait to see it in the daytime.

I yawn and stretch my arms above my head. As my eyes are closed, I didn't see his reflection behind me, so he startles me when his arms wrap around me, and he lays his chin on top of my head. I jump and he laughs.

"Sorry, I didn't mean to startle you. I just couldn't resist."

Fuck, is this the start of it. I put my hands over his that are resting on my tummy. He doesn't move them, which is fine by me. I lay my head back on his shoulder and watch us in the reflection of the glass. I smile at him watching me and when he winks at me, it does funny things in my tummy. "Would you like a drink, Pink?"

"Oh yes please. Do you have any hot chocolate? I always like to have a hot chocolate to take to bed."

He laughs at me and kisses the top of my head and then the side of my neck. I need to pull away before he starts going where he shouldn't. Just then, the phone rings in the apartment and he leaves me so he can answer it. Saved by the bell, literally. He finishes on the phone and calls the elevator up. It's our bags from the car. I forgot about them. He brings them in and then carries mine for me. As he passes, he takes my hand and leads me to a room. We walk in and it's beautiful in here.

"This is your room. I will leave you to unpack your stuff and I will see if I have hot chocolate. If I don't, I will get some brought up for you." He leaves, closing the door behind him. Wow, this place is huge. It's bigger than my room back home in LA. I take out my cell. There is a message from Poppy.

Hey VI, just checking in to see you got there safely and all is okay. Xx

I quickly type back.

Just arrived and all okay. Xx

I think there is a time difference from LA to here because when I saw the clock in the living area it said it was eleven fifteen but when I took my phone out just now it was eight fifteen. My phone has changed to eleven twenty. So, LA is three hours behind New York. Good to know. One thing I did worry about at first was if it would bring back any memories from my time here, but I can honestly say I could have been anywhere at all, because I never saw the outside, apart from the day I was rescued but then we were only put into an RV, and I was in no state to take any notice of my surroundings. There's a knock on the door. I haven't even moved yet. I've been sitting on the bed. The door opens and he walks in with a mug and places it down on the side table.

"One hot chocolate for my lady. I have put some sugar on the side in case you need to sweeten it. I have no idea if it's sweet or not." I know I keep saying this, but how can he be a monster. I wonder if I got it wrong. Maybe his papa was rich and left him a lot of money. He did say he was going to sort out his papa's house. I never asked him anything about it.

"Why thank you, kind sir. Now I will be able to sleep." I yawn just as I say it and he smiles at me. "I didn't know there was a time difference. I hold up my cell to show him the time just as a message pops through.

We both look as it dings. It's Ryker. I see the look on Steve's face. He goes from smiling to angry. I scowl at him. What's his problem? He knows we are friends. He gets up and leaves the room.

"Good night," I shout. I get up to see if there is a lock on the door. There is, I turn it quietly. I feel a little safer now. I then spot the chair by the dressing table. I move it under the door handle so no one can come in. I know I'm paranoid but the look on his face just then had me scared. I tried not to show it but inside I started to panic in case he did something. He looked furious at seeing Ryker's name. I read the message, the bit you could see.

Hi Vi, had a good time last night. Let's catch…

Ah, now I see why he was mad. I never told him I saw Ryker last night. Then again, I don't have to tell him, he doesn't own me and it's none of his business. He has no right to be angry at me. I don't reply to Ryker. Instead, I take out my pj's and get ready for bed. I open a door and there is a bathroom, phew, I don't have to leave the room. I wash my face, taking my makeup off, and then brush my hair. I climb into bed. I pick my cell up.

Hey Ryker. Yeah, it was good to catch up. I'm in New York. Can you believe it? I'm with Steve. He's been really nice and has a plane and a lovely apartment right on the top floor. I will be back in a couple of days. See you soon. Xx

I don't care if Steve's angry. I like Ryker. In fact, after seeing Steve so angry like that I've just realized I really like Ryker, again, and I kind of miss him. Why didn't I see it before? I say I'm not attracted to his type but then I don't have a type. Unless it's a bad boy type. I'm a fool. That makes me more determined to find out what I can about Steve and to give what info I can to Poppy. If he is who I think he is, then I need to put a stop to his trafficking. To save the girls he uses and stop him using them again.

I settle down to sleep. I hear a noise and it wakes me; I think it's the handle on the door. Fuck, I don't know what time it is but why is he trying to get in? I scoot up to the headboard and pull my knees to my chest and throw the comforter over me. Like he doesn't know I'm fucking in here. Then there's a light knock. I don't answer, I don't want him to know

I'm awake. He knocks again, slightly louder but not too loud. I'm shaking like a leaf, my breathing is starting to get erratic and my heart is racing like a horse, I want to curl up and hide. I do just that. I get off the bed as quietly as I can and crawl under it. I hide. I wait and wait. I don't hear him. It feels like I've waited forever when I finally decide to get back on the bed. He must have gone. I try not to make a noise just in case he has his ear to the door. I knew this was a bad fucking idea, coming here. I stupidly thought I could trust the monster. I quietly lift my cell to see what time it is. It's three twenty-two. Why the fuck is he awake and trying to get into my room at this time?. I feel sick. My tummy is hurting and I'm sweating, wrapped up in the comforter. I don't know if I can sleep. What if he tries to get in again?

I wake up to knocking on my door and I fly up and scoot to the headboard again like I did earlier. I can see it's light outside, the room is so much brighter. I obviously did fall back to sleep but I don't know for how long. I pick my cell up from the bed. It's ten sixteen. Fuck, I can't remember the last time I slept till this time. Only I didn't get much sleep. I'm sure I was awake half the night from him trying to get in.

"Pink, you awake. Can I come in? I have some breakfast for you and some coffee."

Fuck, I don't want him to see me like this.

"Pink, are you awake? I'll leave it out here. Come get it when you're ready."

I don't move. When I think he's gone, I dash to the bathroom, grabbing my stuff from my bag. I take a very quick dip and then put my face on and do my hair. I can't let him see me without my makeup. It's my mask and what if he recognizes me? I go dark today. It's how I feel. I have dark eye shadows and dark purple lips. I put on my grungy overalls, but I do put on a bright luminous green tee. I move the chair quietly and then unlock the door as quietly as I can. I open it but it creaks. Fuck. I peep out and he's standing there, leaning against the wall. He doesn't smile. He looks pissed. I jump as though surprised to see him.

"Oh crap, you scared the life out of me. What are you doing there?"

He frowns. "I was waiting for you. I made you breakfast, and it was going cold, so I covered it. I knocked on your door and told you it was here."

Oh crap. "Sorry, I was in the bathroom for a while. Just had a shower and got dressed. Had to do my face, you know how it is." Well, actually he doesn't.

He cocks his head. "You look beautiful and I'm sure under all that you are even more beautiful. Come, now you're ready. Let me take this to the table and we can eat. I've already been out for a while. Had a run in the park." He doesn't look like he's had a run. He's in jeans and a tee which is tight and shows off his abs. Not anything like Ryker's but still he's ripped. He takes the tray and walks off with it. I guess this means I need to follow. I walk behind him.

"You don't look like you've been out running," I try to make small talk.

"That's because it was a while ago and I've had a shower and changed since then and made you breakfast."

Okay then. That's telling me. After breakfast, which was a little awkward, I get up to clear the dishes. I then walk over to the windows to look out.

"Oh, my goodness. Look how beautiful it is. Wow, that's a huge park out there. I wondered what the blackness was last night. It's stunning. How can that huge park be in the middle of this mass concrete jungle? I'd love to go walk in there."

He comes up behind me.

"That is the famous Central Park. It's something like six miles long. I'm sure you must have seen it in movies. There are so many movies and TV shows that film there. It's also not safe to be in at night, but it will be good to walk through during the day. I have to go out soon on business. You could either go for a walk in there or wait for me and we'll go together later on." He puts his arms around me like he did last night, and I lean back into him.

"Hmm, this is nice. I like you in my apartment, Pink. You bring color into my life like nothing ever has." I can't see any reflections this time with it being light out. But I can feel him smiling. He gets ready to go out. He gives me a card to operate the elevator. I don't even know what floor this is, I know it's the top floor, but we are so high up, you can see for miles. He gives me a kiss; it's a long, heated kiss and I get butterflies in my tummy, but I also feel nauseous. I pull away before it goes too far.

"Right, you get going. I'll come down with you and I'll go for a walk in the park. Meet you back here later."

He sulks like a big kid because I pulled away. But he takes my hand and we travel down. On the sidewalk, he pulls me to him again and kisses me hard. Then he leaves. I walk to the crossing to see me over the road. He turns to watch me, and I smile and wave. I wait until he's gone around a corner. He's on foot at least. I move quickly. I'm on the park side of the road but I head in his direction. I have no idea where he's going because I have no idea where I am. I see him down a road as I walk near the park railings. I wait until I see him turn again. I cross over, luckily the lights just changed. I run down the road he went down, and I know exactly where he turned, right near this blue car. I slowly look down the road and he's not there. Fuck, I cautiously go down. Then I notice him right up ahead but over the other side. I follow, keeping low, so I'm hidden behind the parked cars. If he turned, he wouldn't see me, unless my fucking hair is on show, that would give me away immediately. I pop up and watch him turn again right near that white car. I stay on my side and as I approach where he turned, I watch him through a car window. He goes into a house just up the road. I watch him ascend the steps. It's right by that black truck. I move down the road where he disappeared into the house, and I note the house numbers. I stop before I get anywhere near the house, and I count the numbers in the sequence I've been following. I turn and walk back the way I came. I need to get back to the park. Once in the park, I get my cell out and I message Poppy.

House number 22650 W Sixtieth street. Check this out. Track the location I was just at.

I start to walk around the park. I grabbed a map at the entrance near the circle and that statue. A man wanted ten dollars for it, I told him no, but he gave it to me anyway. I walk for a long time. It's so beautiful in here and there are so many people doing all sorts of things. I come across the Belvedere Castle and go up to the top. I love this. Then I watch young boys around turtle lake with strings trying to catch the turtles. The little blighters catch one, so I ask them to let it go. The other turtles come up to take the food, then disappear again. I sit watching it all. I love it here. I look at my cell and see it's almost three. I've been here forever. I need to head back. He will be worried if he's back and I haven't given him my cell number. I don't want him to track my cell.

There's a message from Poppy.

Are you okay? What is this address? I have someone looking into it. Please let me know you are safe.

I am safe, yes. I just wanted you to check it out. Don't worry about me. I will explain all when I get back.

I reply but then I delete the messages to and from Poppy. If he was to get into my cell, I don't want him to see.

I step off the elevator and into his apartment. He comes barreling toward me.

"Where the fuck have you been? I've been here just waiting, not fucking knowing where the fuck you were or even being able to get in fucking touch with you. I've been fucking worried sick thinking something fucking happened to you or you got fucking lost." He's shouting and swearing at me right in my face, towering over me to intimidate me like I'm some little girl. I cower away from him, backing up, but he just moves with me. The look of anger on his face scares the fuck out of me. I think he's going to hit me at one point and I raise a hand to my face. Then I think of Poppy and what she would do. I stand up tall, making myself look bigger and I push back. I poke a finger in his chest, getting him to give me space. The look on his face is comical. Like he can't believe I'm coming back at him, well I'll show him.

"Don't you dare fucking scream in my face like I'm ten years old again. Who the fuck do you think you are? You don't own me. I'm a free woman and can do what the fuck I like. So back the fuck off or I leave right now, and you will never fucking see me again. Yes, I can fucking say fuck as well."

Wow, I feel empowered and in control, just like Poppy told me to be. He looks kind of shocked. He stands staring at me, not speaking, but looking at me quizzically. He runs his hand through his hair, then he starts to laugh. He laughs so hard he bends over. I stand with my arms folded over my chest, staring at him with my head cocked. I don't laugh. He looks up to me and laughs even harder. I just wait and tap my foot. He then stops laughing and the next thing I know, he's assaulting my mouth with his. He's taking it hard and frantic. He bites my lip and I squeal, that hurt. I push him off me. I've had people treat me like this in the past and I am not going there.

"That fucking hurt, Steve," I say, wiping at my mouth and see blood on the back of my hand.

He looks at me, not quite knowing what to say or do. He's scaring me, to be honest. I can give as good as I get now, I'm not the stupid, naive little girl I used to be and I'm sure he could overpower me if he wanted to. I turn and walk to my room, where I lock it behind me. It's a good fifteen minutes before I hear his knock.

"Pink, please open the door. I'm sorry about the way I just reacted. I was scared. So fucking scared, I've never been scared of anything since my papa, but you scared me. I thought something had happened to you and I've only just found you. Please open the door."

I go into the bathroom to clean up and redo some of my makeup. I make him wait for ten minutes. Then I open the door and walk out. I have to step over him as he's sitting leaning against the wall next to the door. I get myself a water from the kitchen, as I turn, he's standing there leaning against the wall with his arms folded.

"I'm sorry. Please accept my apology. I was just scared and that's a really new feeling for me. Believe me." He gives me a small smile and I just shrug my shoulders. He walks to me and stands in front of me. He crouches slightly, placing his arms around my waist and joining his hands at my back. He bows to my face. "Do you accept my apology, Pink?"

I look at him and nod. He smiles, then leans in and kisses me very gently this time.

"You were hot as fuck giving me what for. It really turned me on, which is why I kissed you like I did. I'm sorry I hurt these gorgeous lips," he says, peppering me with kisses between each word and being gentle where he bit me.

"Okay, apology accepted, this time, but you scared the crap out of me coming at me like that. I thought you were going to hit me or something. I'm sorry I shouted back, but don't treat me like a little kid, okay?" He nods.

"Are you ready to go out and see the sights now? I don't have any work left for today, but I will have to do some tomorrow." He plays with a strand of my hair between his fingers.

"Yes, I'm ready."

We head out and I tell him about the park and what I saw. We spend the day doing all the tourist things. We stop at an amazing steak house for dinner, then we spend time with me in awe at all the people in Times Square. It's late when we get back home, and I go straight to bed. Locking my door and putting the chair up against it like last night. I've had a great day.

He did it again. He woke me up. This time it was two fifty. He was trying the door again, only this time he wasn't being quiet about it. I scooted back again, thinking he was going to force it open. Then I hid under the bed like last night. I must have got uncomfortable and woke up under there banging my head, not realizing where I was. I climbed back into bed, and it took me ages to get back to sleep. He's just woke me up by knocking again. It's light out this time. It's déjà vu. I do what I did yesterday, get ready before leaving the bedroom. This time, he has the breakfast set out on the table for us to eat.

"Why have you tried to get into my room the last two nights early in the morning hours?" I ask as soon as I sit down. I want to know. He said he would respect me and my wishes. He carries on buttering his toast before he looks at me. Then he takes a bite before he decides to answer. He shrugs.

"I was just testing the waters. Have you any idea how hard it is for me to sleep in the next room. Knowing the girl I'm mad about is in a room next to mine. I couldn't help myself. I thought if your door was unlocked, it was a sign you wouldn't mind me coming in. I just wanted to lie next to you." He shrugs again.

"It's a good thing the door has a lock on it, then. If it didn't, you would have presumed incorrectly. I told you, I hardly know you and I'm not like that. I need time. You scared the life out of me, so much so I hid under the bed. I've not slept well the last two nights here because of it." He looks hurt and upset.

"I'm sorry, I didn't want you to be scared. That's the last fucking thing I would want. I shouldn't have done it; I should have been able to control myself. This is all new to me too. I'm not used to having a woman sleep in the same place as me, but not in my bed. I'm learning. Shall we go out to see more sights today? Then we can get our flight back later this evening if that's okay with you? I have to slip out for a little while. I won't be long. Will you wait here for me this time, so I don't panic thinking you are lost or hurt? New York can be a very scary place. As you saw yesterday with the number of people there are."

He sounds really genuine.

"Okay but I will come down with you, have a quick walk around the zoo I spotted on the map yesterday, then come straight back. If I'm not back when you get back, I promise I will only be in the zoo area. Is that okay?" He gets up and kisses the top of my head.

"Perfect."

We both head down together. I cross the road again at the crossing like yesterday and he waits to make sure I'm across before going in the same direction he did yesterday. I walk into the park but then double back to walk the direction he is walking. I can't see him, so I need to be careful. I get my cell out and message Poppy.

Track my cell for a few minutes.

I come out near what I now know is Columbus Circle. I spot him going down the same road as yesterday. I follow, only this time he heads in a different direction. I stay behind, low and follow. It's a different road, but another house he goes into. I count the numbers and just as I get a little nearer, he comes out. He looks both ways, then goes farther up the road. He didn't see me. I was on the opposite side of the road; the thing is, there was a woman I could see only a little of and I swear it was Vera. I nearly had heart failure when I saw him come out. I follow again and this time he goes into another house on another road. I make a note and I head back to the park. I run in the park and head to the zoo just in case he comes looking for me. I'm shaking. What if it was Vera? I message the house numbers and road names to Poppy. She's going to wonder what I'm doing.

I'm walking around the zoo looking at the animals when I feel some-one behind me. I suddenly turn, ready to roundhouse whoever it is, it's

Steve. I should have known he'd find me. I've only been here about half an hour.

"Hey, you, that was quick. I don't feel I've been here that long." He smiles and kisses the tip of my nose. We walk around hand in hand for a little while, then we leave.

I had a great time in New York. We're on our way home on the jet. I will see Poppy first thing tomorrow. I need to tell her what I think. I'm almost sure the houses he went into were trafficking houses. I need Poppy to look into them. If they are, then we have him.

Twenty

Steve

I'VE HAD A GREAT TIME IN NEW YORK WITH HER. SPENDING THAT time watching the awe on her face at all the new sights. Sights she's only seen on the TV and now she's gotten to experience them in real life, and I was able to do that for her. It was me putting the awe on her fucking beautiful face, I just wish it was put there with me fucking her. I know I spooked her a few times, and I nearly ripped her fucking head off as soon as she walked in, because she wasn't home when I got back. That was out of order. She was right, I treated her like a little girl, but I was terrified. Me. Fucking terrified. That's something I never thought I would say. I'm just not used to these feelings. I was frantic, thinking someone had taken my Pink, and was going to do God knows what with and to her. I wanted to go out and kill whoever had taken her. Rip their fucking heads off. I was so angry because I had no control. I now know I was feeling like that because it's what happens with my girls. We take them. We literally rip them away from society and their families, never to be found or seen again. I had visions of that happening to Pink, and me not having control over it. I was losing my mind. I even ripped some of my hair out, pulling on it, thinking it was happening to my girl. I think nothing of it with the girls I do it to. Maybe that's because I don't literally do it. My men do it and I don't actually see what happens to them. I now know what their loved ones must feel, Yet I feel no remorse for it.

When she walked in like nothing was wrong, I just flew at her. The look on her face was one of utter fear and panic, she cowered away from me. I hated being like that, but I was relieved she came back. I then saw the moment on her face where she realized she didn't have to take this from me and she fucking turned on me. Well, I found it hilarious. The first thirty seconds, I wanted to rip her head off for daring to speak to me that way. Then as she went on, getting in my face and pushing me back with her finger, I was elated, and it turned me on big style. My fucking cock was rigid. How she didn't notice I have no idea, but then she was ranting in my face, so I guess she wouldn't think to look how turned on I was. When she went to her room, I rushed to mine. I needed to have a fucking jerk before I went and did something to her. I pulled my jeans and boxers down and I grabbed him. I couldn't wait to get into the bathroom. I stood behind my door. The relief I felt when I started to pull on him. I looked down and watched my hand moving up and down and over the tip. The cum was seeping out into my hand, lubricating it. He was standing tall and proud with his huge purple head staring at me. I licked my lips. I banged my head on the back of the door as I tugged harder and harder. I closed my eyes and I pictured her.

She was sitting on the chair with her legs spread wide open. I imagined her pussy to be hairless, with just a little pink strip down the middle to match her head hair. I could visualize her so clearly in my mind. She would suck on her finger and trail it down her naked body to her pussy, where she would insert it and play with herself as I looked on. Then she would suck the same finger, making noise to let me know how much she was turned on by watching me. I would stand with my cock in hand pumping away in front of her while watching her fingers repeat the same path. She would pull her feet onto the chair with her knees spread wide. I would watch her play with her clit and watch those fucking luscious pink lips pucker up with the noise and her breathing getting more and more labored. I would bat her hand away, not wanting her to climax. Then I would pull her head forward, making her lower her legs and I would put my cock on her lips and spread my cum over those pink juicy lips and watch as her tongue would dart out to taste me. I would then fuck her mouth until my cum was spewing down the back of her throat. She would look up into my eyes all the time and I would watch her, mesmerized by her mouth and tongue.

Once finished, I'd kneel in front of her and spread her legs so wide, lifting them over my shoulders and I would bury my face deep inside that pink pussy. Spreading her lips with my finger and tonguing her clit. She'd be squirming on the seat, sliding back and forth. I'd insert my fingers and find her G-spot. I would make her climax so hard she'd scream at the top of her lungs, calling my name. I'd lap all the juices flooding out of her. Once I licked her dry, I'd take my cock and play in her pussy folds, up and down and around and around not quite entering her. Just to get her going again. My cock would be rock hard yet again from tongue fucking her pussy. I would grab her by the ass and pull her forward, impaling her with my cock as she landed on my thighs. I'd grab those ass cheeks and squeeze them while making her rise up and down on my cock. She would ride me as I impaled her with every bounce onto him. In no time, we would be riding out mind shattering orgasms together. Her pulling at my hair screaming my name, jutting her fucking beautiful globes into my face where I'd suck on a nipple so fucking hard and nibble it. She would scream and scream until she nearly passed out and I'd empty my cum deep inside her. Once she was on her back, spent, I'd then tongue her pussy one last time, savoring the taste of us mixed together. Together forever.

My mind was so vivid with all that I hadn't realized I was shouting her name as I was squirting my cum all over my hand. It dripped all down my arm and all over the floor. I thought to myself, *God, I can't wait to be able to do all that with her.* I can see her being a real firecracker when she's thick in the throes of passion. I hoped she didn't hear me shouting and grunting. Fuck.

We are sitting outside her building. I don't want to say goodbye, but I know I have to.

"It was a great few days away. It would be great if we could do that a lot more. What do you think?"

I see the look of panic cross her face for a fleeting second, then it's gone. I frown.

"It would, I agree. Just I have two jobs and it's not that easy to get away like that. They were both very good about the short notice, because, well, I've never really had any time off for a long time. I would definitely love to do it again though. I had an amazing time with you. Thank you, Steve."

She leans in and kisses me. This is the first time she's ever really instigated a kiss. That's fucking progress in my eyes. It won't be long before I'm in her panties. I can feel it. My cock starts to get rock hard. I shuffle slightly to try to maneuver him into a comfy position. She pulls away and looks at me quizzically. I look to my cock then back to her, raising an eyebrow in a sorry. She looks down and I see her eyes go wide. She smiles, then kisses my lips quickly.

"Okay then, time for me to leave. Sorry," she says, smiling at my cock.

The little witch. She has to know she does this all the time to me. I think back to my room and the images I had of her on that chair. That is not helping my situation. Maybe I need to try to move this along a little bit faster. Start by worshiping her body 'cause I feel for the first time ever I want to do that. I want to lick every inch of it and feel every bit of it. Right, time to head home.

I've just walked into my Santa Monica home, and I have images of her in here the other night. She was throwing up. I think there was more to it than the shock or the food. I definitely feel there is something underlying happening there. I check my watch. It's still not too late, almost ten. I walk into my office and suddenly remember the stuff in the safe from my papa's house. I had forgotten about it, and I should have gone back to check the place was bulldozed and all flattened now. I've been too wrapped up in Pink and my business in New York. The good news is we've opened seven more houses. I just managed to visit three that are all in the same neighborhood and they are booming. You would never know what went on in those houses. They look like every other house. I had the walls insulated and it's all soundproofed in every room, so the neighbors don't hear. The only thing is that if any of the neighbors are nosy and see men coming and going at all hours, it may raise suspicion. I checked out the areas before purchasing them, and most of the houses are residential but there are an awful lot that are second homes and not lived in all the time. I have two of my houses positioned between such houses, which is perfect. The other one does have a full-time resident, but it's a young man who is out most of the time working his ass off to pay for his house that is way over his budget.

There are a lot of new girls now, and I have recruited some new men, well my men have recruited new men. All of them vetted. Vera is in one of the houses and she's doing a good job, just like she always does. It's why I pay her good money and give her a cut of the profits. She is overseeing the three that are close together. They are raking it in as the word gets out. I think back to the last couple of days and when I thought Pink had been taken. It's the first thing that comes to mind, because it's what I know. I know how it all works. Most of my girls are coaxed with a promise of fame and fortune in the US, they mostly come from eastern Europe. They are the ones that want the American dream. Easy pickings. Some of the girls are kidnapped, but not as many as we used to do. That's why my automatic thought was Pink had been taken. I know there are a few smaller trafficking rings around, but mine is the biggest, and it's growing like wildfire.

I've given instructions to take the other rings out and burn the premises down. I have lined up more properties to purchase. I've been thinking of buying a hotel. Used specifically for my trafficking. Not a place that just anyone can check into, just the customers, for as long as they want. I will have different options on a menu for them to choose from. They can check in for a day or a week, whatever they fucking want. It's genius. I've got two hotels I'm looking at. I want them to have private underground entrances, strict rules on what can be brought in like no cell phones, and a lot of soundproofing to be done. I thought about turning them into exclusive hotel clubs. Either with membership or pay as you go. I know doing this will bring in the big bucks. This will bring in a lot of the A-listers and B-listers, the millionaires and the billionaires. These will be huge business for me.

I open my walk-in safe and look at the shit from his house. I knock a journal by accident, and it lands on the floor. I pick it up and it's open on a page dated just before I was born, and I see Kirill mentioned a few times. I start to read it. I can't believe what I'm reading. I walk to my desk and sit, reading it properly. Apparently when Kirill was fucking and had my papa there, they quite often fucked the same women at the same time. I could never imagine sharing Pink with any fucker. I'd kill any fucker that touched her other than me. One of these women was Dimitri's mama. Apparently, they both fucked her but when she got pregnant, she had the baby, then Kirill killed her. That was a couple of years before I was born but my papa put it in this section. I pour myself a vodka, a large one. It goes on about my papa having feelings for one of these women they fucked. He started seeing her on the sly, so Kirill didn't find out. He would fuck her every chance he got. He and Kirill had fucked her at the same time once or twice but then it was just my papa. This woman got pregnant. It was with me. My papa was happy. I've never known him to be happy. He wanted to marry this woman. He told Kirill, who just laughed in his face and told him what a fucking fool he was. It jumps to me being born to Oksana. I like that name. I never knew my mama's name. Papa always said she was a whore and died in childbirth. He was bitter and angry all the time. If I asked who my mama was and for him to tell me about her, he would backhand me and throw me into the basement. I soon learned to keep my mouth shut.

When I was born, my papa was happy, he had a son and heir. A son that could have carried on his name and become someone in the Bratva. What a disappointment I must have been. I laugh to myself. When I was a few months old, my papa had a visit from Kirill. Apparently, my papa was too smitten with me and didn't do his job as he should, which led to Kirill being shot. It was only a superficial wound in the arm, but they could have killed him. Kirill visited my papa and told him to get his fucking head on straight, that having a kid didn't stop him from doing his job. They argued about it, then apparently my mama walked in with me in her arms. My papa said she froze on seeing Kirill and that when Kirill saw her, he went mad and started to lay into my papa. My papa didn't know why but Kirill beat him so bad that he couldn't talk for a while. He needed his jaw wired together. My mama became a different woman after that encounter and my papa knew there was something wrong.

Once he was mended and was able to talk, one night he forced her to tell him what that was all about with Kirill. Why the fuck did he take a beating for her? She broke down and told him that he wasn't the father to her baby. She told him Kirill was the father. My papa went mad, and he snapped her neck, right then. He couldn't believe it, but he knew something wasn't right. He wrote about how my eyes were the same color as Kirill and Dimitri's and how he thought it odd, as he had brown eyes and my mama had green eyes. He said there was no way he would give me up and he didn't think Kirill knew the baby was his. He wanted me, he wanted to keep me so I would carry on his name, without anyone knowing. Why the fuck should Kirill have all the kids and women.

I pour more vodka. I can't believe what I'm reading. Is this fucking real? Kirill is my papa. My real papa. All this fucking time, I lived this shitty fucking life while Dimitri and Igor had everything they wanted. All this time my papa beat me and treated me like a fucking rabid dog because in the end his hatred took over and he hated me for who I really was, not his blood. It wasn't my fucking fault. But holy fuck, I'm second in line, it should have been me ruling Bratva all along after Kirill died. Not Igor. Igor who is my fucking real brother. Does he know? Did he find out and that's why he tossed me aside? I bet he fucking knows. Now I know why I have the same eyes as him and Dimitri. We are all brothers. I'm a fucking real Ustrashkins. How the fuck did I not know? This is blowing my mind. I should be the Pakhan, it should be fucking me. I don't need to kill Igor and his family. I just need to take control from him. He's my little brother, after all. A real fucking brother. He's ruled all this time when it should have been me. ARGHHHHHHH. I scream at the top of my lungs. I'm fuming. I start throwing shit about and breaking what I can. I need a release. I need to get out of here and break something or someone. I need out.

I leave the apartment, grabbing my jacket as I do. I walk to the pier. It's a good twenty-minute walk but I need to walk to try and shake off this destructive feeling inside me. I want to find a woman and fuck her so hard it kills her. I want to find a thug and beat him so hard, making him bleed and cracking his skull when I've finished. I want to find Igor and rip his fucking head off. He was never meant to be the Pakhan, after Kirill killed Dimitri, it would have gone to me.

I bypass a liquor store. I look in as I walk past. I double back. One, there was a fucking woman with pink hair, and two, I need more vodka. I'm going to sit on the beach and try to fathom out what I just read. It's all jumbled up inside me. I walk in and the pink hair turns around. Fuck, she must only be about twelve or something. I'm glad I don't really want to take my anger out on someone that looks like my girl. Just then I see a young white guy looking shady. He has on a Starter cap and a big fuck-ing puffer coat. We're in fucking LA. No one wears puffer coats. He looks dirty. His jean shorts have holes in them and are dirty, his sneakers are old and dirty, and I can see holes in the side of one of them. He's moving from foot to foot in the same spot, slightly jittery. I wonder if he's alone. I move around to the beers, and I can see up in the mirror on the wall what is going on in the shop. There is the pink girl who it looks like she is with her mama. Then there is another guy, he is black and has a Starter cap on. I see him nod to the white guy in the puffer coat.

I watch it play out. The white guy moves up to the guy behind the register just as the young pink girl leaves with her mama. He pulls out a gun. I watch the other black guy move to the white guy. He hands over a backpack, which I didn't see in the mirror. I hear them shout, telling the clerk to empty the register and put the cash in the bag along with ciga-rettes and spirits. They throw another backpack at him and tell him to move it. I quietly move around the store and make my way to the exit. No, I'm not leaving. I'm going to show these two punks not to mess with me. They are either that fucking stupid or that fucking high, because neither of them notice me. Fuck it.

I walk up to the white guy who has the gun and I tap him on the shoulder. He spins around with the gun in his hand. I disarm him in one swoop, bending his wrist right back, breaking it. He screams out. The black guy has tried to bypass me. The fucking pussy was leaving his partner. I trip him up while I still have hold of the white guy's wrist. He falls face-first into the closed door. Yes, I closed it before I moved over to them and put the closed sign on. I bring my foot up to the back of the white guy's knee and I make him fall forward while snapping his leg. I let him go. I have the gun. It's not like he can do much with a broken wrist and leg.

I grab the black guy by the scruff of his neck and lift him up to his feet.

"Please don't hurt me. Please. I didn't have the gun. It was his idea. I don't even know him. Please don't hurt me."

I don't believe him for one minute. This guy is the leader. He gave the signal to the other guy. I put his head through the door window. Then I pull him back and I break his legs, both of them. Now he can't run. I throw some cash down onto the counter and ask the clerk for a bottle of vodka and tell him to call 911. I tell him to wipe the footage, I don't want the police to come knocking. He's shaken up, I can see that, but he does what I ask. I move the guy away from the door and I leave. There, I've done my duty and released some anger.

I feel much better. I sit on the beach, but I don't drink my vodka. I decide I need a clear head. Alcohol never helps me. At least I broke some bones without fucking killing anyone. I head back to my apartment. The fresh air and the violence have worked wonders. I can now sit and think about things. There is no way Igor will believe any of this if I approach him. Even if I show him what was written down in the journal. Even if he did believe me, he wouldn't give up being the Pakhan. No way. I know he says he doesn't really want it and who knows, maybe he would give it up with having five kids. Maybe this could be an out? Would he really? I don't fucking know. Do I chance speaking to him and showing him? Maybe we can take a DNA test, or do I kill them all as planned? I think it has to be the latter. We don't even make small talk these days. I still wonder if he knows and that's why he distanced himself from me and treats me like shit.

I couldn't fucking sleep last night. One, I was having vivid thoughts of Pink again and what I'm going to do to her, so I was coming a lot last night and, two, I made a few calls and have some of my men meeting me tomorrow, the loyal-to-me Bratva men. I have some things to discuss, and I have a lot of money and promises to help me do the talking.

I'm on my way to walk Pink to work. I arrive and wait. There is no sign of her. I thought she said she had a shift today at the coffee shop. I head there to see if she's already at work. I look through the window until I see that other woman is coming from the back. She jumps at the sight of me. I mouth sorry, she comes to the door.

"Vi isn't in today," is all she says and shuts the door, locking it.

Fuck her and fuck, where is she? I needed my Pink fix to help me through today. I have some tough decisions to make.

Twenty-One

Vidana

I COULDN'T SLEEP MUCH LAST NIGHT. I WAS THINKING ABOUT STEVE and our trip. I was thinking how when I confronted him and faced up to him, he really enjoyed it. I thought he would have been the opposite. I messaged Poppy to tell her I need to see her urgently. She's meeting me at the refuge at ten. I spend time in my room until then. I head out to meet her, all the while looking around me to see if I'm being followed. After following Steve the last couple of days, I see how easy it is to follow someone and them never know. I reckon with his job he could follow anyone around and never be seen unless he wanted to be seen. I grab a Starbucks and a muffin as I walk to the refuge. I walk to Poppy's office and knock. I wait this time, there is no need to rush in.

"Come in," she shouts, and I do. She looks up and smiles. "It's not like you to knock and wait for an invite." She laughs, having a slight dig. I laugh back. "Before we start on what you want to see me about, I have some news for you. We found your mama and your sisters." I gasp, placing my hands over my mouth.

"Now, before you get too excited, listen to me. It's not all good news. In fact, I'm fucking fuming."

Oh god, I feel tears forming in my eyes. I wipe them away. She hands me a tissue.

"Right, your mama moved far from where you lived. She moved to another old mining town far away, I suspect where no one knew her or who she was. They have all been living in squalor, Dana. Your sisters are not in very good health. All of them have health issues. I don't have it confirmed yet, but they all seemed malnourished at first sight and very dirty.

Your mama is the opposite. She is healthy and looks extremely good. My men have intercepted your sisters and they are on their way here. They are being looked after and have all been cleaned, clothed, and fed. They should be here tomorrow."

I squeal and get out of my chair and move around to hug Poppy.

"You're amazing, Poppy. I don't know what I would do without you. I would probably be dead if it wasn't for you and Igor and now thanks to you two you are probably saving their lives." I cry hard.

"I need to prepare you, Dana. You've been through it, and you've helped so many others through it." She grabs my hands, standing up. "Your mama has been using your sisters. Our men spotted different men coming and taking your sisters out. Some on their own, some would take two or three. They haven't seen anyone take your youngest sister, Zoya, so we think she is okay. My men started to follow, and they were appalled at what they found. Your sisters were taken to a salon for intimate services. These places have been popping up all over Russia. It is legalized prostitution. But these particular salons which are behind steel doors in an apartment block are for the selling of young children, to use their bodies. Your mama would allow your sisters to be taken and she would get a cut of whatever they made."

I scream out, I can't believe our mama would do that to her own children. I collapse to the floor. How can this happen to all of us? How can it be? I cry curled up on the floor. Poppy sits next to me and pulls me to her side.

"It's okay, Vidana, they are safe now. They are on their way here. Nothing will ever happen to them again. I need you to have your meltdown now, because when they arrive tomorrow, they will need you to be as strong as you can be. The strongest you have ever been. They will need you, Vidana, they will want their sister and you can show them that there is life after the abuse. I'm so sorry, sweetie." She hugs me to her to let me have a meltdown.

After my sobs subside, I look up to her.

"What about her, Poppy? The vile thing called Mama. I hope she dies a horrible death." She looks at me with sorrow in her eyes and nods.

"Igor gave his men the go-ahead to destroy her. He wished it was him doing it. He was beside himself, knowing he could have brought you all here with Svetlana, and none of this would have happened to any of you. He thought by eliminating your papa, you would all be safe. In reality, it was your mama that you all needed saving from. Your mama is dead. Our men gave her a slow, painful death, one to reflect what she has done to her children. I will not go into it but just know she is no longer alive and able to harm any of them." I smile inwardly, knowing she's gone. I hate her for putting them through this. Using their little bodies. It's funny, I still think of them all as being little, but they are mostly grown up now. I need to mentally prepare myself for their arrival.

"Let's get you a coffee and then we can talk more. Do you want to stay here or come with me to the dining room?"

"I'll stay here please, Poppy. I can't face anyone right now."

She leaves to get us coffees. I get in the chair and sit crying. Not for the loss of my mama, but the loss of my sisters' souls. I have to help them regain them. They have a long road ahead of them. Poppy is gone for a good twenty minutes; she must have gotten held up with something. It gives me time to get into my head the reality of our lives. They may blame me for leaving them. They won't know what happened to me. There is no way Mama would have told them anything other than I ran away and abandoned them. I need to make sure they know it wasn't like that. I suspect Dominika will be the most upset and will probably hate me. I have to tell them what happened to me and how Igor and Poppy saved my life and now they have saved theirs. Poppy arrives back with the coffee.

"Sorry, I got stopped and had to just sort something out. Before we move on, do you want to move back in here for a while, so you can be with your sisters? It's completely up to you but I want you to know there is a room for you if you do. Now, have a drink, then tell me what you wanted to talk to me about. I presume it has something to do with the addresses you messaged to me."

I nod and take a few sips of my coffee. I wipe my eyes and compose myself and then I tell her everything I know about Steve and his alias Alborz. As soon as I mention that name, she rises from her seat and starts to pace. She grabs her cell and tells Igor to meet us here. Oh fuck.

"Poppy, please don't hate me for not telling you sooner. I just wasn't one-hundred-percent sure it was him. Then following him and seeing Vera; I knew one hundred percent it was him. Please don't hate me."

"Oh, Vidana, I'm angry because you put yourself in danger like that. If he had caught you following him, you could have ended up back in that business of his or worse still, dead. But I don't hate you, sweetie, you are brave and stupid, that's for sure." I smile at her.

"I keep thinking I must have Stockholm syndrome. I am so attracted to him, but he was never my abuser. I know he was in charge and his voice saved me but is it the same thing?" She thinks for a minute before speaking.

"There is no way of knowing, to be honest. Stockholm syndrome is a thing, but it can come in many forms. You said his voice practically saved you. That is the same thing. You have this fixation on him. It's understandable."

"But he treats me so well. I told you the other day he is so nice. Is there a bad side to him? I think he's in love with me and I love him. He's a monster and I think I'm a monster for loving him. It's making me think there is something wrong with me. I also love Ryker but in a different way than Steve, I'm so confused with everything." She hugs me to her.

"There is nothing wrong with you. You think he saved you, but he didn't. He put you in that place to begin with. He did this to you regardless of if he touched you or not. I think it's more adoration because his voice saved you and kept you sane. Giving you something to hang on to instead of just giving up. I think it's definitely Stockholm syndrome, it's not love you feel for him. It's probably love you feel for Ryker." Just then, I feel nauseous, and turn as the door opens and Igor walks in. He looks annoyed and I get up and grab the trash can to throw up. I get handed a tissue, It's Igor's hand. He's not angry, at least not with me.

"I'm sorry Igor. For everything." He smiles and then he takes hold of me, he pulls me in gently and hugs me to his strong chest. I feel uncomfortable, but I don't move. He suddenly pulls away.

"I'm sorry, Vidana, that was inappropriate of me. I just needed to hold you, to let you know nothing is on you at all. You were innocent in all of this. I'm the one that is sorry for not taking you all when I brought Svetlana. I should have just killed your mama and brought you all back. I didn't know it was your mama you all needed saving from. Svetlana never said a thing. Then again, Svetlana was the most selfish person I ever met." I look up to him and nod.

"Thank you, Igor. I should never have blamed you when I got here. You have helped not only me but now my sisters and I shall be forever grateful to you both." He nods and takes a seat. I run through everything I know about Steve. I tell him my initial thoughts where I questioned if he, Igor, knew about it but just didn't tell Poppy. Was he into the sex trafficking also? I watch as his jaw tightens and clicks, the angrier he gets. He looks at me with sorrow and then such disdain at my suggestion that he knew or had something to do with it.

"I knew we had someone on the inside, but I would never have suspected Steve. He runs the Darvish Cartel. It's his fucking cartel."

"Wait, that's the name the doorman at his New York apartment used. He called him Mr. Darvish. I thought it was odd as it didn't sound Russian with his papa being Russian."

"He's as fucking American as they come, yes his papa was Russian. He's not even fucking Iranian. How the fuck did he pull this off and right under my nose? I knew he was pissed at me for overlooking him when I took Andrey to be my man at arms and Ivan to be my third. I only took him on as my man at arms after they got killed because I trusted him. He was the only person apart from Dimitri I ever trusted. I know we grew apart when my papa made me who I am today, but I still considered him a brother when we were growing up. I should have known he would betray me. He must have an ulterior motive. There is something that drove him to do this. He wants to be in control. He always wanted to be in control. He tried to control me as kids, always planning what we were going to do and when, as though looking after me. Well, I guess this is where he found control. He knows I abolished all sex trafficking when I took over from my papa. I didn't know my papa was into it until I took over. I killed everyone involved. It sickens me. I would never have any dealings with sex trafficking, Vidana. Never." I smile at him, and Poppy gets up and walks behind him. She puts her arms around his neck and kisses his head.

"She just had to know for sure, Igor. Vidana didn't really know any of us, and in her head, you took Svetlana away and killed her papa." He kisses her hand, then turns back to me with such sorrow.

"Those addresses you gave Poppy, I had them checked out last night. I had men undercover go to them. They are used for sex trafficking. You did good, Vidana. I can't tell you what you have just done. We will be able to bring down the Darvish Cartel once and for all. They are one of the biggest sex traffickers. I know they take girls, some so very young from their families. Some of his men offer money to them, promising them a good life, others are just grabbed off the streets and their families never see them again. Grabbed like you were Vidana. I just can't imagine anything like it, or what you went through. You have just helped us immensely. Doing what my men couldn't do. You found out who was behind it. I can't thank you enough. Now you have told me this, I suspect Steve will have some kind of plans in place. I have my men following him. I told him I didn't need him today, but that I need him first thing in the morning. I know it's a lot to ask but if you see him today, do you think you can just be normal with him?"

Oh god, I don't know. I know too much and now I have confirmation of those houses. I know it's him a hundred percent. I don't know. I start to breathe heavily and start to shiver. I know this means I'm going into shock. Poppy moves quick. She's out the door fast, but returns with a warm blanket. She smothers me with it and wraps her arms around me.

"Breathe with me, Vidana. In and out. Slow breaths, follow me. In… and out… in… and out… that's my girl. You're doing great." Igor passes me some water and I sip it slowly. I can feel myself calming down. I nod,

"Yes, I can do it for today at least, I think."

"Great, just don't go anywhere alone with him. Poppy mentioned he has an apartment in Santa Monica, and you stayed in his apartment in New York? Do you know the addresses by any chance?" I tell him the name of the building but that's all I have.

"Thank you, Vidana. You have been amazing and let me tell you now, anything you ever need or want to help you and your sisters, all you have to do is ask. Please, never, ever be afraid to ask either of us. We are here for you and your sisters, always. I also have to tell you because I don't know if you ever knew but…" He looks to Poppy, and she nods. "I know you have gone through so much today and I hope this is a little joy for you, our eldest daughter Sabina, well, she is your niece. You are family, you are her aunty and you and your sisters will always be welcome in our home. Sabina was the result of me and Svetlana, it should never have happened. She lied to me about her age. Anyway, I am grateful we have Sabina. I will tell you the story when all this is over, and I will introduce you to her when you and your sisters are ready. She will be thrilled to have aunties and some who are not much older than she is."

I cry, oh my god, I have a niece and I never knew. I won't question why they have never told me, not yet anyway, but…

"I didn't want to tell you until I thought you were ready, Vidana. You have shown me what an amazing, strong, selfless woman you are, and I would be grateful for Sabina to have such an amazing role model like her aunt Vidana," Poppy says, squeezing my hand. Igor leaves, I suspect he has a lot to get organized on how to take Steve down. It sounds like it's going to happen very quickly. Igor obviously doesn't mess around, especially when it comes to sex trafficking.

"Poppy, how are you going to have room for all the girls if you take down Steve's sex ring? You don't have the room for my sisters and me to stay if you are going to have all these new girls arriving any day now. I don't want to be a burden on you. But…"

She stops me. "You and your sisters will never be a burden on us. I have been setting up another refuge this last couple of years. That's why I've been so busy. It's not far from here but it's ready to take on twice as many girls as we can take here. This will be my base. I have the other one staffed and I have an amazing lady looking after it. They are all set for any new girls. If I have to open ten refuge centers, then I will, to help girls like you out. I will gladly kill any man I ever see mistreat a female, or knowingly mistreat one. You say Steve, as far as you know, didn't hurt any girls personally, well that's one thing and he's treated you with respect. He can't be all bad, just bad enough to own the sex ring and take all the wealth from it. That's bad enough in my eyes." I am in awe of her even more. How she has the time with her big family, I will never know.

I stay at the refuge for the rest of the day helping out. I need to keep my mind active. I'm excited for my sisters to arrive but I'm also apprehensive about it. Not knowing the reaction I will get from Dominika, Iskra,

Clara, and Zoya. Just saying their names has tears streaming down my face. I'm also really hiding here, from Steve.

I know I have to leave at some point and I'm sure he's going to be waiting for me somewhere. I stay later than normal, trying to avoid him. I walk out, keeping a firm grip on my fanny pack and not looking around at anyone. I have my AirPods in and I walk fast toward home. I hope he isn't around. I really don't want to see him. I make it to my building with no sign of him. I breathe out in relief, taking a pod from an ear. Just as I pass the seating area in the lobby, I hear my name and I automatically freeze. Fuck. It's him. I turn slowly to see him standing by a chair. He smiles widely at me and walks over.

"Hey, gorgeous, I missed you today. I waited for you this morning to walk you to the coffee shop but there was no you. Sybil said you weren't in today." Fuck, he went looking for me. It's like he's stalking me, or it feels like it. I smile, not trying to look nervous.

"Hey yourself. Aww, did you? Yeah, I was at the refuge all day today. How are you?" He looks at me funny, then leans in to kiss me. I automatically step back; he pulls back and squints at me.

"What's wrong?" He cocks his head.

"Sorry, nothing. I'm just tired, it's been a long and challenging day. I'm drained." I step forward and raise up on my toes to kiss him. He smiles as I do. He pulls me into him and kisses me harder.

"God, I missed you today. I wanted to see you so badly. After spending all that time with you in New York, I felt lost without you today. Do you fancy coming back to mine for the night? I could get a chef in to cook you something nice. I don't know if I will see you tomorrow. I have to be at Igor's early."

"I missed you too. Can we have a rain check though please? I ate at the refuge and I'm exhausted. You know I didn't sleep well in New York." I raise my eyebrows at him. "If you're not working late tomorrow night, we could go back to yours. How does that sound?" I rise up to kiss his lips again. I'm trying to be a little provocative and sensual, but have no idea how to do that, or even if it's working. "Okay, but I have missed you. Not even a quick drink or a little snack?" I smile at him and shake my head.

"I'm going straight to bed. I have a big day again tomorrow. I'm at the refuge all day, we have some new girls arriving plus the new girls that arrived today, and they need me again tomorrow. I really am sorry. Let's make a date for tomorrow night. I should be finished about eight thirtyish if you can drop by." He pulls me into him and I have to look up as he speaks.

"Okay, you get your beauty sleep, not that you need any and I will try to get to you tomorrow evening. I don't know what Igor has planned but I will try to get away. See you tomorrow, Pink. Sleep tight." He kisses me hard and long. I break off and walk to the elevators.

I walk backward smiling and waving at him, so he doesn't know the sickness I'm feeling from being in his arms, or the fact that my breathing is now starting to get erratic, and I feel like I want to faint. I am not doing that here in front of him. I blow a kiss and walk into the elevator. I press button nine and breathe out slow and steady as the doors shut. I breathe in and out. Just then, the doors open, and he's standing there. My eyes go wide with shock.

"Just one more kiss, then I will leave." There are others in here and some huff in disgust and some cheer and clap. I'm embarrassed. I give him a kiss, then push him out. I watch the doors close and breathe out as the elevator finally starts to ascend. It's going to be a long night.

Twenty-Two

Steve

I PULL UP AT IGOR'S. IT'S REALLY FUCKING EARLY. I MISSED SPENDING time with Pink last night but there is something not quite right again. I could sense it with her and she stepped back when I went to kiss her. Why the fuck would she do that? She looked terrified when she saw me. It was only fleeting, but it was there nonetheless. When I opened the elevator door, I saw the panic on her face, again it was fleeting. She's hiding something. I hope this day goes to plan. I put in the code for the gates to open. It doesn't work. I put it in again and nothing. I press the buzzer, nothing. I press it again. Nothing. I get out of the car, and I hear a shot. Fuck, it's going down. I call for backup, telling them code red at the Hill's. They know where that is and what it is, it will take them at least twenty minutes to get here, just enough time. I scale the gates and rip my jeans on the razor wire as I pull myself over the top. I jump down and stay low to the ground. There are no lights on, someone cut the power, which is why the gates wouldn't open. I need to stay low; I don't want either side shooting at me.

I move closer to the house. I can hear shouting. I'm not sure whose men are shouting. I hear gunfire again. It's coming from upstairs. I enter the house through the open doorway, I stealthily move around. I see Igor's men running around. There's gunfire again. I edge up the stairs with my gun drawn. Suddenly someone fires and I turn to see a figure in black with a black balaclava covering his face. I shoot to kill. I don't fucking care, he fired at me and luckily he's a shit shot, he missed, even if it was an intentional miss.

I edge farther up the rounded staircase, I get to the top and carefully peep round the corner, there's no one around. I edge along to where I know Igor's room is. I enter very carefully but it's empty. I don't hear the kids or anyone, just some running. There's a dead body in here, again covered from head to toe in black. I pull off the balaclava, fuck. I check the rest of the rooms upstairs and apart from the odd body all dressed the same, there's no one around. I head to the back staircase and slowly edge down. I see one of Igor's guys at the bottom. Why the fuck are there so many of Igor's men here? He only ever has the two stationed at all times. He didn't call me for backup, which is protocol. I hover over the man, looking around all the time. I feel for his pulse, I can see he's shot, but it doesn't look like it would have killed him. He opens his eyes, he's ready to fight until he realizes it's me.

"Where's Igor and the family? Are they safe? How many men?" I whisper.

He nods that they are safe, holds up his hands to let me know eight men, I've killed one and seen four, so that leaves three remaining.

"Igor?" I ask.

"Safe room, basement," he whispers.

"Hold tight, play dead if you have to until I get back, he closes his eyes and I shoot him in the head." I edge around to the kitchen.

I see another of our men on the floor, and also another in black. Fuck. At this rate, they will all be dead. I move to the basement, just then, the door opens, and I step back and fire. It was one of them, fuck, that leaves one. The gunfire would give me away. I run down the stairs, there are two of them in black. I fire and both drop dead. That's nine. I hope that's everyone. I know about this safe room, Igor showed me how to work it if I had to. I press the button near the stairs that you wouldn't know was connected to anything. It's an intercom.

"Igor, it's Steve. I wave at where I know the camera to be so he can see me. There are nine perps dead, and all ours from what I've seen. I called for backup before I came over the gate. They should be here any time now." I sit on the stairs and wait. I know it will take a few minutes for him to get out of the room. The safe room is underground. The entrance is behind a brick wall, you would never know it was there. It opens and Igor comes out with his gun raised.

"It's just me. These fuckers are dead. I got them both in the head. The others I've seen are dead, there were nine. I don't know if that's all of them. Our guys did a good job, but they all seem to be dead as well." He nods.

"I got the one in our bedroom and the rest of them upstairs. Poppy got the kids to safety first. The triggers went off around the perimeter, all of them, so I knew there were a few entering. She got them all safe, and I pretended to be asleep when the one entered my room. I shot him in the head. I got the others before joining Poppy. I didn't know how many there were. With all the triggers going off, I reckoned it had to be a lot of them. Are you sure that's all of them?" I shake my head.

He goes to the intercom and tells Poppy to wait until she hears from him. She tells him she's seen two others heading out of the house and onto the grounds. Fuck. I head up the stairs with Igor following me.

"We could do with them alive, so we know who is behind this," he shouts to me.

I spot them and run after them. Igor isn't as quick as I am with his bad leg, but he has an amazing aim. He fires, one goes down, he got his leg. I fire on the other doing the same, he goes down. I did aim for his head, but got his shoulder instead. Fuck. I stand over the one Igor shot. I would have shot him again if it wasn't that Igor caught up. Igor rips his balaclava from his head, he spits right into Igor's face.

"Fuck, he's Iranian. Who the fuck are you? Who sent you? Who do you work for?" He doesn't speak, he just laughs. Igor punches him, knocking him out. We move to the other one that I shot. Igor pulls his balaclava from his head. He recognizes him right away, I see it.

"Igor, that's Tavok. He's one of ours. No wonder he ran, the fucker. He knows what's coming."

"You work in the arms division. What the fuck are you doing coming here trying to take me and my family out? Who the fuck do you work for? You know I will get it out of you one way or another. You've heard the stories, I'm sure. Well, let me tell you, they are all fucking true."

Tavok automatically looked at me when Igor asked who he worked for, I saw the slightest of nods. That fucker gave me away just with that one slight look and nod. Igor would not have missed that. Fuck. I shoot him in the head. It's the least I could do to spare him the torture he would endure, and he did me a favor after all. Igor looks to me.

"What the fuck."

"Game's over, brother. This fucker just gave you the nod. I saw it and you saw it." I disarm Igor. "In the house, Igor. We have things to discuss." I see the sneer on his face. The fucker thinks he's got me. *Wrong, brother, I got you and your fucking family.*

I have the gun in his back, so he knows not to try anything. I know all his tricks. Who the fuck do you think taught him most of them? We walk back through the kitchen door, and I walk him to his office. I sit behind his desk with the gun still pointed at him as he sits in the chair before me.

"Steve, what are you doing? Why are you doing this?"

"Ha, if only you knew, fucker."

"Believe me, I do know."

I cock my head and squint my eyes at him. Does he know?

"Tell me what you know, Igor. Please enlighten me."

"I know you want to kill me and my family. Poppy will never come out unless she knows I'm safe. She will wait till backup arrives. Poppy's a strong woman, who will protect our kids at any cost. Alborz Darvish, do you know that name, Steve? It was brought to my attention that Alborz is the leader of the Darvish Cartel. The funny thing is, not many people have actually seen him." He's watching my face for any giveaway. He knows alright. I have no idea how he knows, but it doesn't surprise me. What I am surprised at is that it's taken this long. I smile at him.

"Please carry on."

"That's it. What more do you want?" I play with the gun, letting him know I can shoot at any time. "So, what's the plan, Steve. You going to kill me and my family, and then what? You want to take over Bratva? Is that your big plan? You always wanted the control, even as kids you always tried to control me in every aspect of my life. You wanted me to be a wimp and fail. You were always jealous. Then when I killed Kirill and took over, you hated it. You went off the rails. I know you used to get drunk and spout off about how it should be you leading the Bratva and one day it will be you. Do you think I don't know everything? That's why Andrey was made my man at arms and not you the first time around. You were so bitter and twisted because you couldn't control me. Wanting to be me had you so bitter. The men hated you. Your papa was no better. My papa hated him. Come on Steve, what's the big plan?" This fucker is trying to goad me. I have the fucking gun here aimed at him; I have the power and the control. He knows it and I know it, yet he's sitting here like a cocky bastard, thinking he has the upper hand because he knows shit.

"You know nothing, you dumb fuck. It was me that planted the seed, letting you know Kirill killed Dimitri. It wasn't fucking Kirill, you dumb fuck. I fucking killed Dimitri. I was the one that set up the sting, I…"

"You fucker." He flies out of his chair and across the desk at me. I hit his head hard with the gun. I'm not killing him until he knows the truth. Then I will gladly put a bullet in his head. I push him off the desk. He must have blacked out for a minute. He comes round as he slumps to the floor. He rises up, rubbing his head and sitting back in the chair.

"I will carry on. I wanted Dimitri gone, then I was going to kill Kirill and you, so I could take over. I knew you would kill him if I told you he killed Dimitri. You idolized Dimitri like he was some big fucking super-hero you looked up to. It made you weak and soft as shit. I tried to make you a man. I was the one that tried to make you more like me. At one point, I wanted us to rule Bratva together. You were just not good enough, or at least you weren't back then. Once Dimitri died, you seemed to man up and became more like Kirill. That's when I knew I had to kill you as well. Then, well, Poppy arrived, and I do like her. She's much better than you will ever be at running Bratva. Then you had all these fucking kids. It just got more and more complicated. I should have done it as soon as you killed Kirill, but I needed the men to know it was me and I would then rule. It just got harder and harder. I decided to start the cartel years ago, to set up a sting using Svetlana and her sister, but then that fucking failed. Who knew a woman would foil the plot. That's Poppy for you. You got a good one there, but she would be more suited at my side than yours. So, I planned this, but fuck me, even this went wrong." I get up and grab his vodka bottle from the table at the side. I keep my eyes on him at all times in case he tries anything. I grab two glasses and place them on the desk and then the bottle. I sit and pour us both a drink.

"Here, one last drink for old times. We did have some fun growing up, didn't we, Igor? I laugh at the shit we got up to until my papa found us. You don't even know the times I was beaten and put in the basement for days, do you? Or the times he would bring his whores down there and have me fuck them while he watched. Apparently, that's what your papa used to do to my papa all the fucking time. They even shared the whores, including yours and Dimitri's mamas." I laugh.

I watch as his eyes squint at me. He leans forward and takes the glass of vodka. He knocks it back in one. I join him, raising my glass in salute to him and down it. He takes the opportunity I thought he would. Only he dives to the floor instead of diving for me. The fucking pussy. What I didn't know was that someone was behind me until I feel the gun at my head.

Igor pops up and he's holding a gun. Fuck. I didn't see this coming.

"Turns out you're not as good as you thought, Steve. My beautiful wife here." He nods his head in my direction, which means she's pointing the gun at my head. "Well, let's just say she's far better at this than you are. Now put the gun on the table barrel first. Don't try anything because she will pull the fucking trigger at the slightest move."

Great, I have both of them with guns on me. Well, my life wouldn't be worth living if I did survive unless they both died. How the fuck did I not see her or the door she came through? I just fucking got up to get the drinks. What timing.

Just then, I hear some noises. I didn't call for backup, it was a lie. Some of the men come in with guns raised. Fuck, I am dead for sure now. I grab the bottle and pour myself another large vodka. I salute him with my glass again.

"To your good health, Igor, my brother."

"You are not my fucking brother, Steve. I know you like to think we were like brothers growing up, but it never happened that way. You tried to rule my fucking life, which is why I dropped you when I did. You were vile, Steve, you had ideas beyond you."

I start to laugh; he furrows his brows. Yeah, that's right, Igor. I'm mad.

"Well, for your information, BROTHER," I grit out. "We are actually real fucking brothers. I am your older brother, the middle son to Kirill. He fucked my papa's woman, constantly apparently. She fell pregnant, telling my papa I was his. In fact, I was Kirill's. My papa was smitten with me when I was born until the day Kirill visited and beat the shit out of him for slacking at his job. He ended up with a broken jaw and couldn't speak for a while. Once he could, he asked my mama what was wrong, because she was being very strange to him. She broke down and told him that I was, in fact, Kirill's baby. My papa lost it and snapped her neck there and then. He treated me so bad, even the neighbors were concerned for me. I only just, in fact, this week, found out Kirill was my real papa. My papa never, ever told me anything, not even my mama's name, as you know. I went back to his house and retrieved stuff from his safe. There were these journals. He has all the details of all the kills he and Kirill did and then it gets to my birth. When he found out I was Kirill's and not his, he lost his mind. Apparently, he wanted to keep me to take out his anger of Kirill on me, Kirill's son. In his mind, he was paying back Kirill by me being fucked up constantly. All the times I was beat up and told you I had been fighting with the kids from school or Bratva. It was all from him. So, you see, I knew all along I should be the one to rule the Bratva and as I am Kirill's second born, well, it is my right to rule Bratva and you need to step down. What do you say now, little brother?"

I see him trying to take in what I just said. The moron. He can be dense at times.

"I don't believe a fucking word you say, Steve. It's all bullshit as usual. Now do you have anything else to tell me that isn't bullshit? Something more plausible than you being my fucking brother. In your dreams maybe," I huff out and then laugh aloud.

"What else is there to tell? Unless you know something you're not telling me?" I see him nod to Poppy. She gets on her cell and ask someone to come in. My eyes go wide as Pink walks in. I jump out of my seat.

"What the fuck? Why are you here Vi, did they hurt you? Tell me, are you okay?" Just then, Poppy puts the gun to my head.

"Sit down, fucker. She is perfectly fine. Now, are you going to answer, Igor? Is there anything else you need to tell him?"

Now I hate this bitch too. She and the kids need to die. The other men are standing at the door with guns pointed, ready to shoot, so it's not like I can do anything anyway. If I was to take one of these out, the other would still be around and I don't want to put Pink in harm's way. I look at her, really look at her and she looks okay, not terrified or breathing erratically like she does. In fact, she looks so composed right now. She's not afraid of them, it's me she's afraid of. It's always been me. My instincts were right, but what has she got to do with any of this? She smiles at me nervously. What the hell is going on?

"Pink, just tell me you're okay. I just need to know. Is it me, Pink? Is it me you are scared of? Why? I have never harmed you. I'm in love with you, Pink. You must have realized I'm in love with you. I've never been in love with anyone in my life. Pink, just tell me what is going on."

I see the turmoil on her face. She is conflicted. I'm so confused as to why she is even here. She's looking at me sympathetically, and I don't know why. Poppy digs the gun into the back of my head, warning me. I sit back down. I take the bottle of vodka and pour myself another one. I down it in one. I may as well try to go out shit-faced.

"Guys, you can leave us for the time being. I will shout if I need you or if you hear any commotion, come back." He dismisses his men.

"Is there anything else you want to tell me?" Igor asks again.

He must know or he wouldn't keep asking me to tell him. I wonder if I can take out Poppy from behind me then get to Igor. What if he takes Pink and threatens to kill her? I've just spilled my guts out about being in love with her, which in our line of work means she is collateral. Would he do that? She's obviously here for a reason and she's not scared of them. Is that because she just thinks they are nice people and doesn't really know them and doesn't know she's in danger? But surely, with the guns drawn and pointing at me, she would be in a bit of a panic, wouldn't she?

"I don't have anything more to say. I've told you I'm your brother. My papa's journals have it all documented, if you want to read them and we could do a DNA test. That's it from me."

Igor lowers his gun, knowing Poppy has hers at my head. He foolishly put it in his waistband at the back. I could easily disarm Poppy and shoot him before he manages to grab it. I stand up slowly.

"Pink, talk to me. I know this is scary with the guns and all that, but that's not on me. That's these two. Don't let them fool you. They are not the saints they make themselves out to be. They make money doing illegal stuff, you know what Bratva is like. It's these two you need to be scared of."

"I'm not scared of them, Steve, nor am I that scared of you. I got a call to come here and so here I am. Poppy, what was it you wanted me here for? I came as quickly as I could. You said it was urgent on the phone and that you were sorry to have to do it this way and drag me into it. What is this?"

"As Steve, or should I say Alborz Darvish, of the Darvish Cartel is not coming forward with the information just yet, I just wanted you, sweetie, to hear it from him and not be fooled by him. You needed to know." She shoves me again in the head, hard with the gun. "You may as well talk now, Steve. You know we know."

Fuck, I knew when Igor mentioned the name earlier that they must know, but until she just called me by that name, I wasn't a hundred percent sure. There was no way I was going to say anything until I knew they knew.

"You got me," is all I say, staring at Igor. "We are still blood brothers, whether you want to believe it or not, Igor. We had great times as kids, but you were a fucking pussy. It was me and Dimitri that covered for you all the fucking time when Kirill wanted to whip you into a man, a man like him. You didn't have it in you back then to become the Pakhan, I still don't think you have it in you now. Poppy is more of a Pakhan than you, but you need to hand it over to me. You obviously know it's my cartel, and you know we are, or should I say, I am huge now in the US. The Iranian side was a cover-up so no one would suspect me, an American white guy, would be the one running it. Well, I did, and I have run it successfully. If I become the Pakhan, I will join it all together and rule this fucking country, not just LA. With Pink by my side, I can do anything."

He laughs at me. Really laughs.

"You are delirious, Steve. You honestly think I am just going to step down and let you take over. Even if I wanted to, I wouldn't. You would run the Bratva into the ground and make a mockery of us all. You're not a leader, you've clearly shown that. You may think your cartel is successful, but let me tell you, your six houses have all been taken down this morning in New York City. I know there are more, but they will fall as well. That is why Vi is here, or should I say, Vidana. She needed to know that with her help we were able to take you and the cartel down. The Darvish Cartel does not exist as of right now. You are the last living one, yet to be killed."

I don't flinch at anything he says. Internally I am fucking screaming, and the anger is building right in my gut, I can feel it close to exploding. He's destroyed it all. After all these years, he's destroyed what I built up, just like that. I see Pink look to him. She's got that puzzled, conflicted look on her face. I need to get her on my side and take these two out. She said she wasn't scared of me. Then it fucking hits me like a semitruck. He said her name. Vidana, not Viya like she told me. She lied. Then it fucking hits me again.

"Pink, are you Svetlana's sister, that Vidana?"

Her eyes go wide. I fucking knew there was something about her. She nods.

"Do you know who I am and what I do or did?"

She nods again.

"How?"

She looks over my head to Poppy. Maybe looking for confirmation that she can tell me.

"Yes, I know who you are. I saw you once through the crack of a door. I was being raped as usual by an old disgusting man and you were outside the door shouting at someone. I saw the side of you, but it was your voice. You are American, which I found odd, as all the other men were Iranian. It was your voice that helped me survive the rest of the time in there until I was rescued. For some reason, I fixated on you and your voice. That day in the coffee shop when I dropped the pot. It was your voice. I knew straight away it was you. I needed the proof though, for myself. It's why I managed to pluck up the courage to speak to you, to get to know you. I felt sick all the time in your company, it brought back so many memories of being constantly raped, earning money for you. Of letting men fuck every hole I have on my body, of all those vile, disgusting men touching me any way they wanted and physically ripping me internally and beating on me. Every day, countless times a day. I would have died if it wasn't for your voice, Steve. I fell for you in some perverted way. I have been told it's a Stockholm syndrome effect, even though you were not my actual abuser. It's still by association. So, you see, spending time with you, as much as I wanted to, it physically made me sick. Each time you kissed me, I wanted to throw up. I did it because I needed to know myself if it was really you and that you were Alborz, the sex trafficker, the fucking monster, as I call you, the man who broke me first. The vile, filthy fucker that has no regard for women and their bodies. How the fuck can you say you love me; you broke me in ways no one should be able to break. You run a sex trafficking ring? How then, Steve, can you possibly love any woman? It can't be possible. You just think you love me. I thought I had fallen in love with you, but it's not love, it's the fine line between love and hate. Now I know it's you, I know I hate you and could never love you. You are a vile disgusting, mother fucking monster, Steve, and I hope you rot in hell for all the pain and damage you have done to not only me, but the countless other girls you destroyed. I hate you, Steve."

At hearing her words, I feel sick myself. When I thought she had been taken in New York, I was thinking the worse and imagining her being used and it made me despicably angry, and I would have not hesitated in killing anyone who touched her. Now I know she was raped day in and day out at my hands, I feel sick to my stomach. I feel shame and remorse. I want to kill every fucker who laid a hand on her. Yet they did it because I let them do it. I let them violate her body in unthinkable ways. It sickens me. I need to save her. I need her to know that it's not me and I would just worship her. I need to get it through to her, I love her so much. I'm brought out of my thoughts by Igor laughing. He's fucking laughing at my self-pity. I pour another glass of vodka and down it. Distracting them. Poppy laughs at him laughing and Pink joins in. They're all fucking laughing at me. They're fucking mocking me. All of them. I jump up, turn, and take the gun from Poppy. I palm her in the nose, breaking it and sending her flying backward. I turn the gun on Igor, it all happens so fast, he's trying to grab his gun, but I shoot before he manages to lift it to shoot me. I hear Pink screaming my name and look at her as Igor goes down. His gun is thrown in the air, and I watch as Pink catches it and before I can comprehend what she is doing, she shoots.

Epilogue

Vidana

EVERYTHING HAPPENED SO QUICKLY THAT DAY, I WILL NEVER forget what I saw. When Poppy called me, she asked if I would come over, but she warned me it might be dangerous, and that she wasn't forcing me. It was my decision. She said hopefully it will give me closure and sate my mind once and for all on Steve. It could have also gone the other way. Upon hearing what he had to say, I could have just fallen at his feet. But I knew I didn't love him, after returning from New York, I knew he was the monster I suspected him to be. He allowed men to violate my body time and time again, with no regard to me as a person. It was all on him. He had me taken from my home and he was the one who kept me there to be used. Once I heard him say it was true and I could see for myself the look in his eyes when confronted, I knew this had to be done once and for all. To hear Igor saying they had destroyed the cartel and that Steve was the last remaining one, I wanted to cry with joy. I just didn't yet, I needed to stay composed. I saw the horror in his eyes when he realized who I was. That horror turned to anger fleetingly, but then to sorrow. I think the sorrow is for what had happened to me at his hands. When he was saying he loved me, I felt sick. I wanted to throw up on him. I went into a rant at him and told him I hated him. I can categorically say I do. I thought I loved him, but I now know once and for all I definitely didn't. I realized it was Ryker I loved. For the last few years, he has been there for me.

I was lost in my thoughts after having my rant at him when there was a commotion. He attacked Poppy, knocking her out, and then turned and shot at Igor. He went down, but his gun was tossed in the air. I caught it, and before I knew what I was doing, I aimed and fired at Steve. I have never even held a gun, let alone fired one. I just instinctively put my finger on the trigger and aimed. Everything happened in slow motion. Igor going down, the gun in the air, me firing and Steve going down with a hole in his head. I killed him. I dropped the gun and screamed at the top of my lungs. The other men came barreling into the room with guns raised. I dove to the floor and curled up into a tight ball. There was lots of shouting in Russian, I could understand every word. I didn't look up. I stayed curled up for what felt like an eternity.

Suddenly there were hands on me, and I screamed, trying to shake them off.

"Wait, stop, don't hurt her. She's terrified. Be gentle. Help me get to her."

It was Poppy. I looked up as someone was helping her move to me. She had a rag at her nose which was bloody, but she was safe. I jumped up and hugged her so tight. I was hysterical, crying so hard. She was safe. She was alive. I was scared Steve was going to get up and shoot everyone, including me. Poppy pulled away slightly so she could look in my face. "Did you get hurt? Did you get shot?" I shake my head but I look down and see blood splatter on my clothes. I check myself just in case I did get hurt. No. I look around as she does, and I see Igor on the floor. I scream as Poppy rushes to him. It must have been his blood, as he was next to me. Steve fired and he must have shot Igor. Thankfully, I see him being helped to a sitting position. He's holding his shoulder. There's blood everywhere. I look to him for hope and clarification. He nods to me and smiles.

"I'm okay, Vidana. I think you just saved our lives." I look to the desk where Steve was standing but, he's not there. I move slightly so I can see around it and onto the floor. He's there. My hand flies to my mouth to stifle yet another scream and I screw my eyes shut while crying. I can't unsee what I just saw. He lay there on the floor with his eyes open. It looked like he was looking at me. There was a hole in his head. Anyone would be proud of that shot. I had no idea where I was shooting. I just knew if I didn't shoot, he would shoot us all. Or shoot the others and take me with him for a life of God knows what. I would be his hostage because I would not willingly stay with him. I had to do it. That image will forever be ingrained in my brain. I will learn to come to terms with it, because I know I have saved countless girls from going through what I went through and probably saved an awful lot of lives.

That day is one I will never forget, yes, because I killed the head of a cartel, but it was also the day my sisters arrived at the refuge. I stayed at Poppy's house for a few hours. She saw me to a room where she got me clean clothes and I had a long soak in a bath. When I was finished, I fell asleep on the bed. I think the shock and adrenaline took over. I woke up screaming at the vision of Steve with a hole in his head. Poppy came rushing in and sat talking to me for a while. Her daughter, Sabina, came in. She was beautiful. Poppy had asked her to come up because she wanted to introduce me to her. Sabina knew Poppy wasn't her real mama, they didn't want to hide that from her ever, so they had told her recently. They told her about me, her aunt Vidana and she wanted to meet me. Just before Sabina arrived, Poppy told me the mess was all cleared up as though nothing happened and that the children didn't hear or see anything. She told them that there was a bad man who hurt Mama's nose and hurt Papa's shoulder but that everyone was safe. She came barging into the room like a little bull in a China shop. I could see Svetlana in her, but only slightly. Thankfully she was all Igor. There was no mistaking that. She sat on the bed next to me and I hugged her to me.

"Hello Sabina, it's lovely to meet you. I'm your aunty Vidana or aunty Dana, whichever you want to call me." She was very chatty and didn't want to leave me. We went and ate together in the kitchen. Igor came in, I stood up and ran to him and hugged him to me. I don't know why but I just needed to do this. He looked down and smiled. I froze.

"He was right, you know. I always thought it odd he had your eyes." He nodded.

"It's time to get going if you're up to it. We need to get to the refuge. It's a big day today. A package from Russia." As soon as he said that, I realized my sisters were supposed to arrive today. Sabina didn't want me to leave but I promised I would come see her and we could spend time together. Poppy, Igor, and I went to meet my sisters. As excited as I was, I was also terrified. It was hard for all of us. I got my sisters back, but I know I had lost Dominika for the time being. I needed to do a lot of work with her, more than the others. One thing's for sure, I was not going to leave them like Svetlana left me. I would be there for them for as long as they needed me.

It's been three years since that day. My sisters are all doing so well considering what they went through, but with the help from me and the refuge, we got them there. Dominika still struggles, but she's feisty like me. She now works in the coffee shop I used to work in. Iskra has gone to university, Klara and Zoya are both still in high school. To say they are all a handful is an understatement. Sabina is in high school with them. It's weird having aunties going to your school, but she loves it. She's a little star with her dancing. She's the world solo champion, three years on the run and Zoya has started dancing too. It's great seeing them all grow up, worry-free. They are young enough to enjoy their youth.

I moved out of the refuge last year. They were fine with that and, in fact, they all moved in together on the ninth floor of Igor and Poppy's building. I did offer to buy a house for us all, well Igor offered, but they were happy. They knew I needed to get on with my own life. I still have pink hair. Sometimes I go blue, sometimes purple. Ryker loves me changing it to different colors but especially the pink. He always loved the pink. I moved into a house with Ryker last year. We are engaged. Poppy was right, the first time I gave myself to a man, which was Ryker, on my terms was everything she said it would be. He was the most patient and gentlest person with me. It took us a long time to get to the point of making love for the first time, but the wait was worth it. He worshiped my body. I can honestly say with all my heart, I love him, and I think I did right from the beginning, but just didn't realize it. My life is perfect in every way. To come from what I went through to have this fulfilled life is just amazing. Poppy, Igor and all the kids have been a huge part in our life with us being related to Sabina. They welcomed us all with open arms and have done so much for my sisters. I will forever be grateful to them both for that. I also got promoted by Poppy and I was made manager of the refuge. A full time paid job.

Sabina

I love my parents, don't get me wrong, but I don't like the life they have, it's not for me. All I ever wanted to do was dance. I know my body has changed over the years, but I still dance. I am never giving it up. Mama and Papa don't want me or my siblings to do something we don't want to do. I know what they do. It's dangerous sometimes. They are Bratva after all, but there is no way I want to be associated with them. When I turned sixteen, they let me go to college in New York at the world-famous New York Dance Academy. I know, sixteen on my own in New York. As if my parents, being who they are, wouldn't have me watched, well, guarded. It's why they let me go. I was accepted young because of my achievements at being a world champion for a number of years.

I've been at the academy for three years now. I'm almost nineteen. My parents have been to visit me so many times along with my sisters and brothers. Our family is huge now. My aunty Dana got married two years ago. She now has a lovely little boy, my cousin, and I adore him. She's visited me with Uncle Ryker a few times and, in fact, so have all of my aunties. I still can't believe I have five of them. I love them all and I do miss being away from them. It's been a long three years, but between them all, there is always someone visiting me.

I haven't told any of them, but I met this boy at the academy. My parents think most of the boys at the academy are gay. How wrong they are. There are a few, but not as many as they like to think. So, Tad is the love of my life. I know I'm only young and have my whole life ahead of me, but we are in love. I've been seeing him for just over a year but haven't told my parents. I'm sure they must know. They have guards watching me. I told them I have a lot of friends that are boys, but like I said, they think most of the male dancers are gay and think their daughter is safe.

I've just been out with Tad, and we are walking home. We haven't met each other's parents yet, for obvious reasons. I live in an apartment my parents bought just near the academy and Tad will always walk me home whenever we've been out. He doesn't know who my family is and that I am probably being constantly watched. I have a lady who is kind of like a nanny, if I was a kid. She comes daily and makes sure the apartment is clean and she cooks meals for me. How will I ever be independent if they don't let me live my life alone? I've told them so many times I do not need a babysitter. I'm old enough to leave home if I want to. I have nothing against Barbara, and she is a lovely older woman, but I need my own space with no one looking after me. I'm going to have the talk with Mama.

Just as we get near my apartment, a lady approaches us. I step forward to see if she is okay. She looks nicely dressed and doesn't look harmful. She only looks to be in her twenties, not much older than me. It just so happens we stopped next to an alleyway and I hadn't realized. I didn't see anyone else until I hear a scuffle and turn to see Tad being dragged away down the alley. I can defend myself. With parents like mine, there was no way any of their children would not be able to defend themselves but as I turn to run after Tad down the alley, the woman, or I can only presume it's the woman suddenly pulls my hair back and before I know it, there is a cloth smothering my face. I fight, with everything I have, trying to get her to let go, scratching her hands and arms until everything goes dark.

THE END

Reviews

I really hope that you enjoyed this fictional story. Reviews are lovely!
Honestly, they are! And they also help other people to make an
informed decision before buying this book.

I would really appreciate it if you took a few seconds to do just that.
Thank you!

Find Me and Follow Me. Xx

Amazon - https://amzn.to/2H5QquX

Facebook - https://bit.ly/345Ydlr

Instagram - https://bit.ly/2SZVcwt

Goodreads - https://bit.ly/37di1oI

BookBub - https://bit.ly/3j6AmWV

www.lyndathrosby.com

Lynda Xx

Books by
LYNDA THROSBY

Catfish
A dark, gritty, romantic thriller (this book contains graphic scenes) for
18+ only.

The Best Day of My Life
A sweet, single dad of twins romance.

Chef
A semi-dark romantic thriller.

A Christmas Wish
A sweet Christmas fairy tale novella.

More about Lynda

Lynda lives in Cheshire in the UK with her husband Peter and cat Bailey. She has two grown-up daughters and has two beautiful granddaughters.

She runs a successful financial business with her husband.

As a young teenager, Lynda used to read horror books with a love for everything Stephen King and James Herbert. She has always wanted to write and even wrote horror stories at age thirteen.
A little later, she started reading Jackie Collins and Jilly Cooper and has always had a love of books. This then exploded with *Twilight* and *Fifty Shades of Grey*. Oh, and the introduction of e-readers.

In her spare time, she has a season ticket for Manchester City Football Club and goes to all the home games. She loves going to concerts and the theater. She goes to the cinema at least once a week. When the weather is nice, you can see her gliding down the road on her Harley Davidson 1200T motorbike. Traveling is also high on the agenda, and her dream is to visit every state in the USA.

＃ Acknowledgments

I wouldn't have done this without the help and support I got from my family.

First to my husband, who makes time for me to write by running our business and the continued support he gives me, encouraging me all the way.

Thank you to ellie from My Brother's Editor - for editing and formatting my words, you have no idea what your words mean during the process.

Thank you to Rosa from My Brother's Editor for proofreading my words, such a huge, huge, help as always.

Sybil Wilson from Pop Kitty for the amazing cover as usual.

My family and friends who read the books and give me feedback.

To those special readers that can't wait for the next book to come along. You make it all worthwhile, knowing you are as excited to read my words as I am to write them.

Thank you to everyone who supports me and reads my words.